If Kisses Cured Cancer

T.S. HAWKEN

Seahawk
Press

Published by Seahawk Press 2018
First Published: In Australia, April 2018
Copyright © 2018 T.S. Hawken

Disclaimer

Every effort has been made to ensure that this book is free from error or omissions.
Information provided is of general nature only and should not be considered legal
or financial advice. The intent is to offer a variety of information to the reader.
However, the author, publisher, editor or their agents or representatives shall
not accept responsibility for any loss or inconvenience caused to a person or
organisation relying on this information.

A catalogue record for this book is available from the National Library of Australia.

Cover Image: Eliza Selkirk
Cover Design: Sarah Bürvenich, www.sarahmachtsachen.com
Book formatting services by BookCoverCafe.com

ISBN:
978-0-6482558-0-2 (pbk)
978-0-6482558-1-9 (e-bk)

Acknowledgements

The idea for this book formed when my wife Tara fell ill with cancer at the age of 29. Her fighting spirit, kind nature and positive outlook have been beacons of hope in those stormy seas. Tara, you somehow always find light in the darkness. I hope that influence is present throughout these pages. I love you. Let's stay together 'til we're ghosts.

To those who read early versions of the manuscript and gave amazing feedback, I am forever in your debt. Those people, in no particular order, are: Eli Helm, Emily McDiarmid, Stew King, Nikki Hawken, Tom Grayling, Jodie How, Di Parker and the ladies of the Harvey Bookies Club. You all contributed essential ideas that shaped the personality of the locals in Ocean Heads.

To Dmetri Kakmi, whose professional editing advice brought the story from a clunky pile of junk to something I can be proud of - thank you, thank you, thank you.

To Simon Camp at Gold Gully Farm for giving me a writing refuge when I needed it most, you're a bloody legend. I can't wait to set up in the tent again sometime soon.

To Sarah Bürvenich, Stacey Whiteford and Eliza Selkirk, who all helped in creating the cover of If Kisses Cured Cancer, you are absolute gems.

Finally, to you the reader. It's no exaggeration to say that without you, this book is nothing but noise being shouted into the abyss. I hope you get something from these pages. If you never look at an unattended shopping trolley the same again, then I have done my job.

For Tara, always...

One

That sick feeling creeps into Matt's stomach again as he hits the highway. Every weekday is the same. The moment he leaves the coastal road at the edge of town, a tightening fist squeezes his bowels. Matt doesn't know why. He thinks maybe he drinks too much coffee.

Smooth-barked eucalypts line the road, creating a separation between the bitumen and farmland. A heat haze shimmers off everything, like ghosts trying to escape the furnace of an already baking day. Matt doesn't take any of this in. His mind is numb. He passes cars, looking dead ahead on automatic pilot. For two years he's done this drive. The weather changes, but the road doesn't. Rain, hail, or shine, the traffic lights still turn red when Matt nears them. The white lines still divide him from the oncoming cars, full of smiling faces driving down to the freedom of the coast.

Rusty and beaten-up, Matt's Holden swings into the Optitel car park. He checks his watch and swears under his breath. Late. Again.

Matt skulks through the building, taking the long way to avoid walking past Mr James's office. Phone chatter drones around the customer service hall. Cubicle workers all sit with their faces lit by computer screens, speaking in apologetic tones. Taking a seat in his own grey-walled box, Matt is about to put his headset on when a voice booms in his ear.

'Nine minutes!'

Matt leaps up. His heart almost bursts through his ribcage. He turns to see Mr James standing barely a foot from him, florid cheeked and double-chinned. Matt double takes, trying to figure out where his boss had come from. It's like he's some kind of corporate Vietcong, ambushing employees among the jungle of partitions.

One

'Do you know how much time nine minutes each day adds up to, in a two-hundred and sixty day working year?' Mr James asks.

Matt is sure he is about to find out.

'Thirty-nine hours.' Mr James's eyes lock onto Matt's. 'An entire week of work. Would you like to have three weeks holiday this year instead of four, Mr Pearce?'

'Umm, no sir.' Matt answers, averting his eyes.

'Well I suggest you turn up on time, then.' Mr James holds his hand out to Matt. 'Do we have a deal?'

Matt stares at the hand for a moment, before shaking it. It feels like he's holding a sweaty Christmas ham.

'Great!' Mr James's tone turns glib, as he drops his ham to his side. 'I won't keep you any longer. Happy servicing.'

Matt eases himself down into his chair and watches Mr James stride away in a swish of polyester. When he was younger, Matt's parents had told him he could be anything he wanted. Matt is unsure when company cog had hit his list of dream jobs. Maybe the memo had slipped past him, like so many other things in his twenty-five years of life. When he had finished high school, Matt's plan was to get a job and save to travel. All of his friends were doing it. Unfortunately, his jobs were sporadic and parties too many. When it came time to leave, the travel train passed by his stop and picked up everyone but him. His biggest trip was scraping up enough money to move into his uncle's vacant unit, when his parents left for Tasmania because the town was getting too busy. Emails, blogs and social media became the only way to keep in touch with European adventures he might never experience.

Matt puts his headset on and answers the first call for the day.

'Good morning. Optitel customer service, my name is Matthew. May I start with your name please?'

'My name is Sue. I want to know why my home phone is cut off,' her voice is sharp and angry. 'I've paid my bill.'

Matt holds back a sigh. When he first started working for Optitel, he thought it would be interesting to talk to people all day. But nobody calls customer service in a good mood. The callers' problems aren't too bad if you look at them as singular cases, but they are always a crisis to the caller. Compound this day after day, week after week, for two years and it grinds even the brightest enthusiasm to muck. That sick feeling from the car rises in Matt's stomach again.

'Okay Sue,' Matt says. 'May I have your last name and the phone number which has been cut off, so I can pull up your file?'

Sue tells Matt her number and last name.

One

'Do you mind holding while I look up the information, Sue?'

'I've already been on hold before I spoke to you. Am I being charged for this call, even though it's your fault I have to ring from my mobile?'

'I'll have to look up that information too, Sue. Please hold.'

Matt clicks the line over to mute. This is a pretty standard call. He pulls up the information and sees the bill has indeed been paid. It was paid two weeks late, which is why Sue's phone has been shut off. Line disconnections happen all the time. The company will charge a reconnection fee to get it back online if the bill payment was late. He also sees that yes, Sue is being charged for this call.

Matt sucks in a deep breath and delivers the news. He is sorry, there is nothing he can do. Sue goes ballistic. She raves like it's the end of mankind.

'This is ridiculous. You put me on hold for fifteen minutes to tell me there's nothing you can do? This is a joke!'

Matt wants to agree with her. He wants to tell her the company should be more understanding. He wants to reassure her. He wants to tell her it's obscene how Optitel treats their customers. But it's not company policy to do so. The training manual tells him to follow the script in this situation and to explain in a firm but polite voice that the terms are set out clearly in her contract. The worst thing is that Matt knows there is something he can do. If Sue complains enough and threatens to close both of her phone accounts and go to another provider, then he can reconnect her for free and give her a rebate on her mobile for this call. He wills her to say the words, but she doesn't. She just swears at him and hangs up; another dissatisfied customer.

After a few more calls Matt gets up for a cigarette break. He doesn't actually smoke, but he noticed in his first few months at Optitel that smokers get to take three, no-questions-asked breaks during the day to fuel their addiction.

Outside, Matt leans against the wall in the courtyard shade. Even in the shadows it's hot enough to melt the fat off a T-bone. A crumpled cigarette sits unlit between his fingers. It has lasted a year and a half so far.

The courtyard door bangs open and a familiar face squints in the sunlight. It's Z. Not her real name, but she uses a cigarette holder like Zsa Zsa Gabor, so Matt had taken to calling her that when they first met. In the last year, he has resorted to addressing her simply as Z because like most Australians he doesn't have the patience for calling people by their full name, made up or otherwise. The rest of the office has taken up calling her Z as well. Even Mr James, who normally addresses people as mister

One

or mizz calls her by her nickname. In an office full of employees that rarely make it past six months, she has been at Optitel the entire two years that Matt has. He has no idea how long she was here before he arrived.

Z is a lanky six-foot-two, with closely cropped hair, thick-rimmed glasses and a smile that comes across as more of a scowl. The wrinkles around her eyes make Matt think she's pushing forty, but considering the amount of age-inducing nicotine she inhales every day, she could be in her early twenties for all Matt knows.

'Still being a soft cock and not lighting that thing?' Z nods at Matt's hand as she takes out her cigarette holder and loads it.

'Still trying to use cigarettes to groom the perfect phone-sex voice?' Matt replies dryly.

She lights her cigarette, takes a long drag and blows smoke into the air with a flourish.

'Absolutely, darling. Have to keep our callers happy somehow.'

The pair stand quietly for a moment, watching Z's plume of smoke dissipate into the scorching air.

'How have you lasted in this place as long as you have?' Matt finally asks when he can't take the silence any longer.

'What did you do this time?' Z cocks her head, seeing right past Matt's question.

'Nothing.'

Z raises her eyebrow in scepticism.

'I was a little late.'

'Again?' Z shakes her head like a disappointed parent. 'Seriously Matt, it's not that bad if you just put your head down and do what you're told to do. It's hardly inspiring work, but at least it's work.'

'Having Mr James breathing over your shoulder doesn't help.'

'Please, he's a puppy dog.'

'With the breath to match,' Matt frowns.

Z barks a husky laugh, taking another drag through her cigarette holder.

'How were your calls this morning?' Matt asks, shifting the subject away from his own troubles.

'Just another day in company service,' Z smirks.

This is the first time Matt has heard Z use the term. He tilts his head and thinks on it for a moment.

'Not a bad way to put it,' he says. 'We're not serving the customers, are we?'

'Don't take it to heart, darling. We're doing what we can for them.'

Matt stares again, not sure what to say. *Are they really doing everything they can?* He would stub out his cigarette to end the conversation, if he was any kind of normal person. Instead, he just puts it back in his pocket, nods goodbye and walks inside.

Sitting at his cubicle, Matt takes call after call for the rest of the day. On a notepad to his left he scribbles mindlessly: *customer service or company service?*

Before he leaves, Matt opens up his company email and writes an open letter addressed to everyone at Optitel.

Sometimes we need to ask ourselves: can we do things a better way?

90% of our calls have a dissatisfied rating. Why?

Maybe it's because we are serving our own needs as a company, instead of putting customers first.

But if we have no customers, we have no company.

We're running the risk of losing our business, because we treat people like they don't matter.

It's time things changed.

Instead of only giving rebates when someone threatens to leave, why don't we give them straight away?

If we know we can save someone money by switching them to another plan, why don't we do it automatically?

If company policies are restricting us from doing the right thing, why don't we just change the policy?

It's time we delivered true customer service, instead of just company service.

It's time to turn things around, or die a slow death.

Serve the people.

The rest will follow.

Matt hovers his mouse over the send button for a few moments, before letting out a long sigh and minimising the window. He's never had the courage to step outside the lines, so why start now? It's not like it would achieve anything, except maybe cause him to lose his job.

Matt hangs his head and stands up to leave. At least it's Friday - two days breather before this all starts again.

Two

Matt has no trouble waking up. While a lot of people like to sleep in on Saturday he finds it hard. When he *has* to get up it's a struggle. When the option is there to sleep in, his nattering brain won't let him.

Switching on his stereo, Matt inserts a Bob Marley CD. Happy reggae riffs float around the room. It's been a long time since Matt has listened to this album. It used to be one of his favourites. Lately, he's forgotten the joy that Bob injects into him. Matt hums along with the song, *Jammin'*. When he was younger he thought the lyrics were 'pyjamas'. He was singing it one day when his friend started laughing hysterically.

'Why would Bob Marley be singing about pyjamas, you idiot?'

Matt had shrugged. It didn't matter, he liked the song no matter what the words were but he had to admit, *Jammin'* made more sense.

Jamming around the room, Matt begins to tidy up. He straightens pillows, vacuums the floor and wipes the bench tops. Dirty washing, which has been piling up for weeks, is shoved in the washing machine as *Redemption Song* wanders out of the speakers in his lounge room. It almost looks like a respectable unit by the time Matt is done. He feels a sense of achievement surveying his work.

Pulling some boardshorts out of his top draw, Matt decides to head down to the beach for that swim. He may as well get some exercise while he's on a roll.

It seems like everybody within a few hundred kilometres has come down to the beach today. Swarms of people carry multi-coloured beach umbrellas and towels down the long winding stairs to the sand at the bottom of the cliffs. Those who have neglected to wear thongs face the hot-sand dash down to the cooler tidal zone, where most people are setting up. Some throw down their towels mid run and jump on top of them for relief, before picking them up and dashing again.

Looking out of the corner of his eye at a group of tanned girls in their bikinis, Matt picks his way down to the water's edge. He might be in a good mood, but he's not stupid enough to smile and say hello to them. Chubby white men shouldn't bother attractive girls as they soak up the sun. Safer to just slip into the ocean.

The water is cool against Matt's skin. Even in summer the ocean never gets much warmer than the mid-twenties. Goose bumps rise on Matt's arms and legs, but he dives under, submerging himself completely. After coming up and sucking air into his lungs, the cold seems to ease. It always does once your hair is wet for some reason.

Floating on his back just beyond the breakers, Matt lets the water wash away the working week. His fingers pucker into waterlogged prunes as the sea swirls around him. Matt's eyes start to drift closed in relaxation, when a tennis ball plops next to his head. Startled, Matt gulps in a mouthful of seawater. Coughing and spluttering, he searches for the bottom with his feet. Dry retching, the salt of the ocean burns his throat.

He can hear laughter from the beach, as a buff, twenty-something male stands on the water's edge watching Matt struggle.

'Hey mate, chuck us the ball,' the man shouts.

Having recovered from the fright, Matt assesses the green ball that interrupted his relaxing float. He picks it up, swimming in a little so he can plant his feet on the bottom. Hurling the ball as hard as he can toward the shore, he strains his arm. The throw falls pathetically short of its mark and the man has to walk forward to retrieve it. Instead of voicing any thanks, he shoots a look of scorn at Matt, picks up the ball and runs back to his friends who are waiting and laughing. The jeers remind Matt of the kids at school who used to call him 'Custard Arm', because he was hopeless at any kind of ball sport, especially cricket. While some people seemed born to blaze the ball down the pitch at lightning speed, his efforts were always slower than a wet fart. It had served as a major disappointment to his classmates when he had moved to town from New Zealand as a kid. The star sportsman of the school, Chris McGee, had declared that 'all kiwis are great at cricket' and invited Matt onto the team without the need for a trial. In his debut match, he had been carted for two sixes and three fours in his first over. Matt was relegated to the bench after that. The only time his teammates spoke to him was when they asked him to say 'deck six', then sniggered when he did. When Matt finally realised his accent made it sound like he was saying 'dick sex', he closed his mouth and refused to talk. It had taken an entire year to get more than a few words out of him and, even then, it was mostly whispered. Maybe that was one of the reasons Matt had decided to try customer service in the first place - he always felt like he had something to say, but was afraid to say it. His job provided a script and willing participants in conversation. A structured safety where he thought no problems could arise. His first day in the job had robbed him of that notion, but by then he was committed.

Matt lets out one more half-drowned cough as he makes his way up the beach. A short dip in the ocean was enough. He needs to go food shopping anyway.

Three

Matt had thought that everyone on the planet was at the beach, but he was wrong. The rest of the population is at the supermarket. He walks in with bare feet. The cold tiles send a chill through his soles and up his legs. It doesn't matter how hot it gets outside, the supermarket floor is always freezing. Matt knows the soles of his feet will be black with dirt by the time he's finished. He doesn't mind. Matt prefers shopping with bare feet in summertime.

Locals groan around each aisle of the supermarket complaining about the crowds. Matt overhears two older women talking. It never used to be this busy, they say to each other. It never used to be this *commercial*. The sea-changers have interrupted their sleepy life and no one is happy about it, except the sea-changers. Down from the city they have flooded in over the years to set up life along the promising coastline. A simpler life, a quieter life: the family life. It's better to live with salt in the air than smog and the new highway reduced commuting time to be the same as crawling bumper-to-bumper from the CDB to the inner suburbs. The locals say the intruders brought the complicated life along with them and grumble every day about blow-ins, long lines and carbon-copy retail sprouting up to destroy family businesses. New residents walk around with permanent smiles on their faces not talking to anyone else, like an upside-down mirror of their neighbours' mouths, which won't stop moving with gossip. Matt doesn't feel strongly about it either way. He just wishes it was quicker to get bread and milk.

Pulling a trolley out of the neat stack, Matt wanders into the fruit and veg section. Scanning the produce racks, he sees the lettuces are almost out, the capsicums are deformed and the strawberries have a light fuzz of mould on them. The weekend is a terrible time to get fresh fruit. He looks around at the people: swinging their baskets, touching and squeezing the avocados, putting their grubby fingers on the bruised peaches. Matt doesn't like shopping. It always feels like such a mundane chore that is wasting his life. He doesn't have anything better to do right now, but because he *has* to shop he loathes it. There is never anything new or exciting in this place. It's just another rut carved out before him.

Matt looks down at his still empty trolley. He watches in envy as a woman pushes her full one past. Ripe bananas sit on top of a fresh loaf of bread. There are eggs, milk and toilet paper. Everything Matt needs. The woman abandons her cart near a stack of carrot bags. She walks over to the deli, taking a ticket, standing there, looking up at the digital number display. There have to be at least ten people in front of her. Matt longs after the trolley that is sitting there. He is about to get on with his own shopping, when a different woman walks past and starts pushing the full cart away.

What?!

Perplexed, Matt watches the retreating trolley roll away, pushed by a pale girl with black hair. 'Girl' isn't the best description. She is around Matt's age, her pigment-free skin standing out against her raven hair. She is thin, dressed in a black t-shirt and tightly fitting jeans. Matt turns around, back to the woman who was formerly in possession of the trolley. She's still standing there, looking up, waiting for her number to be called. Matt doesn't know what to do. He feels like he should go over and tell the woman what just happened. Looking around, he checks to see if anyone else has seen the theft. It's only him. Matt is at a loss. Is this some kind of silent crime that happens often? Working on impulse, Matt starts to follow the pale girl who is now walking towards the checkout. He hides behind a stand full of corn chips and watches her put her bounty on the black conveyer belt, divided from another person's shop by a white plastic baton. She looks calm, placing her jar of honey, pasta sauce and Hokkien noddles down in line. She doesn't look around. She just waits like any normal customer. She's a professional. A professional trolley thief. The girl turns her head to look at the magazines to her left. Matt can see she has green eyes like a cat, or a witch. Her nose is small and curves up slightly at the end. She looks beautiful in her calmness, yet as cold as the supermarket floor.

Matt turns around and looks back toward the fruit and veg section. The woman at the deli has now noticed that her food is missing. She's spinning around in circles, scratching her head, like she's thinking: '*where on earth did I put my trolley*?' She doesn't look angry, just confused. Matt watches her, amused by the reaction. She has no idea what just happened. Matt feels a small tingle of power, knowing the answer to something that's so baffling to another person. He thinks about telling her what happened, but dismisses it. The trolley thief at the checkout is a lot more interesting.

Again, he watches from behind his corn-chip camouflage. The trolley thief is almost done. The last of her items - which are not her items - are being placed in reusable bags that she has pulled out of her handbag. An environmentally conscious, trolley-thief witch. She pays with a credit card and pushes her haul out of the automatic doors. Matt is lifted out of his voyeuristic spell as the doors close behind her.

He wants to run after her. He wants to see where she goes and what kind of life she leads. But he just stares at the doors, imagining he was the kind of person who could do something like she did. An outlaw. A rebel without a cause. A trickster. Matt takes one step forward, then stops, letting her go. He still needs to get some food.

Four

Back at his asbestos unit, Matt unpacks the groceries. Images of the trolley thief start flitting around the edge of his mind. Her eyes, her skin and the unusual aura she had about her. She was odd; that went without saying. Yet there was something about her that was irresistible. She is proof that chaos doesn't consume you if you don't play by everyone's rules. For a moment, he imagines the lady whose trolley was stolen getting home, with a look of complete bewilderment still on her face, telling her family about the mysterious disappearance. Her extra hour of shopping that day is well worth the mileage she gets out of telling the story to all of her friends. The thought helps Matt rationalise any negative feelings against the trolley thief. She isn't hurting anyone. She's simply bending social conventions to suit her life. But she is gone. Any fantasies he might have of running into her again are just that: fantasies.

Shaking the thoughts of her away like dandelion spores, Matt puts the groceries away into their proper places. Once he's finished, he walks aimlessly around the unit looking for something else to do. Going outside is out of the question, it's hotter than the hairs on Satan's ass out there. At least the old evaporative cooler that buzzes in the corner of the lounge room provides a small shred of relief.

Matt notices the local paper that has been sitting folded on the coffee table since Wednesday. It's routine for him to take it out of his letterbox each time it's delivered, leave it on the table unread for a week and then throw it in the recycling when the new one turns up. Since today has been a day of unusual happenings, Matt does the unthinkable and actually picks it up to have a look. At first it seems like the same old paper he has seen for years – the local cricket team had a win against their arch rivals, someone caught a big fish down at the boat ramp and the RSL club have changed their dinner menu for the new year. Hard hitting current events. Then, Matt comes to the 'letters to the editor' section and an entry catches his eye. It reads:

Stop Stealing My Flowers

To the callous thieves who have been taking flowers out of my garden, please stop. I work very hard to get my rose bushes budding and my azaleas blooming. I spend money on seeds and hours with dirt on my hands. Picking what is not yours as you walk past is a crime. You are stealing. Please think twice before robbing an old man of the only joy in his life. Your mindless actions are what is wrong with society. I hope you're happy with yourselves. Stop your nefarious ways now, before you stoop to robbing banks.

Sincerely, William Keats

Matt reads the letter twice, half smirking at the ridiculousness of the situation and half feeling pity for William. He knows the garden. It is huge and full of amazing flowers. People who walk past have been picking them for years - including Matt's mum from time to time before she left town. Bill, as the locals know him, and his wife Mavis used to see people do it and smile and wave. They might even come over and say hello. But a few years ago, Mavis had died. While the flowers around the garden continued to bloom, Bill's presence had turned into one of bitterness and mistrust, especially towards out-of-towners who couldn't call him by his name. It looks like the constant picking of the flowers has finally seen Bill crack. It's a shame really. They are such beautiful flowers and, before Mavis left, Bill had always been quick to have a laugh. An idea starts to form in Matt's head and, before his usual self-conscious voice can tell him not to bother because nothing will come of it, Matt opens his laptop and starts writing.

My Flower Stealing Shame

Dear Mr Keats, I am so very sorry to say that I am one of the people who has been taking your flowers without permission. I had no idea that you felt this way, and you're right to say that I just wasn't thinking when I did it. I do have an interesting story to share though. Recently, I picked a big bunch of your roses for my girlfriend. We moved to town last month to settle here and we love it. I wanted to give her the perfect gift to go along with the engagement ring I had just bought her. After a very nervous wait, I proposed Friday when she came home from work. She said yes! I have no doubt that your lovely flowers helped with her positive reply. What woman could say no to her lover holding freshly cut flowers in one hand and a diamond in the other? I would love to repay you somehow. Could I drop $50 in your letterbox? Even better, perhaps you could put out a donation bucket for anyone who picks a flower. Encourage people to be honest in a trade of give and take. Maybe some gold coins could then be spent on new gardening supplies? I'm sure you need to cut some flowers away anyway, so those bushes don't get too crowded. You might even leave pre-cut bouquets in another bucket so people won't take ones you're trying to groom. Just a thought anyway. I hope you allow the joy of your flowers to be spread wider than your garden. You may be surprised at what people will give back in return, if you give them a way to do that.

Best Regards
Eric Arthur-Blair

Matt stops. His gut tells him that he should delete the letter, but then an unbidden question pops into his head: *what would the trolley thief do?* He doesn't even have to think to know the answer. Matt immediately creates a fake email account for Eric and sends it to the editor of the newspaper. He regrets it almost as soon as he hits the 'send' button. Surely the letter will be spotted for a fake right away. Eric Arthur-Blair seems such an obvious pseudonym that it will scream hoax. Matt starts to worry that somehow it might get traced back to him. He starts to worry that Bill will take the suggestion hard and it will upset him. After a few moments of panic, he realises he's being silly. It's a harmless prank and, besides, the editor will never publish something that is so obviously a load of rubbish.

As the stress of being found out fades, a slight thrill runs through Matt. He actually pulled the trigger on something, instead of just sitting in the status quo. Maybe it was the lingering enchantment from the trolley thief that made him do it. Matt doesn't know, but he likes the feeling. It feels good to have written something other than a work email. At school, he used to be obsessed with short stories. His Grade-Three teacher wrote in a report once that he had 'a towering imagination'. Matt's mum had stuck it on the fridge as a badge of honour that was higher than any of the A's he had received for maths or science. In high school, he'd won the Year Ten creative writing competition. The box of Cadbury Favourites he'd received as the prize tasted sweeter than anything he'd had in his life. But his enthusiasm had been chipped away after he started submitting to 'real life' publications. Rejection slip after rejection slip had clogged up their mailbox at home. One letter back from his favourite magazine had actually said 'please stop sending us stories'. Eventually, Matt gave up trying to chase a goal that seemed intent on destroying his ego through death by a thousand paper cuts. Instead of writing he started to spend his time reading, escaping from reality rather than living his own. It wasn't so bad, really. Rather than being a writer he got to be a Hobbit hunting for gold, or a space captain searching for new planets. Instead of reaching for the stars in real life, he got to fly through them in his dreams.

Five

Falling, Matt's arms flail above his head. He plummets feet first into the yawning darkness of eternity. The rush of air and water surges all around and the fall continues, on and on. The crashing rocks rise up at terminal velocity. Sandstone and whitewash stretch apart open arms. Just before he hits, Matt shudders awake. The disappointment is overwhelming. No nightmare is as scary as this mundane world on the wakeful side of reality. No nightmare could compare to Mondays.

Five

The car won't start. Matt tries for fifteen minutes before he lets his head rest in defeat on the steering wheel. He regrets revving it so hard on Friday afternoon when it was pushed to its limit. Matt could call the RAC, but they might be hours. He can't call in sick. He doesn't have any days left. There is no choice but to run for the bus.

Mr James is standing at his cubicle when Matt arrives. All Matt can stammer is that it isn't his fault, before he is interrupted.

'Laying the blame elsewhere is a weak excuse,' Mr James tells him. 'If we deny responsibility for our actions, then we take away our power to change for the better. You're a coward, Matthew. You do not have what it takes to improve yourself. This is your second and final formal warning. One more slip up, no matter how small, and you're done at Optitel. Now get to work.'

When Matt sits at his desk, there is already an email in his inbox from Mr James. It's addressed to the head of the HR department, with Matt cc'd in for his benefit. The email details the nature of Matthew's last two warnings. It says that despite strong mentoring from Mr James, Matt refuses to fit into Optitel's company culture and is not fulfilling his latent potential. There are so many big words in the body of the email it is clear that it has been designed to make Mr James sound smarter than he really is. Matt would find this comical, if his job weren't on the line.

Matt's eyes flick to his draft folder where his email about company versus customer service is lurking, ready to be unleashed. To stop himself from committing career suicide, he clicks open the internet and searches 'interesting ways to kill yourself'. The first entry says that falling through a bunch of chainsaws would be bound to make headlines. Another forum suggests hiring hitmen on every continent around the world, then trying to evade them. To make things even more exciting, the bounty should be high enough that the hitmen will also subcontract out extra hitmen, creating a freelance army to hunt you down. The dark humour jolts Matt out of any serious intention of further searching.

He minimises the window, puts his headset on and pushes the flashing light on his phone panel to start his work day. The first call is an elderly lady who cannot understand the charges for directory assistance. She thought directory assistance was supposed to be a free service. Of course, this would be the case if she had used the unadvertised, recently changed number for free directory assistance. However, she had chosen to use the new upgraded assistance line advertised on TV, which connects you directly to the number you want for another extra fee. The lady sounds close to tears on the phone and says that her husband is going to rip shreds off her. The bill is so much more than usual. Matt's heart goes out to the old lady. He feels like she's been tricked. This shouldn't have happened. He pauses, looking at the notepad next to his desk with the words 'customer service or company service?' written on it.

'Did I hear you say that you want to close your account?' Matt asks her.

His pulse starts racing a little faster.

'Oh no, I didn't say that. I'm just sorry I didn't know the free number.'

'Because if you were going to close your account with us, then I can offer you a rebate on the disputed charges and provide you with the correct free directory assistance number. You did say you wanted to close your account with us, didn't you ma'am?' Matt presses.

The woman pauses for a few moments. 'Um, I'm not sure.'

'That's okay, ma'am, I understand you're very angry. I'll go ahead and refund those charges as long as you stay with Optitel. Would you like me to do that?'

'Oh, yes please,' she says, finally catching on. 'I may have closed my account otherwise. Thank you for your wonderful service. I'll remember to call the right number in the future.'

'You're welcome.'

The call puts Matt in a better mood. He feels like he's done a good deed. Maybe inching out of protocol isn't so bad. The job could be so much easier if they were allowed to do the right thing, instead of the profitable thing. The trolley thief would approve.

Matt decides to reward himself with a fake cigarette break. Z is already out in the baking heat of the courtyard, sucking cinematically on her Zsa Zsa stick, as if she has a bubble of air-conditioning around her.

'Well you look different,' Z says in her husky tone, 'did you get a haircut or something?'

Matt takes out his crumpled cigarette, smooths it off and holds in between his fingers, trying to do his best James Dean impersonation.

'I don't know what you're talking about.'

Z's eyes narrow.

'Wait, I know what it is. You're smiling. Well spank my ass and call me Kitty, I don't think I've ever seen a real smile on your face before! It suits you.'

Matt puts his head down, trying to stop himself from smiling even more.

'Did you get your dick sucked on the weekend or something?'

Matt's smile drops.

'No! It was just an old lady.'

'You let an old lady go down on you? Gross!' Z teases.

'No, on a call, just then. I helped her get some charges refunded. It just feels good to help someone for once.'

'Well good for you, keep it up.' Z expertly flicks her finished cigarette out of its holder and into the bin by her side. 'Just remember, nobody satisfies our customers like I can,' she gives an exaggerated wink and leaves the courtyard.

When Matt gets back to his desk he is determined to help the next customer out any way he can. This time it's about mobile phone charges. A higher bill than expected, charges for voice mail, charges for reconnection when the line has dropped out, charges for data usage over the designated plan limit.

Matt lowers his voice.

'Can I be honest with you, sir? If I was you I'd be angry about this too. I work for Optitel and my mobile phone is with another provider. I won't say their name, but they have a red logo. Looking at your usage here, I would say that a fifty-dollar plan with them would more than halve your bill. Coverage? Well our coverage is better, but it appears the vast majority of your calls are made in the city and that provider has excellent coverage in urban areas. Yes sir, I am able to cancel your plan. I'm sorry I couldn't be of better service.'

Matt's heart is thumping when he hangs up. His fingers are tingling with excitement. This is what customer service should be like, serving the people rather than the company. The rest of the day flies by. He issues advice to the best of his knowledge to get customers what they deserve. He actually has people thanking him at the end of phone calls. His last success for the day is convincing a woman to roll her home phone into their business account, along with mobile and internet usage. That way, calls between all of those lines are free of charge and they get a discount for online. It will save them hundreds of dollars a year.

When Matt steps onto the bus, his head is held high. He hums to himself as he flops down into the seats that smell like dirty socks. He taps his knees, mimicking the drumbeat of *Stairway to Heaven* by Led Zeppelin, which plays in his head. Today was a good day.

Six

Black tar squishes beneath the Holden's tyres as Matt pulls out onto the main road. The incessant heat has softened the bitumen so much that it feels more liquid than solid.

Thank god the cool change is due to hit tonight, thinks Matt.

He winds down all of the windows, to get as much air as possible circulating through his would-be incinerator of a wagon. The RAC had come and fixed the problem with the car last night. Apparently, the starter motor is buggered. They showed him a little trick where if you tap it lightly with a hammer it puts the brushes back in alignment to get things going. Matt doesn't know what 'the brushes' are, but he doesn't need to know. He can work a hammer and that's all that matters.

The roads are practically empty, as if people have gone on strike because of the tiresome weather. It's an easy 100km/h drive up the highway. At the start of the city, Matt eases back to a normal speed. The whomp of air coming in the windows dies down to a whistle. The radio now seems ridiculously loud. Matt turns it down and continues to listen to the angelic voice of Jeff Buckley. It's one of Matt's favourite songs: *Lover, You Should've Come Over.* The lyrics make him feel like someone has put into words how love should feel. Not that Matt has been in love. He just assumes that's what it must be like. He did have a long-term girlfriend once. Helena. You couldn't call what they had 'love'. It was a more an acceptance of each other's company. They'd mostly bonded over alternative music, getting a thrill out of introducing a new band the other hadn't heard of. They'd listen to records, but hardly talk, making out when Helena wanted to. After one drunken high-school party they'd lost their virginity together in the back of her sister's car. The relationship had crumbled not long after, because Helena had taken interest in a guy from university that was worldlier and more daring in his musical tastes. The only exposure Matt has had to romance since has been through movies, music and pornography. He suspects they're not strictly true-to-life representations, but doesn't have the first-hand data to prove it. The only other sexual encounters he has had were hazy, alcohol-fuelled things, where he had been able to work up enough courage to approach a girl and she'd been inebriated enough to invite it. The details of each one are hard to fully remember, but at least none had taken place in the back of automobiles.

Matt is at his desk by 8:45 a.m. He thinks about coffee but the idea of shoving a scalding brew into his body is beyond comprehension. He gets a cold can of Coke out of the vending machine in the kitchen instead.

When Mr James comes to his desk, he's actually smiling. Matt wraps up his call and looks up to his boss. As if by conditioning, Matt's stomach growls in nervous protest and his fingers start to twitch.

'Matthew. I'm glad our little talk yesterday got through finally. Not only were you on time today, but I've received two emails from the feedback department saying that customers have called in to express their thanks for the help you gave yesterday. Well done. I wonder if you might be able to step into our orientation training today, to take some new employees through a few exercises?'

Matt simply nods and forces a smile. He hates training exercises. It's like he's being punished for helping people. There are only ever two kinds of people at training: those too stupid to understand what you're saying, or those who think they know better already and don't listen.

'Okay then, see you at 2:00 p.m. in the conference room. Bring your 'A' game,' Mr James says.

A small amount of bile rises into Matt's mouth. His 'A' game? *Some people are just born wankers*, he thinks.

The dreaded prospect of saying something wrong in front of a pack of newbies makes the morning plod along at an agonising pace. His hands tremble every time he considers the afternoon and what he's going to say. Lunch is hard to push down. A lack of saliva in his mouth means Matt has to chew his sandwich into a gummy pulp, before swallowing the ball of bread and lettuce. It's a major battle of will to consume the last of it.

With a pen and notepad tucked under his arm, Matt makes his way to the conference room. He knows he isn't going to use the stationery, he just doesn't want to look like he's going in unprepared. Something in your hands means something to contribute. You don't go into battle unarmed.

The group of new recruits looks like a roll call of talent-show rejects. There's the man-child with a baby face covered in shaggy red stubble; the girl dressed in a pink latex dress, who is chewing gum at the speed of light; the teenager wearing a suit two sizes too big for him; and the likely-single mum with blue tattoo lines for eyebrows that make her look like she's shocked to be there. Those are the ones who at least make some kind of eye contact when Matt enters. The rest sit with heads down, doodling notes that don't need to be taken. Mr James is standing at the front with a whiteboard on one side of him and a computer and telephone hook-up on the other. Z is there as well. She gives Matt a surreptitious wink, which puts him at ease. A least she's there as back up if needed.

'Ah, Matthew,' Mr James booms. 'Thanks for joining us. Everyone, this is Matthew Pearce, he's been a call centre employee with Optitel for the past two years. He'll be able to share some at-the-coalface advice that will prove valuable when you're down in the mines.'

He laughs at his own joke in a pig whine and motions for Matt to take a seat against the wall. Mr James then proceeds to give his 'you're very lucky to be working for such a great company' speech, before going through the basic operations of the system. Word for word this is the same speech that Matt listened to when he first started his training. Even the jokes are scripted. Matt zones out and looks at the people in the group. Under the stark fluro lights, every purple blotch of imperfection and poorly applied clump of foundation shows up on their disinterested faces. Pink Latex Girl is scribbling notes, while Red Stubble looks up at the ceiling. Big Suit is picking his nose. He finds what he's digging for and scrapes a green booger out with his index finger, studying it closely before wiping it under the desk he's sitting at.

Just another bunch of revolving-door employees. Matt wants to scream: 'get out now, before they crush your souls!'

'Matthew,' Mr James says.

Matt jerks his head up, out of contemplation.

'Would you mind fielding a call on loudspeaker to show our new friends how it's done?'

Matt stands up without comment and goes over to the phone. Those present perk up with some interest. A small buzz of tension beats into Matt. What if he stuffs up? He starts to picture the class in their underwear to help relax. Big Suit is wearing a G-string, Red Stubble is in red boxers and Tattoo-Eyebrows doesn't seem to be wearing anything at all. Her saggy tits flop around like a pair of potato-filled stockings. Now pleasantly distracted, Matt looks down at the computer screen. He selects a waiting call and picks up the receiver. The line is dead. He clicks the button a few times, but nothing happens. Matt clicks again and puts the person back on hold.

'I don't think it's working, Mr James.'

'Nonsense. I hooked it up myself.'

Matt answers another call and clicks on the loudspeaker function, which just crackles white noise. He hangs it up, then repeats the process just to prove his point. Z leans in and tries to get it working, but can't.

'Well, it appears we have a technical difficulty,' Mr James laughs falsely. 'It seems even the pros can get it wrong sometimes. Never mind. Thank you, Matthew. We can listen to some calls from yesterday instead.'

Matt goes white. Yesterday.

Mr James leans over Matt's shoulder and takes the mouse in his hand. The smell of spiced cologne makes Matt want to vomit. Mr James pulls up some files. He double clicks on Matt's name and then selects a call.

'In order to ensure Optitel maintain our excellent customer service, your call may be monitored or recorded' a woman's voice says.

Matt swallows a lump in his throat. When you don't hear the message at the start of the call yourself, it's so easy to forget.

'Thank you for calling Optitel, this is Matt. Can I start with your name please?' Matt's voice sounds whiney to his own ears.

Matt sits there, with his head down. He doesn't even need to listen. He knows what's coming. The first one is the call with the old lady who had trouble being charged for directory assistance. It plays all the way through without Mr James stopping it. Matt looks up to see some puzzled looks on the faces of the trainees. He swings his head to his boss. Mr James is sitting there, with his arms crossed over his chest, a smug smile on his face. His eyes are saying: 'I've got you now, you little oxygen thief.'

Matt looks over at Z. She stares at him with her mouth open.

The next call starts. Matt listens to himself tell the man to go with another mobile phone provider because it will be cheaper. He can't take his gaze from Mr James, who is sitting there, licking his lips like a brute lizard. *He knew*, Matt thinks. *Why is he doing this?*

As if in answer, Mr James stands up. He moves casually to the computer, leans over Matt and hits the mute button.

Six

'Now, my friends. I thought that rather than the same boring training drills, we could have some fun this afternoon. Today is Matthew's last day at Optitel. He's being fired for poor customer service skills, poor attendance and for not following the script we professionally provide. Optitel is a good company and we only want good people working for us. We want team players, not lone wolves. Let Matthew be a model of what not to do in your job here. Do not take matters into your own hands. Do not stray from the script. If you step out of the boundaries, you will become lost like him.'

Matt's whole body has gone numb. He can see the amused looks on the trainees' faces. The smiles that say: 'We're better than you. We might look stupid, but you are stupid'. He looks back to Mr James, who is smiling malevolently.

'Matthew, I wish I could say it's been a pleasure, but it hasn't. Now please report to HR and they will brief you on your departure. Please everybody, a round of applause for Matthew's ignorance.'

Mr James starts clapping and the others follow, except for Z who just stares at Matt with a sad look on her face. Matt gets up and all but runs out of the room. The sound of flesh-slapping palms chases him out into the hallway. He feels dizzy. He feels ashamed.

He feels angry at being embarrassed like that. Most of all he feels worthless, like he really is a waste of the air he breathes. By the time Matt gets back to his desk, one of the human resource managers is there, waiting. Matt is handed a small box in which to pack his things and is told that because he has been terminated, he will qualify for social benefits without a time gap. His departure gift is an Employment Separation Certificate and a business card with the address of the nearest Centrelink office on it. Welfare, government support, The Dole. He'll be supported by his own taxes until he can find a new job.

Impotent anger flares inside Matt. He wants to yell, to scream that all he did was help his customers. But he just packs his meagre tidbits off of his desk into the tiny box in silence. He looks up to the HR person who is staring out over the room with a distant look, like she's giving Matt his privacy while he says goodbye to his cubicle. Before Matt stands to leave, he opens his email draft folder, finds his note about customer versus company service and hits send. It's one last silent flip of the bird, before he heads off into the abyss of unemployment.

Seven

Matt doesn't know how he got home, but he must have driven. His car sits clicking heat in the driveway. He stands on the steps of his apartment with his head in his hands. The stifling temperature of summer pushes into his brain. In the distance, a rolling crack of thunder rumbles like a stalking beast. Looking up to the western sky, he sees the black and purple maelstrom looming on the horizon. Matt turns and looks back to the door of his house, then back to the car. The wind begins to sweep up in pace and the surrounding air drops in temperature. It won't be long until the storm breaks.

A strong gust of wind rattles the fence. As if he's in a trance, Matt walks down off the steps and gets back into his car. It's only a few minutes until the Holden rolls into the lookout car park. There's not a soul in sight. Everyone is hunkered down in the sanctuary of their homes. Out to sea, the swirling black clouds gallop toward land. The sea is a frenzy of white caps and swell. The sky and ocean are two mirror storms, linked together by forks of lightning. Each blast of luminescence is followed by a gut-vibrating clap of thunder. Inside the Holden it's warm and safe. Outside it's cold and dangerous. Without hesitation, Matt opens the door and steps out into the fury of nature, letting reality cloak him. It isn't raining yet, but the moisture in the air is palpable. The gale rips the car door out of Matt's hands, slamming it shut. The noise is drowned out by wind and thunder. Standing to face the storm, Matt watches as darkness descends on the coast. He trudges foot over foot toward the lookout, the wind buffeting his body. Stepping over the railing, he jumps down onto the grass. His feet inch toward the cliff edge. Matt makes it right to the precipice and leans over, looking down. Below, waves explode onto the rocky point with such ferocity that it sends a shudder through the cliff. A shower of white spray shoots up to meet the first droplets of rain coming down from the sky. Matt watches with overwhelming sadness welling inside him. The storm smacks into the cliffs like a black fist. Matt is almost pushed onto the ground by the wind and rain that pours down.

A deep sense of sadness soaks into Matt's skin. Rain stings his face like tiny daggers, mixing with the tears now flowing down his cheeks. The icy air numbs his body, matching the feeling within. He looks over the edge, down at the rocks and the violent sea.

He can't even hold down a shitty job. He's stupid. He should have made something of himself by now. What that 'something' is Matt isn't sure, but it seems painfully obvious that he should have started working toward it long ago. Now it's too late. He's no longer new and shiny. At twenty-five he's wasted material.

Guilt churns Matt's mind as the rain comes down. He has no right to be depressed. No right to be on this cliff edge. He never lacked security or opportunity. His parents had been middle income. Never hungry or in need of shelter, life had been comfortable. He had never had any real struggle. He was never abused, never beaten or molested. He was loved. Is loved. But love and security hadn't amounted to inspiration, or happiness. It only amounted to walking a mundane path without any real connection. He doesn't feel like an interesting individual, or even part of something bigger. He's nothing: a capsule of emptiness.

The waters below look up with a black smile of promise. Matt sits down, sobbing.

People will say: '*Why did he do it? He had a roof over his head, money in the bank. He had a normal life.*'

Yet Matt hasn't even been able to maintain that with any kind of enthusiasm. He has no purpose, no goals and no prospects. Even then, there is no real reason for him to want to jump. He's not a refugee, or a victim of violence. He wouldn't be able to explain it if somebody asked. It's a feeling of heaviness that can't be shaken off. Like having all the opportunity in the world and letting it slide by has been a crime against himself.

Matt doesn't want people calling him a coward after he dies. It's guilt on every side no matter which way he looks. The only way out is down.

A flash of lightning blasts into the sea, splitting the waters momentarily. The sizzling ocean revives Matt's thoughts back to life like a paddle shock to the heart. He gasps in breath. *What is he doing?* He shouldn't be here. He turns back and looks up at the wooden railing of the lookout. Another burst of lightning illuminates the sky, followed instantly by a rage of thunder. He takes one last glimpse down and then inches himself back along the slippery grass to safety. He lets the rain pelt into his face. After what feels like an age, he picks himself up and climbs back toward the car.

Shutting the door behind him, the warmth inside envelops his soaked body. Still staring out at the roaring cold outside, Matt starts to punch the steering wheel. His hands thump into the plastic again and again. Bones crunch with each strike, sending pain shooting up his arm. It's the first real thing he's felt in a long time. Finally exhausted, Matt collapses back in his seat.

It's night when Matt turns on his car and rolls out of the car park. The worst of the storm has blown past. It's still raining, but the intensity has gone. The road is slick and shiny. Distorted streetlights reflect off puddles in the gutter. The pedestrian crossing ahead glows green. As the Holden nears, the lights turn red. Matt can't believe it. There isn't anyone around. He looks left and right. Not even a bird. Matt looks up at the red and narrows his eyes. Why is he letting something so stupid control him? It seems ridiculous. He's fed up with following rules that don't matter. Matt eases his foot down onto the floor. He is breaking the law as he rolls through the red lights.

Matt's eyes flick up to the rear-view mirror. There is another car coming up the street behind him. His heart sinks: the cops. The wagon pulls up to tailgate him. The headlights behind are almost blinding in the mirrors. Matt's heart beats hard against his ribcage. He blinks and looks ahead, seeing his driveway. Clicking on his indicator, he slows the car and pulls to the curb. The wagon behind glides past without dropping any speed. It wasn't the police after all, just another white Holden. His heart is still thumping.

Matt looks back to the rear-view mirror and stares at himself. He is drenched. His face is blanched white, hair plastered onto his forehead. He smiles. A spark shows in his eyes that he hasn't seen before. He'd just broken the law and gotten away with it. He'd been caught at Optitel and paid the price. But not this time. In a silly way it feels empowering, like he's finally taken his destiny into his own hands.

Maybe life can be more interesting, if you're willing to make it that way, Matt thinks. An image of the trolley thief flashes unbidden into his mind. It makes him smile again. He looks down at his hand, which is now swollen like a black and purple boxing glove. Each thump of his heart sends a throb of pain through it. Feeling the skin and knuckles gingerly, he doesn't think anything is broken: just bruised. It will heal and fight another day.

Eight

Matt sleeps like the dead. He doesn't dream, doesn't snore, doesn't twitch. He's a breathing corpse wrapped in a duck-down doona. Contemplating killing yourself is exhausting. It's 11:00 a.m. before the light of the post-storm day gets bright enough to wake him up.

Still lying in the security of body-warmed sheets, Matt reaches over to his mobile phone and dials the number for Centrelink. A machine answers, delivering recorded options. 'Dial 5 to report an over payment' seems the most promising to get him through quicker than normal. Matt knows from

Optitel that some callers get ranked as priority. Those where the company may be able to recoup some extra money normally get top billing. Once you're through, you don't go back into the queues until your call is resolved.

It's only two rings before someone picks up. After a brief exchange, Matt is transferred to the correct department and is surprised that The Dole has now been repackaged into a more confidence-boosting term: Newstart Allowance. His customer service representative's name is Gerard. Gerard sounds like he has tissue paper shoved in his nose and is reading direct from a script next to him. Matt rattles off his personal details in a monotone to match Gerard's. Yes, his employment status has changed. Yes, he has a Separation of Employment Certificate. No, he doesn't own any assets.

Gerard explains that because Matt has registered his intent to claim, then should all other requirements be fulfilled, Newstart will be back paid to today. He needs to visit an employment services centre so they can assess his skills and provide career recommendations, then every two weeks Matt must lodge details of jobs he's applied for. Other than that, he can do as he pleases. Matt takes down his call receipt number and is about to hang up, when an idea strikes him.

'Gerard, do you like your job?' he asks.

Eight

'I'm sorry?'

'Do you like your job? I used to be in customer service and I hated it. People yelling at me all the time for things I had no control over. Being part of a system so rotten that you feel sick. I ended up getting fired and that's why we're talking about The Dole, I mean Newstart. To be honest it's quite a relief to be on the other end of the call. I just wanted to let you know I've been in your shoes and I appreciate your help.'

'Oh,' Gerard says before pausing. 'Well, thanks. No, I don't really like it, my job that is.'

'Wait, Gerard,' Matt stops him. 'Remember this call is probably being recorded. Don't elaborate. I'll just say that I understand how you feel.' Matt pauses for a few moments. 'Hey, is it possible to have my employment interview with you in the closest office?'

'I'm sorry, we're not the ones doing the advising. That's all outside contractors totally separate from us.'

'You're kidding?' Matt says, surprised.

'We just help provide monetary support. I should also mention that the one employment advice provider I can see listed here in your area is a paid service.'

'What? Really?'

'Yeah, I know. Sorry. There's one in the city that's free. If you'd prefer them I can get you a booking for tomorrow. They're called Job Smart.'

'Okay, do you know which one is better?'

'Honestly? I have no idea. Like most things it probably depends a lot on the person you get.'

Matt sits silent for a few moments, weighing his options.

'Matt?' Gerard asks. 'I can't do it over the phone because it's not my job, but if you don't have any luck with these guys, I can head down there one weekend and catch up for a beer to talk options with you. You seem like a good person and I'd be happy to help.'

'Really? You'd do that?' Matt is astonished.

'Sure.'

'I dunno mate, I don't want to impose.' Matt says, feeling weird about asking a stranger for his time.

'Well, you need to go to these guys anyway to tick the box in our system. So, give them a go first. If it doesn't work, it'll give me a good excuse to head down the coast for the day. I've been meaning to for a while anyway.'

'You sure? Really sure?'

'If it makes you feel any better, you can buy the beer,' Gerard laughs.

'Okay then. Deal. Thanks Gerard.'

'Of course. Just email me a time and place to catch up one weekend and I'll be there. In the meantime, try to enjoy a little time off. If you need anything else in terms of Centrelink, hit me up directly. I'll help where I can.'

Eight

Gerard provides a direct number for his desk and an email to reach him on.

'Unreal, thanks so much, Gerard. You've been a great help.'

After Matt hangs up he feels odd, like he's just agreed to meet someone on a Tinder date. He's hopeful that things might turn out well if they catch up, but some part of him is thinking Gerard might be a serial killer. Still, it's worth the risk. If Gerard can help Matt figure out what he wants to do with his life, then it could be the best chance he ever took. If Gerard is a serial killer, at least he'll die in a more interesting way than throwing himself off a cliff. He might even make international news one day when he's found in a sealed drum with the rest of the bodies. Matt sighs and looks at the time: 11:20 a.m. Laying back onto the pillows, Matt puts his hands behind his head. He now has nothing to do and all day to do it.

Nine

The supermarket is surprisingly quiet. While the weekends are busy in store, lunchtime on a Wednesday shows that this once small town is still far from big. Matt walks around the aisles without purpose, trying to decide if there really is something he genuinely wants. Every time he walks up behind someone he holds his breath, hoping it will be the girl. It never is.

The aroma of rotisserie chicken draws him toward the deli. Matt lets his body lead him, shutting out any chatter in his mind that might distract him from the smell. He closes his eyes, picturing a delicious sandwich with wads of butter melting over the meat. The image is followed by a memory of eating roast chook sandwiches down on the foreshore as a family with his parents. His Dad is laughing, making jokes, excited about his new job and how great it is that they're out of Auckland. He'd already landed a big client for the company. Talking about farming equipment in a Kiwi accent seems like it's a bonus in the sales game. They assume he's worked the land as a sheepherder on some mountain somewhere. If he could only find someone to watch the rugby with, instead of that bloody AFL aerial Ping-Pong shit, things would be perfect. He gives Matt a playful nudge and steals a chip out of his hand. Matt leans in and takes a bite from his Dad's sandwich, grinning through a mouth of chicken and gravy. Matt likes making his dad laugh. Through all of this, Matt's mum looks out to sea.

'You know, I've been thinking about going back to work myself, now that Matt's settled at school,' she says, picking up a chip and studiously dipping it in tomato sauce.

Matt's dad's smile drops a little.

'Why would you want to do that?' he asks, 'We're doing well. You can be a lady of leisure.'

'Yeah, but I'm just at home all day, Vincent. I want to find something to do.'

'So take up painting, or something. You always were the artiste of the family.'

'I guess,' she says, putting the chip in her mouth and chewing.

'What's wrong with painting?' Matt's dad asks, becoming annoyed at his wife's mood.

'Nothing. I like painting.'

'Then what's the real issue, Kate?' he asks, impatient.

'I just want to contribute something to the family. Something real.'

'Raising Matt isn't a contribution?' Vincent says, like Matt isn't even there. 'It's one of the most important things you can do!'

'I know that,' Kate says, looking at her son. 'But he doesn't need me twenty-four-seven like he used to. And it would be nice to have something for myself. Just of my own.'

'Well, there it is. Miss Independence.'

'It's not just about that. It would be social interaction with other adults. We could afford to go home every now and again.'

'Why would you want to go home?' Matt's dad is angry now.

'Dad -' Matt tries to say.

'Quiet, Matt. Your mum and I are talking.' He turns back to his wife. 'So you're home sick. That's it. But this is our home now, Kate.'

Matt gets up and walks away, down to the sand where the sound of the waves drowns out anything else in the world.

The memory fades off and the sliding doors of the supermarket open as Matt leaves. Heading out the doors he sees a stack of this week's local newspaper. Remembering the email he sent off on the weekend, Matt curiously grabs a copy and flicks it open to the letters-to-the-editor section. There, in bold type, is the title of his missive: **My Flower Stealing Shame.** Matt can't believe it. They actually printed it. He looks around, suddenly self-conscious that someone might be watching him and suspect what he did. No one is watching him though. He puts the paper back in the stand before someone looks his way.

It's just a stupid letter. He rationalises in his head. *Who cares. Nothing will come of it anyway.*

Matt starts walking up the street, detouring the long way home to help put his mind at ease. He walks past an apartment block that used to be Jimmy Wilson's house. Jimmy was one of Matt's best mates in primary school, but they'd drifted apart as Jimmy started to get into footy and Matt showed zero interest in the sport. 'Not liking footy is like not liking meat pies', Jimmy had told him angrily one day. When Matt said he didn't really like meat pies either Jimmy had given him up as a lost cause. At least he had his books. Matt wondered what Jimmy was up to these days. Probably off gallivanting across Europe like most of his past high school companions.

Matt smells Bill's garden before he sees it. The potpourri scent reminds him of his grandma, Shirley. Shirley lived up in country New Zealand before she died of what Matt had thought was probably loneliness. His family visited once every few years, but the equivalent of two weeks out of two hundred left her on her own most of the time. She had refused to go into an old-folk's home. When the local meals-on-wheels provider found her keeled over among the dahlias in her back yard one hot-summer's afternoon, she was already decomposing. The family had only been back one time since, for the funeral. Matt supposes her grave has the same lonely feeling to it that Shirley's house did much of the year, visited only occasionally by relatives who prefer to get on with living, rather than thinking about the dead.

When he rounds the corner, Matt stops short. In full bloom are the same big, purple dahlias Shirley used to have in her garden. Around them is a Technicolour mix of gardenias, grevilleas, bougainvilleas, kangaroo paws and lavender. A bucket filled with bouquets of summer blooms sits on a small table next to the fence. A cardboard sign hanging underneath reads: *Flowers, Gold Coin Donation.* Bill had done it! He had seen the reply to the letter and had already put the advice into action. A woman is browsing through the offering on the table. She selects a bouquet, takes out her purse and slides a few coins into an ice-cream container next to the bucket. As the woman walks away, Matt sees Bill stalk up and check what's in the container. He huffs a little and walks away, back into the garden to tend his flowers. Matt crosses the road, keeping out of sight. He watches another woman walk up, take some flowers and offer a ten-dollar note into the container. Bill once again returns as the woman is leaving, checks what's inside and huffs off again. It seems like the old man is in a worse mood than ever.

Matt stands behind a power pole, taking in the scene with mounting curiosity. He can't figure out why Bill should be angrier, now that people are paying for the flowers. The same scenario plays itself out three more times, with different men and women, always producing the same result. Matt remembers his father's words from his earlier memory: 'What's the *real* issue, Kate?'.

There is only one bouquet left in the bucket when a larger set woman comes along and looks at the wares. She pauses for a few moments, before looking around to see Bill. She waves at the older man and calls for him to come over. From his vantage point Matt can't hear what the two are saying, but the tone is friendly and after a minute or so Bill claps his hands and trots over to a bush full of flowering snapdragons. He clips off a fresh bunch and brings them over to the woman. The pair share a few more minutes' conversation, before the bigger woman gives Bill a hug, puts a gold coin in the tub and walks away. Now Bill is beaming. Matt is about to leave when a man dressed in jeans and a t-shirt walks up to the flower table. Bill gives him a smile and a hello. The man replies with a silent nod, takes the bouquet and drops some money into the tub. Bill's smile turns into a scowl as the man walks away without further interaction, or even so much as a thank you. The old man slinks back among his flowers and Matt takes it as his cue to head home.

Back in the apartment, Matt rummages through his drawers. He needs to see if he can fix this situation. It's Matt's fault Bill put the bucket and tub out there and, if it is only going to make Bill unhappier, Matt needs to try to make things better. Not even stopping to make himself some lunch, Matt heads out the door and down the street. It's not long until Bill's garden comes back into sight and smell. Matt takes up his position across the road. The bucket on the table is almost full again. From a safe distance Matt watches the old man put a few more bouquets in and then dust off his hands. His head turns up to the sun and he wipes his brow. Glancing up and down the street one last time, Bill heads into the house. This is exactly what Matt was hoping for. Waiting for a bit longer, just to make sure Bill isn't coming back, Matt crosses the road. He takes a permanent marker out of his pocket and flips over the sign at the table. On the back side, he writes in neat script:

FLOWERS, GOLD COIN DONATION.
ASK ME FOR A SPECIAL BUNCH FOR JUST $5
- Bill

Matt puts the sign back with his message showing, slides an envelope into the ice-cream tub and resumes his secretive post across the road. A few people stop at the table and exchange a bouquet for some gold shrapnel. Most look around before they do, presumably to see if they can catch sight of Bill for the special bunch offer. After almost an hour in the scorching sun, Matt is starting to fantasise about chicken sandwiches again, when he finally sees Bill come out of the house. A teenage boy at the flower table also sees him, waving his arm and calling out Bill's name. Bill looks puzzled for a moment, like he should recognise the someone calling out to him, but doesn't. He walks up and the boy points to the sign and says a few words. Bill looks at the sign for a long time, before the boy asks him a question again. Bill nods, scurries off and clips some prime flowers off one of his many bushes. When Bill presents them to the boy, the boy's hearty thanks can be heard clearly across the street. Matt can even hear him call the old man 'Bill' again. As the boy leaves, the older man looks at the sign again, shakes his head and goes back to his garden. Matt hopes he hasn't made Bill worried that he might be getting dementia or something. His concerns fall away when the next person who comes up to the table calls out to Bill again. They have a long talk, before Bill heads away and brings back a beautiful bunch of Australian natives. The pair laugh together as Bill collects his five dollars. He moves to put the note in the tub when he notices something inside. Taking the envelope out, he opens it and his eyes go wide. Bill looks around, to see if he can see who put it there. When he doesn't, Matt watches him take a fifty-dollar note out of the envelope, along with a small scrap piece of paper. Matt doesn't need super eyesight to know what it says. It's a message from Eric Arthur-Blair, saying he must have missed Bill, but thanks for the flowers for his fiancé and that he hopes all of his customers are stopping to have a good chat with such a giving man. He knows that a proper hello is probably worth more than the money itself.

Ten

Sitting, waiting for his appointment at Job Smart in the city, Matt looks around the room. It's like the dregs of society have all come down to get together and mope. Most of the people have more tattoos than teeth, as if ink is more important to their happiness than dental hygiene. The prevailing fashion outfit of choice is tracksuit pants and a singlet. There are a lot of professional-looking people waiting as well. However, Matt chooses to focus on the characters that make him feel better about himself. Since he doesn't know anything about them personally, he can only go on appearance. There is a young boy standing with his dad whose haircut is bordering on child abuse. It's shaved at the sides with a big long mullet running down his back. His dad has the same styling. *Some people are just doomed from the start,* thinks Matt.

No one makes any eye contact, like there's some unspoken, collective sense of embarrassment at being there. The carpet is a deep navy colour with yellow swirls and red triangles randomly set into it. It reminds Matt of the carpets in cinemas and casinos, which seem to be designed to absorb any visible trace of stains, by being too ugly to stare at in the first place. Matt is moving his eyes along one of the swirls trying to find where it starts, when his name is called.

Matt looks up to see a portly man holding a black clipboard. His stomach is flopped over his belt like a big sagging teat, which is held in check by a tightly tucked-in, beige button-up shirt. The man catches Matt looking at him.

'Matthew Pearce?' he repeats again.

Matt nods his head and stands up. He feels no sense of achievement at being called. Everyone's number comes up sooner or later.

'My name is Simon,' the portly man says, as he leads Matt into a tiny meeting room with two chairs, a table and a computer. 'Take a seat,' he instructs, indicating one of the worn chairs.

Keeping silent, Matt sits and waits for Simon to finish reading what's on the clipboard in front of him.

'Okay, so it says here you have just departed a job in customer service, is that right?'

'Yes,' Matt nods.

'Do you have any other experience that's worth mentioning?'

Matt casts his mind back to his job as a dish pig at a local restaurant after he finished school. His mum had lovingly called him an 'underwater ceramic technician'. Matt doesn't think Simon will be impressed by the title. There was also the time his dad hooked him up with a labouring job with a builder mate of his, Bruce. After three days of carting timber and bricks, getting splinters and bruises in the process, Matt had sat down with Bruce for an end-of-the-week stubby. Bruce had kindly told Matt that he wasn't a labourer's asshole and that maybe he'd feel more at home in the office with his wife. That had lasted six months, filing paperwork and answering calls, before Bruce's wife had made a none-too-subtle pass at Matt. He'd made his excuses and immediately started looking for other work.

'Not really,' Matt says to Simon.

'Right, well, this won't take too long then.'

Ten

Simon shuffles the mouse on the desk in front of him, bringing the computer to life. He opens what looks like a CV template. Under work history he types in Optitel, Customer Service, along with a generic job activity description.

'What school did you go to and what was your final score?'

'Ummm, Belmont High School and eighty-six.'

Simon looks at Matt suspiciously, but writes down the school and score anyway.

'Contact details?'

Matt tells him and Simon completes the document. He hits print and the pathetic excuse for a résumé comes out on the desk.

'My advice,' Simon says, handing Matt the single piece of paper, 'is to look on the internet and classifieds section of your local newspaper and apply for any customer service job you can find. I will also keep a copy of your CV and forward it to any company that lodges customer service opportunities with us. There are plenty going around, so we should be able to find you something soon.'

Matt takes the paper, disappointed.

'That's it?'

'Not unless you have any skills you forgot to mention.'

'Well, it's just,' Matt trails off.

'Just what?' Simon looks at his watch, then at Matt.

'Well, I was hoping to do something other than customer service. It didn't really suit me.'

'Didn't suit you?' Simon purses his lips. 'Look, here's the problem. No one is going to take a chance on someone they don't know that only has work history in one job and no other education. So, it's that or going back to study.'

'Okay,' Matt says, thinking they're getting somewhere. 'What about study? What are my options there?'

'Matt,' Simon leans back in his chair. 'This is Job Smart, not Study Smart. I only get paid my bonus if you get placed in a job. You don't appear to be an idiot, so why don't you jump online yourself and look up study options if that's your deal?'

'Because I'm not sure what I want to do.'

'Then figure it out,' Simon stands up.

'But-'

'I'll do you a favour,' Simon interrupts him in a tired voice. 'I will sign the form for Centrelink that says you did your duty and came here. If you want to keep that cheque coming in, apply for jobs that you're not qualified for. Not by a lot, but a little bit. If you get a job offer from a customer service job and you turn it down, then your benefits get cut off, so don't even apply for those. Use your time gainfully unemployed to pull your head out of your ass and look for something you actually want to do. But you need to do a favour for me.'

'What's that?' Matt asks sheepishly.

'Stop wasting my time and get out of my office. It's morning tea.'

Matt exits the office with his piece of paper in hand, feeling dazed from the whole experience. There's a good chance that if Matt didn't figure out an option other than a dead-end job, he might end up like Simon, with his next snack break the most exciting thing to look forward to in the day. Sitting down in his car, Matt takes out his phone and looks up Gerard's number.

Want to catch up for that beer? he texts.

Gerard's reply pings through a few seconds later, saying he's busy this weekend, but the next one sounds good. If Matt sends through a picture of his proof of the meeting, Gerard can get his payments happening in the meantime. Matt would have thought that being offered free money would have made him feel a little bit better. It only makes him feel more worthless. Maybe he should find a barber, get a mullet and be done with it. He shakes his head and starts the car. Suicide would be a more rational option. He just hopes something worthwhile will come up soon.

Eleven

Friday night is fish n' chip night. Ever since Matt was a young kid, his parents would buy dinner at the end of the week: greasy, battered fish and chips. They used to be wrapped in old newspapers, so your fingers would turn black with print by the time you finished your meal. Since then, safety concerns about ink poisoning meant your order had to be wrapped in new, white paper with a grease shield in the middle. So much for recycling. Matt tries to think when was the last time he'd spoken with his parents. A month? Maybe two? Like staying in touch with his high school friends, Matt had every intention of making calls and writing messages. But when he went to do it, he realised he didn't have anything to say. He knew what they were up to from their social media updates and he hadn't done anything exciting himself to report. It was like the internet had lulled everyone into this fake kind of contact, where they didn't actually speak with each other, but still felt like they were somehow involved in everyone's lives. Matt had missed a few calls from his mum recently. She'd leave a message saying how everything was great in Tassie and that they thought of him all the time. He'd text back saying he's sorry he missed the call and all was good on his end. He should give them a call this weekend and let them know that he was looking for work. His mum's advice would undoubtedly be 'you can do whatever you set your mind to,' and his dad's witty response 'as long as it doesn't involve the gift of the gab.' He'd tried to bring Matt to work once, but after Matt stumbled through his first conversation with the boss, his dad began answering questions for him, to save his son the embarrassment. Even when he said to the lunch lady that Matt would love a meat pie, Matt kept silent. He didn't want to embarrass his dad either.

Matt picks up the phone to place his fish n' chip order. The phone is engaged. After a few minutes Matt tries again. It's still busy. Either the shop is flat out, or the phone has been left off the hook. Sometimes the second is a symptom of the first. The new owners don't seem to like taking phone orders when they're under the pump, so they cut the line off to avoid interruptions to their face-to-face customers. After three more tries, Matt decides to bite the bullet and just go down to order. The alternative of not eating his routine meal is out of the question.

As Matt pulls up in front of the store, it's apparent that they're extraordinarily busy. Since this is one of the few 'fast food' options in town, the result in summertime is a constant line out the door. This is especially bad on the weekends. The place is called The Fish Tank; an apt name since the wide-windowed shopfront means anyone can peer in from the street. Aquatic scenes are painted on the bottom half on the window, depicting a crayfish in a chef's hat, smiling as he eats a juicy yellow potato chip. Taking his place in the queue outside, Matt peers in the window to see the fryers stacked full of baskets, bubbling away with orders of dim sims, battered savs, flake and scallops. White, oil-splattered dockets are pegged to the end of each basket, indicating whose order is being cooked. Closest to the window, a pimple-faced teenager sweats over a hotplate stacked with burgers, eggs, onions and grilled fish. Matt watches as a drop of

Eleven

sweat drips off the young cook's nose and evaporates in a hiss between two souvlaki pitas.

The line creeps inside. The bell attached to the entrance doesn't ring, it just jingles a little as each new person entering the shop leans on the door to keep the exit clear. The man in front of Matt grumbles that there should be a local's queue, as if his money is worth more than the other hungry people waiting. The smell of fresh fish mixes with vegetable oil and melted beef fat to create an aroma unique to coastal fish n' chipperies. Matt looks at his watch. He's already been waiting for thirty minutes and he isn't even close to ordering.

'Phone order for Russell,' a skinny woman with a florid complexion yells from behind the counter.

Russell doesn't answer, so she repeats the call once more before putting the white food parcel into the bain-marie to keep it warm. So, the phone wasn't off the hook. You just had to be lucky to get through.

The line inches forward again. Matt overhears the girl taking the orders say that it is an hour wait for food.

'You can go and have a beer at the pub while you wait,' she offers.

Matt looks at his watch again. He's starving. At this rate, he'll collapse in line from low blood-sugar before he can even get to the front.

'Number eighty-six!' the woman yells, as another basket of food is dumped onto the wrapping bench.

A burly man in a black muscle-top gets up to retrieve his order. A southern-cross tattoo wobbles on his sunburnt bicep as he picks up his food.

'Phone order for Russell,' the woman screeches again, looking around at blank faces. 'Order for Russell?' she catches Matt's eye.

You would think that since Matt has eaten here every week since she started, that the woman would recognise him. She doesn't. She seems desperate to get rid of this order.

'Sorry, did you say Russell?' Matt steps forward tentatively.

'Piece of flake, minimum chips and a fried dimmy,' she says.

'Yup, that's me,' Matt says without thinking. 'I must have missed your first call.'

'That'll be $10.50.'

In a nervous daze, Matt hands over his money. *It isn't stealing*, he justifies in his mind. *I'm still paying for it.*

With the steaming bundle in his hands, Matt marches out to his Holden before the real Russell turns up. He sits is his car and looks into The Fish Tank window for a few moments, debating whether he should go back in and admit to his crime. His stomach murmurs that he should count his blessings and run. His stomach is right. Matt starts up the car and heads home.

Fish and chips have never tasted so good. Drizzled tomato sauce on chips and tartare on fish, the food slips down his gullet almost singing in delight. Matt feels charged. It isn't just the Coke he's drinking to wash down his food. His head is abuzz with possibilities. Worthless rules and etiquette had been thrown out the window and life seems lighter as a result. First the red light, now this. He hadn't been caught. There is no chance of him being caught now. This must be how the trolley thief feels when she gets her supplies.

Morally, Matt feels fine. He hasn't harmed anyone by driving through an empty pedestrian crossing. He'd paid his bill at The Fish Tank. There are no victims here. Maybe Russell would be a little upset, but Matt has no doubt the shop will make up for their mistake. They were so busy there was no way they could keep track of every single order. Victimless. Ethically sound crime. It is an interesting concept.

Sitting back, chewing on his crispy dim sim, Matt lets out a contented belch. He could get used to this, amusing himself with little pranks. Matt wonders if being constantly amused and being happy feel the same in the long run. If he could just watch movies, read books and steal chip orders without stopping to ponder about how he was doing nothing of substance with his life, would that sense of worthlessness still be there? Could he just engage in so much entertainment that he could eventually become content with the cycle? Maybe, but he'd have to win lotto or something. Even if he wasn't waiting for his fish, chips and dim sims anymore, he still had to pay for them. Centrelink won't cover that forever.

Twelve

The supermarket is packed again. Like some kind of doorbuster sale, people are pushing in lines, snatching products off the shelves and generally throwing any kind of shopper's etiquette out the window. Matt would turn around and leave now, except the chicken in his fridge has been picked clean and he has no bread left to make a cold-chip sandwich for lunch. Add onto that needing luxuries like toilet paper and he really has to get some things.

With his blinkers on, Matt weaves through the bakery section and slips two loaves into his trolley.

He almost adds in a dozen donuts that sit on the shelf alluring him with promises of glossy-icing pleasure, but stops and looks down at the list in his hands. He learned a few years ago that whenever he went shopping hungry he always spent twice as much and came home with junk. If he wants to avoid blowing his man tits out any more than he already has, he needs to write a strict list to keep him on track in the land of temptation. Scanning the list, Matt groans inwardly. If he wants to get everything on there it's going to take him hours of bunting through the aisles. He looks around, seeing if there are any abandoned carts full of food ripe for the picking. Last night's chip heist has emboldened him to make the day-to-day that little bit more amusing. It's not like the trolley-theft idea is an original one, but creativity isn't sitting high on Matt's priorities right now. His stomach grumbles again. If a trolley doesn't have bread in it, he'll have to add his own.

Matt decides to walk into the fruit and veg section. There's more space there to see opportunities and more people to obscure himself among if he makes a wrong move. Matt's hands shake in anticipation as he watches a man leave his cart next to the strawberries. He steps forward into the crush of people wanting mushrooms. A minute's hesitation costs Matt the option and the man

Twelve

leaves with his trolley and newly acquired shiitakes. Matt changes his focus to another trolley packed full of goodies, until he realises there's also a kid sitting in there. That might be a bit hard to explain at check out.

Matt almost decides to just bite the bullet and do the shopping on his own, when he spots her. The trolley thief. She's hovering next to the milk fridge, eyes intent on something near the self-serve nut dispenser. Matt follows her line of sight to see a trolley, unmanned in the herd of people. Matt looks back to the girl again. She steps forward, all cat-like grace. A lioness hunting her prey. With barely a sideways look, she walks right up to the trolley and pushes it forward. It's beautiful, like watching a professional among amateurs. She strolls away with the cart, plonking two loaves of bread and a dozen colourful donuts onto her bounty before heading for the counter. Matt is paralysed. He knows he should be going after her. His brain is screaming at him: *go now you idiot, you'll never get a chance like this again.* But he's glued there, staring glassy-eyed toward the counter. When the witch eventually gets through the check out and through the doors, Matt comes to his senses. He blinks, looks around and the sound of the world comes rushing back into the vacuum he's been occupying. Leaving his own bread sitting on top of some ears of corn, he heads for the exit. He's not letting her get away so easily this time.

Walking quickly out into the car park, Matt cranes his neck, searching for her. She's not in the first row of cars, so he moves to the next section. Looking left and right he finally spies her black hair, bobbing at the back of a pale-blue hatchback as she loads her bags into the back.

Without even thinking, Matt walks towards her. Forgetting that he doesn't like confrontation, he nears the hatchback and says in a clear voice.

'Excuse me, but that's not your shopping.'

Thirteen

The trolley thief looks up at Matt with an icy glare as he approaches. The emerald of her irises seems to draw Matt inside them. They are a mix of primal desire and intelligence, like an animal whose instincts outweigh any normal thought.

'That's not your shopping,' he repeats.

She straightens up, puts her hands on her hips and narrows her gaze.

'Of course it's mine. I paid for it.'

'But you didn't shop for it. I saw what you did. You stole my trolley.'

'Your trolley?'

She looks down at the bags in the back and rifles through the contents, taking out a small, plastic pink container.

'I suppose these are your tampons as well?' she snaps.

Matt's cheeks flush the same colour as the packet in the trolley thief's hands. He takes a step back, caught off guard. He always feels uncomfortable when confronted with women's sanitary products. It's as if a piece of wrapped-up cotton could gouge out his eyes. Maybe it's because he doesn't know enough about them to dispel any silly notions he has about their use. Maybe it's just that the associated image of a bleeding vagina isn't something he wants to envisage. He banishes the thought and renews his resolve.

'They're not yours either,' he manages to say. 'I saw you.'

The girl snarls a little, her nose wrinkles up resembling a tiger's and her eyes flash with anger.

'What are you going to do? Call the cops? What would you say? This woman paid for some groceries that aren't hers? That's not stealing. It's not a crime.'

Thirteen

Matt is stunned. He looks down at the groceries in the back of the car wistfully.

'Look,' he says in a conciliatory tone. 'I'll be honest. I wanted that trolley for myself. I saw you do what you did last week and thought I'd give it a try. But I chickened out. Then I saw you again. You're... amazing. I can't stand shopping.'

The girl's expression changes a little at the words, like she's surprised to hear them, but still doesn't want to back down.

'Surely there's some stuff in there you don't want that I can have. I'll pay you for it. There's more than enough for the both of us,' says Matt hopefully.

The two stare at each other, trying to figure out the best move to make.

Matt pulls out his wallet as a show of his intentions. The girl looks down at the bags, then back to Matt again. She seems undecided.

'You can keep the tampons,' he adds.

The comment makes a faint smile appear on her lips. It isn't enough to show teeth, but her straight line of red lipstick tips up at the edges just a little bit.

'Okay, but I get to say what you can have. And you have to take what I don't want.'

Matt isn't in any position to bargain. He doesn't want to go and waste more time in the supermarket. He just nods.

Without any further exchange, the trolley thief leans into the back of her car and starts sorting through her bags. She empties one out neatly into another and starts placing things like oranges, apples and pears inside the empty one. It looks like she's splitting everything she can right down the middle. Matt stands, tapping his foot nervously, looking around to see if anyone is watching what's going on. No one is paying the slightest attention to them. It takes the girl a full five minutes to separate the groceries into two distinct groups: four bags for her and four for Matt, including one with a fresh loaf of multi-grain bread.

'Here you go,' she says, lifting them out of the car again and putting them on the ground. 'I've tried to be as fair as I can. You get the pasta, I get the rice. You can have the soft drink and chips, but I get to keep the milk. Deal?'

Matt holds his hand out in agreement. They shake hands. Her grip is firm and much warmer than her skin tone suggests.

'How much do I owe you?'

'Eighty-three dollars.'

Thirteen

Matt flips through the cash in his wallet and pulls out eighty-five in notes, handing them to the girl.

'Nice doing business with you,' she smirks.

Shutting the boot of her car, she moves to the driver's-side door, leaving Matt standing there with his groceries at his feet.

'Wait!' he says, looking down at the shopping. 'These are your enviro-bags.'

The girl peers over her car to inspect them. She pauses for a few moments as if weighing her options.

'You can bring them back for next week's shop. I'll meet you here next Saturday morning at 10:00 a.m.'

To punctuate the statement, she gets inside her car and shuts the door. Matt picks up his new bags, while the engine turns on. He steps back, letting her reverse out. As the blue hatchback drives away, the girl gives a quick wave in her rear vision mirror.

Waving back, a thought occurs to Matt: *I didn't even get her name.*

Fourteen

Matt lays his groceries out on his kitchen bench to take an inventory. Close to everything he needs for the week is there. A few extra treats, like chocolate flavoured Yogo and mini-portioned Twisties packets indicate that the woman who did the shop must have children. There are some things on the bench that Matt wouldn't buy in a million years. The floral-printed toilet paper seems a bit excessive for its actual function and there is no way he'd ever use something called *paprika*. Regardless of the few excess pieces, it was well worth the non-effort to shop this way. It isn't something that could be done to the same person twice, but if he chose a busy time and a new target each week, potentially Matt could forever avoid the tedium of picking out his food. All he has to do now is go to the corner store for some milk. Easy.

Having finished his food audit, Matt's thoughts return to *her.* He can't believe he confronted her, let alone talked her into sharing the groceries with him. His body is still trembling from the encounter. Matt holds out his shaking hand, trying to make it go still with a force of will. The effort actually makes the trembling worse. Just then, a loud knock sounds at the door. Matt jumps so high it feels like his hair grazes the ceiling. A dozen paranoid thoughts race through his head. *It's the police. They caught us on CCTV. Someone recognised me and reported me. But I didn't even do the stealing. It's her. She wants her things back. How could she know where I live? She really is a witch.*

The knock at the door sounds again, this time accompanied by a husky voice asking: 'Matt? Are you home?'

Matt lets out a long, relieved breath. It's Z, but what is she doing there? She doesn't know where Matt lives either. He makes his way to the door, doing his best to compose himself.

'Z, this is a pleasant surprise.' Matt says, trying to act nonchalant.

'You look like you've had your butthole licked by a ghost,' Z says, taking a step back to look Matt up and down. 'Is everything okay?'

'Yeah fine, fine,' Matt waves her off, laughing at her strange way of showing concern. 'It's been a weird week. Do you want to come in?'

Z walks up to Matt and rests a hand on his shoulder. 'Seriously, is everything okay? I've been trying to get in touch, but you're a difficult man to get a hold of.'

'I've been fine, really. All normal. No worries.' Matt lies, turning around and walking back into the house to avoid any eye contact. 'Come in. Do you want a beer?'

Z looks at her watch. 'It's barely lunchtime, but sure, why the hell not?'

Matt goes to the fridge and grabs two cold beers, popping the tops off and handing one to his lanky friend.

'How's everything going at work?' Matt asks, trying to steer the conversation away from him.

'It's been a madhouse since you left,' Z says sipping her beer. 'That little email you sent out caused quite a stir. Two other people have already been fired for working outside of the script. You've become quite the hero in there after word got out about why you got the sack. Everyone is trying to give their own version of 'true customer service'.'

'You're kidding?' Matt is stunned. He had completely forgotten about his email rant. 'How'd they know why I got fired?'

Z smiles wryly.

'Someone leaked the recordings of your calls to the entire company, along with a few embellishments about how you stood up to Mr James when he told you you were through.'

'You didn't?'

'Me? Nah, no one knows who it was,' she gives a wink from behind her thick-rimmed glasses. 'They covered their tracks well, sending everything by an email routed to look like it came from an IP address in the Philippines. Mr James had a conniption when it happened. He sent around a company memo saying not to open emails from suspicious sources as they probably contained viruses.'

Matt looks at Z like he's seeing her for the first time. She was the closest thing he had to a friend at work, but it wasn't like they hung out, outside of the office. He is taken aback that she had cared enough to track him down and check up on him.

'So how *did* you find my house?' Matt asks, curiosity getting the better of him.

'Like I said, not easily. I figured you would have a mobile phone with Optitel, but nope. I had to look at your expired records in the Optitel system for any old phone numbers you had. The only one under Matthew Pearce was registered here, so here I am.'

'That's a lot of effort just to come and check that I was alright,' Matt says, arching an eyebrow. 'You don't have a crush on me, do you Z?'

'Please,' she scoffs, taking a sip of her beer. 'You're not old enough, or female enough, for me.'

Matt almost chokes on his drink. It's the first time Z has made any reference to her sexuality. There were of course rumours around the office, but Matt had passed them off as shallow, based only on appearance. Just because a woman had short hair didn't mean she was gay. Her casual obsession with asking colleagues about their adventures in oral love had always come across as a little strange, but it was endearing in a weird kind of way. This really was a day of revelations.

'Now, Matt.' Z levels her gaze at him. 'How are you holding up? Really.'

Matt shrugs. 'Oh, you know, I did want to kill myself at first. Almost jumped off the lookout at The Heads, but I'm over that now,' he tries to make it sound like a joke, but the quaver in his voice has it sound more serious than he intended.

'Oh, Matt. What that prick did was so unprofessional,' she steps in and gives Matt a hug.

He returns the embrace awkwardly, mumbling something about being fine. When he goes to pull away, Z holds him tighter. The unexpected tenderness of it makes the lump in Matt's throat burst into a strangled sob. All of the emotions he felt while standing in the storm on the clifftop come rushing back. He cries into Z's shirt, feeling embarrassed about his lack of composure, but unable to do anything about it.

Z holds Matt tightly until he cries himself out. He blubbers for a full five minutes before things finally settle down. Once the tears subside, Z pulls back and looks down at him.

'If you tell anyone that I hugged you, I'll kill you.'

The comment makes Matt laugh despite himself.

'Seriously,' she brushes off the moisture on her shirt. 'I have a reputation to uphold.'

Matt nods, looking around for his beer and taking a sip. He feels incredibly thirsty, as if his display of waterworks has dehydrated him.

'I'm sorry,' Matt starts to say, but Z cuts him off with the wave of her hand.

'Don't you dare apologise to me for being honest. Why on earth did you want to kill yourself, Matt? I noticed you'd been flat at the office for a while, but never thought you'd do something like that.'

'I don't know really,' Matt shrugs. 'I'm in my mid-twenties and have done nothing with my life. I have no prospects, no skills and no idea what I even *want* to do. I have no purpose.'

Z takes a seat, holding her beer bottle in her hand and just listening. Since she doesn't offer any comment, Matt goes on.

'I couldn't bring myself to do it anyway. I knew I shouldn't be there, but knowing and feeling are two very different things. I just feel like a waste of space. My parents would be sad that I'm gone, but I don't feel like anyone else would even notice. I'm just a mediocre blip in a world of extraordinary people.'

Z finally raises her head to speak.

'You know what, Matt? I know how you feel. Believe it or not, I've had similar feelings before. I'm not going to tell you just to cheer up, because that's fucking insulting. I'm not going to tell you that you can do anything that you want to do with your life, because that's a lie. You have options, but they aren't unlimited. And, that's a good thing. It makes your choices to move forward easier.'

The intense look in Z's eyes makes Matt pay close attention to everything she's saying.

'The way I see it, you either get another job in customer service, with a company who actually treats their customers well -'

'But...'

'OR,' Z continues, 'you go back to study to do something a bit less 'mediocre' as you put it.' Z uses her fingers to put the word mediocre in air quotes and the tone of her voice makes Matt regret what he said.

'Z, I didn't mean that -'

'I know what you meant,' she said, 'I know customer service ain't glamorous, but I find glamour in other parts of my life,' she smiles. 'And as for you being "already in your mid-twenties", get the fuck out of here with that bullshit. Twenty-five is young. Life involves eras. The first few you don't realise it because they're mapped out for you - infancy, primary school and high school. But after that you have to make your own eras. They don't have to be forty years of the same thing. Better to mix it up. You can change shapes every five or ten years and still get good at what you choose to do. Be a waiter, be an actor, go and study. But decide and commit to it.'

'That's my problem. Deciding.'

'Wait! I know what else you could do!'

'What?'

'You could find a hot MILF and be her toy boy!'

'Ha. If I were a bit taller and a bit -'

'Longer?' Z provides, holding her hands out in measurement.

'I was going to say fitter!'

'And I'm going to slap you in a minute,' Z says. 'Honestly, I don't know what you see in the mirror, but I see an attractive young man, who is kind, has a sense of humour and not a conceited bone in his body. You don't have a supermodel figure like I do, but you're far from fat. You've got the ultimate dad bod without the drawback of having kids to weigh you down. You're a straight girl's dream.'

'Dream friend maybe.'

'God, you're impossible. '

She takes a swig of her beer, falling silent and swilling the liquid around her mouth.

'You know, I did meet a girl this morning.' Matt offers conversationally.

'No!' Z perks up. 'Do tell.'

'Not much to tell really. I don't even know her name. But we're catching up next weekend to go shopping.'

Fourteen

'Oh, ka ching. You're in!'

'It's not like that. You have no idea. She's... unusual.'

'Unusual is good.'

Matt just nods. He doesn't want to fill Z in on the full details. Even though he's opened up about himself personally, he feels that letting Z into the trolley thief's world of bending the rules would somehow diminish the specialness he is feeling about it right now. It's his and the thief's little secret.

'So, you have something to look forward to then?' Z asks, sensing his discomfort at telling her any more than he already has.

Matt nods again.

'Well, that's some kind of purpose, at least in the interim.'

'I've organised to meet a guy from Centrelink to give me career advice too.'

'I'll take that as a good sign then,' Z says. 'Making plans for the future is the first step in finding your way. Here's cheers to unusual women and new opportunities.'

She holds out her beer. Matt clinks glasses with her, glad that she had cared enough to come and check on him.

Fifteen

Matt can't remember the last time he woke up at 5:00 a.m. This time is normally reserved for farmers and garbage men. Outside, faint blue light rises above the horizon, pushing back the night to herald the coming of the morning sun. Matt pulls himself out of bed. There's no way he'll be able to get back to sleep. He is anxious about how the grocery shopping will go today.

Pulling on some shorts and a t-shirt, Matt wanders into the kitchen. Everything is hushed in the anticipation of a new day. He pours himself a glass of water and lets the liquid wake his body as he drinks. He looks out at the sky and thinks maybe he should get out and do something. It does seem a waste to sit inside on the first sunrise Matt has been up for since Christmas as a kid.

On the lookout, Matt sits and hangs his feet over the edge of the decking. The tiniest sliver of red light is emerging along the horizon. It doesn't take long before the sun shows its face. It's amazing to Matt how quickly it happens. At first, just the hair of the first rays slip into view, rippling along the ocean in a shimmer of orange and red, running to meet the cold sands at the bottom of the cliffs. Then a quarter can be seen, then the full blazing orb. It's less than five minutes before the sun has leapt from the sea and is ascending into the Saturday sky. The glow off the sandstone cliffs is like a bonfire. The natural colour of the rocks enhances the light being beamed in their direction. Matt knows this happens every single day but today it feels special, because he is there to witness it.

A black dog emerges from between two trees behind the lookout path. It comes up to Matt and sniffs his face. He pulls back as it tries to lick him. The dog pants hot breath into Matt's neck, so he reaches out to give it a pat. There is a quick, sharp whistle as a woman runs past the lookout with ear buds plugged in. The dog turns toward its owner and runs off to follow her. As if that first hint of human movement was a signal, other people and dogs appear on the track, walking by the cliff-top lookout for their morning exercise.

With his solitude interrupted, Matt stands up and stretches his arms. Grumbling, his stomach lets him know that it's breakfast time. On the way home, Matt picks up the newspaper so he can check out the classifieds for jobs.

Chewing on Vegemite toast and slurping a cup of coffee, Matt pours over the black and white print for anything interesting. He sees Optitel is advertising. Even the site of the logo makes him feel ill. The ad itself is even more off-putting. *Work in a fun, supportive team environment. Career progression opportunities. Professional on-the-job training provided.* If Matt didn't already know what it was like working in one of those jobs he would probably get sucked into the positive spin on the page. The TV video-hits program *Rage* plays in the background, but Matt isn't paying attention. Matt stares at the phone-sex operator jobs and wonders if he could mimic Z's husky voice and get a gig. Probably not. Matt writes down a few jobs into his Centrelink logbook, which he knows he won't get interviews for. The minimum requirement for a fortnight search is eight jobs, so Matt lists ten. His work is done until Wednesday week. Maybe he'll fall into something between now and then. If not, he'll at least have caught up with Gerard for some advice.

It's only 8:00 a.m. and Matt is thinking again about shopping with the trolley thief. He goes to his shelf and picks up a book that he bought at the local second-hand bookshop during the week. It's called *Zen and the Art of Motorcycle Maintenance*. He had chosen it because of the quirky title. Matt likes how the weather in the book reflects the mental movements of the main character. It serves as a great distraction from his own thoughts. He opens the page and gets lost in someone else's world for a while.

Sixteen

Arriving at ten minutes to ten, Matt is early. He once heard someone say, 'If you keep someone waiting, then you value your time more than theirs.' He doesn't want the trolley thief assuming Matt thinks he is superior to her. He knows he's not.

The car park is busy. People are doing circles looking for spaces. Matt sees someone pulling out of their spot, so flicks on his indicator and waits for them to leave. He doesn't know whether he should wait in the car, in the car park, or in the supermarket. There wasn't any

Sixteen

concrete plan. All the trolley thief had said was to meet her here at 10:00 a.m. Matt decides to walk around the car park to see if he can find her blue hatchback. After an unproductive circuit, he gets back to his Holden. Looking at his watch he sees that it's 10:05. Maybe she isn't here yet.

Deciding to wait leaning on the back of his car, Matt watches the people walking in and out of the supermarket. There's an old man sitting at the front doors selling raffle tickets. There is always someone fundraising at the door of the supermarket. At Easter it's Legacy torches, in spring it's Remembrance Poppies. In between it's a hodgepodge of causes - the footy club raffling a trailer of firewood to raise money for some new jumpers, or Rotary selling tickets for a hamper stuffed with shortbread and a tartan blanket. Today it looks like the man is from the Lions Club and he's flogging the opportunity to win a meat tray. The constant stream of fundraisers has instilled a kind of charity fatigue into Matt. He rarely asks what the cause is for anymore, but if the person at the desk is quick to smile and say g'day without asking him to buy something, then he'll donate his money because of their good manners.

At 10:45, Matt is starting to think that he should just leave. It doesn't seem like she is going to turn up.

Disappointment seeps into Matt, like his shoes are filling with water. His soggy ego can't stand much more rejection. Sighing, Matt decides he's just going to have to go and do his non-shopping alone. He pulls the enviro-bags out of his car and sets off toward the doors. As he draws near, the sight of her exiting with a full trolley takes him by surprise. She's like the dawning sun that he saw that morning. Her eyes are the light and her lips are the warmth. She looks up to see Matt approaching and nods her head slightly. She looks over to the far left and signals silently that he should follow her. He trails behind until they exit the car park completely and start walking down the road toward some back streets. Matt takes in her slim figure. She's wearing a white cotton singlet and cut-off denim shorts with black stockings underneath. There is a black line on the back of the stockings that runs all the way down her calves into red Converse shoes. Her hair is pulled back in a ponytail, revealing two tiny, white ears on each side of her head. They're like baby's ears, freshly made. Matt shakes his eyes away from the hypnotising sight and catches up to her.

'I didn't think you were coming. I was waiting,' he says, coming to her side and matching her pace.

'I couldn't get a park.'

Sixteen

It isn't an apology, just an explanation.

'It took me some extra time to find a person that had enough shopping for two people,' she adds.

'I thought we were going to do it together.'

The trolley thief turns around and her eyes burn into Matt's.

'Two people, standing in the fruit and veg section together, looking inside people's carts as they go past? It's hard enough alone to get the timing right. I didn't want you to ruin it.'

Dejection deflates Matt's growing sense of excitement. 'Oh.'

The girl looks at him and realises she's unintentionally hurt his feelings.

'Look. I didn't want to raise suspicion. Maybe we can do it together next time. I even got you some extra milk and eggs. I did have you in mind.'

'Oh,' Matt's one word sentence is the same as before, but the new tone suggests happiness.

The trolley thief pulls up at her car and stops. Matt holds out the enviro-bags tentatively, like he's going through with some kind of sordid drug deal in this back street behind the supermarket.

'I'm Matt,' he offers along with the bags.

The girl's eyes flick up like the words have stung her.

'I thought you looked like an Ethan.'

'Sorry?' Matt apologises with a question.

'Never mind. I had just attached a name to you already. Now that it's not the same, you feel like a different person.'

Matt has no idea what to say.

'What did you think my name was?' she asks.

'I don't know. You just exist as you in my head, not an entire personality,' Matt lies.

The trolley thief goes on packing food into Matt's bags for him. There's a tension hanging in the disjointed silence. Matt shuffles his feet, watching his groceries go into the bags. He sees a packet of condoms and wonders if it's some kind of signal, or just an unwanted item that he's obliged to take.

'How long have you been doing this? You know, stealing trolleys?' he asks.

'About a year,' she answers. 'When I moved here no one would look at me. I felt invisible, so I thought I'd use that invisibility to my advantage.'

'Where did you move from?'

'Melbourne. It's a lot quieter here. I like it.'

Matt nods awkwardly. Having finished, the trolley thief hands him the now full bags.

'Only seventy dollars this week. The man liked looking for specials.'

Sixteen

'Would you like to go out for dinner tonight?' Matt blurts. He's been thinking about this all week. In his mind, he had sounded a lot smoother, but there is no way he's going to miss this chance.

Putting the bags back on the ground, the trolley thief studies Matt from head to toe with emerald uncertainty. He stands with unease under her glare.

'What kind of dinner?' she asks, finally.

'Fish and chips? We can eat on the lookout. I can meet you, or I can pick you up. My shout.'

She nods slowly, like she's waking up. Matt's not sure if that's a yes or a no, or just contemplation. He takes the money for the shopping out of his wallet and hands it to her. She takes it and slides it into her shorts, still looking at him. Matt feels uncomfortable under her gaze. She's looking at him like she's trying to x-ray into his emotions: lust, mixed with curiosity and good intentions.

'I can meet you at the shop. My name's Joy.'

'You don't look like a Joy.'

She smiles at the joke.

Seventeen

Matt's Holden and Joy's hatchback pull in together side by side at The Fish Tank. Matt has worn his red t-shirt for the date. He doesn't know why, but he always seems to revert to red when going out. It's like the colour is his way of dressing up, without wearing a button-up shirt. Joy gets out of her car and Matt sees she has also changed. She's wearing black jeans and a black top, with a skull encased in a love heart on the front.

Leaning over, Matt unlocks the passenger side and waves for her to get in. Joy settles into the velour bucket seat and shuts the door.

'Are we going somewhere else?' she asks in greeting.

'No, I just wanted to go over the order process with you.'

She looks at him oddly. 'I'm pretty sure I know how the order process goes at fish n' chip shops. We have them in Melbourne too.'

'No, no,' Matt smiles. 'This is like the supermarket. We're going to hijack an order. It'll take us ages to get our dinner otherwise.'

Joy looks out of the car to see the line of customers, which winds out of the shop. She nods her approval.

'Is there any chance I can request some fish? I don't like any of the other stuff.'

'I'll do my best. Basically, I'll go in and ask for a phone order that my 'friend' has called through. We'll have to take what we can get, but you can have dibs on any fish. You stand at the door and wait. Once I've paid, we walk as quickly as we can up to the lookout. It's a couple hundred metres from here, through that little bush park on the other side of the road,' Matt points to the far end of the car park to show their escape route.

'Sounds easy enough. Have you done this before?'

'Just once, but it sure beats waiting. Are you ready?'

In answer, Joy opens her door and gets out. She walks up to The Fish Tank window and stands on her tiptoes, looking inside. The bain-marie fogs up the glass on the inside of the store as steam rises out of the food case. White-wrapped parcels sit in the metal trays waiting for their owners. Names are scrawled on the side of the packets. Matt stands next to Joy, his chin almost resting on her shoulder.

'See anything you like?'

'That order for Russell looks promising,' she points inside.

Sparks of apprehension shoot into Matt's fingers. They start to twitch, like he's back at Optitel, being grilled by Mr James.

'Uh, better leave that one. I'll explain later. Just wait here.'

Pushing past the waiting customers, Matt walks inside and straight up to the counter. He peers inside the loaded bain-marie, seeing if there are some other phone orders in there he can choose from. He can't take Russell's chips off him two weeks in a row, assuming it's the same person. There are three other orders, for Hayden, Grayling and Giddins. Matt can see that Hayden has ordered two pieces of grilled flake. The florid lady at the grilling station sees Matt looking at the parcels.

Seventeen

'Can I help you?'

'Ah, yeah. My friend Hayden phoned through an order not long ago, I'm just seeing if it's ready.'

The woman eyes Matt, like she's supposed to know him from somewhere. Dismissing the thought, she looks down at the food and sees the order for Hayden.

'This is the one. That'll be twenty dollars exactly.'

Matt swaps an orange note for the parcel and turns without any further hesitation. As he exits the shop, he has to bump past a tall man wearing a faded blue trucker-singlet a size too small for him. He smells like bourbon and his thongs make a loud whack as he steps around Matt. The man shoots a surly look at Matt when he pushes past.

Holding up the food as a signal to Joy who is waiting outside, they start to walk along the red-brick walkway that leads toward the bush park across the road. They are only a few meters from the store when there is a shout behind them. Matt and Joy both turn to see the man in the blue trucker-singlet emerge from the shop. He sees them and yells.

'You! Wait!'

'Run!' Joy whispers.

The two take off. Matt tucks the food under his arm, like a piping hot rugby ball. He can hear the man screaming behind them as he gives chase. All Matt can understand is 'Stop!'. His pounding heart and feet drown the rest out. Joy streaks ahead, laughing. Her skinny legs stretch out in long strides that defy the tightness of her jeans. Matt can't see the funny side. If they get caught he's bound to take a pummelling for commandeering this man's food. Barely pausing to make sure there aren't any cars, both Joy and Matt dart across the road and into the park. Almost tripping over the gutter, Matt regains his footing and starts chasing after Joy's already retreating form. The shouts from the man seem to be dying out. Matt turns to see him on the footpath across the road, with his hands resting on his head, like it's too much effort to continue the chase. Not letting up, Matt keeps running. He sprints through the grassy parkland and past a row of bushes, then slows his pace to see where his date has gone.

'In here,' Joy whispers to him.

She's tucked behind a thick row of scrub with her hands resting on her knees. Her normally white face is flushed red and she has a huge smile on her face. Matt pushes into the hiding space next to her. He feels sick.

'That was great. It worked perfectly!' Joy says, as they push further back into the bushes to obscure themselves from view.

'Perfectly?' Matt asks, aghast that she could think that almost getting caught was funny. 'That guy almost got us. That was terrible. I feel like I'm going to throw up. I can't believe he walked in just as I took his order.'

Joy's smile turns to a smirk. Her face pinches to form two cute dimples just below her cheekbones. She starts to laugh.

'That wasn't his order.'

'What do you mean? He was running after us,' Matt furrows his bow in confusion.

'Didn't you hear what he was yelling out?'

Matt shakes his head. The adrenaline surging through his body is muddling his thoughts. He takes a seat on the ground, resting their dinner on his lap. His short breath is starting to regain some of its normal rhythm.

'All I heard was him telling us to stop. I just ran.'

Joy leans down and picks up the package. She rips a small hole in the top end of the paper and pulls out a steaming chip. Looking at it for a few seconds, she pops it in her mouth and starts chewing.

'He was trying to tell us that we forgot our tartare sauce.'

Matt's thudding heart almost stops at Joy's words. *Tartare sauce?*

'I would have stopped running, but I didn't want to ruin the excitement,' Joy grins, pulling another chip out of the paper. 'And besides, I don't like tartare anyway.'

Matt looks up at her, unable to speak. It takes him a few moments to calm down properly. He still doesn't see the humorous side of the situation. His face is whiter than Joy's pigment-free arms.

'Do you want a chip?' Joy offers him the packet. 'They're good.'

'I don't think I'm hungry.'

'Well, there's plenty of food here. You're going to have to help. Maybe we can go for a walk up to the lookout and work up your appetite.'

Matt looks at the branches around them. He doesn't want to leave their security. He doesn't want to go out where he can be exposed. As if sensing his anxiety, Joy leans down and holds out her hand.

'Look, you've shown me a fun time so far. There's a spot near here that not many people know about. Let me take you there and we can eat in peace.'

Matt realises he's acting like a coward. Regaining his composure, he clasps Joy's warm palm. The touch reassures him. Standing up, he reaches into the small tear in the paper packet that Joy has nestled against her chest. He slides out a chip of his own and puts it into his mouth, looking out into the park.

'I hope it's not too far. We don't want your fish to get cold.'

Eighteen

Joy leads Matt along the cliff-top path. They're headed toward a long stretch of bushland that spreads away from the main town of Ocean Heads into uninhabited national park. A waist-high fence and a few feet of grass are all that separate them from the sheer drop into the sea. Walking uphill, the main lookout recedes in the distance behind them. In front, the sun is still above the tree line, but the shadows of the bush are starting to grow longer on the ground with each step forward. Matt and Joy take turns in plucking hot chips from their parcel.

'Where are we going exactly?' Matt asks.

'You'll see,' she answers, striding ahead to take the lead.

It has been a long time since Matt walked up this way. He used to roam in this bushland as a kid. However, his sense of adventure as an adult had only extended to the movie theatre and bars in town. A eucalyptus-tinged sea breeze blends with the smell of dinner. The path winds away from the cliff and down into a short gully. Iron Barks tower overhead, while a mix of saltbush and moonah trees pack together to create a dense scrub on both sides of them. The sandstone track stands out amongst the surrounding bush. Matt's lingering sense of paranoia at being caught fades completely.

'So, tell me about yourself,' he asks as they walk. 'I still don't really know anything about you.'

'No, that's boring,' Joy answers, stuffing another chip in her mouth. Her tiny ears wiggle slightly as she chews. 'I don't want to talk about me. You don't get to know someone from their physical history. You get to know them by finding out how they think. These are the rules: no questions about what we do for work, no talking about the weather and no talking about sport.'

Matt almost stops walking. He looks down at his feet as they press on down the track. The restriction of discussion subjects causes Matt to start chewing his lip with insecurity.

'What on earth do we talk about then?'

'Life,' Joy laughs, like it should be the most apparent thing in the world.

'Life?'

'Or death. There's two big ones. There are plenty of other topics. Whatever you like, just don't ask me what footy team I go for.'

Joy stops as they come to a break in the trees.

'Down this way.'

She steps over the wire fence that is still on their left-hand side. There's a tiny gap in the scrub that looks like it leads back to the cliff again. Joy pushes through, holding her white parcel over her head, so it doesn't get caught on the bushes. Matt follows without comment. He ponders what he's going to say next. This girl obviously doesn't care for the obvious. Ducking under a branch, then squeezing through a gap that scratches against Matt's bare arms, they come out into a clearing. A small patch of grass is matted on the ground, surrounded by craggy moonah branches. The clearing overlooks an uninterrupted view of the glistening sea. Matt doesn't walk over to the edge, but he knows that this part of the coast is very high and steep.

Joy sits down on the grass and opens up the food, spreading the paper out in front of her like an oil-stained tablecloth. Matt stands, taking in the area.

'How did you find this place? I've been living here my whole life and I've never even heard of this spot.'

Joy shrugs her shoulders and breaks a piece of fish into two with greasy fingers. 'I like exploring. I used to go down unknown alleyways in the city. This is no different, there's just more trees.'

Matt takes a seat and looks at his date. She studies her portion of fish before plopping it into her mouth. Her eyes squeeze shut, like she's savouring the taste.

'You don't like rules, do you?' Matt asks.

Joy looks out to sea thoughtfully before replying.

'My dad says that when I was a baby I never used to like being swaddled in blankets. I guess rules are the same thing. Some people like being wrapped tightly by rules, because it makes them feel comfortable. I prefer to wave my arms around.'

Matt looks into Joy's eyes as she talks. He's quite sure that there's no one else like her on the face of the earth.

'So, what you're saying is that you like the freedom of making your own choices?' Matt asks.

'Something like that. I don't like expectations. I like new things. Billions of people have lived before us, so

Eighteen

why keep doing the same things they always did? If I want to learn old things, I'll read stuff on the Internet. If I want new experiences, I'll live in the moment without analysing how or why.'

'But don't you think you have the same instincts as all of those other billions of people? If you just live in the moment, aren't you bound to be driven by the same things that drove them?'

Joy picks up another chip. 'I like this conversation. I wonder if anyone has spoken all of these exact words before, while eating chips, sitting in this exact spot and then said 'Illywhacker.''

'I very much doubt it,' Matt wrinkles his nose at the weird comment.

'Well, see, we're doing something new then.'

Matt just sits and nods. He takes a piece of fish and stands up, walking over toward the cliff. Peering over the top, he looks down at the churning whitewater below. He feels the irresistible urge to jump. It's not the same dark urge to end his life that he had experienced the week before, more a feeling like he'd like to just try it and see what happens. Pushing the sensation away, he steps back again and walks around the edge of the clearing. There are a couple of old, brown beer bottles thrown in the bushes, evidence this place had been frequented by others in the past.

'I don't think we're going to be able to take someone's phone order from The Fish Tank again,' Matt says, returning to sit down with Joy who is licking salt from her fingers. 'They're bound to figure out what happened after that guy had to chase us for tartare sauce.'

'You're probably right. We shouldn't even go back to our cars until after closing time. They might be waiting to throw hot oil on us.'

Her eyes glow mischievously. Matt doesn't know if she's joking or serious. She's probably joking. He takes the last of the fish and eats it, screwing up the paper and setting it to the side so he can take it when they leave.

Joy is looking around at the scrub, still sitting close to him. The daylight is fading to a deep indigo and the first stars of the evening are just beginning to twinkle silver in the sky. He wants to lean in and kiss her, he wants to feel her lips against his, but he doesn't take the leap. He just reaches out and holds her hand. She squeezes his palm without looking back at him.

'Why do all of these trees look like zombies?' Joy says instead.

Matt looks about at the moonah trees. In the twilight, they do look undead. The desiccated bark has holes all through it and their branches wrap around each other, like they're trying to strangle the life out of themselves.

'It's all the salt in the soil that makes them look like that. They're alkaline-based scrub plants.'

Joy looks to Matt like he's just said something wonderful.

'How do you know that?'

'School, I guess. We had to come on excursions out here all the time. There's an ochre mine not far from here. They used to take the pigment from the soil to make paint for tinting the old red-rattler trams in the city.'

'Wow, it's like another universe out here!' Joy says, her eyes going wide with excitement at Matt's useless knowledge.

'I suppose it is,' Matt answers, looking around him with a renewed sense of vision. He used to take all of this for granted.

Joy wriggles around on the grass and lies down on her back. Her black skull and heart t-shirt stares up at Matt, as she looks up at the sky.

'Let's see if we can catch any shooting stars,' she says.

Matt follows her line of vision and realises that the sun has gone down. Only the faintest fingertips of disappearing light can be seen holding onto the edge of the sky. The sounds of night start to echo around them. Crickets and bugs click out their eerie tunes. The Milky Way is flickering above them and a crescent moon sits at its zenith in the sky. Matt settles in next to the strange pale girl, who steals shopping trolleys and doesn't like being swaddled. His fingers reach out to find hers again, intertwining like the branches of the moonah trees around them. Together, the pair look up at the unknown.

Nineteen

It's well past midnight by the time Matt and Joy start to head back. They had stared for hours, pointing out shooting stars, lying on their backs. There was something childish about how excited they both became when they spotted a star, the happiness at finding one undiluted by any intellectual thought. The warm night air meant that the moisture of the grass beneath them didn't bother them in the slightest. Eventually though, a light cloud cover had settled over the night and put an end to their fun.

Every rustle and noise the shadowy scrub makes, sends shivers into Matt as they walk back. He doesn't know what's out there, nor does he want to know. It takes what seems like forever to pick their way through the trees in the darkness, to find the yellow track. Neither of them talk. It feels like silence is the perfect thing to say.

Eventually they come across the familiar walking path and stroll together along the cliff top, down toward their cars.

The row of shops stands out like haunted houses around the car park, abandoned until tomorrow morning. Matt's stomach flutters as he draws near his Holden. He doesn't know what is expected of him here. He doesn't want to part ways without some kind of promise to meet again. Pulling out his phone, he uses it to light their final footsteps on uneven bitumen.

'I'd really like to do this again, Joy,' he stammers. 'I had a good time. Can I have your number?'

Smiling, Joy takes Matt's phone and programs her details into it. She presses the call button and Matt hears Joy's phone ring in her pocket.

'Now I've got your number too. You'd better call me,' she says, 'or I'll tell the fish n' chip shop owners where you live.'

She hands the phone back to Matt and her cheeks form into shadowy dimples.

They stand there awkwardly; looking at each other, like neither of them is sure what to do next. Matt knows he should have the courage to kiss her, but all his courage for the evening has been spent. He wishes he were braver.

'Okay then,' Matt says, looking at his feet. 'I'll call you soon.'

He opens his door and gets into the car. Shutting the door cuts off the tension that was hanging between them. Letting out a big sigh, Matt turns on his engine and lets his headlights shine over Joy. She looks like a beautiful vampire in the artificial light. Matt waits for her to get into her hatchback and drive away safely before he puts his car into reverse.

When he gets home, Matt's phone beeps with a text message.

You should have kissed me.

Matt types out a reply and hits send.

That would have been too obvious.

Twenty

M att has picked the trendiest bar in town to catch up with Gerard. The title of 'trendiest' isn't that special in Ocean Heads, because it's the only bar in town other than the pub. Still, that hasn't stopped the owners from trying to fulfil hipster expectations anyway. Called 'The Conversation' it has no music, no TV and no pool table. In short, no distractions. You even have to check your mobile phone into the coat room at the entrance. The concept is that you should concentrate on the people you're with and enjoy the lost art of discussion,

Twenty

rather than putting up photos on social media of what you're eating. Matt has only been here once and felt self-conscious standing around staring at his feet. But Gerard is from the city and might be into something weird like this. Because he can't take his phone in, Matt waits at the entrance. He texted Gerard the address a few hours ago saying to meet here at 3pm and that he'll be the guy near the front door wearing a black t-shirt and a vacant expression. Matt looks around at the three other blokes near him also wearing black t-shirts and thinks maybe he should have put a flower in his hair instead. Matt is about to send Gerard another text, when he notices a man walking toward the entrance, looking like he is searching for someone. He's short and scruffy-looking, with half a beard on an otherwise youthful face. They lock eyes with questioning looks and say the other's name at exactly the same time. Matt awkwardly holds out his hand to shake Gerard's, thanking him for taking the time to come and help. Gerard takes Matt's hand, just as awkwardly and says no worries, he wanted to come down the coast anyway. They pause in silence for a few moments, standing and staring anywhere but at the other person, waiting for someone to make the first move.

'Ah, I guess we should go in then,' Matt says, indicating the entrance.

'Right,' Gerard says, following Matt through the process of checking in his phone and finding a table among the Sunday afternoon patrons.

They grab an overpriced pint of craft beer at the bar and then find a table near the window. In the centre of the table is a deck of cue cards, each with a question printed on it in case people are grasping for something to talk about.

'So,' says Matt.

'So,' says Gerard.

'So,' says Matt. He decides to make the most of the cards between them and picks one up. 'What do you like most about your job?' Matt turns the card around to show Gerard that's what it actually says and Matt isn't just being nosy.

'Well,' Gerard looks out the window as if trying to find an answer. 'I like being able to help people out. People like you.' He smiles weakly.

'You said on the phone you don't really like it though?' Matt asks, straying beyond the script of the card into real conversation.

'No, not really. It's actually quite depressing. I'm like a counsellor most of the time - talking with people who have just been sacked, or need financial assistance because their partner has left them and isn't paying support. Sometimes they're victims of abuse. A few times I've had to talk someone down from suicide.'

Matt shifts uncomfortably in his chair.

'The worst thing is, we're trained to try and get people off the phone as quickly as possible. We're supposed to direct them to the internet to complete registrations online. I can't bring myself to do it. A lot of elderly people call, so they can't do stuff like that. Some can barely speak English. It's not fair to ask them to try and navigate the bureaucracy alone when half the people in the call centre can't even do it properly themselves. It sucks. It's like we're set up to fail and have people losing their minds at us when they finally get through the hold queue.'

Gerard looks up, suddenly realising he had gone off on a small rant.

'I totally get how you feel,' Matt says, rescuing him from any embarrassment. 'I mean, I know how hard it is to please customers when the system ties your hands. Man, I thought I had it bad though at Optitel. It sounds like a nightmare where you are. It's a lot higher stakes than someone whose bloody Internet reception keeps dropping out.'

'Yes, but Hell hath no fury like a geek with slow Wi-Fi,' Gerard smiles for the first time.

Matt raises his glass and they cheers, bonding over shared miseries.

'We're not here to stew on my problems,' Gerard adds, 'We're here to talk about how you can figure out a way to do something new. I'm assuming you don't just want another customer service job?'

'You assume correctly,' Matt nods.

'Have you had any epiphanies about what you want to try?' Gerard asks.

'No, not really. I mean, I looked at what I'm qualified to do and it's basically nothing. I don't want to work in retail. I don't want to do customer service. I wouldn't last a day labouring. I feel like a bit of a useless whiner actually. I *do* want to help myself, but I don't know where to start.'

'Well, it sounds like you're probably going to have to get some kind of qualification if you're going to do something you want to do. That's fine, you can keep getting Newstart and upskill at the same time. Or, you can go to uni full-time and switch over to Austudy. That's easy enough.'

'Yeah, but upskill to do what? I'm totally lost.'

Gerard frowns, thinking of the best way to start. 'Why don't we consult the cards?' he asks, picking up a new one from the pile and making a show of reading it. 'What is your go-to sex move and why?'

The two share a laugh.

Twenty

'Oh god,' Matt says, 'I won't scar you by recalling my feeble attempts with the opposite sex,' Matt's mind flashes to Joy briefly. He thinks that she would approve of these kinds of discussion starters, skipping past the weather and going straight for the jugular. His thoughts then wander to the times he had been with girls. Drunken fumbles in the dark, failed battles with bra straps, uncoordinated squirming that was over much too soon for any kind of mutual satisfaction.

'Okay, here's one.' Gerard picks up another card from the deck. 'What would you do if you won lotto? I think that one's actually pretty spot on. Matt?'

Matt waves away thoughts of premature ejaculation and focusses on the matter at hand. 'Um, don't know. Probably travel. Go out and see the world?'

'Oh cool, where?'

'Europe maybe, there's something romantic about all of the history there, all of the old places and wars and interesting lives that have unfolded.'

'There you go. I think we might be onto something. So, travel, do you have enough saved to go anywhere now?'

'Of course I do, I just won lotto.'

'You know what I mean!' Gerard says good-naturedly.

'I guess. I've got enough for an airfare and maybe a few weeks, but I feel like at this point I'd just be doing it

to run away from myself, not actually finding out what
I should be doing with my life.'

'Okay, so let's pretend you can make a career from
traveling around. I always seem to see jobs for travel
agents going around.'

'Do you actually travel though?' Matt asks, 'Or is that
more like a retail job?'

'Yeah, you're probably right.'

'You could be a pilot, or an air steward?'

'It would be pretty cool to fly for sure,' Matt says, but
the lack of enthusiasm in his voice belies his disinterest.

'You could be a travel blogger,' Gerard continues. 'Or-'

'A blogger?' Matt interrupts. 'You can actually make
money from that?'

'Sure. You have to be on top of the game, but they do
make good cash from what I hear. Plus, there's the free
travel that companies throw at you in the hope you'll
give them a good rap.'

'I do like writing.'

'Great! What kind of writing?'

Matt considers the only piece of writing he's done in
recent years - the letter to the editor about the flowers.

'Creative writing, I guess. Maybe a hint of journalism.
But I'm not very good.'

'You could get good. Take a course.'

Twenty

'I always thought writing was an art, more of a natural gift.'

'Well, you probably have to have some talent, but I'll bet your fake lotto winnings that the best artists who ever lived practiced like crazy.'

'Really?'

'Of course! Painters. Musicians. Sports people. They all have to train. You just don't unleash your talent on the world and expect to be called a genius. Like anything, you have to work on it.'

'Yeah, you're right,' Matt nods. He was always told that nothing ever comes easy but it always seemed easy for others. It was more likely that hard work was the surest path to success. It's just that a lot of people, including Matt, didn't particularly like hard work, so tried quick fixes to see if they could work their way around it. Maybe it was time to give up those childish ideas.

Gerard pats his pocket for a second before realising, 'If I had my bloody phone on me I'd be able to look up course options!'

Matt's face falls at Gerard's frustration.

'Oh sorry, I thought you might find this place kind of novel or something.'

Gerard takes a thoughtful sip of his pint.

'Well, the beer's good. And having someone to actually talk with face-to-face is quite neat. It sure beats the phone, or trying to hammer out a conversation while someone is checking their Facebook for something more exciting.'

Matt's shoulders drop a little and he has a taste of the beer himself. It actually is really good.

'Anyway, you can look up courses later,' Gerard continues. 'Just Google search it and stuff will come up. At least it's something to hook onto and explore. Even just put in something like 'what jobs can writers have?' and you're bound to get some ideas of how to start. Look at some travel blogs too while you're at it. Get some inspiration. Sound like a plan?'

'Yeah, it does. It's a start at least. Thanks!' Matt clinks glasses with Gerard to show his appreciation.

'Now, let's get to the deeper issues.' Gerard says, picking up another card. 'How would you make the perfect burrito?'

By the time Gerard heads out the door and back to the city Matt feels like he has made a new friend. Gerard says he'll email Matt a few links to writerly things he finds that might be interesting. Matt offers a sympathetic ear whenever the world of customer service gets too much.

Twenty

When Matt gets home he starts thinking about Joy again. A little drunk, he decides to send her a text, only to find he's left his phone back at the bar. After a few seconds of being pissed off, Matt realises it's probably for the best and heads off to bed, ready to start a week of new directions.

Twenty One

Matt's eyes keep roaming to his phone. He'd picked it from the bar as soon as they opened at 11am. Disappointingly, there were no messages from Joy. He spends the rest of the morning browsing 'jobs for writers' on his laptop. The choices all seem to be incredibly difficult to make a career in - journalist, copywriter, blogger, novelist. Every article he finds talks about increased competition and falling wages at the same time. It's disheartening to think about failure before he even starts.

Instead of continuing to dig himself into a dark mood Matt decides to get started on a book that has been sitting on his nightstand for a while - *The Unbearable Lightness of Being*. While it's a good read, Matt can't help but wonder what Joy is up to and whether she wants to do that something with him. He looks at his phone again.

Should he call her, or wait a day or two? It's the ridiculous dilemma Matt has seen played out dozens of times in bad romantic comedies. He should just man up and call her, but he doesn't want to seem desperate.

The day is warm, but windy and overcast. It's what Matt's mum refers to as a desolate day. There is no real character to the weather. It discourages Matt from going outside because of its drabness. There's no sparkle. *Should I text?* Matt thinks. *Nah.* Joy feels like the kind of person who has better things to do with her time than worry about flirt games. After reading the same page three times and not taking in a single word, Matt finally picks up his phone. He knows he's being stupid. He knows, yet he hesitates. It's almost noon. Maybe Joy is free for lunch. She might be happy to take a break from work. Wherever and whatever work is for her.

It excites Matt that he still knows so little about Joy, yet already feels connected to her. He has never been one for hippy nonsense like 'love at first sight', but infatuation after first date is working its way beneath his skin.

He types a single word into his phone and hits send.

Hungry?

The reply comes back almost instantly.

For food?

Of course food.

Yes. Food of the eating variety. I'm going to go down to the Sand Witch Café if you're interested in joining me at 12:30ish.

Matt is always careful that he uses correct grammar and punctuation in his texts. He doesn't like people who substitute numbers 4 letters. Again, it's only a few moments before Matt's phone buzzes a response.

OK. See you for food at 12:30ish. Please bring your runners. I'll explain later.

Runners? Matt doesn't like the sound of that. After their close call Saturday night, he thinks he might give 'order theft' a rest for a little while. He'll have to come up with other ways to get his kicks. Nevertheless, Matt goes to his cupboard and fishes out his running shoes which haven't been used for at least a year. A cobweb hangs in the heel of the left shoe. Rather than risk sliding his foot into a potential venom trap, he cleans it out wearing thick rubber gloves. The spider that might have once been in there is long gone though. Not even it wanted to live so neglected in the back of a wardrobe.

Matt shoves his shoes and a spare set of clothes into a backpack, along with his wallet and phone. He wants to be prepared for anything that Joy might throw at him.

Despite the flat weather, the main street is crowded. Mums are out having their Monday coffee catch ups and tourists, hungover from last night's 'Sunday session', sit eating late big breakfasts at the numerous cafes that dot along the strip. A pack of lycra-clad men walk their hi-tech racing bikes along the footpath. The clicking of cleats serves as a beat to the swaying metronome of their penises, which wriggle in their bike shorts. Matt can't look away from the spectacle. Why people wear such ridiculous outfits is beyond him. Most of the men are older than Matt's father and have either grey hair, or potbellies that hang like awnings over their frightening packages. No one else seems to notice this or think of it as strange.

Matt comes to the Sand Witch Café and sees Joy waiting out front. She stands underneath the sign that has a witch riding a broom, with bristles forming the shape of a sandwich. Joy's t-shirt for today has a photo of the earth and the words DEEP written across it. She has a backpack slung over her shoulder as well.

She sees Matt approaching and walks up with a red lipstick smile. Before Matt can say hello, she grabs the front of his shirt and pulls him into her. Their lips lock into a furious kiss and Joy's tongue snakes into Matt's mouth. The heat of her passion takes him by surprise. Before Matt can become self-conscious about the public display, Joy leans back and pats him on the chest.

'Sometimes I like dessert before my lunch,' she says with a sexy smile.

Matt stands there shocked, with lipstick smeared over his face. Joy laughs at him and reaches up to clean the mess she just left.

'What do you feel like eating?' she asks, wiping away the red smudges on his lips.

'Uh,' is all Matt can manage to reply.

'Nah, I don't like 'uh'. I hear these guys make a mean chicken schnitzel burger though.'

Matt just nods. Joy continues to take him by surprise, even when he is expecting less-than-normal anyway. They walk into the busy café together. Matt looks up at the blackboard hanging above the counter and ponders the numbered choices of focaccias. He likes the look of the Mediterranean Vegetable Medley or Chicken, Avocado and Mayo Delight. He turns to express his opinion to Joy, but she's no longer standing next to him. Matt looks around to find she has walked right up to the front of the line.

'Excuse me,' he hears her say, to the woman at the front of the queue. 'But I have breast cancer. Do you mind if I go before you?'

With a slight look of shock on her face, the woman stammers that of course, by all means she can go first. Without a pause, Joy turns, smiling to the girl serving and orders two chicken schnitzel burgers. Matt goes red with anger and embarrassment.

Happily, Joy comes back to Matt.

'It'll be five minutes. We won't have to wait long.'

Matt takes her by the arm and shuffles her into a quiet corner near the drinks fridge, which buzzes neutrally.

'What do you think you're doing?' he hisses at her.

'It's alright, you got dinner last time,' she says, confused at his anger.

'No. You just pushed in and said to that lady you have cancer. You can't do stuff like that.'

Joy looks dismayed at Matt's annoyance. 'Why not? We push in all the time.'

'That's different. You can't lie about stuff like cancer. That's just wrong.'

'But I do have cancer,' she says, looking at him with an unwavering gaze.

'No, you don't. Don't say things like that.'

'What?' Joy answers, now bristling with indignity. 'I do. I had a partial mastectomy of my left breast last year to remove a grade three tumour.'

Matt's mouth hangs open in shock. He doesn't know if she's telling the truth or not. He doesn't know how to respond.

'I didn't have to have chemotherapy,' Joy continues hotly, 'because they say they got it all and I didn't have any secondary tumours. Is that not good enough for you?' Joy's face is now red and her eyes are getting glassy with pending tears.

Every ounce of anger has been sucked out of Matt's chest and been replaced with a lump of dread. She's not lying.

Before he can even think about apologising, Joy runs out of the café.

Matt stands there like a lost child. The shock of the revelation has paralysed him into inaction. The customers around him seem to be trying to look away, but he catches glances of disdain from everyone close by. One woman's scornful look seems to be asking, *why haven't you gone after her yet?*

The clock on the wall opposite Matt's head ticks away loudly.

By the time Matt gains the presence of mind to pursue Joy, she's nowhere to be seen. He stands with a slumped posture in the middle of the walkway, looking from left to right in the hope of finding some clue to where she's gone. He may as well be looking for a ghost.

A young girl comes out of the café behind Matt and taps him on the shoulder.

'Excuse me, but I think these are your burgers.'

Matt turns to her dumbly and looks down at the food. She presses the brown paper bags into Matt's hands. He has no choice but to take them. Their weight sends waves of guilt up Matt's arms. He stands there for a while longer, looking forlornly at the burgers. The last thing he feels like now is eating.

Taking the bag off his back, Matt slides the food inside and takes out his phone. With his backpack nestled between his feet, he tries to call Joy. The phone rings out. He presses *call* again. After the fourth unsuccessful try, he sends a text.

I'm really sorry.

Picking up his things, Matt starts to walk up the street towards home. What a disaster. The week had begun with so much promise.

As he rounds the corner out of the main street, Matt's phone beeps.

Meet me at Front Beach.

Twenty Two

Rows of cypress trees line the wide lawn that runs down to Front Beach. The sap smell from their bark clings to everything, even with the strong wind blowing. A rocky headland juts out on the northern end of the beach, before bending back into a long bay, protected from the large ocean swells on the other side. Normally this cove is dotted with fishermen and families walking their dogs. Today the standard crowd is replaced with kite surfers, making the most of the blustery conditions.

Matt stands at the top of the grassy hill, scanning for any sign of Joy. He sees her in the sheltered corner next to the cliffs. She is sitting on an old set of wooden pylons that were once a boat ramp during the town's post-war settlement days. The beautiful construction had been replaced years ago with a concrete edifice at the other end of the bay, more suited to launching today's top-of-the-line fishing vessels. Now, the pylons are mostly rotted away. Only a few still poke their heads above the sand line, the rest fade into the shallows.

Approaching Joy, Matt holds onto both of the straps of his backpack, as if he's leaning on them for support. He kicks off his shoes and walks up to her, letting the damp sand compress beneath his toes.

Joy stares out to sea. Her mascara has run from crying. Matt stands next her, watching a kite surfer skim past over the clear but choppy waters. Joy doesn't acknowledge his presence. She just looks outward. Matt waits with a heavy heart. He can't stand having said the wrong thing, but can't bring himself to apologise until she's ready to talk. Matt clears his throat, in case she hasn't seen him, but she continues to sit as the wind ruffles her wild hair.

'I didn't mean for you to find out like that,' Joy says, finally. 'Sometimes I forget about it and then it just slips out. I'm sorry.'

Matt doesn't comment. He thinks that this is one of those times where listening might be the better option.

'It's hard when I remember like that. It's like recalling a nightmare,' Joy continues to look out to sea with red eyes as she talks. 'My mum died from the same thing when I was young, so I always used to check. One day, it was there. I didn't even need the doctors to do a mammogram, I just knew.'

Matt rests his hand on Joy's knee to show his support. It seems a hopelessly inadequate consolation for what she is revealing to him.

'Twenty-eight years old and I had cancer,' she grips Matt's fingers. 'Twenty-eight. I didn't hesitate to have the operation. Better to lose your breast than your life.'

Strands of black hair whip wildly at Joy's face, like they're helping fan the words out of her mouth.

'After they cut it out, I didn't feel any relief. The likelihood of it coming back one day is high. That threat always hangs there in the background, like a guillotine blade waiting to drop.'

Joy lets Matt's hand go, so it falls back to his side. It's hard for him to understand being in the same situation. It is an earth-shattering thing for anyone to have to deal with, let alone a young woman.

'You know, it's funny,' Joy interrupts his thought. 'I kind of like it sometimes. In some ways, I'm grateful for the diagnosis. I look at life differently now. I don't dwell on stupid little things. I'd always wanted to get away and live on the coast, so I did. Before, there had been every bullshit excuse in the world not to do it, but those excuses just dropped off. Today I have a licence to do what I want. I don't feel guilty for being selfish anymore. So, I guess there's that at least. Weird how if you're forced to confront the end of your life, it makes you want to do what you should have been doing all along. It forces you to make the most of the little time you have left.'

Joy lets out a half-laugh and looks at Matt. He tries to smile back and say something comforting.

'I've got your burger,' is all that comes out.

Her new laugh is real.

'Wow, you really have a way with words, don't you?'

Matt shrugs his shoulders. He's never known anyone with cancer, so he doesn't know what to say. Joy stands up off the wooden pole she's leaning against and starts walking toward the grass. Matt follows.

They settle down on the edge of the beach, sitting on the green lawn step, their bums on the grass and their feet still in the sand. It's like they're part of two different worlds. Matt takes lunch out of his backpack and hands one of the burgers to Joy. Mayonnaise and beetroot has stained though the paper, making it pink and soggy. Pulling the wrapper halfway down, Matt bites into his meal and starts chewing, as Joy does the same. A flock of seagulls gather around, watching the pair eat. The bird closest to them is standing on one leg. Matt wonders for a moment if it's a cripple, but when Joy throws a piece of lettuce at it, the other leg comes down to the ground. The gull spreads its wings and gargles an ugly thank you.

The rest of the flock gather in closer, waiting for their chance. Matt doesn't like seagulls; he thinks they're the beggars of the bird world. Joy seems to be enjoying throwing them pieces of her meal, so he doesn't say so.

'How can you be so strong?' Matt asks her instead. 'If I was diagnosed with cancer, I'd be a screaming mess. You seem so relaxed most of the time.'

'I don't know,' Joy shakes her head, flicking a hunk of beetroot toward the birds. 'I *was* a mess at first. I guess you just get used to the idea. I don't think we're built to be hysterical for long periods. After the operation, that urgency was taken away a little bit as well. According to the doctors I'm cured for now, whatever that means.' She bites her burger thoughtfully before pressing on. 'Like I said, sometimes I just forget. I feel normal. I feel healthy, so there's no reason to think about it all the time. It's kind of like living with a kidnapper that you're now comfortable with.'

Matt wrestles to put himself in her shoes. He tries to consider his reaction to something so life changing.

'I do think about different things now,' she continues.

'Like what?' Matt asks.

'Like what do you think happens when we die?'

'You mean do we go somewhere else?' Matt asks.

'Yeah.'

He pauses to give it some thought. A gust of wind whips sand along the shoreline.

'I reckon we'd have to go somewhere,' he says eventually.

'But how do you know that?'

'I guess no one does. It's just a gut feeling I suppose,' Matt takes another bite of his chicken schnitzel burger.

'I think there's nothing. Like we just go into a dreamless sleep forever,' Joy comments.

'What makes you say that?'

'Well, think about it. Every single person ever in history has died. People like Albert Einstein, Plato and Jimi Hendrix. You'd think that out of all of those people, at least one of them would have sent a message by now, letting everyone know they're okay. Surely someone would be smart enough to reassure their family that it's not so bad to be dead.'

'Maybe they can't. Maybe they're too far away.'

'I used to tell myself that. But seriously, what about two lovers?' Joy throws the rest of her burger to the seagulls and looks at Matt, with passion blazing in her eyes. 'You would do anything you can to let the other one know not to worry. If nobody in history has been able to get word back, then I can only think that it's because they're gone completely. There is nothing left of them at all. They're dead, finished, just food for bugs.'

The idea makes Matt feel uncomfortable. There has to be something more to it than the wind and the clouds around him. More than the fleshy body he lives every day in. There has to be some kind of meaning. He just feels it. Maybe it's all those lessons from Sunday school, or the times his mum had dragged him along to mass at Easter and Christmas that had drummed it into him. Even though he doesn't believe in Christianity in the literal sense, he still feels like the idea of an afterlife has some weight. Maybe it's just wishful thinking.

'What about all the reports about ghosts and stuff?' Matt probes.

'But they don't *tell* anyone anything. They just float there and point and maybe wail a bit.'

'What if the spirits can't actually explain what being dead is like in a way that we'd understand it?' he retorts.

Joy's forehead knits together, like she's never considered this angle before.

'What do you mean they can't explain it?'

'Well, try and tell me what zero sounds like, or a hydrogen atom feels like when you touch it.'

Joy looks puzzled. It makes Matt think he's onto something.

'Everything we experience is through our senses, right?' he presses.

'I guess so,' Joy nods.

'Of course it is. The only way I can ever explain anything is in reference to something physical: a taste, a smell, a sight. Even abstract concepts like time come from an understanding of prolonged physical experience.'

'But just because we can't sense it, doesn't mean it's not there either.'

'That's my point. When you die, your spirit is separated from your body. It's a completely new experience. There are no tastes, or smells, or anything. You don't exist the way we do now, through the senses. It's extrasensory, so you can't explain to someone with a body what it's like, because they couldn't begin to comprehend it. You wouldn't even have a voice to be able to explain it either. You have to experience death yourself until you can relate to other dead people about it.'

'I'm glad I met you,' Joy smiles. 'I still don't believe you, but I'm glad you at least gave it a try.'

Matt grins. He doesn't know what he was trying to say either. It did make him feel better somehow though.

'What about God then?' Matt asks, wanting to keep the conversation going. 'If there's nothing after you die, then there isn't a God either.'

'Nope.'

'Then who created all this?' Matt says, exasperated, sweeping his arms out to the ocean and the sky. 'It didn't just pop into existence!'

'Of course it did. That's the big bang theory.'

'But what came before that? What was at the start?'

'Nothing.'

'Nothing will come of nothing,' Matt says, quoting one of his favourite Shakespearean lines from *King Lear*.

Joy smirks, like she understands the reference.

'Who created God then?' she asks, raising an eyebrow. 'Something had to be there at the beginning, so why not just a set of expanding elements, rather than a ready-made God? I'm simply taking out the first, more complicated step.'

'You can't be serious,' Matt scoffs.

'Of course I am!' Joy raises her voice a touch. 'This whole universe evolved on its own from patterns and laws that the universe created itself. It's self-perpetuating. And even if God did exist once, she's probably dead now. Everything dies eventually, even you and me.'

Matt can't agree with Joy, but it seems that they have come back around to the beginning of the conversation anyway. He lets it drop, rather than going over the exact same territory again and again.

'Okay then,' Matt says, unzipping his backpack and reaching inside. 'At least you can give me the answer to one of the universe's other great mysteries.'

'And what's that?' Joy asks, curious. She looks to see what Matt is pulling out of his bag.

'Why on earth did I have to bring these running shoes down here?' he grins.

Twenty Three

'R eady?' Joy yells over to Matt, as he holds the other end of the string. 'Go!'

Matt takes off along the beach, laughing. Joy throws the red and blue kite into the air. The wind catches it and it spirals upward as Matt runs. It spins and twists in the wind. Increasing his pace, Matt feels the string go taught in his hand and the kite rises into the sky. Higher and higher it goes. Joy starts running after Matt.

'Don't stop this time!' she yells as she tries to catch up. 'Keep going, or it'll fall.'

Matt has at least a kilometre of empty sand in front of him, so he keeps running, looking upward at the flimsy nylon construction. Joy had bought it at the two-dollar shop and wanted to see if they could get it to work. Even in this strong wind it's a challenge. The kite is barely two feet across and not very aerodynamic. A yellow ribbon, which had been attached to the tip of its bamboo frame, blew away as soon as they took it out of the packet.

'Oh well,' Joy had said as it rolled into the distance. 'There goes twenty cents.'

Matt's chest is burning from the effort of running, but his will to keep the sorry little kite in the air makes his legs pump harder. He fights back laughter with every step. The kite swoops down toward the sand so Matt runs faster still, jerking on the string to keep it in flight. The kite sweeps up again and hangs gracefully for a few moments.

'I think you got it. I think that's it!' Joy claps her hands as she draws closer to Matt. 'Slow down, let it fly!'

At her words, Matt lets up to a jog and then stops. Transfixed, he stares up to the red and blue triangle, floating against the grey backdrop of the clouds.

'Yes! Look at her go!'

Joy has reached Matt and is jumping up and down with excitement.

'I told you she'd fly. I told you!'

The kite tugs at the string in Matt's hands, signalling that it's okay on its own for now.

With mouths open, Joy and Matt watch with wonder, moving their heads from side-to-side like novelty circus clowns. Flapping above, the imitation bird spreads its nylon wings. The breeze makes it look like a living thing.

'It looks so happy now,' Joy says, reaching out and taking Matt's hand. 'In the shop it was so sad, sitting there on the shelf. It was built to fly, it had just never been given the chance.'

Gliding in curious circles, the kite starts to dip. As the wind backs off, it sinks down toward the sea. Realising what's happening, Matt takes off running again. The kite momentarily lifts up, but it's too late. With a final spinning circle, the kite dives into the ocean.

'Damn it!' Matt stamps his foot.

Dragging it in, Matt pulls the soggy creature in from the water. A small wave catches it, washing it in for the last few metres and depositing it at Matt's feet. Picking the kite up, Matt tries to wipe the sand and water from it. It's hopeless though, the frame has snapped and the nylon is coming undone all around the sides. Joy moves in to Matt's side and looks at it.

'It's ruined,' Matt says.

'It's okay,' Joy says, putting her hand on the kite with affection. 'I'm just glad it got to fulfil its dreams.'

Twenty Four

It has been an exhausting day. Stretching aching muscles, Matt sinks into his couch with a beer in his hand and turns on the TV.

He and Joy had parted with a drawn-out kiss, after spending all afternoon at the beach. Matt had wanted to continue the day and have dinner, but Joy is heading up to the city for the week to spend some time with her dad. It is now Matt's project to brainstorm ideas for their date. He's already nervous about it, since he has no clue what to do. He casts his mind back to think of other dates he's had in the past, but there weren't really any times when he'd asked a girl on a 'date'. It had seemed like such an American thing to do for some reason, something that only happened in the movies. In real life, it was supposed to be a lot more organic. Matt racks his brain for something interesting to do, something unobvious. The only options that pop up are the most cliché things he can think of - dinner and a movie, mini-golf, a candlelit dinner. Nothing he thinks will make an impression.

Matt looks down into the neck of his green beer bottle for answers. Only bubbles and amber return his gaze. There are no epiphanies there. He wonders again what it would feel like if he had been told that he was dying like Joy. There is no escaping the fact that he had seriously thought about ending his life only a week or so ago. Was that any different? The logical side of him says it is a disgustingly selfish thing to throw away your life, when others were struggling with everything they have to keep theirs. But the way he feels about himself has very little to do with logic. His life isn't worth as much as someone else's. He hasn't given anything interesting to the world and doesn't have a lot of promise either. He's not a father, a doctor or a teacher. The more he stares into his beer, the more the feeling takes hold of him again. It hasn't gone away after all. It still hangs there. All that had happened this week was a mere distraction. Amusement. The sense of worthlessness that had gripped Matt still has its fingers wrapped around his neck. He has done nothing with his life. So was that any life at all? If he died tomorrow there would be no footprint left behind. His family would possibly shed a few tears, but those tears would dry in the dust and be forgotten before a single generation passed. There is no Matthew Pearce legacy. He isn't even a blip in history. He is less than a blip. Maybe that is a reason to turn things around. Maybe it's time he looked to his potential and tried to fill it. But what is his potential? What is he supposed to do? What does he want to do? Is being a 'writer', whatever that means, really what he wants? Is what he is *supposed* to do and what he *wants* to do even the same thing? No solutions come to him. Any strand of a good idea seems to just evaporate into another unanswerable question.

There is the promise of a relationship with Joy, the promise of something special. But is that special, really? Haven't millions of other people been in love? That means there is nothing unique about it. It's just another fleeting emotion to slide off into the abyss. He still feels compelled to try though. The same instinct that tells him there is more to life, is telling him to chase her with every fibre of his being. But maybe he's not good enough for her. She is smart, beautiful and interesting - not the kind of person that could have any lasting attraction to someone like him. Any charm he somehow has now will wear off the more she gets to know him.

Matt strengthens his grip on his beer bottle. All of a sudden, he is very angry with it. He squeezes his fist as hard as he can, trying to break the bottle in his hand, but he's not strong enough. Frustrated, he throws it against the wall and it shatters, splashing liquid up to the roof in a splatter of froth. Splinters of glass fall on the ground.

Matt sighs. Too much time to think isn't a good thing. To snap himself out of the feeling, he takes out his laptop and turns it on. Rather than his normal detour to Facebook, Matt double clicks on his word processor program. At the top of a new document, he writes the heading: BEER BOTTLE.

His first line takes Matt by surprise. 'The bottle is dead, since it's no longer able to hold what it was made to contain.'

Not bad. He thinks. *Not good either, but at least it's a move on from writing fake letters.* Rather than linger in philosophical territory, Matt starts to describe the mark that it has made on the wall as a result of its demise. His words are rusty and when he reads it aloud everything sounds childish. Matt doesn't care. At least he's doing something for himself. At least he's doing something that might leave a shadow to show that he was once alive - like the beer bottle that's left its dent on the wall.

Twenty Five

Music drifts over Matt as he lies on the lounge-room floor reading *The Unbearable Lightness of Being*. Having stuck with the book, he has been drawn into a world that would seem drab if it weren't for the emotions and thoughts of the characters. The ideas that the author Milan Kundera raises spark an interest in Matt. He is especially intrigued by the theory of eternal recurrence. The idea basically states that the universe is repeating itself over and over again. By this logic, it might be possible that Matt would live the same life, over and over. If that were the case, he should make it a good, if not interesting life. Right now, his life is so devoid of either concept that Matt thinks if he were forced to live the same path repeated for eternity, then it would be the worst Hell imaginable.

Aside from two toilet stops and a break for lunch that he doesn't taste for thinking, Matt reads the book from cover to cover. It's late afternoon by the time he finishes. Matt feels anything but light afterward. A weighty silence sits in his soul. He knows that the book is fiction, but it still seems real. The world of communist Czechoslovakia was so far from his current sphere of understanding that it may as well have been set on the moon. However, the people still acted like normal, dysfunctional people from anywhere else. The most horrifying thing was that he related to these people while reading it. He wishes he could really live in their shoes, because even though their lives are full of suffering they are romantic sufferings which he hasn't experienced himself. There is nothing romantic about *his* pains. They eat at him. The only hopeful message that Matt can take out of the novel for himself is that when seemingly bad things happen, new doors of opportunity open. Maybe losing his job is one of these times. It has opened the door to reassess his life and even have the courage to ask Joy out that first time. It got him out of the day-to-day grind that was sucking away his soul one breath at a time.

There is a loud knock at the door, jerking Matt from his reflective mood. He gets up, hope rising in his chest that it might be Joy surprising him by coming home from the city early. He opens the door and it's Z. She looks relieved that he's home. Matt's heart drops a little, but he's still happy to see her.

'I quit,' she says in the way of hello. 'I told those fuckers to go and suck a bag of sweaty balls and that they weren't treating people like humans.'

'Beer?' Matt asks.

'Mind if I smoke?'

'Let's sit on the deck.'

Matt goes inside and grabs two bottles from the fridge, before shuffling out onto the two-by-two meter square of 'deck' at the front door. It has two plastic chairs that are barely used. Matt sometimes fantasises about putting a rocking chair out there one day, just so he can pretend he's a hundred-years-old and hang out with a shotgun laid across his lap. He hands Z an open bottle and sits down.

'How'd Mr James take it?'

'Like someone who accepts resignations almost every day,' Z says. 'Still, it would have been nice to have a 'we'll miss you' speech after five years of wading in their stinking trenches. I think he might have suspected I leaked your call recordings.'

'I thought you said no one knew who it was?' Matt asks, feigning shock.

'Please, no one even in the IT department there could have rerouted an IP address with so much elegance. I tell you Matt, doing stuff anonymously really doesn't pay the ego cheques like it should. A lot more could get done in this world if people didn't mind about getting credit. I did it and I'm proud of it.'

Z's bold honesty always puts a smile on Matt's face, no matter what kind of a mood he's in. He watches her stuff a cigarette into her holder and spark it alight. Matt's fingers twitch for the ghost of the cigarette he used to keep in his hand in the Optitel courtyard. He thinks about asking Z if he can hold one of hers, but decides he doesn't want to come across as too much of a weirdo.

'So, what now then?' Matt asks, as Z sucks in a lungful of smoke. Her shoulders drop a few centimetres as she exhales it out into the late afternoon breeze.

'That's why I'm here,' Z says, raising her eyebrow, a smile playing on her lips. 'That email you wrote about company service. It has inspired me to start my own company. *True* Customer Service, contracting to companies who actually value their community. Do you want to be partners?'

The question takes Matt off guard more than Z's announcement of quitting ever could. He leans back in his chair, letting the offer sink in. Working with Z would be plenty of fun, but the idea of re-entering a life of customer service makes his gut churn. Even if he's treating people the right way, the idea just doesn't seize him with the sense of purpose he wants to feel. Still, the opportunity of growing something is much more attractive than starting a dead-end job that he has no control over. He looks at Z again for a long time before answering.

'Can I think about it?'

'Oh wow, that's a no.' Z says, taking a deep swig of her beer.

'No, it's not,' Matt says. 'I'm just a little unsure about a life on the phones. I can see the positives, but I want to be sure. I have this idea that I might try to go back to uni and study.'

'If there's one thing I've learnt in my life,' Z says, setting down her drink, 'it's that if you're going into a big project like this it's either a fuck yes, or a no. Otherwise, there's no way you'll make it through all the pain of setting up and sticking things out until you see the benefits on the other side. It's the same with a relationship. Unless you're ready to go in balls out, don't bother.'

Matt considers the words. Not just about the offer, but what it means for the two other big maybes in his life right now. Dating Joy is practically a no-brainer. His entire being lights up with a screaming yes whenever he thinks of her. It's not love yet, he doesn't think, but it's certainly something he wants to see out. A career in writing is something less obvious. Maybe it's that he knows the crushing feeling of getting rejection slips for things he's tried to have published before. Maybe it's that he knows how hard it is to make a career slinging any kind of words. Maybe it's just that he doesn't think he's any good. But deep in his gut, way down, there's something telling him that he needs to at least try. Now this opportunity from Z has put another 'maybe' in the mix, it's too much for him to process all at once. He wishes he was the kind of impulsive person that can just leap in on instinct, but he doesn't trust himself enough to do that. He stops and looks up again.

'I'd really like to think about it,' he says seriously.

'Fine,' Z waves, blowing smoke from pursed lips like he has already turned her down. 'You've got a month. I've already started setting up the backend stuff and putting together lists of potential clients. I've been interviewing freelancers in the Philippines to help pick up any overflow of calls and have a handful of really great options. Most of them have English nailed better than you and me. Super switched on people.'

'Geez, you have been busy,' Matt is impressed. 'And you only quit today?'

'I don't do anything by halves, Matthew. When the idea took hold I had to start doing stuff at night time and on weekends in preparation. Now it's at the point where it needs my full attention and I couldn't last one more day in that dream-murdering hole. I just need a partner to level me out, act as the soul of the business and help train the team. Someone who really cares about people. Someone like you.'

Matt is flattered. He has always thought of himself as a bit of a misanthrope, mostly because he found it hard to open up to people with any kind of depth. But Z is no bullshitter. If she sees that he is kind towards people, then that's what she sees. Matt knows enough to realise that self-perception is one of the least reliable things someone can have, unless they are a Buddhist monk or something.

Matt swishes his bottle around after trying to take a sip and realising it's empty. His head is full. He needs another drink to help think things through. At least this is going to be a good distraction from twiddling his thumbs, waiting for Saturday with Joy to come around.

'Another drink?' Matt asks Z.

Z looks at Matt like he's just asked if she breathes air. He heads back into the house to grab a new round.

Twenty Six

Saturday can't come quick enough. Even with Matt's deliberation between study and starting a new venture with Z, he finds it hard to make any real headway with a decision. The occasional text from Gerard venting his own customer service woes seems like Matt should nudge toward study. He just doesn't know for sure. Throw in his preoccupation with his new crush and Matt's head is just as muddled as ever.

At night, he and Joy message each other sweet nothings. Matt finds he's always wittier in prose than speech, so he prefers texts to phone calls. Sometimes, sexual innuendo creeps into Joy's messages, but Matt is too nervous to cross the line. He doesn't want to come across as a pervert. His feelings for Joy are almost alien in a way. They're so intense, yet so confusing. He wants to see her, hold her, speak with her. Some dark side even wants to possess her, even though he knows that's a horrible thing to think. All of this has come on so strong and fast that the more cerebral side of him keeps passing off his feelings as borderline delusional. It's just his hormones talking. It's just that she's something new among his boring world. It's just. It's just. It's just that she's amazing.

To get out of his head Matt goes for long walks. Up in the hills at the back of town. Through the shops. Down to the foreshore. Past Bill's garden to see the bustling trade.

This afternoon he's walking past the skatepark where the kids blast around on scooters, skateboards and BMXs. They hang out in groups according to their vehicle of choice. The skater kids are in skinny black jeans and loose white tees, every one of them with long, scraggly hair and caps on their heads. The scooter riders all wear helmets, knee pads and elbow pads. They're mostly wearing shorts and sneakers. The ones on BMX bikes also wear helmets but theirs are covered with scuffed stickers, or tagged with graffiti. They all have flannel shirts with sleeves rolled up to the elbows. None of the groups seem to have any animosity towards the others. They cohabit the space and zip around each other in an ordered chaos that somehow avoids any major collisions. They all seem to get on without written rules, making it up as they go along. Laughing, zooming, falling and rolling to their feet. Free.

Matt walks back down to the main street. He walks past the Sand Witch Café, Bakery, Newsagents, Post Office and Two-Dollar Shop. He remembers when it used to be the One-Dollar Shop but inflation had caused them to rebadge at some point in time. He eavesdrops on snippets of conversation as he goes, to keep any nattering conversations in his own mind at bay. Two blokes are talking about the footy and how the Cats have a good shot at winning the premiership this year. A woman and her friend discuss the weather and how they're looking forward to the change of seasons. The starts of conversations are nearly always the same - *how are you?, what have you been up to?, how's things?, what's up?*. The replies are just as general and repetitive - *I'm good, not much, same as always, nothing new*. It all seems so inane compared with the deeper stuff Joy asks when they're talking.

Matt heads home. He picks up the newspaper in the driveway and flicks to the classifieds. Walking inside and settling in next to his laptop, he plugs in a few jobs he has found that are beyond his experience level. Just for kicks he lists that he's applied to be a dental assistant. Matt imagines what it would be like if he got the job, having to stick his fingers in people's mouths and put that saliva sucker thing into the side of their cheeks. It would be intriguing for a while, but the novelty wouldn't last.

Done with his 'work' for this week, Matt turns to the Letters-To-The-Editor section. There is collective outrage at a proposal to put a McDonalds on the highway. People rave about bad health, big business and branded litter in the streets. There is one letter bemoaning the fact that The Reject Shop will be setting up in town soon. What will happen to their beloved Two-Dollar Shop? Gone for sure. There are complaints about no parking, bad traffic and rude people. A lot of the letters remind Matt of posts he sees on Facebook when people have had a bad day. These kinds of rants aren't a new phenomenon after all. They're just easier to publish now.

Matt decides he should flex his writing muscles and add some difference to the moaning. He clicks open his word processor and starts a short letter.

What if we all knew each other?

Dear Readers,

I've been seeing all of your complaints on this page for a little while now. To be honest, I think a lot of it stems from the fact that we don't know all of the faces around town anymore. We're afraid of change and we're afraid of 'the others' that come with that. But what if we all knew each other? What if we started to make an effort to get to know a new person each day. Not just a token hello or a nod. Not even a 'hello, how are you?'. I'm talking real conversations about real things. I challenge you to ask someone you've never met before one of the following questions this week: What are you passionate about? What has been the happiest day of your life so far? Can you tell me about the first time you ever fell in love? We might find it's harder to complain about people we've shared a laugh or a tear with, especially when it comes to petty things like traffic and parking. Who knows, we might even start being polite to each other again.

Yours in Friendship

Matt is about to sign his own name when he thinks better of it. He doesn't want the embarrassment of people he knows, yet hasn't spoken to for a long while, pulling him up and saying they saw what he wrote. He just wants them to read it on face value and think about it, not attach a face to the message. He thinks about putting Eric Arthur-Blair on the letter, but he'd previously written that Eric was new to town and Matt wants it to seem like the letter is from a long-time local. Yet, he doesn't want to throw someone real in there either. Instead, Matt creates a new fake email account under the pseudonym David Robert Jones. He copies the letter into a new draft, signs off, addresses it to the newspaper and hits send. Z might not like being anonymous, but Matt prefers to keep his head out of any spotlight if he can help it.

Twenty Seven

Saturday comes around and Matt meets Joy at the supermarket. He greets her with a full shopping cart. He'd commandeered it in the frozen food section, from a man that was yelling at his son for wanting ice cream.

'I didn't want to waste too much time on this,' Matt says to Joy as he approaches her in the car park. 'We've got a bit of a drive ahead of us today.'

'Really?' Joy smiles with her crimson lips.

Matt nods, unwilling to elaborate. His anxiety at how today will go overshadows all else.

'How was your week?' Matt asks as they walk through the car park together.

'Depressing. Dad hasn't been the same since Mum died. He tried, but he has always been detached. It got even worse when I was diagnosed. It's like he shut off completely. Like I'm dead already, even though I'm all clear for now. Let's not talk about that. What are we going to do today?'

'It's a surprise.'

'I love surprises!' Joy lets out a squeal of delight and does a little ninja kick in the air.

'Good,' Matt laughs at her display of excitement. 'We can take my car and leave this stuff in yours, if you like.'

'There's nothing that needs to be put in the freezer?'

'Nah, the guy was telling his kid that he couldn't have ice cream because he wets the bed.'

'I'm glad you took his trolley then.'

Matt is glad as well. He'd never wet the bed, but he knows intimately the feeling of being embarrassed in public. His firing at the hands of Mr James is the most recent humiliation and he still thinks about it lying awake in bed at night. His own dad had never had that problem before. He never seemed self-conscious about anything. He'd dye his hair blue for local charity, or dress up as a cow and come to school to promote strong bones during kid's health week. He'd yell g'day out of the window of his car at strangers. He'd loudly declare that rugby was a superior sport to AFL down at the footy ground, just to get a rise out of the folks and engage in a friendly argument. He revelled in being gregarious and outgoing. Revelled in the attention that it brought. Matt preferred to be the phantom at his side, watching his dad's exploits. A lot of the time he felt acute embarrassment on behalf of his father for the things he said and did, but mostly he felt envy, wishing he could be so outgoing. He felt proud that this was his dad. He really should give his parents a call one of these days.

Together, Matt and Joy dump the groceries into Joy's car. He returns the trolley to its corral and clips it back into the row. The one-dollar deposit for the trolley falls out of the dispenser on the push bar and clatters to the ground. Matt looks down at the money. Slowly, he picks it up. Wandering back to Joy, he holds up the dented gold coin and shows it to her.

'What do you normally do with this when you take the trolley back?'

'I give it to the fundraising group at the entrance.'

'Why?'

'Because otherwise it would be stealing,' she winks.

'Well, I'm glad we're on the same moral wavelength,' he smiles.

Walking back to the supermarket doors, Matt drops the coin into a tin marked with a Guide Dog symbol. Upon hearing the noise, a seated man wearing dark glasses voices his thanks and gives a nod.

Joy smiles her approval as Matt rejoins her and they both slide into the beaten-up Holden. The motor chugs to life after some cajoling from Matt. With a squeal of the fanbelt, he reverses out of his park.

'So where are we going?' Joy asks, as Matt heads onto the road and starts driving out of town.

'To the airport.'

'What?' Joy jumps in her seat. 'Where are we going?'

'Calm down,' Matt says, thinking he made a mistake by not qualifying his statement. 'We are going to the airport. That's our destination. We're going to play a game that I made up during the week. That's all you need to know for now.'

Fields of brown grass and cracked soil frame the highway. To the far left a mountain range humps out of the ground, like the shadow of a dinosaur. The peaks are small, a toy version of larger mountains that Matt has seen in National Geographic magazines. If Matt didn't know better, they could be driving in

Africa. Skeletal remains of trees dot the landscape; a reminder that drought has ravaged this part of Australia for over a decade. The only hint of civilisation along this stretch is the occasional service station on the side of the road.

'You know, I've been thinking,' says Joy, looking out the window.

'Did it hurt?'

Joy rolls her eyes at Matt's dad-joke.

'I'm serious. You said back there we are on the same wavelength morally.'

'Yeah.'

'What did you mean by that?'

'I guess I just meant that I don't like stealing. I don't feel like I'm stealing anything when I take those trolleys, because I pay for the stuff. It's a victimless crime.'

Joy falls silent and looks out the window again. Grey telephone poles flash by like a set of visual Morse code messages. Matt turns the radio up as his Jeff Buckley CD clicks over in the player. Joy starts humming along to the start of the first track, *Mojo Pin*. Matt relishes the fact that she seems to know, and like, Jeff Buckley. Someone had once offered an opinion that Buckley sounded like a dying cow. Matt was so offended that he hadn't spoken to them since.

'But we are stealing, really,' Joy says, after a couple of songs have played.

Matt looks to her and then back to the road. She has one leg up on the seat and her chin is resting on her hand, like she's a feminine version of Rodin's *Thinker*. Loose strands of midnight hair are tucked behind her miniature ears. They look like dark feathers of contemplation.

'But we're paying for the groceries. We paid for the fish n' chips,' Matt explains.

'I know. We're not stealing the items themselves,' Joy says slowly. 'We're stealing time.'

'Time?' Matt is confused.

'Yeah, we're stealing people's time. That's far worse than stealing something disposable. Time is the most precious thing we have.'

Matt looks at her quizzically. He's not following her.

'Time's something you can never give someone back,' Joy says, looking concerned. 'We're taking a small amount of someone's life every time we do it. It's like we're committing gradual murder.'

'Oh come on, that's a bit dramatic!'

She sits up straight and turns down the radio.

'No, I'm serious, Matt. Murder is stealing all of someone's time left on this earth at once. We're basically murderers by increment.'

Twenty Seven

Matt lets her stream of thought take form in his own mind. He keeps waiting for her to burst into laughter and say that she was just playing, but she doesn't. He turns up the radio a little to help himself think. He scrolls the tracks along to the last song on the album. It's called *Eternal Life*.

'Well,' he says. 'You've been told that your life might be cut shorter. Maybe we're just evening the balance a little bit? Like stealing a few dollars off a millionaire to buy bread.'

Joy considers the statement and nods slightly. 'I guess that makes me feel a little better. But how do you measure something like that? Who has more life left than others? You can never really know.'

'I guess that's why it's not against the law to murder people just a little bit,' Matt says sarcastically.

'It should be,' Joy grunts.

Deciding to change the pace of the mood, Matt presses eject on his CD player. He inserts Bob Marley. The relaxing reggae rhythms cause him to alter his grip on the steering wheel. The familiar song of *Jammin'* starts playing.

'Pyjamas!' Matt sings as the words kick in. 'I'll wear pyjamas with you.'

Joy looks at Matt like he's gone insane.

'What?' Matt laughs. 'Didn't you know this song is about sleeping? It's a secret fact that not many people know about.'

Joy smiles at his playful tone and absorbs the vibe herself. She starts bobbing her head to the beat, dancing in her seat while the song bounces along. They start singing together.

'Pyjamas! Pyjamas are a thing of the past.'

The lyrics send the pair into a giggling fit. Both of them are gasping for air, with tears running down their faces. It lifts the atmosphere of the car into a sense of hope. Joy claps along and is singing at the top of her lungs. Matt wonders if this is happiness, or just amusement. It feels like happiness.

The end of the highway comes into view and Matt turns onto the ring road that leads to the airport. Trucks roar around their chassis of song as the Holden settles into the traffic. Matt slows down as they go under a bridge fitted with a speed camera. Once they pass, having evaded the trap, he speeds up to over a hundred kilometres an hour to make up for the lost time.

Twenty Eight

Boarding announcements blare over the airport PA. The large black and yellow departure board clicks over its times and flight numbers. A plane from Hannover just landed five minutes ago, with another from LA due in ten minutes. People are filing in queues, checking luggage and glancing at their watches. The constant hum of a thousand conversations fills the terminal like a swarm of bumblebees.

Matt and Joy don't participate in any of this, they just observe, taking in the sights and sounds. The two wait at the check-in section looking around, before Matt takes Joy by the hand and leads her toward the domestic terminal.

'We can go into the departure lounges on this side without a ticket,' Matt explains. 'They never check. We can watch people come and go. And, we can play the game,' he tells her over the drone of noise.

'What game?' she asks, as a man with a briefcase hurries past, clutching a boarding pass in his hand.

'You'll see.'

Joy and Matt get past security without any issues. Neither of them have bags to check, so it is a simple process of putting their phones through the x-ray scanners before passing through the metal detector. The newsagent on the other side is overflowing with people. Racks of trashy magazines sit on the outside. Without pausing to look closer, Matt leads Joy down the long, wide corridor. Waiting lounges branch off from the main passageway every few metres. Inside these gates, hundreds of people sit waiting, like sheep ready to be herded onto their flights. It occurs to Matt that if he were waiting for a plane he would stand, since he was due to be forced to sit for the duration of the flight anyway. A small café is selling over-priced coffee and ham/cheese croissants, but Matt and Joy bypass all of this. Matt keeps looking from side-to-side, as if he's trying to decide on a good place to sit, dragging the bewildered Joy in tow. He pauses for a few moments outside a toilet, which has a small drinking fountain at the front. After surveying the doors for a few minutes, he shakes his head and pulls Joy along again. They keep walking, right down to gate 16 at the end of the row, where a wide window overlooks the tarmac. Shiny, painted planes roam their grey paddock like moving billboards. There are no people waiting for flights here, only an elderly couple looking out of the window as the jets take off. There's another toilet in the corner, before the window. Matt takes a seat across the hall from the lavatory entrance. Joy sits down next to him.

'What are we doing here?'

'Just wait. You'll see soon. I'll go first.'

'Go first with what?' Joy asks with growing irritation.

Matt doesn't answer. He just sits, tapping his knees. Arching his neck, he peers back down the hall to see if anyone is approaching. There doesn't appear to be. A boarding announcement for DJ841 to Sydney crackles from the speaker overhead. Hearing this, the elderly couple abandon their post and head back toward the busier gates, presumably to board their plane. Matt and Joy are left alone.

'So, while we wait tell me something new about yourself,' Matt asks.

Joy looks up to the ceiling, trying to think of a good answer. She purses her lips and clicks her tongue in her mouth. Both of her palms rest face down on the seat, as she swings her legs underneath it, thinking. Settling on something, she looks back to Matt.

'I used to be afraid of the dark. I had to sleep with the light on until I was almost thirteen.'

'That's not so strange,' Matt says. 'I still get scared in new places when it's dark.'

'What about you? What don't I know about you yet?'

'Hmmm, I used to think that a chest of drawers were called Chester Draws.'

'What?!' Joy laughs.

'Well, it's an easy mistake to make.'

'I guess it is. But that's nothing *really* about you, that's just a little tidbit fact. Tell me something about growing up in Ocean Heads.'

'Ummm, okay.' Matt thinks for a minute. 'I used to have this mate called Tristan. We'd hang out together and talk about the latest book we'd read. It was always fantasy at that stage: Lord of the Rings, The Magician, The Dragonlance series.'

Joy's eyes are locked onto Matt's face as he tells the story, like he's the most interesting thing in the world right now.

'So one weekend we're up in the bush, kind of where you and I were the other day. We were tearing through the Iron Barks, pretending to be elves. We had homemade swords and bows. There was a fake goblin we were trying to track. Its feet, coincidentally, were shaped like a kangaroo's, so we were searching for footprints. As we went through the bush, we found a track. It led to this cave we'd never seen before.'

'I think I've seen the one!' Joy gasps. 'Does it have a really small entrance that opens out into a big cavern?'

'Yeah that's the one? How do *you* know about it?'

'I told you I like exploring, don't change the subject. Keep going.'

'Right, so we find the cave and squeeze through only to find a whole bunch of porn magazines in there.'

'Stop it. What did you do?'

'Well, we were curious kids. We read them from cover to cover, asking each other what we thought of this model, or that one. We read the dirty stories to each other, the jokes. It must have been hours we were gone. We only realised how long when we heard people in the bush shouting our names. We'd missed some lunch that Tristan was supposed to be back for and his parents had gotten worried. We hid the magazines and ran out, calling that there was nothing to worry about. Problem was, when Tristan's parents found us we still had very obvious boners jutting in our pants. Tristan's dad went apeshit. He thought that we'd been fooling around in the bush, that I'd lured his son into some kind of prepubescent, gay relationship.'

'No way?! What did you do?'

'We didn't say anything. We didn't want to let them know about the magazines because we'd get in trouble, so we just spun some ridiculous story. I can't even remember what it was. It obviously sounded like a lie. Tristan's parents forbade him from ever playing with me again.'

'The bigots!'

'Yeah, it sucked. We were at the end of primary school, Year Six, so still hung out a little there, but we drifted apart after that. Funny thing is, for some reason it made me think maybe I was gay for a while.'

'But you were turned on by photos of naked women. That should have been obvious.'

'Yeah, I didn't know. I was just a confused kid.'

'What did you do?'

'Nothing. I kept my thoughts to myself. When I started having wet dreams it was always about women too, so I figured I must be straight. It was a little disappointing actually. I think part of me wanted an explanation of why I wasn't your normal, meat-pie-eating, ball-sports-loving bloke.'

'Well, I'm glad you're not normal. I don't know if there's such a thing anyway,' says Joy.

Instead of answering, Matt puts his hand excitedly on Joy's leg as he sees a man approaching. He's holding a black briefcase. Matt watches out of the corner of his eye. The man looks out of the window at the planes for a while, before walking into the bathroom. Matt gets up, but Joy grabs his arm.

'What are you doing?'

'Just wait,' Matt whispers forcefully. 'I need to see if it works first. You'll get your turn next.'

He pulls his arm free of Joy's grip and again checks that no one is coming, before ducking inside the bathroom.

Inside, there is a long, silver urinal with ads for motion sickness medication and condoms screwed on the wall above. To the right is a set of porcelain sinks with a wall-length mirror above. The man with the briefcase has already locked himself inside the single cubicle that is set into the far wall. Matt has a clear view of the black briefcase, as the cubicle door doesn't quite reach the ground. There is a zipping noise as the man undoes his pants and settles down to do his business. Matt hunches over to see the man's underwear is around his ankles. This is exactly what Matt had hoped for: the sight of matching black shoes, surround by a pair of crumpled pant legs.

Matt is shaking with nervous excitement. Is he going to do this?

Waiting for a few more heartbeats, Matt creeps up to the door as silently as he can. Then, reaching down as fast as possible, he yanks the man's briefcase out from under the door.

'Arggh!' the man on the toilet yells with fright. There's a loud banging and scraping as he fumbles inside the cubicle. 'Wait! Stop!'

Matt turns and runs. Discarding the briefcase, he lets it skid onto the tiled floor before he exits the toilet. As soon as he gets out of the door, Matt contains his pace, back toward the puzzled Joy. He takes his seat.

'Pretend you're kissing me,' he says quietly to her. His heart is leaping out of his throat. 'But watch the door.'

Matt leans in and puts his face close to hers, so he's facing the wall and she has a clear view of the toilet door. Despite her confusion, Joy does as she's told. Rather than pretending, she lets her lips brush his. He enjoys the feeling of her hot breath, grazing his skin. After just a few seconds, her eyes lock onto Matt's with a half scared, half pleased look. Matt smiles against her mouth. Joy closes her eyes and holds the back of his head, pulling him closer into a real kiss. Matt draws in air through his nose and settles into the embrace. He places his hand on her back and runs his fingers up and down her body. Leaning back, he gives Joy a look to see if the coast is clear, but she pulls him in again. Finally, she lets Matt's lips part from hers. Her cheeks are flushed and she's panting a little.

Matt looks back down the hall, to see the man retreating into a crowd of people, clutching his briefcase.

'What did he look like when he came out?' Matt asks eagerly.

'What did you do? He was white as a sheet, clutching his bag to his chest. He then put it on the ground and searched through his belongings. He looked so relieved and happy after a few minutes. Then he looked at us accusingly. It all happened in the blink of an eye. That's when I had to kiss you properly, so I wouldn't give away our cover.'

Joy smirks, looking down the hall to see if she can catch another glimpse of the man.

'What did you do?' she repeats.

Matt leans back into his seat, pleased that his plan has gone off so well. He closes his eyes and tries to steady his breathing. It's like he's just won some kind of game show.

'I waited until he sat down on the toilet with his pants around his ankles, then I ripped his bag out from under the toilet door.'

A giggle of astonishment escapes Joy's mouth.

'What? Why?'

'Well, when I was thinking of what to do together, I thought it would be cool to do some people watching. So, I thought of the airport. Then I thought, what about extreme people watching, when you get to see proper emotions. Seeing others cry when people leave for a holiday doesn't appeal to me, so I thought of this.'

'I don't understand.'

'I wanted to see someone afraid, then relieved and then possibly confused or angry. But I didn't want to actually hurt anyone. So, I figured if you did this, then they wouldn't ever catch you. They'd be hurrying to pull up their pants, then stop to pick up and check their bag before leaving the toilet. Only then, they'd try to figure out what happened and who's going to confront a couple kissing? Not me.'

'You're brilliant!' Joy's eyes are wide with wonder.

Matt blushes at the compliment.

'The only problem is, I didn't get to see his expression. I only heard him yell when I took the bag. So, now it's your turn to do the same so I can watch.'

Fear washes over Joy's face. She starts shaking her head at the prospect.

'No way. I couldn't.'

'Come on. It's easy. It'll be easier to get a target for you too. I was lucky the first guy that went in had to use the cubicle and had a bag with him. Women should work every time. They always have a handbag and they always have to sit down to pee. There aren't any cameras in there. You'll never get busted.'

Joy stares at Matt like she is trying to figure out where all of his strange ideas come from. He doesn't know himself.

'So, what do you reckon? Do you want to give it a try?' Matt nudges Joy.

'Alright then. Just once though. I don't want to get dragged into jail because of you.'

Twenty Nine

Joy executes the bag stealing routine four times before they have to call it quits. Matt doesn't get another opportunity, but he prefers to spectate anyway. The expressions on people's faces are priceless when they exit the toilet. It's a rainbow of emotion all at once, like watching a practical joke show live. Every reaction is unique. The best moment comes when a dignified woman wearing a power suit, emerges holding her sodden bag in front of her. She must have stood up mid-stream and peed all over it.

Matt almost bites off Joy's tongue with laughter while they feign another kiss.

Joy is hooked on the rush it gives her. She keeps begging Matt to do it just once more. When a security guard starts lingering around them, they figure that the gig is up. The pair retreat back to the bustling anonymity of the food court and settle down for a late lunch.

'That was so much fun!' Joy says, as they take a table in the corner. 'I think you're winning the prize for the most original date competition.'

'I'm glad you liked it. I had no idea if it was going to work or not. It's hardly complex stuff, but I was so nervous.'

'Me too! God, the first time my knees were knocking so hard I thought they'd give me away.' Joy smiles, biting into a sushi roll that she'd just bought.

'I would say you're braver for eating raw fish at an airport.'

Joy looks down at her roll with alarm.

'No way. They're always busy here, so the turnover of stock means it stays fresh. Your little McDonalds fat burger there is more of a death trap than this.'

'Uh ah,' Matt shakes his head with a mouthful of McChicken. 'It tastes too good to be bad for you.' He pushes some fries into his mouth for good measure and takes a sip of his Coke. 'According to evolution, my body is designed to only be attracted to things that are good for me.'

'That's the dumbest thing I've ever heard. By that logic people who like going skydiving and swimming with sharks are doing it to improve their chances of survival.'

'Don't argue with science,' Matt says.

Joy just shakes her head and takes another bite of her roll. She chews her food, looking around at the constant flow of people moving about.

'I quite like airports,' she says. 'Everyone here looks happy, like they're just coming back from, or are on their way to somewhere exciting.'

Matt watches a couple walk past. They both have hiking packs on and are dressed in matching mountain gear. He feels a little jealous that they're heading somewhere he is never likely to see. He knows what Joy is saying though. This building is a portal to a wider world. It was built to take people beyond their normal lives.

'So, what are we going to do for our next date?' he asks Joy, tumbling his ice in his cup. 'It's your turn now.'

'Oh, I've got a few ideas.' Her emerald eyes flash with knowing. 'My best one isn't as crafty as your stunt today, but I think you'll like it. It'll be peaceful.'

'Peaceful? Sounds like a good balance to me. When do you want to go?'

Twenty Nine

'How about we get together again tomorrow? Are you doing anything?'

Matt beams. Even if he did have something on, he would cancel in a heartbeat.

Thirty

Matt sits waiting in the gutter out the front of his unit. It's 6:00 a.m. Joy wants to get an early start to beat the Sunday traffic, so Matt is ready to go. His backpack sits next to him, empty. Joy said she would provide the necessary things. All he had to do was wear some sturdy shoes. His trusty Cons are laced firmly on his feet.

The hatchback rattles up the street. Confronted by the red pedestrian lights, Joy barely slows down. She just looks from side to side to make sure it's safe and pushes through. Matt stands up onto the curb, so she doesn't run over his feet as she pulls in. Joy waves hello out of the open window.

'Good morning,' Matt smiles, as she comes to a stop.

'You all set?' Joy replies. 'It's going to be a hot one today. Lucky we'll be there before the heat kicks in.'

'Glad to see you're dressed for the occasion then.' Matt laughs.

She's wearing her standard skin-tight black jeans with a navy singlet top. Her alabaster skin stands out against the dark colours.

'Just get in,' she says, after looking herself up and down.

It's not long before they're heading in the exact opposite direction they travelled yesterday. The hatchback wraps along winding coastline. It is the start of The Great Ocean Road: a scenic tourist drive which twists and turns right down to the Twelve Apostles, one of Australia's most iconic landmarks. Those impossible stacks of limestone are more than a three-hour drive away, so Matt dismisses it as the destination for their date.

'I packed us a lunch,' Joy says. 'No burgers today. We've got nuts, salad, cheese and some bread rolls.'

Matt looks back to see the fare stacked next to two bottles of water and a pair of walking shoes.

'My Sherlock Holmes instincts tell me that we're going on a hike somewhere,' Matt comments.

'Very observant, Dr Watson,' Joy says. 'It's a place where my dad used to take me camping as a girl. It's always deserted, even at this time of year.'

Matt smiles his appreciation. After the excitement of yesterday, a relaxing stroll will do him good.

The drive is stunning. On the right-hand side, sheer granite cliffs loom high above the car, stretching back into dense bushland. On the left, the road drops away just beyond a metal guard rail, down into the sea. Around every corner, unwavering views of Bass Straight are revealed. The ocean is clear and calm, with just a few puffy, white clouds hanging in the sky. Occasionally, a motorbike whips past them at breakneck speed. Matt never ceases to be startled by the roar of their engines. Riders lean hard to arc around the tight hairpins and suicidal blind corners that typify this route. It's a miracle that none of them skid over the cliff into the sea.

Just before they reach the hamlet of Lorne, Joy and Matt get caught behind a caravan. There are no opportunities to overtake, but being in no hurry, it doesn't bother them in the slightest. To pass the time, Matt tells Joy about his old job at Optitel and his spectacular dismissal. Whilst Joy thinks the story is funny, she loathes the cruel ambush played by Mr James.

'That guy will get what's coming to him one day,' Joy sneers. 'Karma can be a right little bitch.'

'I dunno,' Matt shrugs. 'I don't feel like I was doing anything wrong, but technically Mr James was right to fire me. I don't really care. He did me a favour in a way.'

Matt leaves out the part about wanting to kill himself afterwards. He's embarrassed to talk about it with Joy, since she seems so enamoured with life.

'So, what are you going to do now?' she asks.

'I'm a bit stuck on it. Someone else at Optitel just quit as well and has asked if I want to start a customer service company with her that treats people like gold. Sub-contract to new companies and that.'

'Sounds interesting. At least you'd be doing something you believe in.'

'Yes and no,' Matt says. 'I think I'd like working with Z. She's a classic lady. But I think I'd be grasping to help people understand a new app, or whatever they're calling in for. It just doesn't excite me. You always hear about people who leap out of bed in the morning excited to get to work. I want to feel that, or at least look forward to something I'd be spending most of my time doing.'

'Well, what do you think your *thing* might be?'

'I quite like writing. It would be pretty cool to do something like that,' Matt keeps his tone as neutral as he can, in case Joy thinks it's a terrible idea. Even to him it seems somewhat frivolous and self-serving.

'That's a great idea!' Joy slaps the steering wheel cheerfully, surprising Matt. 'Then you can write me sonnets. You could be Australia's next bush poet, like Henry Lawson, or Banjo Paterson.'

'Ha! I don't know about that. I've never been out bush, like the outback and stuff.'

'Well, you could start your own movement. You could be a coast poet.'

'A coast poet?'

'Yeah. You live on the coast, not the bush, so you're a coast poet.'

Matt shakes his head at her excitement. 'I'm not anything right now. I don't even know how to write properly. I've never studied it. It seems really hard to earn a living doing it at any rate.'

'So learn!' she exclaims, slapping the wheel again. 'Dreams are nothing if they aren't chased. Who cares if you make money if you love it. And anyway, writing is like talking. Anyone can do it. '

'But not everyone can do it well.'

Thirty

'That's true,' Joy concedes, 'but you have to at least give it a go. You could always wash dishes at night and write in the day.'

'Yeah, my Centrelink contact reckons I could get some kind of support if I do a full-time uni course. Maybe I'll look into it some more.'

Matt lets the conversation drift off with his non-committal answer. They're now out of Lorne and on the winding road again, climbing up a steep incline. Joy's car struggles up the hill, so she drops it back into second gear. It kicks back and shoots forward with a grunt.

'It seems unbelievable that people could make a road here,' Matt comments, looking up at the chiselled stone of the cliff above.

'Don't get me started on that!' Joy says. 'My dad used to regale me with the same story every time we drove through this section of road.'

'Tell me,' Matt asks with curiosity.

'Nah, it's alright, I don't want you to fall asleep on me.'

'No, really. I want to know.'

'If you insist,' Joy clears her throat and puts on her best tour guide voice. 'This road was built by returned servicemen after World War I. It's dedicated as a memorial to all of the fallen soldiers who never returned to Australia. At a distance of two hundred and forty-three kilometres long, it's the world's longest war memorial. The whole thing was dug by hand, using explosives, pick axes and wheelbarrows.'

'Shit,' Matt says in awe, marvelling at the sheer drop next to them. 'Imagine being up here in the dead of winter, trying to cart about granite boulders with frozen hands.'

'Several soldiers died during construction,' Joy continues in her mock tone. 'But it wasn't all hardship. A steamboat ran aground just near here one time and had to jettison its huge cargo of booze. The workers got their hands on it and forced a two-week stop of work, while they had a great old lark, drinking the entire lot. Five hundred barrels of beer and one hundred and twenty barrels of whiskey, in one big party.'

'That's awesome!' Matt laughs. 'They deserved it. There's no way you'd get me out here in the mud and rain to make way for more tourists to come down to the coast.'

'When I think about it now, it is a pretty cool story, but when you're a twelve-year-old girl, it's not so interesting. Bless dad. At least he tried back then.'

By now the car is passing cypress trees on the approach to Apollo Bay. Joy doesn't stop. She just keeps going through the town. For Matt, this is as far as he's ever come before. He loves the carvings that line the foreshore. They are cut right out of old tree trunks, still rooted in the ground. It's like they're tree-spirits escaped from wooden shackles.

'How far have we got to go?' asks Matt.

'Not far. We're parking up in the Cape Otway Forest and then it's on foot from there. I hope you're feeling energetic.'

Matt is. It seems the blue sky just goes on forever.

Thirty One

Mountain Ash Eucalypts grow like prehistoric giants along the walking track. Even on this hot day, it's cool under the canopy of trees. The Eucalypts stand like sentinels over the smaller, flowering Blackwoods, resembling the protective image of parent and child. Willy Wagtails and Bristlebirds hop around on the forest floor, chirping in the carpet of moss and ferns. Matt can't believe his eyes. He hadn't known there was a full-blown temperate rainforest so close to home. The stark contrast between this scene and the savannah-like fields spanning the drive to Melbourne yesterday, makes it seem impossible that the two could exist in the same country, let alone the same state. Even the cliff-top trees of Ocean Heads are completely different from this.

The lightweight pack is easy to carry on Matt's back. Joy walks ahead of him with her own small bag. Her hiking shoes look comically big in contrast to her narrow-cut jeans, but Matt wishes he had worn something similar. His normal pair of Converse shoes will give him blisters by the end of the day.

They meander through the forest, down steep embankments, through narrow gullies and rock hop over a stream, which babbles down through a tangle of brown and green foliage. Setting along the riverbank, Joy leads upstream, letting the moist soil soften their footfalls. There isn't another person in sight. Joy had been right. Even at this busy time of year, no one seemed to come up this way.

Matt can hear the dull rush of falling water, as they follow the stream upward. Dappled light is shining through the trees. A filter of green permeates everything around them. It's like a David Attenborough documentary.

The ground rises more as they go up. Matt is sweating from the effort as the pathway turns into a small rock face. Water is funnelling through the middle of the wall. Joy climbs up, around the side. Matt grapples for branches that are sticking out of the rocks, almost falling at one point when a tree root breaks off unexpectedly. Hearing him swear under his breath, Joy turns around to make sure he's okay.

'It's not far now,' she says, her forehead beading perspiration. 'Just over this little rock ledge.' She turns to face the precipice and lifts herself up. Matt can't believe how nimble she is in those pants.

Struggling, Matt clears the last rocky obstacle and gasps in astonishment. Spread out before them is a hidden valley. The trees offer cover for the most part, but in the centre, bright sunshine beats down onto a small billabong, which spreads back to another rising rock face. The water looks black and cool. A small waterfall trickles into the pool, producing a colony of delicate bubbles, which float on the surface. The water is touched by the fingertips of ferns that grow around the banks. Joy sits, resting atop a smooth boulder.

'Not a bad place for lunch, hey?' she says, recovering.

'Not bad at all,' Matt says, internally flabbergasted at this slice of utopia.

Joy sits on the rock with her head in her hands, panting.

'You alright?' Matt asks.

Thirty One

She looks up with a forced smile. 'I think I'm a bit dehydrated from the walk. I've got a splitting headache. Can you pass me some water?'

Matt lets his backpack slip off his shoulders and fall to the ground. He grabs a bottle of water and hands it to Joy who gulps it down hungrily. She wipes her lips, seemingly satisfied. Matt takes off his shoes and socks and walks over to the edge of the water. Crouching down, he cups his hands into the pool and splashes his face. It's instantly refreshing.

'It's a pity we didn't bring our swimmers,' he says. 'I'd love a dip right now.'

Joy gives him a coy look, as she pulls a rug out from her backpack and spreads it out on the ground.

'There's no one else around. I don't mind if you want to go skinny dipping.'

Matt looks at the water and then back to Joy. Swells of hopeful nerves shiver inside him.

'What about you? I'm not going to show you some skin unless you show me yours.'

'No, I don't like taking my shirt off anymore,' Joy looks away, embarrassed.

It takes a few moments for Matt to understand her reluctance. Her breast cancer operation must have left her with some scars. In an effort to disguise his slip up, he splashes his face once more.

'It would be a shame to waste the opportunity,' Matt says, his eyes lingering on the billabong.

'Really, I don't mind if you go in,' Joy says. 'I'll watch from here.'

'You just want to check me out,' Matt jokes.

'Maybe,' she laughs.

To keep her laughing, Matt stands up and starts dancing around the clearing, slowly taking off his shirt.

'Wooo!' Joy claps. 'Put on a show!'

He peels the t-shirt off and swings it around his head, throwing it at Joy. She catches it and holds it over her face. Stealing sneak peeks out of the side, her eyes reflect the colour of the trees above her. Swaying his hips theatrically, Matt unzips his pants and lets them drop to the ground. His actions are more funny than sexy. Humour is the only way he can overcome the insecurity he feels in his own body. Resting his thumbs inside the elastic waistband of his boxers, he looks to Joy, raising an eyebrow.

'Take it off!' she hoots.

Instead, Matt turns and jumps into the water with a loud splash. The fresh water envelops him as he descends beneath, immersed in a deepening silence. Holding his breath until his lungs begin to tingle, Matt pushes back up toward the surface. Bursting into the world again, the sounds of nature mixed with Joy's giggles come into his ears.

'You're a tease!' she yells out to him, as he breaststrokes over to the waterfall.

Matt didn't have the guts to stand naked in front of Joy. The prospect of it is terrifying. If he thought about it, he'd realise he'd never been naked sober in front of a girl before. Matt stands under the waterfall. The weight of cascading water pummels his head and shoulders. After washing his neck and underarms free from the grit of the walk, he swims back to the rocks near Joy, feeling like a new man. Getting out of the water, Matt's chest is now heaving from the cold rather than from the exercise.

'It's chilly in there!' he says, walking up to Joy, dripping wet. The hot sun filtering through the trees helps warm him.

'I'm sure it's not that cold,' Joy teases him.

'Really?'

'Yeah, you're just a big sook.'

'We'll see about that, won't we?' Matt says, wrapping Joy in a wet bear hug.

She squeals with fright as his damp body covers hers. Matt nuzzles cold kisses onto her neck as she fights to wriggle away from him.

'No, stop it!' she giggles.

Instead of stopping, he reaches down and picks her up in his arms. Holding her against his chest, she's surprisingly light. He walks her toward the water's edge.

'Don't you dare!' she says, half seriously, half looking at the water with excited anticipation. 'Matt, don't you do it.'

Without warning Matt jumps, taking her with him into the pool. They crash into the water together. Joy gasps when they come up for air.

'Oh God, oh God. It's cold!' she pants, kicking her legs hard underneath the water to keep herself up. Her smile has gone.

'I told you!' Matt smiles.

'That wasn't funny,' Joy splashes water at him, paddling back to the rocks.

As she gets out, her wet singlet clings to her body. Her soaked jeans drip water, the denim sucking onto her legs with their new weight. Matt thinks she looks incredibly sexy.

'I can't believe you did that,' she says, flashing an angry look at Matt, who's still treading water in the pool. 'How on earth am I going to walk back like this?'

'It's okay, you'll dry,' Matt says, trying to calm her down. 'It's only water.'

Joy isn't listening though. She stomps over to Matt's clothes and picks them up.

'What are you doing?' Matt asks, eying off his dry t-shirt and pants.

'It' okay, it's only water,' Joy huffs, throwing them into the pool at him.

He tries to suppress his smile as his clothes land in the water. He knows they'll dry in the sun, so he just stands there, watching as they become saturated and sink to the bottom. Once they are submerged, he dives down and picks them up. Joy is standing with her arms crossed, glaring down at him as he nears the bank.

'Are you happy now we're even?' he asks her. 'It's going to be a long walk back if we're not talking to each other.'

In response, Joy sits back down on the rug despite her wet clothes. She starts pulling out their lunch in silence. Matt takes the hint and gets out of the water. He dries off as much as possible before re-joining her.

'Look, I'm sorry,' he apologises, sitting down. 'I thought you'd think it was funny. How can I make it up to you?'

Joy thumps down a bread roll next to Matt.

'Come on. Please. I'll give you a foot massage or something.'

He doesn't want her to be in this mood for the ride home. It seems like a waste to spoil such beautiful surroundings by holding a grudge.

'Well... a foot massage would be nice,' Joy admits, the sour gloom lifting slowly from her face.

'A foot massage it is then,' he beams. 'Right after lunch.'

For such simple fare, lunch is very tasty. The cashew nuts and cheese are a perfect savoury dessert, after eating salad and bread. Matt finishes his bottle of water, before refilling it again in the billabong.

When he gets back to Joy, she's stretched out, reclining on a moss-covered rock with her feet in the air. She wiggles her toes at Matt.

'I'll have my rub down now, servant.'

'If I don't do a good job, will you punish me?' Matt mocks.

'If you're lucky.'

Matt checks that his t-shirt and pants are drying in the sun, before easing back down next to Joy in his boxers. He wedges himself against a tree for support and takes her heels in his lap. Her feet are slick from the moss, so it's easy to knead her toes. He presses into the arch of her foot. Joy throws her head back and lets out a light moan of pleasure. Glad that his efforts are producing a result, he continues. The sun's rays fall down on Matt's skin, warming his body. He closes his eyes and relaxes into the task. While his fingers push and rub, Joy's moans get louder, taking on a distinct sexual edge. Her sounds of pleasure arouse Matt and soon there is a swell inside his damp boxers. Hoping she won't notice, he props Joy's heel onto his thigh and raises his other knee in an effort to cover his groin from view. The shift, however, makes Joy fall silent. Opening his eyes, Matt sees Joy looking at him mischievously. Her eyes trace his entire body, from his face to his lap.

'Are you enjoying this, servant?' she coos, sliding her foot down and pressing it against his groin.

She moves her foot lightly up and down. Matt's cheeks flush with the stimulation.

'Don't,' he manages to whisper. 'Don't play with me.'

'You're mine, young man,' she smirks. 'I can do what I wish.'

With surprising dexterity, Joy grasps the waistband with her toes and pulls it down to expose the tip of his hard manhood. Matt's legs start to shake with tension, but a rising lust inside him pushes back any nervousness he thought he would feel. Raising his hips, he lets Joy work down his shorts with her toes. She pushes her slippery foot along his length. This time it's Matt who lets a murmur of desire escape his lips. Encouraged, Joy continues her motion. Her movement is languid but insistent. Matt watches her as she shifts her feet together, closing around his member. He looks into her stunning eyes. This only serves to inflame the urgency building up deep inside him. Joy bites her lip, revealing how turned on she has become. She lets her stare roam back down to where her feet are sliding back and forth. Matt arches his back, letting the feeling grow more intense. His breathing becomes laboured.

Joy curls her toes, letting the tips graze over him. Her movement quickens. The curve of her feet is hot against him. The escalating pressure is too much to contain. With a final groan, Matt's eyes squeeze shut with a shudder. He twitches backward, moving away from the insistent Joy. The pressure of her skin against him has become too sensitive to bear. Matt sucks in the sweet air and slumps back onto the ground, spent. He lets his eyes flutter back open. Joy is smiling sweetly at him. Matt doesn't know what to say. His whole body is warm and tingling all over.

Joy looks down to the mess Matt has made on his stomach.

'Maybe you'd better go for another swim,' she purrs.

Thirty Two

The blue hatchback motors back towards civilisation. The peace of the afternoon has lulled them both into a reflective silence. A line of traffic crawls along the Great Ocean Road. Tourists and day-trippers are heading to the city after a weekend of play.

Matt sits in silence, contemplating the moments that took his breath away in the forest earlier that day. His hollowness has been replaced with a sense of contentment. It amazes him that such a fleeting physical act could result in such euphoria. He keeps sneaking glances at Joy out of the corner of his eye as they trail behind the traffic. A satisfied grin is etched on her face, which grows wider every time she catches Matt looking.

'What are you staring at?' she finally asks.

'The most beautiful woman alive.'

Matt knows the words are corny, but he doesn't care. He means it. She is remarkable. Joy looks away upon hearing the comment, a veil of darkness falling over her features.

'What's wrong?' Matt asks, noticing her change of expression. 'Did I say something wrong?'

'No, it's okay,' she says, shaking her head with a sigh.

'It doesn't seem okay.'

Joy tightens her grip on the steering wheel and glances at Matt.

'No, it was a nice thing to say. Never mind me, I'm just sad that I have to go back to work this week,' she says.

'What do you actually do for work?' Matt asks. 'I still don't know.'

'It doesn't matter what I do. My job doesn't define who I am,' Joy answers cryptically as she concentrates on the traffic. 'It's just a way to make a living.'

'Yeah, but it's still a part of who you are. I mean, when you meet someone, it's standard to ask what they do. It helps position them in a certain place in your mind and tells you what kind of person they are.'

'Well, I don't like being put in a box because of what I do to earn a living.'

The answer doesn't satisfy Matt, but he knows that repeating the same line of questioning won't get him anywhere. Maybe Joy is embarrassed about her occupation. Matt is about to ask her if she's a stripper, but fresh in his memory is her reluctance to swim naked, so he dismisses the idea. He focuses on the road. The vehicle in front of them brakes cautiously around every sweeping bend, the taillights flickering on and off in a staccato rhythm. Exhaust fumes float from the car before vanishing into the air, like hot breath on a cold night.

'Don't they say that if you can find a job that you enjoy, then you'll never really work a day in your life?' Matt presses, thinking of his own situation and how he'd love to find something he's passionate about.

Joy backs off the accelerator as they start to roll downhill in their endless car conga-line.

'Who are *they* exactly?' asks Joy, glancing at him. 'And why do *they* know what's best?'

'I don't know. Conventional wisdom I guess. It's just what you hear people saying.'

'So, by *their* logic, doing worthwhile things isn't very hard. If you don't have to work at something, then it's easy. How can that be so satisfying?'

'Because it's fun. Like being an actor,' Matt says without much thought.

Joy shakes her head.

'Not everyone can be actors. Some people still have to pick up the rubbish, pump the petrol and dig holes. If everyone was an actor, then nothing would ever get done. Not everyone can live their dreams.'

Matt leans back in his seat.

'So, does that mean I shouldn't try to be a writer? I should just look for a menial job that serves a function to benefit society?'

'That's not what I'm saying at all,' Joy shakes her head. 'What I'm saying is that just because I'm a boring old secretary during the day, doesn't mean that my job isn't important in the overall scheme of things. More importantly, just because it's what I do for money doesn't mean it defines who I am. I'm Joy the *human*, not Joy the *secretary*.'

'So, you're a secretary,' Matt smiles.

'No actually, I'm a teacher, but that's beside the point.'

Matt is surprised by this revelation. It's frustrating, but also compelling that Joy is like this, always leading him on paths he didn't think he'd go down.

'Where do you teach?' Matt, asks, happy that Joy is finally revealing a little about her normal life.

'Here and there.'

'You really are a secret squirrel, aren't you?' Matt says, exasperated.

'What? I do relief. It's hard to get steady work on the coast. Everyone wants to be down here. Besides, it suits me. I don't like getting attached to the kids during the full year. It's too sad to see them go off to Christmas knowing you won't be a part of their lives anymore.'

Before Matt can ask more, Joy changes the subject.

'I think it's a great idea for you to be a writer, Matt. Really.'

'But you were just saying that not everyone can do what they want.'

'I talk rubbish most of the time,' Joy laughs. 'Just because it's not possible for everyone to do what they want, doesn't mean *you* shouldn't try. The world needs writers after all, so why not you? Beautiful arrangements of ink will always be more permanent than any fleeting business deal or momentary sporting achievement. In a sense, art is one way to achieve a certain degree of immortality.'

Matt catches sight of the big roundabout that leads into Ocean Heads. The day is almost over. He wishes the road would just go on forever, so their conversations could be infinite. The blue hatchback exits the roundabout and hits the home stretch towards Matt's place.

'What do you mean immortality?' he asks, as the familiar pedestrian crossing comes into view.

'I mean that artists who leave something behind can still talk to the living. Their work is the only certain message they get to send back from the grave. Maybe that's all the afterlife there is, having left a lasting mark on the world.'

It's an interesting thought. Matt does like the idea of leaving something behind, but only great artists change people's lives and leave a lasting mark. He feels like he's destined to be mediocre at whatever he does. At least a mediocre customer service operator helps people a little in their day-to-day, even if it isn't exciting. That's more meaningful than creating things that will never be seen, or affect the world in any way.

Joy pulls up to the curb, out the front of Matt's grey unit.

'I'll find out about some courses this week, 'Matt says, reaching for the door handle. 'The more I know the easier it will be to make a decision. Thanks for today, I had such a great time.'

He leans in for a goodbye kiss. Their lips touch and Matt thinks that if he had to live one day of his life over and over again, repeating for eternity, this might be it.

Thirty Three

Matt shuffles down the steps of his unit. He needs some fresh air. All week he has been going cross-eyed looking at university courses, online degrees and other study options. He never realised how competitive the world of education was until he saw the list of Google ads that came up in his browser after a quick search. The overwhelming choice has given Matt a dull pain in his eye that is threatening to become a migraine. He hopes the glow of the sun can burn away the headache caused by the glow of his laptop screen.

As Matt walks aimlessly down the street, he starts turning over the options available to him. The most promising is a university in the city that is well regarded and has a last-round intake of openings before the study year starts in a couple of weeks. It's close enough to drive to, has government supported placements and if Matt studies full-time he'll be able to claim Austudy for the duration of the course. An Arts degree would let him major in writing, English literature, or journalism. He can even try out units in each strand during his first semester before he makes a decision on which one to dedicate most of his time. Every time Matt thinks he's made a decision, Z's face pops into his head, looking disappointed that he doesn't want to work with her. He starts to rationalise why customer service is a safer choice and why that's probably a good thing. But writing seems like it will be much more fun. Matt despises decisions.

The Ocean Heads primary school comes into view. The play equipment is empty; its faded yellow fibreglass slides and metal fireman poles look sad without kids climbing on them. They must all be in class. The school had taken the monkey bars down years before, after Leigh Armstrong broke his wrist on them. Matt had been in his class and remembers Leigh coming to school with a white cast that went up to his elbow. The kids had started calling him Notso after that, as in not-so Armstrong. Notso didn't mind his new nickname. He thought it made him sound like a Japanese Samurai. Notso always was an optimist. Matt notices with disappointment that the seesaw in the school is gone now too, no doubt due to some unfortunate accident and an angry parent threatening to sue unless it was removed. Matt thinks it's a pity that things have shifted so much that safety has replaced all fun at the school. There has to be some kind of compromise. Surely the lessons learned in the playground are worth a few skinned knees here and there. Safety versus fun. It's not quite the same as Matt's customer service versus writing dilemma, but it does have a similar vein running through it. It seems finding a good balance doesn't stop just because you've graduated to an adult era in life.

Matt wonders if Joy ever works at this school. He never got to ask if she taught primary or high school, but she'd said 'kids' when she referred to the students. Matt looks at his phone, thinking he should text her again about how much fun he'd had last weekend. The date on the screen pops out at him. February 14th. Valentine's Day. *Shit.* Matt can almost bet that Joy would heap distain on the day as a 'greeting card' holiday, made up by the chocolate companies and florists around the world. Still, he'd much rather risk her thinking he was a foolish romantic than her actually being disappointed that he didn't think of her on Love's big day. God, it's much too soon to be dropping any kind of L word in there. Should he just let it float by without noting it at all? Out of the question. He needs to do something, even if it's a small gesture. Matt turns up a side street, heading uphill towards a familiar destination.

The scent of Bill's garden hits Matt's nostrils as he strolls up the road. He figures that a '$5 special' bunch of flowers is enough to show he cares for Joy, but not so over the top that he'll come across as some kind of desperado. The footpath is jammed with people when Matt rounds the corner. It's a last-minute Valentine's Day rush for flowers. Men and women alike are milling around a long row of trestle tables crammed with blooms of every kind and colour. Bill is zipping around the garden, trying to replenish stocks that are being snapped up faster than he can work. Every time someone takes a bunch of flowers he yells out a big thank you, taking a moment to shake their hand and have a very short chat if they're close enough. He looks ten years younger than he did barely a fortnight ago. He's smiling, energetic and even looks to have had a haircut. Matt waits patiently, taking in the whole scene with a mix of awe and satisfaction. Change chinks into the multiple ice cream tubs that are laid out between bouquets. People also slide in notes - fives, tens, even twenties - tipping outrageously when they are paid personal attention by Bill. As Matt nears the front, he looks around for something that Joy might like. Nothing cliché like roses for her. He searches with his eyes, since it's hard to roam up and down the row of tables with all of the people. Nothing seems to jump out. Matt hears a man in line behind him ask someone: 'Can you tell me about the first time you ever fell in love?'. He turns around to see the two and wonders if the question has come from his most recent letter to the editor, or if it's just a coincidence because of the day. Instead of eavesdropping further, Matt turns back to scan the flowers. He's about to give up and just take the closest bouquet, when Bill walks up with a couple of bunches in his hands to pop in an empty bucket.

'Matthew Pearce?' He stops, eying Matt up and down with an unsure look.

'Hi Bill,' Matt nods. 'Busy day?'

'I haven't seen you in years. My God you're a man!'

'Something like that,' Matt says shyly. 'How have you been?'

'Never better, never better!' he says. 'Did you see that letter in the newspaper a few weeks back? About the young fellow who used my flowers to propose to his missus?'

Matt stops, wondering if it's some kind of trick, but the honesty radiating out of Bill tells him it's not.

'I did see it, Bill. Glad that you decided to take the advice and start charging for the goods. You'll be able to retire on this day's takings alone,' he smiles.

'Ha!' Bill slaps his knee like it's the greatest joke in the world. 'I don't even care about the money. Never did. I give all this to the Salvos.' He rattles the ice-cream tub closest to him. 'I'm just glad all these people can share in Mavis's garden. She'd have loved to see this, Matt.'

Bill looks around with true pride in his eyes at the people.

'I never would have opened it up like this if it wasn't for that letter,' the old man says. 'Funny how just a few words can turn your life around. I was trying to keep this all for myself, like they were stealing parts of my Mavis away whenever something was picked. That fellow Eric put me straight and showed me just how wrong I was. This place that Mavis loved so much is now making more people happy than ever. It's like her spirit gets bigger the more flowers are spread around.'

Matt is taken aback. He stands silently for a while, looking at what Bill sees. Dozens of people, probably hundreds during the day have come to this garden to share in Mavis's and Bill's legacy, something they built together. And it was his letter that helped inspire it.

Even a few mediocre sentences from any writer *could* make a difference in people's lives. Matt just shakes his head in wonder. This was Bill's doing, but he is glad to have played his part.

'Your mum Kate used to come by and always have a good old chat with Mavis,' Bill says as Matt continues to look at the people picking bouquets to their heart's content. It's a wonder they haven't picked the garden bare. Indeed, some of the bushes have nothing but leaves on them at the moment, but Bill doesn't seem to mind one bit. 'How is your mum going anyway, I haven't seen her in a few years I reckon?'

The question snaps Matt back to attention.

'Yeah, she and dad moved to Tassie a while back. They're loving it down there. I'll tell her you said hi. She'll be stoked the garden is going so well.'

'And what about you, then? Are you looking for a little gift for your lady love?'

Matt blushes at the way Bill frames it, but doesn't correct him.

'A special girl, yeah. She's a little different though, Bill. I really don't know what to get her. Not something that everyone gets.'

'Hmmm, that's a tough one,' Bill scratches his chin like he's having a think.

'What's her name?' Bill asks.

'Joy.'

'And would you say she's a day person, or a night person?'

Matt has to think about that. Most of his time has been spent with her in the day, but that one night laying in their secret hideaway on the clifftop, eating fish and chips feels special. Like it was the true start of their relationship.

'A bit of both. She's at home in the day or the night,' Matt replies, not wanting to commit to one or the other.

Bill continues to scratch his chin for a few moments, before his eyes light up and he clicks his fingers.

'Wait here!' he says, running off.

It's not long before Bill comes back with a huge bunch of sunny, yellow flowers, intermixed with dark pink ones that bloom in an unusual pattern. He holds them out to Matt.

'Moonbeam Coreopsis and Autumn Joy,' Bill announces. 'Should be just about perfect for a girl who shares her name with a flower and lights up any time of day or night.'

Matt can hardly speak. They're perfect. He fumbles for his wallet then stuffs a twenty into Bill's hand as he takes the bunch.

'You're a lifesaver, thanks Bill. Really.'

'Glad I could be of help!' The old man smiles as brilliantly as any of the sights in his garden.

'Me too, Bill.' Matt says, turning to go. 'Me too.'

As he walks back down the street Matt pulls out his phone and sends a text to Joy.

I've made my decision. I'm going to uni to study writing. Am going to send in my application this afternoon! Want to have dinner to celebrate?

Only a few more steps along the footpath and a reply buzzes in his pocket.

Yes, and yes! That's amazing.

It really is amazing. Matt thinks to himself. *I actually decided to do something, all thanks to an old man and his flowers.*

Thirty Four

Matt rolls down the street, counting letterbox numbers so he can find the right place. Joy lives in the new estate in town, where every house looks the same. Covenants dictate the homes' colour schemes, styling and even choice of plants. The only differentiation between buildings is the colour of their front doors and the shape of the letterboxes. When this area was first subdivided, nobody in the 'old town' wanted to live there. They called it 'the ghetto'. However, over the space of five years all of the city dwellers built new kit homes in the estate and property values had soared. Land, which had once been a potato farm, had now become prime, half-acre slices of suburban living. Since the pricing increase, locals changed their nickname of the area to 'mortgage hill,' because none of them could afford to buy there without going into major debt.

Matt spots the golden numbers he's looking for and pulls up to the curb. Joy comes out the front door before Matt can even get out of the car. She's wearing a red knee-length dress and black heels. Her legs are sheathed in black crochet stockings. They look long and slender. Matt exits the wagon as she approaches. She tucks a loose strand of hair behind her tiny ear and looks up demurely at Matt.

'My god, you look... stunning,' he manages to say, feeling inadequate in his trusty black jeans and red tee.

'I'll take that as a compliment, Mr Writer,' Joy smiles and presses in close to kiss Matt on the lips. Their mouths remain joined for a long moment, as they sigh into each other.

'We'd better get moving,' Matt says, pulling away unwillingly. 'Our booking is for seven o'clock. We were lucky to get in considering it's Valentine's Day.'

'It's Valentine's Day?' Joy frowns, looking sincere in her ignorance of the date.

Matt opens the door for Joy, revealing the bunch of flowers propped up on her seat. She stares down at them, like a deer in headlights. Matt's stomach churns. He's done the wrong thing. It's the first time he's ever seen her looking indecisive. He starts talking, to fill in the silence descending between them.

'A funny story about those,' Matt stammers. 'The old man whose garden they came from, Bill, wrote a letter to the newspaper telling people to stop stealing his flowers when they went past. I saw it and wrote a fake reply, saying that I proposed to my fiancé with some roses I'd taken.'

Joy snaps her head towards Matt with murder in her eyes.

'Oh! No! I'm not proposing. I mean, it was just a lark. I wrote in the letter he should start charging people for the flowers. So he did, and people from all over started visiting his garden.'

Matt bends down and picks up the flowers. Joy steps back, looking at Matt like he's holding a loaded gun.

'He told me today that he had been clinging to the flowers in the garden after his wife died, but now he's glad that people are sharing in their beauty, or something. Point is, my letter changed his life. He's happier now. I helped do that. My letter did. It made me realise that even if I don't write anything great, I can still have a real effect on people. That's why I enrolled in uni.'

The last words start to soften Joy, so Matt continues.

'Anyway, I got talking to Bill and said I didn't want to get you anything obvious. So, he chose these. They're Moonbeams and Autumn Joy. I thought you'd get a kick out of that.'

'Moonbeams and Autumn Joy?' Joy asks, reaching out and stroking the tops of the flowers with her fingertips.

'Specially picked.' Matt adds, seeing her expression shift.

Joy slowly takes them in her hands and pulls them close, inhaling their summery scent. She looks at them for a while longer.

'These flowers made you want to enrol in uni?'

'Well, what they symbolise anyway.' Matt says, not wanting to make things too literal.

'Thank you, then,' she says, looking up at him and holding his gaze. 'And happy V-Day, even though it's a crock of shit.'

The statement breaks the tension Matt was holding, making him break into the giggles.

'Let me just put these in water,' Joy smirks at him. 'We don't want to miss our table.'

The restaurant isn't too far. It's the town's only worthy sit-down dinner destination: an Asian Fusion establishment called Black Thai. Joy and Matt are greeted by the owner as they enter the swinging doors. She is a tiny Asian woman called Mali, who has been in town longer than most of the locals. When she speaks, her accent is an over-compensated drawl, which would be at home in an outback pub. Mali even uses words like 'strewth' and 'fair dinkum' as her way of letting people know that she's a true blue Aussie sheila, despite her Asian heritage.

'G'day Matthew,' she says. 'How are ya? It's been a long time. How are your folks?'

'Good thanks, Mali,' Matt nods and smiles. 'They're still in Tasmania.'

'Too bloody cold in Tassie for me,' Mali jokes. 'They must be crazy down there. I miss seeing them.'

'I miss them too, Mali. This is Joy. We have a booking for two at seven.'

'Yes, I saved a special table for you, Matthew. You're in a quiet booth in the corner,' she winks at Matt. 'Do you want the special banquet for two?'

'Does that come with your famous Choo Chee Prawns?'

'Plus, spicy Pad Gra Pow, sticky rice and lychee dessert,' Mali confirms.

'Is that okay with you, Joy?' Matt turns to his date.

'It seems like you've got it under control,' Joy smiles. 'Sounds fine to me.'

Mali shows the pair to their booth and they settle in to the sounds of traditional Thai music. Matt knows for a fact that they only play it for the atmosphere, since Mali's favourite singer is really Elvis. An old, gold-framed painting of the King of Thailand hangs on the wall next to their heads.

'Would you like a drink?' Matt offers, pouring Joy a glass of water from the pre-supplied carafe. 'If you want something stronger, I'll go to the bar.'

'Well, we're celebrating, so I'll have a Johnny Black with ice.'

Matt almost spills the water that he's tipping into his glass.

'Whisky?'

Joy just smiles, sipping her water daintily.

Shaking his head in wonder, Matt goes to the bar and orders a beer and a whisky. On his return to the table, he falters when noticing a familiar figure enter the restaurant. Matt is awash with dread. It's his former boss, Mr James.

Ducking his head down to avoid being seen, Matt fumbles with the rattling glasses and slides back into the booth. Without even looking at Joy, he pushes her whisky over to her and hides behind the menu. Mr James is the last person he wants to see. If luck had been kind, he'd never have spotted the man again in his life.

'What's with you?' Joy asks, eyeing Matt. 'You're acting strange, did you slip something in my drink?'

Matt smiles weakly at her joke. All colour drains from his face, as he watches his nemesis sit down at a table on the far end of the crowded restaurant. Mr James is engrossed in his phone, poking at the screen with his sausage-like fingers, unaware of Matt's presence.

'Seriously, Matt. What's wrong?' Joy waves her hand into his line of sight.

Matt has to use both shaking hands to bring his beer up to his lips. Why he is still so scared of Mr James, he has no idea. The man has no authority over him anymore. Matt continues to stare over, willing him to leave.

'Matt!' Joy clicks her fingers. 'What is it?'

'It's Mr James,' Matt says under his breath. 'My old boss.'

'That slime ball who set you up?' she hisses, following Matt's gaze. 'That one with the phone, wearing the cheap yellow tie?'

Matt nods slowly. 'I don't know what he's doing here. Maybe he's down on holidays or something. He lives in the city as far as I know.'

'It doesn't matter,' Joy says, clasping her hands over Matt's. 'He's just another diner. Forget it, we're here to celebrate. That's all behind you now.'

A waiter arrives carrying an ornate aluminium bowl of rice, which he places onto the table. Steaming prawns and fragrant vegetables follow. Matt relaxes when someone stands in front of them, blocking the view. He unfolds his napkin and spreads it onto his lap, letting the smell of spice clear his head. He looks across at Joy and forces a smile. He takes the serving spoons and heaps some rice and prawns onto her plate.

'Make sure you try these, they're Mali's specialty.'

Joy nods, drowning her rice in lashings of the sauce. She takes a fork, then skewers a prawn, putting it in her mouth.

'Oh wow, wow!' Joy murmurs while chewing. 'This is incredible!'

Matt isn't listening. He holds his fork absentmindedly, looking at Mr James again. Joy continues to eat the meal, staring down her date. After five minutes of silence, she stabs Matt's hand instead of a prawn.

'Ouch!' Matt jerks his hand away. 'What the hell was that?'

'Is that grotesque man more interesting than me? We're here to have a good time, not wallow.'

'I'm sorry, Joy,' Matt rubs his hand to ease the pain. 'It's just distracting having him there. It's like he's polluting the room.'

'Do you want me to go over and say something?'

'No!' he protests. 'I'll just ignore him.'

Shovelling food into his mouth, Matt starts to chew and fake-smiles with stuffed cheeks. He makes a show of washing it down with his beer and takes another mouthful.

'So, what are you going to major in at uni?' Joy queries, trying to spark up the conversation.

'I'm not sure,' Matt manages through his rice. 'Either journalism or creative writing I suppose. I'll wait and see how the first semester goes and decide from there.'

'I think creative writing. It's freer.' Joy sips her whisky. 'Journalism restricts you to the facts. That's boring.'

'I guess so.'

'Who are your favourite writers?' Joy asks. 'You know, Ernest Hemingway and Hunter S. Thompson both started as journalists, so I guess it holds some merit.'

Matt doesn't answer. His stare has reverted back over to the far end of the room. He can't shake his inward feeling of self-disdain. It's as though Mr James is whispering to him that he is stealing oxygen again, that he's not worth the skin that he lives in.

'That's it!' Joy huffs, dumping her handbag on the table and rifling through its contents. She pulls out a pen and paper and starts scribbling. The frenzied activity brings Matt back to the present.

'What are you doing?'

'I'm getting my date back,' Joy says as she writes, looking over at Mr James.

'What? What are you going to do? I don't want to talk to him. Just leave it.'

'Do you want another beer?' Joy asks in response. 'I'm going to get you another beer.'

She stands up and folds the piece of paper into her hand.

'What? No, please Joy, just stay here.'

It's too late. Joy is already negotiating her way through the tables. Matt doesn't want to make a scene by following her. He slouches down into his seat so he can keep an eye on the situation. Walking over to Mr James, she leans over and whispers something into his ear, pressing the folded note into his hand. Mr James' eyes follow Joy, as she saunters to the bar.

Matt adjusts himself so he can see Mr James reading the piece of paper. The man's eyes widen and his face goes red, as he screws up the note and shoves it into his pocket. Looking over to Joy at the bar again, Mr James catches her eye. She acknowledges him with a nod and wink. Without hesitation Matt's old boss gets up off his chair and walks toward the rest rooms.

At a complete loss, Matt starts to stand up, however Joy signals for him to stay seated. Matt's heart thumps like a drum. His head thuds with confusion. After a few moments, he watches Joy walk a quick loop near the toilets, before coming back to the table. She sits down and catches Mali's attention, waving her to come over.

'What's going on?' Matt beseeches, ahead the owner's arrival.

Joy ignores the question and looks to the approaching Mali.

'Is everything okay, Miss Joy?' Mali asks as she attends to them, 'How is the Choo Chee?'

'Oh, it's wonderful Mali, thank you,' Joy smiles. 'But I was just in the ladies' room and there's a man in one of the cubicles. He's making some odd noises. I think he might be playing with himself. I thought you should know.'

'Oh!' Mali gasps, standing as tall as her four-foot-ten stature allows. 'I'm so sorry Miss Joy, I'll have someone check it out.'

Before Matt can stop her, Mali scurries away and pulls two of her bigger waiters to the side. Matt watches in horror as they march toward the toilets. Joy sits down with a smirk and takes a swig of her whisky.

'This ought to be fun.'

From the corner of the room, there's a loud bang of a door followed by a bellow, which disturbs the atmospheric Thai music. An instant later, Mr James is being dragged from the ladies' bathroom, grasping at his open pants.

'Wait! There's been a mistake,' he pleads, fumbling with his zipper. 'I thought I was in the men's.'

'No mistake!' Mali yells back. 'You're a dirty man. You have a small penis, like a cashew nut.'

'No!' he struggles again. 'I was set up.'

'No set up!' Mali snaps. 'We don't serve wankers here. If I see you anywhere near my restaurant again, I'll call the police. Now get out of here before you spend the night in jail.'

Struggling and kicking, Mr James is thrown out onto the street to a crescendo of applause from everyone inside. The clapping subsides and people return to their meals. Matt casts a questioning look at Joy.

'What on earth was written on that note?'

'Just an invitation to meet me in the ladies' room. I suggested he get started, so I could perform unspeakable acts on his body.'

'You're kidding?' Matt is bug-eyed.

'Well, it was a bit more detailed than that, but you get the idea. Now, can we enjoy our night?'

Matt sinks back in the booth, both impressed and shocked. He's about to express his gratitude when Mali approaches, cradling a bottle of champagne.

'I'm sorry, Miss Joy,' Mali says, offering the bottle. 'You shouldn't have to put up with that in my place. Please take this as a token of apology.'

Before either of them can protest, Mali pops the cork and pours two glasses of sparkling champagne. Joy nods her head in appreciation and raises a toast.

'To creative writing.'

Thirty Five

Matt lets his car idle on the street. He and Joy reflect on the evening and laugh about Mr James being caught in the act. Joy is tipsy from the champagne and lets out a snort mid-laugh, which sends her into further fits of giggles. Her dark hair swings around her shoulders, rippling with movement. The effect reminds Matt of the ocean's peaks and troughs in moonlight. Before the happiness of the car can abate, Joy opens her door.

'Come in for a drink,' she orders, as she steps onto the nature strip. She shuts the door behind her, slicing off any chance of a negative reply.

Following her wish, Matt joins Joy in the short walk to her house. She takes a solitary key out of her purse and slides it in the lock of her home. With a flick of her wrist they're inside. Warm light welcomes them toward the interior, which is simple but comfortable. A tatty, brown suede couch sits out of place on a large blue rug. In the corner of the lounge, a stereo is propped next to two milk crates full of old, vinyl records. Framed photos and paintings line the cream-coloured walls. Matt recognises one of his favourite works by Vincent van Gogh, *Almond Blossoms*. The flowers Matt gave Joy sit on a table against the wall where someone would normally have a TV.

As Joy bangs her cupboards searching for glasses, Matt meanders along the walls, looking at the art Joy has on display. Curiously, there are no photos of her to be seen anywhere, just depictions of nature shown in different lights.

'I've got beer, or red wine,' Joy announces, placing two different sized bottles on the kitchen bench.

'I'd better not have any more,' Matt looks up from the wall of images. 'I have to drive.'

'So, stay,' Joy answers, twisting open the bottle of beer and sliding it across the bench.

Matt moves over and takes the cool glass in his hands. He sidles onto a bar stool and leans on the counter. Joy stands on the kitchen side, pouring herself a glass of red. The wine's colour complements the shade of her lips, as she holds it up to take a sip.

'How long have you been living here?' Matt asks, keen to make conversation.

'Hmm, a while. I managed to get in before the prices got ridiculous, but not so early that I could afford good furniture,' she quips, indicating the mismatched ensemble in the lounge.

'It's a lot better than my place,' he comments, looking around at the decor.

'It's not a competition, it's just somewhere to shelter from the rain,' Joy says aloofly.

Drink in hand, she walks over to the stereo and bends down to flick through her records as Matt watches from his stool. Finding what she's looking for, she slides the large black disk out of its sleeve and lays it on the turntable of the stereo.

'I just love old records,' she explains, as she picks up the needle arm in a pincer grip. 'I enjoy the process of actually putting music on, rather than pressing a button.'

A brief crackling sound resonates in the speakers, before three descending base notes introduce The Doors' song, *People Are Strange.*

'It even sounds better this way,' Joy adds, standing up and swaying her hips, spinning around as she takes another sip of wine.

Matt watches her dance, losing himself in the hypnotic motion of her body, which swirls up and down like the liquid in her glass. Kicking off her heels, Joy's stocking-clad toes sink into the shagpile rug.

'Come and dance with me,' she beckons with a curled finger.

Leaving his beer, Matt walks over and stands next to her. He shuffles from side to side with the beat. His arms hang at his side, swinging, as his body struggles to keep time.

'That's not dancing,' Joy laughs. 'That's bobbing. Here.'

She puts her glass down on the ground and drapes her arms over Matt's shoulders. The sweet smell of pinot noir floats between them as their bodies find a natural rhythm. Resting her head on Matt's chest, Joy lets his movement rock her around. Slipping his arms around her waist, Matt's hands rest at the top of her bum. His fingers stray across the silky fabric as Joy shifts her weight from foot to foot.

As a new song revolves over, Joy brings her lips to Matt's neck. The heat of her touch lasts for a drumbeat, when Joy kisses again. With every second beat, she lays her lips onto Matt's skin, covering him with a lazy percussion of warmth. They press their bodies closer, all the while grinding their hips in circles. Matt reaches up to the nape of Joy's neck, burying his fingers in her hair. He meets her mouth with his, searching for the taste of wine. The music sways a soft organ melody. The kiss intensifies and they stop dancing, letting themselves slide to the floor. Matt eases his weight on top of her.

With eagerness building, the passion of their kisses increases. Lying on her back, Joy reaches to her side and unzips her dress. The soft touch of silk gives way to tingling skin, as Matt releases Joy from her material shell. Scarlet fabric is cast aside and again their mouths rove over each other. Matt fumbles to undo Joy's black bra. She withdraws from his kiss as he unhooks the clasp.

'Turn off the light,' she whispers to him.

Shaking his head slightly, Matt sinks his head back down to her neck.

'I want to be with you. All of you,' he breathes into her ear. 'We all have scars, it's what makes us human.'

Joy's body tightens as Matt peels away her lingerie, revealing bare skin in open light. He leans in and kisses her again. His lips trail down her body. Seeing the puckered pink flesh around her left side, Matt neither lingers, nor moves away too quickly. He kisses her all over, moving across to the other side, teasing her nipple before returning to her neck. He drinks in every inch of her form. Sitting up, Matt pulls his shirt over his head and lets it drop to floor.

Matt traces his fingers from her neck, over her chest, never looking away from her face. As he massages her body with both hands, Joy's muscles relax. She opens up fully, the walls of uncertainty crashing down.

Thirty Six

The chill in the early morning air is more fresh than bitter. It's a reminder that winter is coming, but autumn is still wedged in the way. By early March, the weather will become unpredictable, but for now it's mostly sunny days. The cold wind blows last night's dreams from Matt's mind as he strolls along the cliff-top walk. It has been a week since his dinner with Joy and that unforgettable night together.

They had spent almost every night since then in each other's arms. Today, however, he had woken up alone.

Joy has gone to the city to 'do a few things' and won't be back for a few days. To distract himself in her absence, Matt is going to begin a short story. It will help polish his writing. He has no idea what to write about and is hoping a morning walk will provide some inspiration. Pulling his hoodie up to protect his ears from the cold, Matt crunches over gravel to his familiar lookout spot.

The sea is blanketed with white caps, the onshore wind fanning specks of foam from shore to horizon. Waves cross over each other in a messed-up slop that no one would want to surf. The beach is all but deserted. The only signs of life down in the bay are a man and a woman going for a morning jog along the shore. Pulling his phone out of his pocket, Matt takes a photo of the ocean and texts it to Joy.

Good morning. You're not missing anything down here, but I miss you.

Holding the phone in his hand for a few minutes, he waits for the alert of a reply, but it doesn't come. Maybe she's not up yet.

Still lacking inspiration, Matt stands there, thinking maybe he should write a story about stealing groceries and meeting a girl. After all, everything he seems to read on creative writing says the best stories are ones based in fact. He turns the idea over in his head, but dismisses it.

There's no suitable ending and eventually the story just seems boring. He wishes he'd done some more exciting things with his life. Something more interesting to write about, or at least embellish. Checking his phone again, to no response, Matt's rumbling stomach reminds him that it's breakfast time.

Matt chomps on some Vegemite toast and watches the morning news. As usual, sadness and insanity has enveloped the world at large. The only human-interest story is about a man who has grown a pumpkin weighing close to five hundred kilograms in his backyard. The news ends on this shallow high, before switching to the daily swill of soap operas and talk shows. Flicking off the television, Matt switches on his computer. Resting his fingers on the keys, he stares at the blank digital page which stares back. The cursor blinks on the lonely canvas, waiting to be joined by letters. No letters come.

Glancing at his phone again, Matt realises he didn't ask Joy a question in his first message; it was only a statement. He composes another text with busy thumbs.

What are you up to today? I'm trying to write but can't think of anything. Got any ideas for me?

A buzz of reply comes through instantly, but it's Z, not Joy.

Got an answer for me yet? Things are coming together and I want to approach clients.

Matt had been racking his brain for the last week trying to figure out how to tell Z that he's decided to study instead. A text is too impersonal, but face-to-face too terrifying. He thinks maybe a phone call or Skype might work, but he needs to figure out what to say first. Matt ignores the text for the meantime, promising himself he'll get back to her soon. His thoughts turn to Joy again and Matt wonders if maybe she's ignoring him. Surely not, but that gnawing feeling that he's not worthy of her is never far below the surface. *God, it's going to be a long day,* Matt thinks.

Dinnertime comes around, but Matt isn't hungry. Joy still hasn't replied to either of his messages. Matt's hands remain propped over the keys of his laptop, waiting for a brainwave to strike for his story. For hours he has sat, without a single thought. The page reflects his ideas: blank. It's like he is a Buddhist monk, deep in the meditation of nothing. No enlightenment comes from his exercise, just a dead feeling of underachievement.

Pacing around the house, Matt turns on the tap in the kitchen and guzzles water from the spout. It's seven o'clock: still not too late to call. He picks up his phone and instantly puts it down again. *Surely if she wanted to talk she would have seen the texts and replied.*

After two more trips from the couch to the tap, Matt finally dials her number. Before it completes a full ring, the line cuts to Joy's message bank. Matt hangs up before the beep. There's no point in leaving a message, he doesn't want to seem desperate.

The quickness of the phone going to the answering service tells Matt one of two things. Joy is either on the phone, or she has it turned off. It could even mean she's run out of battery. *Maybe she's forgotten to take her charger to the city*, Matt reasons. It would explain why she hasn't answered. *That must be it*, he decides. He's being neurotic.

Opening the fridge, he pulls out a green bottle of Heineken: liquid dinner for one.

There is no savouring of taste, no relishing the fizz of bubbles on his tongue. Matt flops down on the couch and channel surfs the telly. The first three channels he sees are playing pointless reality shows. Matt doesn't even pause to watch them. He doesn't watch TV for reality, he watches TV to escape it.

The fourth station shows more promise - a crime show. The detective suspects the killer may be a real, live vampire. Perfect. Matt would trade pointless non-fiction for pointless fiction any day of the week. As Matt watches, his day of numb meditation continues. Suddenly, his phone springs to life. Matt leaps for the device, looking at the screen before being flooded with disappointment. It's Gerard.

'Hey, G,' Matt says, calling Gerard by his new nickname. It was as if customer service people suited single-letter titles for some reason.

The sound of crying is the only answer on the other end of the phone.

'Gerard? You okay mate?' Matt asks, turning off the TV and sitting up.

'I don't think I can do this anymore,' Gerard finally manages on the other end.

'Do what, mate? What happened?'

'This job is killing me, I had a call today where a teenage girl doesn't qualify for support because her parents earn too much, but her dad is abusing her. She can't get out, doesn't have any money and doesn't have a job. I couldn't do anything for her, just refer her to a case worker. We're failing people. Every. Single. Day.'

'Oh, man. I'm sorry to hear that,' Matt says. He searches for a way to solve Gerard's problem, but there's no easy fix.

'Have you thought about quitting?' Matt asks, probing for options.

'All the time, but it would feel like I'm just opting out on these people.'

'But if you can't help them because of the system, you can't help them. Wouldn't you be better off in a job that makes you happier, maybe pays more money and you can give to charity or something on the side if you really want to help? There has to be something you can do.'

'Maybe you're right,' Gerard says, pulling himself together. 'My life is nothing like some of the cases I talk to. They have real problems.'

'Your problems are real too, G.' Matt says. 'If you feel them, they're real. Don't try to fob them off. Address them. Quit and find something else.' It's easy to give decisive advice when Matt isn't the subject of the decision.

'More like find something else, then quit,' Gerard says. 'Unless I get fired I wouldn't be able to get Newstart. I can't afford to just go jobless. Plus, I only know customer service. It's not like I'm just going to go and work for someone like Optitel after what you've told me.'

Optitel. A light sparks on in Matt's head. Before he gets too ahead of himself, he takes a deep breath and tries to assess whether it would work. They seem like the perfect odd couple. There's only one way to know for sure.

'Gerard,' Matt says, 'I think I have an idea. There's someone I want you to meet.'

Thirty Seven

M att sets out on foot toward his local watering hole: The Ocean Heads Hotel. Not a very inventive name, but then pubs don't need clever marketing. All they require for success is to sell cold beer and have live sports-betting on big screens. This simple combination attracts the Australian male like moths to a flame.

Matt looks at his phone screen which glows in the cool night air, helping to light his way through a dark patch of street. There's nothing new to be seen in the way of messages or alerts. The radio silence from Joy is nauseating. At least Z and G are free for the night and have agreed to meet him for a drink.

The stink of cigarettes heralds that Matt is near his destination. In years gone by, smokers stayed inside and fumigated the interior of the pub full of second-hand exhalations. However, due to clean air regulations, they now all hover outside, blowing death-clouds into the faces of passersby. At the end of the line of addicts is Z, sucking down a lung snack through her signature holder. She sees Matt approaching and flicks her cigarette onto the ground, crushing it underneath a white-sneakered foot.

'Thought you'd let me down in person, huh?' she says in way of a greeting.

'We'll see, Z,' Matt says. 'We can have a chat after a drink. I've got another friend coming as well.'

'The girl?' Z asks, curiosity lacing her question.

'Nah, she's up in the city.' A pang of longing hits Matt. 'This is a guy friend, I think you'll find him interesting.'

'I didn't think you had any friends,' Z gives Matt a playful punch on the shoulder.

Matt doesn't take the bait. A couple of months ago, Z would have been right.

The smell of stale beer on the carpet is a welcome change from the nicotine outside. This area of the hotel is reserved for drinking and betting. In the corner of the room a few pathetic old drunks talk with some younger, slightly less pathetic drunks. Give it a few years and you won't be able to tell the difference between the two groups. A handful of builders are having their after-work drinks in a pack to the right. In a U-shaped nook to the far end, men are hunched over betting cards while they look sideways at rows of screens, showing the greyhounds and trots. One of the punters straightens a little when a race starts on the middle television. The dogs leap out of their box and give chase to a fake furball designed to look like a rabbit. Matt tells Z that the bistro side of the hotel is a different affair to this. In the past, they used to offer good honest pub food, like ten-dollar steaks and chicken parmigiana. However, since the influx of money into town, the menu has gone upmarket, boasting designer dishes of Atlantic salmon with 'vegetable symphonies', or braised-lamb cutlets with a red-wine jus. The more detailed the name of the dish is, the higher the price it commands. The result is like a curtain of economic separation: wealthy families dining in the bistro, undisturbed by the proletariat clientele in the bar. The only place where they mingle is the pokies room in the middle.

Happy on the bar side, Matt and Z head to order a round of drinks. Gerard is standing on the edge of the long timber bench, where it curves away into the TAB nook. He's watching the sports screens on the wall with his hands wedged in his pockets. The way his eyes flick from one screen to the other indicate nothing on there is holding much interest.

'I hear the Honey Badgers have a great team this year,' Matt says as they edge close enough to hear.

'Huh?' Gerard looks at Matt, confused for a second before recognition brightens his features 'Oh, hey! Who are the Honey Badgers?'

'Never mind, I was taking the piss.' Matt says, reaching out to shake Gerard's hand.

Matt stands back again to reveal his lanky-limbed companion.

'G, this is Z. Z, meet G.'

'It's a regular alphabet in here,' Z says, looking at Matt, before offering Gerard a polite hello and handshake.

'G works in customer service at Centrelink,' Matt explains further. 'He helped me get set up on the dole and gave me a few career pointers.'

'Oh, so you're the genius who thinks Matt should follow his passions?'

The dry tone of Z's voice makes Gerard pause.

'Don't mind her,' Matt says. 'She's a sweetheart once you get past the sarcasm and the dick jokes.'

Nervous about what he wants to say next, Matt turns and orders a round of beers for them. He has one safely in his hand before venturing forward.

'So, I've officially applied to study writing at university.' Matt lets it out before taking a deep sip of his drink.

Gerard's 'That's great!' reply is offset by Z's 'I fucking knew it.'

Matt downs half his pint before continuing.

'The positive here is, that I think I have a solution to both of your worries.'

Gerard and Z perk up at the announcement.

'G happens to be amazing at what he does,' Matt continues. 'He cares a lot about people, but most importantly thinks his current job licks a bag of sweaty assholes.'

Z gives a semi-amused grunt. Gerard almost chokes on his beer at Matt's language.

'Now, Z happens to be searching for a partner in a new customer service venture. One that promises to only take on clients who want to treat their customers like gold. She needs someone to help be a kind of moral compass in the business, help train the staff and probably temper her potty mouth on the phones.'

'Fuck off,' Z says, proving Matt's point for him.

'I thought you guys should go through the pint test to figure out if you might be a good fit to partner up, so that's why we're here.'

'What's the pint test?' Gerard asks.

Thirty Seven

'He means if we can have a pint together and enjoy it, then we might not kill each other if we go into business,' Z explains.

'Oh, right' Gerard says.

'What's the worst tasting shot you can think of?' Z asks Gerard with a serious look on her face.

'Um, I dunno, maybe Green Chartreuse?' he offers.

'That is suitably repugnant,' she nods, before turning to the bar and slapping her hand on the wood. 'Three shots of Green Chartreuse!' she yells out to the barman.

Before too long a trio of shot glasses are lined up in front of them. Z picks one up and salutes to the other two, indicating they pick theirs up. Without any further word, she downs hers in one gulp, staring down Matt and G to do the same. Matt sips his lightly before half-retching and falling back to his beer. Gerard throws his shot back, slams the glass down on the bar and gives his chest a slap to ease the burn.

'One more?' he asks in challenge.

'I think this might work out after all,' Z says, appraising Gerard in a new light. She holds up her fingers to the barman indicating two more shots, before looking at Matt and his quarter finished attempt. 'Fucking lightweight.'

When the next round arrives, Gerard and Z finish them off without hesitation. Z puts her arm around Gerard's shoulder.

'Right, so about this company,' she says, half party, half business.

Matt's friends settle down into a conversation about 'mission statements' and 'value propositions'. He takes it as his cue to wander into the TAB and browse the form guides tacked onto the walls. Looking up the details for the next race, he pulls a win/place slip from a slot in the bench and starts filling it in with the provided pencil. Cannington. Greyhounds. Race three. Number five. Matt has no real clue what the numbers and x's on the form guides mean, so he picks out a dog he likes the name of: White Whale. Inserting his form into the machine at the payment window, his stub comes shooting out and the teller asks for the money. Pushing his five dollars over the counter, Matt returns to the bench to watch his fortune run out in front of him.

The greyhounds are being led out toward their starting cage. At the bottom of the screen, Matt sees that White Whale is paying eighty to one. His heart sinks. Only a three-legged donkey would be paying those odds. *Oh well, it's only five bucks.* Matt thinks. He looks over to Z and G, who are starting to get animated. The apparent positivity of the conversation puts Matt at ease. He has dodged a guilt bullet in letting either of his friends down and instead may help them both come out happy.

Without any real hope of success on the race side of things, Matt leans against the bar and orders another beer, one eye still on the screen. The gates go up and the dogs shoot out onto the track. White Whale is slow off the mark. Matt groans in disappointment. The pale hound chases the rest of the pack with its tongue hanging out of its mouth. Around the first corner one of the frontrunners stumbles and falls. It curls into a ball and the rest of the dogs trip over it, twisting into a canine snarl of snouts and legs. White Whale jumps over all of them unscathed and Matt leaps out of his chair.

'Go!' he yells. 'Go you good thing!'

G and Z stop their discussion seeing his excitement and crowd behind him, one at each shoulder.

'Who do you have?' Gerard asks.

'The white one with the French flag colours.' Matt answers, eyes glued to the screen.

By now some of the other dogs are running again, but his bet has a huge lead. The pack sprints toward the finish line. Hope rises in Matt's chest and bursts out of his mouth in a resounding '*yes!*' as White Whale crosses the gate as the undisputed winner.

Matt slaps the bar in a burst of uncontained excitement. His mates both clap him on the back. Matt's body is jittery with exhilaration.

'How's it paying?' Z asks, sharing the excitement.

'Four hundred bucks from five!' Matt smiles. 'Do you guys need any investors?'

The three share a laugh.

'A new jug of beer will get you a thousandth of a share,' Z says.

'You're on,' Matt says, collecting his winnings and buying two. 'It's nice to have things going the right way.'

Thirty Eight

Vomit splatters the sides of the toilet bowl. Matt has been glued to the bathroom floor all morning. The cool tiles against his bare legs don't help him to feel any better. The roof and walls are spinning in his hungover haze.

Gerard pokes his head into the room.

'You sure I can't get you anything mate? A lemonade icy pole? A cheeseburger?'

The thought of food makes Matt retch into the bowl again.

'I'm never drinking again,' he mumbles.

'Z just put a stack of coconut waters in your fridge for when you're feeling up to some fluids,' Gerard says, still from the doorway. 'We're both going to scoot off. You sure you're going to be right?'

'I'll be fine,' Matt says. 'Just need to get some sleep.'

How those two are still standing is beyond Matt. They'd gone drink-for-drink with him last night and stayed up in his lounge until the wee hours of the morning, solving the world's problems through ideas about better customer service. They'd even come up with a roll-out plan where Gerard could hold onto his job until they'd pulled on enough clients to cover a living wage. Z had woken up to the alarm clock of Matt's first spew around 10am and proceeded to whip up a buffet of bacon and eggs for everyone. Matt couldn't even go near the smell and had migrated to the bathroom instead. Gerard had come in not long after looking dusty, offering a bacon and egg sandwich to Matt. It had sparked another purge of vomiting as Gerard looked on. He had set about grabbing some fresh towels for Matt and wrapping a blanket over his shoulders, making him as comfortable as possible. Matt had shooed him away in the end, preferring to suffer alone.

'See ya later, Lightweight.' Z calls from the hallway behind Gerard. 'I'll shoot you a text later to make sure you're still alive.'

'Yep,' Matt says into the toilet bowl, the word echoing back up to him.

After another hour driving the porcelain bus, Matt gathers himself enough to stumble over to the couch. He locates his phone and checks to see if Joy has been in touch. Nothing. Scrolling through his sent messages from the previous night, the nausea rises again and he has to dash for a dry heave into the kitchen sink. At 11:00 p.m., 11:36 p.m., 1:12 a.m. and 1:28 a.m. he had sent a hopeless stream of texts to Joy, telling her how wonderful she is and how his *'manhood aches for her'*. Manhood? God. The last text is barely even a message. It's just a mash of words that make no sense whatsoever.

Hobbling back to the couch, with his liver punching him all the way, Matt flops down and holds a cushion to his chest for comfort. This can't just be a normal hangover. He must have food poisoning. But then, Matt can't remember having had any dinner. He closes his eyes to see if he can sleep off the affliction, but it makes the room spin more.

All day Matt languishes on the couch. He only peels himself off to make runs to the toilet and finally start to drink Z's coconut water in the fridge. Surprisingly, it helps a lot. By late afternoon his sweats have died down and he's starting to feel like something resembling a human being. He texts Gerard and Z, letting them know he'll be ready to catch up for another beer in three to four years, but that generally he's okay now.

There is solace in the fact that Joy is due back tomorrow. At least he'll be able to go around and say hello, or she'll have found her phone charger and they can laugh at his stupid texts from the past 48 hours. Hopefully.

Thirty Nine

Ten, eleven, twelve o'clock. Each hour that passes without contact from Joy is a razor slice across the wrist of Matt's psyche.

What if something is wrong? What if she's been in a car accident?

Scenes of mangled metal flash through Matt's head.

Don't be stupid. I'd know if something like that had happened. How would I? No one would know to call me. Don't be so stupid. She's fine.

Matt gets into his Holden and fires up the ignition. It's a five-minute drive to Joy's house. The choice between that and another hour of paranoia is no choice at all. To his dismay, the driveway behind the gold numbers of Forty-Two Adams Way is empty. There is a small brown oil stain on the concrete, where Joy normally parks her hatchback. Staying for a few moments, Matt rolls onward. He'll look like a stalker if he's sitting out the front of the house when she arrives.

Taking the long way home, Matt drives past the beach. His heart hurts. He can't believe he's feeling this way after such a short time. It's like some twisted separation anxiety from the only good thing that's happened to him in ages. The worst thing is, there could be nothing wrong at all. It's all in his head. He's being a sook. An overanalysing freak.

Or am I? He thinks.

The mostly blue skies are showing a hint of threatening rain to the far west. It can't be much more than a squall. By the look of the clouds, it may even just blow out to sea. Pausing in the main car park overlooking the bay, Matt watches with envy as a surfer pulls on his wetsuit in a weird, jumping-dance kind of way. The freckle-faced teenager looks like he hasn't a care in the world. Flashing a quick smile at Matt, he picks up his board and turns to run down the wooden steps. Matt realises he's never seen a scowl on the face of someone heading out into the ocean. He wishes it wasn't too late for him to take up the sport. It looks like a form of physical freedom in which he could lose himself. But everyone he's seen start surfing in their 20s just looks like a fish out of water, flapping around and gasping for air.

Watching the sea usually brings Matt a sense of calm, but today is different. The waves remind him that life can come in and suck back whatever it likes without any warning. Matt puts his car into reverse and heads home once more.

Back in his lounge room, Matt flips open his laptop and logs on to the Internet. Aside from the filters of junk in his email, one message helps lift his spirits. He reads happily that he's been accepted into his course. The first classes start in just a week. His enthusiasm is tempered by the fact that he doesn't have anybody immediate to tell. Gerard and Z maybe, but theirs would be short text congratulations, rather than a proper diversion. His mum will be happy. He forwards her the message from the university, adding a single line: *Guess who's going back to study!*

The exclamation point is about as much excitement as Matt can muster. He picks up his phone and sends a text to Joy as well.

I got in. How's the city? When are you back?

She's already supposed to be back.

Matt's phone starts ringing. With a prick of anticipation, he looks down at the screen. The name isn't the one he most wants to appear, but it's welcome nonetheless. Matt clicks on *answer*.

'Hi Mum.'

'Hi, Honey. I'm online and just saw your email come through. That's great news!'

'I know. I'm really stoked. Finally, I'm going to do something I want to do. That Optitel job was killing me.'

Matt's chirpiness sounds fake to him, but his Mum doesn't seem to notice.

'But what are you going to do for money?' she asks with concern. 'Do you need us to lend you some?'

'Nah, it's ok. I'll be getting Austudy and I have a little bit saved up. I'll be right.'

'Are you sure? We can buy your books or something.'

'I'll let you know if I need something. It's fine, really.'

'Well that's exciting, isn't it? You always were a good little writer,' she encourages. 'It's good to see you nurturing your talent.'

Ever since Matt had gotten an 'A' in English in his first year of high school, his mum had considered him 'a good little writer'. When he'd really started trying to submit work to publications she was as supportive as any loving parent could be, assuring him he'd get his break soon. That inflating of his spirits only made the rejection slips harder to receive. It meant he felt like he was letting her down as well as himself.

'How's everything with you guys?' Matt asks. 'How's dad?'

'Oh, you know your father, he's happy when he's got a fishing rod in his hand. He's down at the pier now trying to catch us some dinner. It's really great down here. I've been helping run art classes down at the Senior Citz centre to keep busy as well. When are you coming to visit?'

She is always trying to get him to go down and spend time with them.

'I'm not sure now that uni is starting next week. Maybe mid-semester.'

'It's so good to get a call from you.'

Matt doesn't want to remind her that she's the one who rang.

'So how is everything else?' she continues. 'Not too many touros in town now that the summer holidays are over?'

'Nah, it's alright. Everything's great actually, couldn't be better.'

No use in dumping his worries on his mother. He doesn't want to mention Joy. Whenever there is even a hint of him seeing a girl, Matt's mother seems to lose her mind. Ever since the Tristan incident it's like she suspects that maybe he really is gay and is just waiting for him to come out. He thinks she would be relieved mostly. But, like any mum, she talks about having grandchildren 'one day' with a misty look in her eyes.

'Oh, that's good,' she says.

Matt can't think of anything good to say, so rather than waffle on he decides it's best to cut things short.

'Anyway mum, I'd better get going. It's so good to talk.'

'But...'

'I've got to go into the university and get all my ID cards and books and stuff.'

'Make sure you let me know if you need any money. Really. I'll pay for your ticket down here too. We'd love to see you.'

'I'd love to see you too, Mum. I promise it won't be long until I come down.'

'Okay, love you.'

'Say hi to dad.'

Matt hangs up his phone. He does miss his parents. It's funny how you forget just how much until you hear someone's voice. Even though they hadn't caught up properly, it's reassuring to know that someone is truly happy for him and wants nothing but good things for his life.

Matt looks around at his empty house and thoughts of Joy come to the fore again. He runs his hand over his face, trying figure out what to do next. Maybe he really should go out to the university. With the semester starting soon, there is a lot to organise in a short time. Matt looks at the clock. He should be there by mid-afternoon.

He can even stop by Joy's house again on the way, just to see if she's there.

Forty

It has been three more agonising days with no word. The process of getting ready for study has provided some relief from waiting for Joy to call. There are even a few moments when Matt reads his new study guides and coordinates his tutorial schedules when she falls completely from his thoughts. But one glance at his inanimate phone jolts Matt back to reality.

He contemplates calling the police to lodge a missing persons report, but doesn't know what he'd say. He doesn't even know Joy's last name and he can't very well call and say: 'My friend Joy is missing, she hasn't replied to my texts.'

Every trip down the street, every errand needed running, ends in a loop past her house. The same distinctive brown oil stain is the only evidence that there is supposed to be a car in the driveway.

Matt has taken to listening to Jeff Buckley on repeat in his car. As pathetic as he knows it is, he just can't help but let the music welcome him into its arms. *Grace* kicks in as he rounds the corner of Adams Way. It's his third drive-by for the afternoon.

From halfway down the street, Matt spots the blue hatchback. It's there! An initial wash of relief filters through Matt, but a few seconds later he realises it's not the only car in the driveway: a navy BMW is parked behind it, sitting there like a dark metal omen.

Pulling up on the opposite side of the street, Matt sits staring at the house. He knows he should just go in. It could be another teacher from one of Joy's schools, or a friend from the city. The churning in Matt's stomach tells him otherwise. Jeff Buckley sings high, piercing notes.

A shadow of movement appears in the window by the door. Slumping a little in his seat, Matt watches as a man in a suit and tie steps out of the house. He looks like a button-down businessman in his mid-thirties. The man turns back to the door as Joy appears in the frame. He leans in and kisses her quickly on the lips, before waving goodbye. Joy closes the door without seeing Matt watching them.

Hesitating for a few seconds, Matt switches off the engine and steps out of the Holden. A numb sense of instinct makes him cross the street toward the man who is just about to get in his car. Matt prepares himself for a confrontation.

As Matt steps on the curb, the man notices his approach. He turns to Matt with a disarming smile.

'Hello there.'

The friendly greeting makes Matt pause.

'Hi,' he manages to say, coming to a stop in the driveway.

The man looks closely at Matt.

'Are you here to see Joy?' he asks.

'Yes.'

Matt's monotone answers belie the undercurrent of anger welling inside.

'You must be Matt.'

Completely taken aback, Matt stands there for a few seconds.

'I am. I'm sorry, you are?'

The man smiles broadly again and holds out his hand.

'I'm Peter. Nice to meet you, Matt. Joy has told me a lot about you.'

'She has?' Matt is perplexed at this turn of events. 'Are you a friend?'

Peter looks back to the house and his facial expression turns guarded, like there's some kind of conspiracy he has to hide.

'Something like that,' he answers. 'I'd better let Joy explain. I have to go. Hope to see you again.'

The words are the final offer of exchange as Peter ducks into the security of his car. Matt stands and watches as the navy BMW eases out of the driveway and down the street. His head is a jumbled knot of uncertainty. Like a man on death row, Matt makes his way to the front door. A brief shuffling can be heard inside before Joy swings the door open. Her slight smile turns to a look of shock.

'Oh Matt, hi. I thought you were someone else.'

'Peter?'

'What?'

'I just ran into him in the driveway. Who is he?' Matt tilts his head to one side, trying to act as casually as he can.

Joy stands with her hand on the door, her face white and eyes wide. Her chin starts to tremor a little and tears begin to well in her eyes. Normally, Matt would melt at any sign of emotion from Joy, but this time a fire of suspicion is stoked inside him.

'Who is he, Joy?' Matt asks, wrestling to keep the monster of jealously from rising inside him.

A tear starts to slide down her cheek as she stares at Matt, not saying anything. She adjusts her grip on the door. Joy opens her mouth to say something but stops and hangs her head in silence.

'Joy? Who is Peter?' Matt repeats.

Joy doesn't answer. Her vocal silence speaks volumes that Matt doesn't want to hear. Unchecked rage starts to grow inside him. He clenches his fists at his side, trying to force the blood to pump around his body. Matt's racing pulse starts to throb in his ears. Joy refuses to meet his questioning glare.

'How could you do this?' Matt finally yells. 'We've only been together for barely a month and already you're running around with someone else? I thought we had something!'

Joy's head is in her hands as she starts to really cry. Her body is shaking, her legs barely holding her up. Matt feels no pity.

'What is he to you?' Matt shouts at her, anger pouring out of him. 'What? Your city fling?'

Joy looks up, suddenly cold in her stare.

'You don't know anything,' she snaps at him.

'Then tell me!' Matt shouts back. 'I deserve to know at least!'

She pauses for a few more seconds, before whispering harshly.

'He's my husband.'

Matt staggers backward like he's been punched in the face. It's worse than that. If someone had hit him, he'd be able to feel something. Instead, it feels like his body is a vacuum. There is nothing inside. Silence rings in his ears, before the reality crushes him like a landslide.

'What?' he looks at Joy in disbelief.

'He's my husband,' Joy repeats. 'That's why I've been in the city. Seeing him. We've been separated for almost a year but now he wants to give it another try. He wants me to move back with him. I'm going to go, Matt. I owe it to him. You and I are finished.'

'You. I...' Matt can't talk. He hunches over as his muscles crumble. He can't respond, so Joy continues.

'You should just delete my number and forget about me, Matt. You and I can't happen.'

Joy stiffens her back and lets go of the door, showing her strength.

'You can't do this to me,' Matt starts to plead.

'I can do what I like,' Joy cuts him short, 'I have cancer. I can do what I want.'

The excuse is repulsive and wrong, but Matt has no response. He just stands there, gaping at her, trying not to cry. Joy doesn't say goodbye. She simply steps back into her house and shuts the door.

Forty One

Unsure how he got home, Matt lies shaking on his lounge room floor. The whole world has just imploded into a succubus of sorrow. The depression he had felt on the night of the storm pales in insignificance to this feeling. This is real. This is justified.

He keeps running through what Joy had said so coldly to him, while Peter's false smile strobes in his mind.

A rational person might dismiss his sorrow, saying that they'd only been together for a couple of months. They would say that time heals all wounds and that there are plenty of other fish in the sea. But that's not right. Joy isn't a fish; she is the sea. The fact that they've never spoken about the weather means that Matt knows who she is deep down. Or at least he thought he had. Nothing makes sense. Nothing matters.

There is no cohesion to Matt's thoughts. They just run over the top of each other, like animals in a stampede, fighting for survival. In their frenzy to escape, they claw each other to death.

Matt struggles to deny the truth of what she said. It can't be right. *How can she be married?*

But what does he know, really? That she had once lived in the city, she is a teacher and she has survived breast cancer. She has a father who is distant and a mother who passed away when she was young. That is it as far as personal details go. The spiritual details had seemed so much more important, but if he'd pressed her for more of her life story maybe he wouldn't be in this mess.

Maybe this is his fault somehow. He is useless, revolting. Maybe this is warranted punishment for being such a disconnected twit. This is all he probably deserves — hurt. She had cheated on him. No, that isn't right. Technically, she had cheated on her husband with him. But they were separated. Being cheated on wasn't in the physical act; it was in being lied to. She had cheated Matt.

Forty One

Matt desperately wants to pick up his phone and call Joy and tell her he hates her and that she's ruined his life. He doesn't have the guts to actually do it though. He doesn't even have the courage to text her.

She's so beautiful. She wouldn't do this on purpose.

She's a bitch. He hates her.

Matt starts to cry. He feels like a baby. The spiral of self-pity spins right down into his bone marrow. His sobs are so deep that they rip at his throat. Dribble oozes from his mouth and over his quivering lips. He cries and cries. This isn't how things were supposed to go.

An hour of tears brings a desert of numbness. He doesn't feel better, he just feels limp. Getting up off the floor, Matt goes to the kitchen and gets a glass of water. Before he can finish drinking, anger bubbles into him. He wants to bite the glass in two, but instead he just drops it into the sink and it smashes. A million splintered reflections sit in the stainless-steel bowl. Turning the tap on, Matt washes away the smallest parts, before he starts to cry again.

Forty Two

Matt can't sleep, yet all he wants to do is sleep. It's been two days since he's gotten out of bed for any longer than a few minutes. The horrible beast of consciousness gnaws at his thoughts. His body is heavy, like his veins have been injected with sand. Waves of despair come and go, but the undercurrent is numbness. Apathy is his new equivalent of happiness. It's the best he can hope for.

Music used to lift his spirits, but now every song just reminds him of Joy.

The bitch. She's ruined Bob Marley.

University starts today — Matt realises as he looks at the date on his phone. He's supposed to be embarking on a new life towards some kind of achievement. He sits up and considers going to school. Not today. He'll go tomorrow.

If only Joy would call to apologise, so that he can hang up on her. He swallows his poisonous spite and hopes she feels it in her own blood. He was perfectly happy until she came along. Well, he wasn't, but he was happier than this.

He hopes that he'll choke on his own vomit in his sleep and Joy will read about it in the newspaper, knowing she caused his death. No one would find him for weeks, until the stench of decomposing flesh permeated the neighbours' house. Matt knows he shouldn't be thinking these things, but he thinks them anyway.

The cupboard is bare. Even the butt of the stale loaf of bread is inedible. He should probably just starve to death. That is more pathetic than choking on vomit. It would be a fitting end to a life that has just wasted away into a bag of bones.

Stop it. You're being a baby. Man up.

The last time he had contemplated dying he had decided to make things more interesting and not follow the rules. At first it had helped, but then that had just led to this.

His time is running out again. He's sick. His brain is turning against him. There is no cure that he can think of. He doesn't even want a cure anyway.

Maybe he needs to go and steal some minutes back to give him some extra life. It would be better than wallowing in the grey of asbestos.

At least the supermarket has beer.

Forty Three

Matt takes off his shoes in the car before he goes into the supermarket. He wants to experience the cool of the vinyl floor on his feet. He needs to feel a sensation that is easy to recognise.

Standing in the fruit and veg section, Matt lets the chill penetrate his toes. It helps make him feel like a normal person. Waiting next to the lemons, he allows two potential targets to go by without taking their trolleys. Neither of them seems like the right option.

Half an hour passes. It doesn't occur to Matt that he could have just done his own shopping by now and it would have taken less time. That's beside the point. He needs to take it away from someone. Matt waits, as motionless as the potatoes behind him.

The perfect mark rolls past with his groceries. A young man, about the same age as Matt: healthy, happy, his hair blow-waved into smug blonde curls. He has plenty of minutes to spare someone else. The man is wearing a Ramones t-shirt. Even better. Matt can't stand people who wear the t-shirts of bands they have probably never listened to.

The laden trolley is left sitting near the deli cheeses, as Ramones Tee heads off to grab some bread.

Now.

At an even pace, Matt walks in and glides away with his catch. It's too easy. Pausing for a moment next to a rack of canned beans, he decides to turn around. Pushing his load toward the shelves of bread, where its rightful owner is standing, Matt sidles up right next to him and leans over to pick up a loaf of multigrain. The man looks at him and smiles hello.

Matt doesn't acknowledge him. He wants the man to look down and see his groceries. He wants him to pick a fight. He wants so badly to get caught, so he can hit something and feel flesh connect with his knuckles. The man just walks off after getting himself some hotdog buns. Matt stalks after him, pushing the trolley and watching as Ramones Tee goes back to the cheese. The man looks around for a while. He walks right around the display searching for his groceries. Matt can't take it. This isn't fun. It's like all the novelty of this has been sapped out of it and he's now seeing it for the petty thing it is. If Joy were here at his shoulder at least they'd be sharing the moment, but she's gone for good. Alone, this all just seems ugly.

Pushing the trolley back over to the cheese, Matt lets it come to rest against the display.

'Hey mate,' he says to Ramones Tee. 'I think I grabbed your trolley by mistake. Sorry.'

The man looks up at Matt.

'Oh wow, thanks. I was freaking out then. I thought I'd gone crazy.'

'Nah, not crazy mate. Just lost.'

The man walks over and inspects the contents of the trolley.

'Yeah, that's mine for sure,' he says, before looking around. 'Where's yours then?'

'I'm not sure,' Matt shrugs. 'Some girl must have taken it. I'm not sure I'll ever get it back.'

'Really? That's odd. Oh well, maybe you should just go and get a new one. There's a big rack of them over there.'

'Yeah,' Matt says, looking back to the outside world. 'Guess I'd better start all over again.'

Forty Four

A cold chip sandwich. Matt's breakfast, made from last night's leftovers. The wad of bread and potato is bland but satisfying as it trudges down into his stomach. The carbohydrates help Matt work up enough energy to make the trek to his first set of classes. It's time he got back on the horse and at least this one is all saddled up and ready to go. He has a journalism lecture and a literature tutorial.

Matt yearns for a flint of inspiration to spark him into action. He's ready and willing. He needs this more than ever.

On his way to university, Matt detours past Joy's house. The blue hatchback sits idle in the driveway, cold and alone. The curtains are drawn and no sign of life stirs inside. She is probably in the city in Peter's flashy BMW. Barely slowing down, Matt drives past and stares his scorn at the brick façade.

Forget her. Forget her.

But Matt can't forget, the wound is still open and weeping.

The tunnelling warrens of corridors at the university are hard to navigate. Matt feels like an explorer, searching for a lost treasure as he hunts for the lecture theatre he's already supposed to be inside. The room numbers are divided into decimal points for some reason: 26.1, 26.4. It makes no logical sense, they aren't fractional rooms; they're whole ones. Eventually he gets to Lecture Theatre Three. He can hear a monotone voice droning inside. Matt cracks open the door and enters with his head bowed. He waits for the lecturer to pause and make note of the late entry, but the monotone just continues on about compulsory tutorial attendance and essay assessments. Not wanting to interrupt anyone's attention by walking up the back, Matt takes the closest empty seat and sits down.

Allowing himself to settle in, Matt surveys his surroundings. Tiered seating spans the small amphitheatre. A sparse arrangement of people fans out among the black-seated rows. Some groups are sitting together, but by and large people are keeping to themselves, focussing on the lecturer whilst scribbling notes. Matt notices he's the only person sitting in the front row. He is right on the edge, like an askew little toe that means nothing to the foot of the student body.

Still talking steadily, the lecturer clicks a slide over on his laptop, which is projected onto a large screen. He looks up to make sure the right display is on before turning back to the class. He is a short man with dishevelled curly hair and glasses. A red bow tie sticks out like a still propeller at the top of his shirt and his navy jeans are hitched above his waist. He looks more like a stand-up comedian than an intellectual.

'Now that we have our housekeeping out of the way,' he says to the class, 'let's start with an introduction to Journalism 101.'

Matt sighs with relief that he hasn't missed anything important. It's like he's turned up at the movies and skipped the previews. A few more students sneak through the doors and slump into empty seats around the theatre. Their uncertain looks around the room tell Matt they're just as dubious about this learning caper as he is.

The lecture drags on with scraping monotony. The subject matter is dry and boring. The first rule of journalism is to make sure you capture the main lead of the story in the opening sentence. This is an art. One must avoid adding superfluous adjectives or personal assessments. Keep it clean and devoid of commentary. Matt takes notes to avoid falling asleep. Despite the comment that distilling stories into as few words as possible is an art, Matt thinks it sounds more like surgery. Clean, efficient, cutting. It does make sense; it just doesn't sound very fun. The lecturer's flat delivery does nothing to lift the ideas above being basic information. There is no interaction or question time; it's simply a presentation of the facts. For Matt, the hour can't end quickly enough. He would get up and leave, but he doesn't want to be rude, so he listens and takes notes. As soon as the lecture ends, Matt snaps his notebook closed and rushes for the door.

There is a two-hour break until his tutorial. Not really hungry for lunch, Matt decides to take a walk around the grounds of the university. The sports fields stretch out in a flat lawn, away from the main student buildings and over to the road, so he doesn't bother heading that way. Instead, threading between the library and the block of lecture theatres, Matt looks for somewhere quieter and hidden. The size of the campus is quite impressive. There are residence dorms, labs and separate faculty buildings for each department of learning. Walking in the general direction of the Arts block, Matt comes upon a small lake. In the middle of the calm water is an island full of dead trees. On the far bank, a small sandstone chapel is nestled amongst some tall reeds. Matt looks around, trying to figure out how to get to the chapel, but there doesn't seem to be any easy route, other than walking right around the lake. In lieu of making the pilgrimage over, Matt sits down on a park bench by the water's edge and deposits his bag next to him. Deciding he may as well appear like someone who is thirsty for knowledge, he takes out the book his literature class is supposed to be reading: *The Sorrows of Young Werther* by Johann Wolfgang von Goethe. He opens the first pages and begins to read. It's in the format of letters from one young man to another. The hopeful first lines send a chill of expectation into Matt.

How happy I am to be away! My dear friend, the heart of Man is a strange thing!

Matt ploughs through the first few chapters. By page 34, the book already has the whiff of tragedy. This excites Matt even more. He is always attracted to stories without redemption; they're truer to real life.

The unstable nature of the main character, Werther, magnifies Matt's own turbulent emotional state. He seeks out the publishing information at the start of the novel. It was first released in 1774, nearly two hundred and fifty years ago. It dawns on Matt that the feelings, hopes and dreams of people seem to have remained the same through the ages. We all want to love and be loved, yet we are destined to be alone in what we experience. No one can truly know the journey we go through except ourselves. Still, we try to share it. We want to feel like we have purpose. We all want to *achieve* something bigger than ourselves, yet we don't seem to ever be able to agree on what that purpose is. It seems to Matt like we are our own worst enemy in our pursuits. The clash between emotions and rationality muddies our judgement, but it's not clear which side is better. If you're all head and no heart you can dissect decisions and work on a path towards doing amazing things. But if you're emotionally cold in your actions you tread over other people in the process. Does being rational necessarily mean that you're emotionally cold? Matt isn't sure. Characters in books are often painted that way, but real life is infinitely more complicated than could ever be captured on a page. Then there are those people in real life that Matt always seems to admire, who just seem to be running on instinct. Artists like Jim Morrison, or Charles Bukowski, or Vincent van Gogh. Yet, those people all seem to implode in their fierce flare of life. They suffer and they die. They achieve greatness but never get close to happiness. It's not clear to Matt which is actually better. Greatness or happiness. Is it best to find a balance of somewhere in between? Half way between rational and emotional. Half way between great and happy. And how do you find it? What's the key and is that key the same for everyone? Matt thinks that maybe if he reads enough and lives enough, maybe he'll start to understand. He looks at the date of the book again and shakes his head. Maybe no one understands and all of this writing is people trying to see if they can figure it out, if only for a small space in time.

Matt looks up from his book. All this time and thinking and we all still seem to be searching for the same things. All of this technological development to bring people together and we're just as disconnected as we've ever been. Struggle, love, separation and death. The themes stay the same. Only the settings change.

A duck quacking kicks Matt back into the present. His eyes focus on the chapel and the lake in front of him. Maybe the setting hasn't changed too much after all. He flips the book back open. He still has some time to finish the next chapter.

Forty Five

Matt practically runs to his tutorial. He was so immersed in Werther's sorrows that the real world had fallen away. It almost seemed like the book was written specifically for him. The main character had fallen in love with a married woman and felt the pain of an unrequited relationship. Werther's feelings are Matt's feelings. There was someone who knew exactly the impact emotion could have: the soul-sucking vacuum of despair it could create. The author Goethe must have been through it to be able to describe the feelings so well. The realisation that his experience has been recycled throughout history again and again gives Matt a strange kind of solace. He's not alone in the core of what he's going through. The situation might have its own small nuances, but the result is the same. Life will go on. It will hurt, but if he just grits his teeth and keeps going things will hopefully improve. If it hadn't been for the distraction of a duck flapping into the lake, Matt might have stayed inside the book all day.

The small tutorial room is packed to capacity. A woman stands at the front, sizing up her students. She has a shaved head and her sleeves are rolled to the elbows. The woman flicks a glance at Matt as he steals through the door.

'Take a seat. We're about to begin,' she commands.

Matt shuffles into a row and manages to squeeze between a girl in a floral dress and the wall. He looks at her and flashes an apologetic smile as he stuffs his bag under the seat and pulls out his books and pens.

'Okay, everyone,' the woman with the shaved head calls for silence. 'My name is Dr Florence Byron. I'll be both your lecturer and tutor this semester. We normally don't have tutes in the first week, but I find it's better to get cracking right away. Now, who's started reading the first text?'

Matt is among a handful of students who raise their hands.

'That's not too bad, I've seen worse showings,' the doctor nods. 'Who of you few scholars are enjoying the read?'

Matt is the only one who leaves his hand in the air. He looks around, surprised. The sea of unappreciative young faces around him suggests that maybe he's out of touch.

'Great!' Dr Byron exclaims with a wide smile, clapping her hands together. 'I can see that I'm only going to like one person in this class. That'll make my job easy.'

Matt blushes at the comment that has drawn all eyes to him. He lets his hand fall.

'What's your name?' the doctor asks.

'Matt.'

'Matt,' she repeats. 'Why do you like Goethe's story? What draws you to it?'

Matt pauses for a few moments, not liking the attention. He runs his fingers over the cover of the book to gather his thoughts.

'It's, ah,' he tries to find the right word. 'It's stormy.'

The girl next to him lets out a laugh at his comment. He thinks he's said something wrong.

'Stormy!' Dr Byron exclaims, sending everyone silent. 'Have you been reading the study guide?' she raises an eyebrow in his direction.

'No,' Matt shakes his head, confused.

The tutor takes a pen and writes the words *Sturm und Drang* on a whiteboard next to her.

'Sturm und Drang!' she bellows in a German accent, veins popping out of her neck.

The entire class jerk up in their seats at the outburst. Having had the desired effect, the doctor laughs.

'Thank you. Basically translated, this German phrase means 'the storm and the stress'. It was a sub-branch of the Romantic Movement that Goethe was linked to for a brief time. It's a testament to young Matt here that he picked up on the nature of the work. Now, one of those people who doesn't like what they've read so far, tell me why. Call out.'

'It's too sappy,' someone yells out from the back of the class.

'It's depressing,' the girl next to Matt voices her opinion.

'Good,' Dr Byron nods. 'Engagement, that's what we want here. I'd rather you hate something than be ambivalent. There are no wrong answers, unless you disagree with *my* opinion.'

There are a few giggles at the comment, but she presses on.

'You should know that the author himself hated this book at the end of his life as well. He was only twenty-four when he wrote it. A literary baby, yet it still became arguably his most famous work and one that resonates the most strongly in young readers. He renounced it later in life, as he grew more mature. Goethe said it was part of a movement that was 'everything that is sick'. Why do you think he thought so?'

Matt is relieved the focus of the class in now off of him and into discussion. The size of the room makes the tutorial much more intimate and special than the lecture he had just attended. It feels like he is part of something. He thinks about the age of the writer of the book. Younger than him, yet he had been able to pen a masterwork like this. Still, he called the work 'sick' later on. Could you change so much in your lifetime that you actually hate your former self? Maybe this is what Z was getting at when she said that people's lives have eras. The idea encourages Matt. He hasn't written a book that he can renounce later on, but he hates the way he's authored his own life so far. Maybe he will look back on that and realise he was sick. That he needed to adjust his mindset and work toward being a different, better person. Or, maybe he simply has to become comfortable with the idea of who he is, rather than second-guessing his ideas and feelings as legitimate.

Doctor Byron nods along as students make comments, before she holds up her hand.

'Some interesting ideas there,' she says. 'I think a big contributing factor to his loathing of this book is the fact that it spawned a series of suicides around Europe. People would dress the same as the main character Werther and top themselves.'

Matt sits up at this comment. He hasn't yet been able to finish the book, but he'd guessed that it might end in sadness. Still, to kill yourself over a book seems a bit extreme, even to Matt. Could writing really have *that* kind of effect on people? He hadn't thought about the danger of putting out ideas into the world like that. Yet his own conception about what he should and shouldn't be doing with his life had brought him to the cliff's edge once already. They were simply ideas at their heart. His own narrative about himself. Who is he to say what else would affect him in such a way?

'How do you think that made Goethe feel?' Dr Byron asks.

'Like he was responsible for them dying?' Matt offers.

'He's not responsible,' counters the girl in the floral dress next to Matt. 'They're ridiculous for getting so caught up in the romance of suicide.'

'Do you think he's responsible, Matt?' asks Dr Byron, facilitating the discussion.

'I'm just saying that's probably how he felt. Like, would they have killed themselves if they hadn't read the book? Thoughts can be like a virus if you can't shake them off.'

'Yes!' Dr Byron says. 'Richard Dawkins' idea of memes goes something like that. That ideas leap from one head to another until they can form cultures, or destroy them. I know if I'd written something that people had killed themselves after reading, I'd feel pretty shitty.'

'But you have to take responsibility for your own actions at some point,' Floral Dress counters. 'We all have free will when it comes down to it.'

'It certainly *feels* like we have choice, doesn't it?' Dr Byron adds. 'One thing you don't have a choice on is that you need to read this book. All of you. Next we move on to *Heart of Darkness* by Joseph Conrad.'

Matt packs up his book and leaves. He's glad he came today. It's like discussing dark ideas is the best way to keep them out of your head, revolving around and around until they make you mad.

Forty Six

The bed envelops Matt's body as the words envelop his mind. He races through the pages with gasping breath. Werther is at the height of his suffering, contemplating either murder or suicide. For the moment, Matt's worries are forgotten in the expanse of Goethe's writing. As each page turns, the story of fate unfolds.

The ending wrenches Matt's soul. Werther's death is at once a release and a sentence. The inevitability of his demise doesn't ease the force of the blow, it enhances it. Matt stares at the last lines, wishing they weren't true, but knowing there is no way to change the ending. The mastery of the writing disheartens Matt. There is no way he could ever dream of creating something so great. It makes him want to put down his pen before he has even written a line. At least he'll never have the power to make people want to kill themselves, unless it's through boring them to death. He tries to put himself in the author's shoes, finding out the news of each suicide. He can't even fathom how terrible that would be. At least Matt doesn't want to end his life over a book. The thought of death now terrifies Matt. It scares him for the same reason he had first thought of suicide — he has done nothing of note with his life. Maybe it was because he had been told by society that he could be anything that he wanted, that he had chosen nothing. He had been drowned in a sea of choice. Now that the field of options has been narrowed with age, Matt feels a conviction that writing is the only way out. He can claw out of the doldrums using a pen as his shovel. There is just one glaring problem — he isn't any good.

That isn't entirely true. You can't be categorically bad if you haven't written anything. Yet, he knows that there is a long way to go before he can compose something worthy of print. At least that is the beauty about writing, the *delete* button is there to help you improve.

He needs to keep Joy out of his thoughts, but she keeps intruding: her eyes, her lips. It isn't just her bodily parts though, that isn't even scratching the surface: her voice, her laugh. Those attributes are too worldly as well. They are nothing. It is the sum of the parts that makes her so great; the sum of her spirit as well as her flesh. But they are now something that will elude Matt forever. They will haunt him like an unfinished sentence. There is nothing he can do now. He knows it's wrong to fight for her. She has made her choice. Matt tries to fix Peter as an object of hate in his mind, but can't. He doesn't even know the man. All he can muster is detached resentment. She has made her choice.

Matt tries to figure out what he's going to do now. His new course is something, but it won't fill in every hour of every day. He needs to keep busy with action to keep away from the grinding of his own thoughts. The nights will be the hardest, and the weekends. It's Friday. Matt calls Z to see how things are going and if she's around for a beer.

'You've called 1800 GANGBANG,' Z answers in her best phone sex voice. 'What's your fantasy?'

'I want to meet a lesbian at the pub for a drink and convert her back to the land of dick.' Matt says in his own husky voice.

'All of our lesbians are busy working right now,' Z continues with the character. 'But there's a sissy boy here that might fill the hole. I mean role.'

'Hello?' Gerard's uncertain voice appears on the line. 'G, it's Matt.'

'Oh, thank God,' he sounds relieved. 'I actually thought Z was putting me to work for a second.'

'We could use the money!' Z yells in the background. From the ambient noise on the other line, it sounds like Gerard has just switched the phone onto loud speaker.

'No clients yet?' Matt asks.

'Not even close,' Gerard says. He sounds worried. 'Z has us working on some standard call scripts that we can put out to show we know what we're talking about. But it's hard when there's not a specific company to work towards.'

'Once we get the first customer, we'll be fine,' Z cuts in. 'It doesn't help that you ruined my big marketing plan for launch.'

'*I* did?' Matt asks.

'You did. I figured we'd be working together, so I was planning to release your little manifesto email on the web, along with your call recordings. I'd then put out a press release saying you'd gone rogue and had started your own company. You were our poster child, Matt. Now that's all gone to shit.'

314

'Oh,' is all Matt can say.

'It's fine,' Gerard adds in. 'We just need to work to make it happen. We'll get there.'

'I guess that means you don't have time to come and meet me for a drink then?' Matt asks.

'Well,' Gerard begins.

'Not even close,' Z cuts in. 'While bleeding heart here works for Centrelink during the week all we have are nights and weekends to make this happen. He can drink and sleep when we get paid.'

'If it helps you guys out, I don't mind if you release that stuff of me with the company name attached. I'm cool with it.'

'Told you,' Z says.

'And I told you,' Gerard voice sounds tired. 'We're billing ourselves as a newer, more honest customer service company. If we start telling lies about who is involved with the company, then we're going against everything we say we are.'

Matt thinks on the problem for a few seconds, while G and Z bicker between themselves about marketing just being white lies anyway.

'Hey guys,' Matt says into his phone. 'Guys!'

'Sorry, Matt,' says G. 'What's that?'

'What if you put out that stuff and I committed to writing the call scripts for anyone who comes on as a client?'

'Really?' says Gerard.

'Sure. I have to start building up my writer's résumé anyway and I know customer service, so I can do it.'

'We can't pay you,' Z yells from the background again.

'I'll take payment in beer and love advice then, at least until you get some cash flow happening.'

'Love advice?' Z's voice is closer to the phone now. 'What's happening with that girl?'

'Her name's Joy,' Matt says. 'And it turns out she's married.'

'Oh,' G and Z's voices sound together.

'We'll be there in an hour,' Z says. 'I'll bring some Green Chartreuse.'

Forty Seven

Matt's head is throbbing. The mixture of a Chartreuse binge on Friday and trying to study this morning has his brain cells screaming in surrender. White noise hampers his every effort at concentration. Z and G had been great at cheering Matt up while they were over, but their advice had amounted to a total of five words: 'forget her and move on.' It's the same advice Matt would give anyone in his situation. But actually living that advice was proving difficult with her face hiding in every shadow of his psyche.

Now late on Sunday afternoon, Matt walks with rolled-up jeans along the water's edge at the beach. Ripples of tide sweep over his feet and dissolve the shining footprints he has left behind. The thumping sounds of the surf mix with the squawk of seagulls.

Up ahead, a family is playing with their dog, running back and forth to the water's edge. Two children sprint as hard as they can up the beach to their parents, who sit happily watching on a blanket in the sand. The blonde-haired mother picks up a tennis ball and throws it back to the water's edge. The excited bark of the dog matches the enthusiasm of the children's laughter.

Petty jealousy spears into Matt. He was once part of a nice little family unit, but he has grown out of it. He remembers running around with his parents on this same beach, going fishing, thinking his father was the biggest, strongest and smartest person on the planet. As he grew older, it was a tough learning curve to realise that his mum and dad were nothing but normal humans like everyone else. Sometimes, Matt wishes he was a little kid again, safe with his parents. Happy in his blissful ignorance, living in this quaint seaside town before it changed. His happiest memories are of little things, like pretending to be asleep in the car on the way back from fishing trips, so his dad would carry him inside and put him to bed. He'd then peek one eye open to see his dad watching him. They'd smile at each other and then the light would go out and he'd really go to sleep. Matt wishes sleep came so easy now.

The dog's bark yanks Matt out of contemplation. He glances over to the family again to see the husband and wife kissing. Their kids are occupied building a sand castle. The woman lovingly watches them play. The father turns his face toward Matt walking up the beach.

His face is familiar, but from this distance Matt can't quite make it out. Something is tugging at him, telling him that something in this scene is wrong. That man shouldn't be here. It's something about his smile.

With a growing sense of unease, Matt walks toward the family. The blonde woman leans in again, kissing the man playfully on the neck. However, the man pulls away. He's now seen Matt approaching. He watches Matt for a few moments. His big smile fades and he stands up.

It's Peter: Joy's husband.

Matt struggles to understand the situation. Peter. With another family. With another woman. He studies the children. They have sandy blonde hair like the woman and broad smiles like Peter. It can't be right.

Peter leans in to whisper something to the woman and then waves to Matt, who now stands rigid, just metres away. He wants to rush at Peter. He wants to tackle him onto the sand and smash in his face with a rock until his blood stains the beach red. Again, Matt looks at the children. He can't move.

Peter leaves his family and walks toward Matt, who is clenching his fists into balls of fury. Matt struggles to hold back his anger. He can't attack someone in front of his children. Matt knows this intellectually, but intellect has no influence here.

'Matt, hi!' Peter says glibly as he approaches. 'What are you doing here?'

'I live here,' Matt hisses lowly. 'What are *you* doing here?'

Peter turns to look back to the woman, children and frolicking dog.

'I'm just spending some time with my family,' he shrugs. 'How have you been?'

'What about Joy?' Matt says, deadpan, wanting to lash out at the man in front of him. 'Isn't Joy your family?'

Peter furrows his brow. He looks Matt up and down to assess the situation.

'I guess you could say that,' Peter scratches his head. 'Have you not seen Joy today? I thought I'd enjoy some time with my wife and kids at the beach after visiting her.'

The rage is too much for Matt to contain within himself.

Forty Seven

'What are you talking about? Joy is your wife,' he snaps. 'Who is that?' he points at the blonde-haired woman.

Peter looks as confused as Matt feels. He turns back and looks at the woman sitting on the blanket.

'What are you doing?' Matt roars. 'You're cheating on Joy!'

The lady looks up at Matt's outburst, but he doesn't notice. He only has eyes for Peter, who is standing in front of Matt with his palms held up defensively.

'What?' he whispers. 'I think you've got the wrong idea here, Matt. Why would you say I'm married to Joy?'

'Because you are, you creep. She dumped me to get back with you and you don't even seem to care. Now you're running around behind her back in my hometown. What kind of person are you?'

Matt is shaking from head to toe. It's all he can do not to punch Peter in his smiling face. The blonde-haired woman approaches. Leaning over Peter's shoulder, she rests her head next to his ear.

'Is everything okay, honey?' she asks.

'I'm not sure,' he says to her. 'This is Matt. He seems to think I'm married to Joy.'

The woman looks at Matt like he's insane and dangerous.

'Why would you think that?' she says, almost to herself.

Matt's disorientation is frightening. The gamut of emotions swirling inside him threatens to overwhelm him.

'Because she told me,' Matt manages to say, between gritted teeth.

The three of them stand there, looking at each other in a showdown of misunderstanding. Peter turns to his wife for a moment.

'Can you give us a few moments, honey,' he says to her. 'I think I'd better clear this up.'

As soon as the woman is out of earshot, Peter looks back to Matt, putting his hands in his pockets.

'Matt, I think you have your wires crossed here,' he looks down at his feet. 'I'm probably overstepping the mark, I really shouldn't be telling you this, but I feel like I need to, at least so you understand what's going on. I'm a family friend of Joy's. I've never been romantically linked with her, but I have had to spend a lot of time with her recently.'

Peter visibly holds his breath, like he's trying to contain what he's about to say, but can't. Finally, he lets it out in a rush.

'I'm her oncologist. Joy is dying. The cancer has come back and spread throughout her body. I'm really sorry. I thought you knew.'

The words are too much for Matt to bear. He reaches back with his fist before swinging it forward with everything he has, smacking Peter in the nose.

Forty Eight

As Peter crumples to the sand, Matt turns and runs away. He doesn't hear Peter's wife cry out, or see the blood pouring from Peter's nose into his hands. He doesn't register the throbbing ache in his right fist, as his feet carry him along the beach toward the staircase. All Matt can think of is Joy. *Why would she lie? Was she lying? What's happening? Dying? She can't be!*

The world has lost all lucid meaning. It's a dream. It's a nightmare.

Matt doesn't stop running. He bounds up the steep stairs two by two, puffing into the car park, red faced and sweating. Still he runs, across the street and up the road, back towards the sanctity of home.

The cool interior of his house is welcoming, but gives no respite to the questions battling each other in Matt's brain. He draws all of the curtains and sits in the darkened lounge room, trying to recover in a shrouded cave of uncertainty.

Matt's pulse is racing. His breath ragged. His nerves destroyed.

What is going on? What did I just do?

He needs answers, but none come. Every solution just begs another question. Guilt hangs in his chest like a tangle of loathing. Until today, Matt has never hit anyone in his life. He's still not sure why he did it. If Peter was telling the truth, the news is disastrous. If he was lying, it solved nothing.

There are no happy endings here.

Matt looks at his hand, which is now swollen and shaking. It looks like a stranger's hand. His knuckles are now dimples in a swollen glove of skin. Rushed breathing is starting to settle, but the turmoil in Matt's heart grows.

No light shines through the windows. The curtains prevent the afternoon light from bringing any illumination into the room. The outside world is a mystery.

Matt stands up, but wobbles on his feet. He stumbles over to the kitchen to lean on the bench for support. He needs to make his brain function. He needs to figure this out. Standing and staring in the darkness, it's like writer's block has overcome him again. He waits there in a daze for the ideas to strike. He waits an hour. He waits two. The sun sets.

Standing in pitch black, Matt doesn't move. Night has fallen and all is silent. The calm of the dark is no comfort. A loud knock at the door startles him like a horror show interlude. Matt straightens up and turns toward the noise. Again, the knocking cuts through the quiet of his unit.

As though the sound has kick-started his body, Matt walks over to the wall and turns on the light.

'I'm coming!' he yells out at the insistent knocking.

Matt opens the door. Peter is standing there with two black eyes and a swollen nose. His fist is poised to knock again. Matt flinches backward, expecting to be attacked.

'Matt,' Peter holds up his hands in peace. 'Joy told me where you live. We need to talk.'

Matt doesn't know what to say. He looks at Peter with a mixed sense of embarrassment and fear. After standing still for a few moments, he steps back to reluctantly welcome Peter inside. Peter makes his way into the lounge room and sits down on Matt's couch, trying to establish a sense of truce. Matt positions himself in the kitchen, deliberately putting some space between them.

'Do you want a cup of tea?' he asks, not wanting to seem too standoffish.

'I'd prefer something stronger if you have it,' Peter answers. 'Anything to take the edge off my throbbing headache. You've got quite a punch,' he winces with a smile, his tone friendly.

'I'm sorry, I...'

'It's alright,' Peter waves off Matt's apology. 'You didn't know. It's not your fault.'

Matt considers the left over Chartreuse on the top of the fridge before grabbing two bottles of beer instead. He already feels sick enough. Matt takes the drinks to the lounge and offers one to Peter. He sits on the floor at the foot of the couch, staring down into his lap.

'Look,' Peter begins. 'There is no easy way for me to say any of this, so I'm just going to give you the truth. It's best you know it all. Joy lied. I've just been with her all afternoon and she's a mess. She didn't know how to react when she found out. She doesn't want you to get hurt.'

'It's a bit late for that.' Matt snaps, but Peter holds up his palm to silence him.

'She's not herself right now, Matt. She's afraid and alone. She thought she had beaten the cancer, but it's come back with a vengeance. Her father has basically shut down. He can't stand to watch his little girl deteriorate like her mother did. He has cut off all communication with Joy. He won't talk to her. He and my dad have been best mates since school. Joy and I grew up together. It's hard for everyone. She should be in hospital, but she won't stay there. She told me that you were caring for her. It's the only reason I let her come home. She lied to both of us.'

Matt looks up at Peter, whose expression is open and pleading. What he is saying doesn't sink in. It just sluices on the surface of Matt's skin.

'This whole thing's a mess, mate,' Peter continues. 'She can't stay by herself. She needs someone to be there in case something happens. I know you haven't known her for very long, but from what she has said you two are very close. I know she's hurt you. She pushed you away to save you the pain of losing her. She doesn't think it's fair.'

'That's not her decision to make,' Matt says.

'You're right, it's not. But as twisted as it sounds, she thinks she's doing you a favour.'

Matt stares into space, as Peter keeps talking.

'Now that you know the facts, I'm going to ask you to make the decision on your own. Joy will never make the first move here. She's too stubborn. You need to be the bigger man. I know it's not fair that I'm putting this on you, none of this is fair, but you have a choice. You can either forgive Joy and spend what time she has left together, or you let me know it's not your place and I'll take her back to the city. I can't let her stay here without support.' Peter takes a sip of his beer as if to wash the words out of his mouth.

Matt doesn't know how to respond. He just stares at Peter and takes a deep breath. The walls of the apartment seem smaller than ever.

'You don't need to let me know now,' Peter says, standing up with a sigh. 'But you do need to let me know soon. Joy has maybe a month or two at most.' He moves over to the kitchen bench and puts his half-empty beer on the countertop. 'Her body is holding up okay at the moment, but she'll go downhill quickly. I've seen it too many times. I'll leave you alone. Think about it.'

Taking his wallet out of his pocket, Peter slips out a business card and leaves it next to the bottle.

'Call me, Matt. If I haven't heard from you in a couple of days, I'll know all of this is too much. I won't judge you. It's not an easy situation. I just need to know so I can make sure Joy is as comfortable as possible.'

Without another word Peter leaves, closing the door behind him. Matt looks down at his unopened beer. He lets it fall to the ground.

Forty Nine

If Matt thought he was confused before, he doesn't know what to call this. The real story about Joy and Peter brings him zero solace; it just makes him angry.

Joy's cold stare and tone when they last spoke had not revealed any sadness, only the look of someone who had been caught out. She had looked healthy. It didn't appear there was an insidious disease devouring her within. Matt knows the history of her illness, but it's difficult for him to compute that this person is the same vibrant Joy he knows.

What am I going to do?

It was true that he and Joy were close, but now he's not so sure. At the moment, he feels rejected. If she had wanted to depend upon him, she should have called him, should have asked for his help. She should have told him. Instead, she had discarded him. Maybe she knows instinctively that he isn't a real man. That he can't handle being her pillar of strength.

Can he really go back to her, grovelling on his knees? Can he meet her again and hold his head high? He had attacked her doctor and friend. He had cried like a baby when she'd broken up with him. Could he have acted more pathetically? He was a joke of a human being. He should have sensed what was happening.

The biggest question is one that Matt isn't prepared to ask himself honestly: *Am I willing to watch my love die, while I stand by, helpless?*

It would be safer to forget that Joy exists. It would be better to accept that she doesn't want his help and let Peter take the responsibility. No one could blame him for walking away. But then, he could blame himself. He is good at that.

Matt stands up to get a drink of water. His body is screaming for the numbness of alcohol, but there's no way he can handle any kind of booze right now. If he starts he might never stop. He has a decision to make.

Right now, he doesn't think he can face her. What would he say? It's an impossible situation with no positive outcome. There is too much water between them to bridge the gap. The rushing torrent of excuses grows wider as Matt starts to rationalise.

He's only known her for a short time. She doesn't want him. How can he take care of her? He can barely take care of himself. How can she possibly be better off in his arms, than being tended to by professionals? Matt has no experience with cancer, or any real sickness. He would be even more scared and lost than Joy. His support would be no support at all. It would be a drain. Besides, she had hurt him by sweeping him aside.

Matt takes his phone out of his pocket and hits dial. He needs an outside opinion.

'Did you already hear?' Z answers with excitement on the other end.

The question throws Matt off guard.

'What?'

'I put those calls and manifesto up this morning. It's Sunday and we've already had five genuine queries from potential clients. The website is getting a thousand hits a minute. If it keeps going like this I'll have to upgrade our server. I hope you're ready to start writing those scripts.'

'Oh, that's great.' Matt manages to say, his voice weak.

'Matt?' Z says, suddenly deadly serious. 'What the fuck is wrong? Are you okay?' Despite her bluster she's a good read of people, especially on the phone when a lack of body language normally makes it hard.

'Nothing, that's great.'

'If you say 'that's great' one more time I'll come around and kick your arse, Matthew Pearce,' she huffs. 'What's happened?'

Matt lays it all out for her. The entire story, from the first time he'd seen Joy until today. He spares no details. It's like he's spewing his problems down into the phone, rancid chunks and all. Apart from a few questions or words of encouragement, Z is silent the whole time. He tells her about the letters to the editor and Bill, he tells her about Black Thai and what happened to Mr James. He tells her about the forest and the airport and the beach today.

'Please help me, Z,' he says at the end. 'I think my brain might melt if I have to think about this any more.'

Z doesn't say anything for a long time on the end of the phone, but Matt doesn't press her. She's clicking her tongue, like she always does when thinking things through. Finally, she clears her throat and Matt braces himself for some hard truths.

'From what you've told me I think that this girl is a liar and a selfish bitch,' Z says.

Matt only nods, not even realising she can't see what he's doing.

'And, you have to get back with her,' Z adds.

'What?' Matt can't believe what he's hearing.

'Matt, I know she's hurt you. What she did was wrong. But it was from a place of fear, not from malice. You clearly love her. I don't know why you have trouble admitting it to yourself.'

'But it's only been six weeks,' he says.

'I don't give a shit if it's been six days,' Z stops him. 'Time has nothing to do with it. Neither does reason. I've just listened to you speak for the last two hours. Every time you talk about her your voice lifts. Every time you talk about the times you were apart, it's like you're speaking from underwater.'

'I'd know if I was in love, Z', Matt says.

'All this fairy-tale horseshit about 'when you're in love you just know' is ridiculous. People lie to themselves about small things. They downright delude themselves if their heart's on the line. Let me ask you this. Do you smile when you think about meeting her for the first time?'

Matt thinks about it. He nods.

'Matt?'

'Oh. Yes,' he says into the phone.

'Do you want to crawl up and die when you picture your world without her?'

The last week or more has been testament to that.

'Yes,' Matt says.

'And do you get a big stiffy when you think about fucking her?'

'Z!'

'Sorry for trying to lighten the mood,' she snaps. 'Am I making my point clear enough though?' she asks.

'Yes.'

'So?'

'I think I need to sleep on it,' Matt says.

Matt can almost hear her silent scream through the phone as the line goes quiet.

'Okay. Sleep on it,' she finally says, 'but time is ticking, Matt. Just try to get your head out of the way for once. Take it from me.'

'Okay,' Matt says.

'And Matt,' Z says before she goes. 'There has never been a relationship in history that was worthwhile that didn't hurt like fuck at some point. Pain is all part of the journey, but the darkest nights have the brightest stars, hopefully their brilliance outshines the rest.'

'Thanks Z,' Matt says.

'You owe me,' she adds. 'When you sort this out, call me and we'll talk about the scripts.'

'I will,' he promises and hangs up.

Matt has no idea how he's going to get any sleep.

Fifty

Matt has to use his headlights while he drives. It's mid-morning, but the grey from above makes it seem like the sun has been snuffed out. Pelting sheets of rain drape over the town, covering it in a wet oppression.

The windscreen wipers on the Holden work at double speed to keep Matt's vision clear. The radio is silent as the rain clacks on the metal roof to its own rhythm. Not even Jeff Buckley has come along for this ride; it's something Matt has to do on his own. There is very little traffic. A few cars hiss past the other way, over sodden bitumen, searching for their own destinations. The passengers are just blurry, inconsequential figures.

Taking it slow, Matt makes sure to indicate at every turn and go easy on the brakes. After a long dry spell the roads are slippery with the residue of summer. Painstakingly, he navigates the route to Adams Way.

Letting the car come to rest in Joy's driveway, Matt watches the raindrops blink through the beams of his headlights. It's like they're little spirits, flashing through the world of light for a mere moment before forming dark puddles on the ground.

Steeling his nerves, Matt shuts off the engine and steps out into the weather. Slamming the door shut with a thud, he hunches his shoulders in a ridiculous attempt to thread a dry path through the downpour, running to Joy's front door. Knocking hard, the wood hurts his hand. There's no turning back now; he's committed.

Matt waits, huddling as close as possible to the house to avoid saturation. He's about to knock again, when the door opens inward. Joy stands there in some pyjama bottoms and a big grey sweater. Her face is slightly drawn. She is thinner than usual, but her eyes sparkle their furious green light. Seeing Matt, her expression wavers. She opens her mouth to say something, but the words are lost in the wind. She holds her gaze on Matt and then looks away. He can see her lips trembling. He stands and waits as the skies empty their tears onto his head. Looking up, Joy's mouth opens again, but words fail to materialise.

Matt steps forward tentatively and wraps his arms around her vulnerable frame. At first, his arms barely touch her body, but then she brings her arms up as well and folds them around his back with determined strength. He hugs her tightly, pulling her close into a soggy embrace. Joy melts into him, pushing her face into his chest. She starts to cry into Matt, burying her sobs in his shirt.

Matt doesn't cry. He is strong. He's a rock. He lets Joy lean on him and weep out her fears. She shakes unspoken apologies with each tremor of her body.

'I know,' he says, resting his chin on the top of her head. 'It's alright.'

At his comforting words, Joy's lament escalates into another wave of grief. She's weeping for the both of them. Her hands grip the fabric of Matt's shirt, like she never wants to let go. He pulls her closer again, letting her know that he's here to stay.

Bringing his hand up to her head, Matt strokes Joy's midnight hair. At the touch of his fingers, she looks up, her red eyes wrapped in a film of tears.

'Can we go inside now?' Matt smiles down to her. 'I'm sick of being out in the storm.'

Fifty

She looks up at the sky, like she's realising for the first time that it's raining. Still without words, she nods and leads Matt inside by the hand. Taking him to the couch, Joy makes him sit down while she goes to boil the kettle. He watches her move around. Every few moments, she looks up at him as though checking that he's really there. The silence between them is not uncomfortable. Nothing needs to be spoken. They both know that, for now, it's enough to be together.

Matt is growing cold on the couch. His body starts to shiver involuntarily. He can hear the kettle boiling and aches for a warm drink. Instinctively, Joy makes a cup of tea. She brings it over and offers it to Matt, before walking off again down the hallway. After a few moments, she comes back with a big doona.

'Take off your clothes,' she says softly.

Putting the cup aside, Matt unbuttons his wet shirt. He slides off his damp jeans. Ever so naturally, Joy removes her sweater and bottoms. There is nothing sexual about it, it's just normal and familiar. She picks up the doona and curls in next to Matt on the couch, encasing them in the blanket. Pressing her warm skin against his, they bask in each other's body heat. Matt lets their breathing sync together. At first, it's a push, trying to match the rhythm of her inhales and exhales, but after a few minutes the pattern settles and it comes naturally.

'So, I was reading the other day,' Matt says after a long while.

Joy cocks her head to the side a little to indicate she's listening.

'It was a Greek myth. About how at the beginning of humanity people had four arms, four legs and two heads. Fearing their power, Zeus split them in two, condemning them to an eternity of searching for their other halves.'

'Well that sounds like a load of crap,' Joy snorts.

'It's not supposed to be true!' Matt slaps her lightly on the arm, chastising her for breaking the romantic moment. 'It's a metaphor.'

Joy turns back around and wriggles into him, leaning her back onto his chest.

'I have two issues with that metaphor,' Joy says in a quiet voice, keeping things conversational. 'Number one, I don't like the idea that we can't be fulfilled unless we partner with a 'soul mate', who may or may not exist. I should be able to find happiness on my own. Sustain myself and be perfectly content with, or without, a man in my life.'

Matt gives her a prolonged hug by way of subtle argument on that point, but she continues.

'Secondly, if Zeus split humans into two halves, I'm assuming one half is a man and one half is a woman. So, where does that leave people who are gay? Are they not entitled to soul mates? Or are they just destined to be unhappy their entire lives no matter what?'

Matt smiles despite himself. He loves how quick Joy is, already looking for problems and taking things to a logical conclusion, trying to see how things might fit in a modern world.

'Well, if you'd have let me finish in the first place, you'd know your second concern is covered. According to the same myth there were previously three genders: male, female and androgynous. Males had two sets of male genitalia. Females had two sets of lady parts.'

Joy laughs at his phrasing.

'And,' Matt continues, 'the androgynous had one of each. So, the other half could be any gender or sex that completes you.'

'Okay, good,' Joy says. 'It's nice to know the Greeks weren't bigots. We could learn something from them.'

'We could learn a lot,' Matt agrees. 'Now, I'd like to address your first point, if you please?'

'By all means,' Joy says, hugging her arms over Matt's.

'I don't think this metaphor has to be about romantic soul mates either. In the myth, Zeus and the other gods were frightened of humans' power when they were united. I think there's a lot to be said for that. People complement each other in lots of different ways. Some are lovers, sure. But there are friends, or business partners, parents and children. Even worthy opponents can sometimes help people find the best in themselves. I think we need other people in our lives to reach our full potential. Not just one person, but many.'

'But your myth also says that people are destined to feel incomplete without someone else. That just strikes me as sad. If people can't love themselves and be content first, how are they supposed to love someone else? How do we know if we really love someone if we're just trying to fill a hole with anyone who helps us *feel* like we're a fuller person? It's like eating a big bag of Nacho Cheese Doritos that are terrible for you, but satisfy your hunger for the moment.'

'I'll be the first to admit that I should chill out on eating so many Doritos,' Matt says, half seriously, half joking. 'But I don't think it's fair to ask people to love themselves completely before they form any kind of relationship. How many people in this world are really content with who they are? Not me, that's for sure.'

'Not me either,' Joy says, surprising Matt with the admission.

'Then who are we to say you have to love yourself first to be complete. Surely you're allowed to find some happiness in others and let them find happiness in you. Some people might not ever learn to love themselves *unless* someone is there to help show them how. If I think to the happiest moments in my life, it's when I was with people like my parents when I was a kid, or the few friends I had growing up, or you. It's when we shut ourselves off from the world that we suffer and stop growing. We need people to remind us that we're enough alone, even if sometimes we don't see it ourselves.'

'Is this your way of saying I was wrong to shut you out?' Joy sounds hurt.

'No!' Matt shakes his head. 'I was talking more about me. I'm trying to say that I need you, Joy. Not *just* you. I think that I need people. Not lots of relationships, but some meaningful ones. I don't like crowds, but I do like company. Are you not a little bit happier when you have someone to share yourself with?'

Joy's prolonged silence after the question makes him look over her shoulder to see her face. She has tears welling in her eyes again.

'Are you not just a little bit happier when I'm here?' Matt presses.

Joy's squeezes her eyes to hold back the tears, but nods.

'Then don't go holding yourself to an ideal of what you *should* be before you let someone in. Be a little bit easier on yourself. God knows I need you to be easy on me. You're enough, Joy. Just as you are.'

'But I don't want to hurt you,' Joy says. 'I don't want you to become a part of me only to have the gods tear us apart again. I don't want to leave you with that hole in your heart.'

'My life's half as much without you anyway,' Matt says in a whisper, like he doesn't want to admit it to himself, let alone Joy. 'I'd rather be whole, even if just for a short time.'

Matt kisses her then. Softly at first, then building to kiss her with everything he has. He lets it radiate out of him. Joy turns around to kiss him fully as well. Matt clutches at her back and pulls her into him, chest to chest. Joy kisses back. Her breath starts to quicken. Her fingernails dig into his back, scratching into him with both pleasure and pain. They gasp as one, finding their rhythm, syncing together. Breathing in and out, in this moment, they feel complete.

Fifty One

Water drips off the eaves outside, sending droplets splashing amongst the garden flowers by the window. Joy is dozing in Matt's arms, purring against him like a cat. She looks so peaceful with her hair resting on the side of her face. Their skin clings to each other's in the light sweat of sleep. The rise and fall of their bodies makes it feel like they're out at sea, adrift on the couch for a raft.

Matt listens as the rain eases to a drizzle. The worst of the cold front is over, but the weather will continue to be cool and overcast for days yet. Winter is approaching in his steady march. Every day will see the sun set earlier and rise a little later. The inevitability of the seasons is a natural paradox; the only constant is change.

Joy stirs. Dragging her lips across Matt's shoulder, she slurps awake. Blinking her eyes, she looks up at Matt. She presses her nose down into his neck and brings her hand up to rest on his chest. After a while she changes position, wriggling her legs out along the couch to lie onto her back. She nestles her head in Matt's lap. He rearranges the doona around them, so he can see her face. She doesn't meet his gaze, staring at the roof instead.

Matt traces her hairline with his fingertips while he watches her.

'Matt,' she sighs, 'what are we going to do? What are we doing?' her eyes finally meet his.

He ponders the question, searching for a deeper answer than the one that rests on his tongue.

'It doesn't really matter,' he finally replies. 'I don't care where we go from here. I just want you to know that I'm here because I want to be.'

'But we can't go anywhere, Matt. I'm...'

'You're whatever happens,' he interrupts, touching her cheek. 'I know what I'm getting myself into.'

'Do you?' Joy sits up, leaving her hand on Matt's leg. 'Do you really know?'

Matt doesn't know, but he doesn't want to admit it. He closes his eyes for a moment.

'I'm just sick of running away from things, Joy. You're the first person in my life that I've felt I can be myself with. That has to mean something.'

Joy doesn't comment. She snuggles back into Matt, guiding his arm around her neck, so his forearms rest on her collarbones. His fingernails brush the back of her earlobe on the left side of her face.

She should weigh more, Matt thinks. As if the mass of her body is something that may help keep her anchored in this world and by losing weight she's letting herself drift off more easily.

'I'm sorry about Peter,' Matt says eventually. 'I feel terrible.'

Joy's body shakes with silent laughter.

'Why are you laughing?' Matt asks. 'It's not funny. I feel bad. I punched him in the nose.'

'I know,' she groans. 'It's all my fault. I'm sorry. He's like a brother to me. I shouldn't have put you in that situation. Rachel was so angry with me.'

'Rachel?'

'Peter's wife,' Joy pauses. 'His real wife.'

'Oh,' Matt remembers the blonde woman.

'You know, it's not the first time he's been hit by a patient's partner.'

'What?' Matt sits up a little.

'He's an oncologist. It's his job to tell people they're dying. Sometimes people react in strange ways.'

'Really?' Matt wonders if she's just saying this to make him feel better.

'Really,' Joy confirms. 'It's like a 'shoot the messenger' reaction or something. He's almost used to it. Honestly, he doesn't hold it against you.'

Matt stays quiet and nods. It doesn't make him feel any better.

'Rachel might though,' she adds.

Now, Matt feels guiltier than ever. He should never have acted so poorly, no matter what.

Again, they lapse into silence. Joy's question still hangs in the air. *What are they going to do?*

The rain patters above, keeping the hush from being unbearable. They both rest, sinking back into a false sense of relaxation. The elephant in the room continues to stalk around them. It's Joy who finally acknowledges it.

'You know, I realise that I'm going to die and I know that the decision isn't up to me, but I just don't believe it. I still don't get it.'

It's a while before Matt responds.

'What do you mean you don't get it?'

'Well, it's like I can't die. I don't know how to explain it. I always thought death was something that happened to other people. I never thought I'd experience it myself. I thought maybe I'd be able to skip it somehow.'

'Everyone dies,' Matt says to the rain outside.

'Yeah, but I don't,' Joy continues. 'I understand what you're saying. Everyone dies: You, me, my mum, everybody. I know this intellectually, but when I think about it properly, I can't understand it. Where do I go? Where does my consciousness go? It's too potent to dissipate just like that,' Joy clicks her fingers to prove her point. 'Even you, right now, you're holding my flesh and blood body in your arms while sitting in your own flesh and blood body. You don't feel like *you're* dying do you? But you are! We all are. We just don't understand it properly. It's like we're in perpetual denial.'

Matt can't answer. He agrees with her, but he won't say it.

'I'm told I only have a few weeks, maybe a month or two and I'm like — that's bullshit. A few weeks! I feel okay. I'm a bit tired and some days I can't get out of bed, but I can still think and talk. This isn't right. It can't be real. I don't have a broken arm with a cast on it, or a cut that I can see getting worse. It's all internal. Maybe if I could see it, then I'd understand it better.'

It doesn't seem real, even to Matt. The entity of Joy is alive in his arms. She's a part of him. For that to cease feels impossible. It can't happen. At twenty-five, mortality is a concept beyond his realm of comprehension.

'So, what are we going to do?' Matt repeats Joy's question. 'What are we doing?'

'For now, we're living, Matt,' Joy pats his arms. 'The rest will take its course.'

'That's not what I meant.' Matt says, 'What are we doing to fight this? I can't just sit here and accept you're dying.'

Joy lets out a big sigh.

'Peter says the cancer is too advanced for me to do anything. It's in my pancreas, my bowel, right through. Surgery would be useless and chemo would just make my last days a misery. He offered to do it anyway and I said no. He wants to try radiotherapy and I said no too. He's grasping at straws.'

'But if there's a chance -'

'There's not,' Joy says. 'I went through the same with my mum. She was so afraid of dying that she spent her last days wasting what time she had left searching for a cure. Trying all sorts of snake oils and faith healing.'

'So, there aren't any alternatives?'

'Kisses,' Joy gives Matt a kiss on his hand.

Fifty One

'Come on,' Matt says, his heart breaking. 'I'm trying to be serious.'

'My mum always said she wished kisses cured cancer. That if love were the answer to everything she would never die, because she had me and dad to give her all the treatment she needed. I would kiss her a thousand times a day, every chance I got, wishing it were true.' She kisses Matt on the hand again, staring at the ceiling. 'But it wasn't enough. No amount of hugs, or chemo, or radio, or apricot kernels, or shark cartilage, or coffee enemas, could stop her body from betraying her. They might work for some people, but not for her. It was her time and she refused to accept it. I can't blame her. I feel the same. I can't be dying. I can't. But I must be. I'll be damned if I waste my time chasing unicorn cures that don't exist.'

'So that's it? You're just giving up?' Matt is angry. Not at Joy, but at the situation. Still it sounds like he's judging her.

'No,' Joy says patiently. 'I'm on a strict no-sugar diet which is supposed to inhibit tumour growth. I'm meditating daily. Peter is getting me some cannabis oil for the pain, and on the off chance it does something more. If it can buy me some time, then I'll be grateful. But if I see a big sugary ice-cream that I want to lick, I'm not going to hold back. I'm not going to get hysterical

351

about dying,' she pauses, reflecting on her last statement. 'I might get hysterical about living though.'

'What does that mean?' Matt asks, seeing a shift in her.

'It means I don't want to act like a patient. I want to go out with you and relish what time we can find.'

'Like stealing minutes?'

'More like stealing moments,' she says with determination. 'Why try to extend your time, when you should just make the most of it instead? We're not doing anything boring from here on out. We're going to take the bull by the horns, carpé the fucking diem and just about any other worn out expression you can think of. It will be Joy and Matt exploring the world!'

'Okay,' Matt says, wanting badly to fulfil Joy's wishes. 'What's the first thing we should do?' he asks.

'New things, novel things, things we've never tried before,' Joy says, 'but also everyday things, things we can do again and again and not get tired of. People should be able to find magic in the everyday if they want lasting happiness. Let's look for that magic, in case I do live forever.'

Joy turns around with a mischievous look in her eyes, pushing him down onto the couch.

'First, I'm going to explore you,' she says. 'We can figure out the rest after I've experienced your everyday magic. Again. And again. And again.'

352

Fifty Two

I 've always wanted to do it.' Joy exclaims from the kitchen, clapping her hands together. 'That's it, we're going, today! How have you never done it?'

'I don't know,' Matt says, shaking his head as he sits on Joy's couch. 'I was always so uncoordinated, I just avoided it.'

'But you live on the coast!' Joy starts searching for her phone on the bench and finds it amongst a pile of magazines. 'Surfing is like the national pastime down here. You can't live at the beach and not at least try it!'

'Well, I never did,' Matt says, folding his arms. 'I'm not sure it's a good idea either. What if you hurt yourself?'

Joy raises her eyebrows at Matt as she clutches her phone.

'What's it going to do? Kill me? Is that the worst that can happen?'

The statement silences Matt's argument.

Over the past few days, Joy had been primal in her lust for Matt. In between him fulfilling her every sexual desire and kink, he was able to retreat home for a breather and some clean clothing. Peter had given him instructions on how to care for Joy. To watch for any signs of mental abnormality, drops in energy, stomach pain, unprompted vomiting, nose bleeds, the list went on. She seemed to be defying any idea of fading away. If anything, her energy was returning. Perhaps it was the cannabis oil Peter had delivered with strict instructions to keep it quiet and under no circumstances say it came from him. Joy took it at night-time before bed so she could sleep through the drowsiness it gave her.

'Look at me, Matt,' Joy presses. 'I'm not going to die without surfing at least once. I'm booking a lesson.'

The waves roll into the bay as they stand on the shore and watch. The day is grey and chilly, but it does nothing to dampen Joy's spirits. Four English backpackers are also along for the lesson. Two guys and two girls, who had refused wetsuits because they consider any temperature in double digits tropical. They all squish their toes down into the sand, crouching next to big softboards, dry-docked on the water's edge. The boards only faintly resemble the small fibreglass craft that Matt has watched the 'real' surfers use. These are twice the size, made of foam with slick plastic bottoms on them. Joy lies down on her board and pretends she's paddling, scraping her fingers along the damp sand. Her grin is as wide as can be and they haven't even hit the water yet. She's wearing a black and hot-pink wetsuit, slightly loose against her pint-sized frame. Matt forces his body into his own neoprene costume. He wonders how many people have pissed in the thing before him, but doesn't voice his concerns. The rubber of the suit sucks against his body, making him feel claustrophobic. Ignoring the sensation, he asks Joy to help him with the zipper. Finally all tucked in, he's ready to go too.

The surf instructor paces around the group with his wetsuit pulled down to the waist, showing off his rippling six-pack. He's one of the local surf heroes Matt has seen in the newspaper. Part Aboriginal, he has a perfect set of teeth and black curly hair. All of the females in the group watch him with drooling eyes. All of the men watch him with barely concealed envy. He sees Matt has finally changed and holds his hand in the air to get everyone's attention.

'Okay surfers,' he announces, 'It's small day out there, ideal for our lesson. But even on days like this, the ocean can be a dangerous place. If you're ever in trouble, hold one hand in the air like I am now and call my name, Dan. I'll come and help. We're going to go for a short jog to warm up. Any questions?'

The sound of crashing waves is the only response.

'Okay, let's go.'

The beginning of the lesson feels like school phys ed class to Matt. He and Joy run along the beach side by side. He is even less fit than he had realised. After one short lap of the beach, Matt's face is burning with exertion. They partner up to stretch, leaning against each other to perform one-legged quad flexes. Once they've worked through their legs, backs and arms, Matt has regained his breath. Dan instructs them all to line up their boards in a row and lie on them. Matt grunts onto his stomach, glad for the rest.

'Alright everyone. Now, I want you to bring your hands up next to your chest and grip the sides of the board. Keep your feet together near the tail. After you've done that, straighten your arms, arch your back and hold.'

The group all follow his cue and, like a pack of self-supporting cobras, they rise up into a snake position.

'Alright, great! This is a good way to get your balance on the waves. Catch a couple of rollers to the sand and brace yourself like this before you try to stand up. Once you're comfortable doing that, it's easy to pop up to standing. Pop!'

Demonstrating his advice, Dan jumps up on his board and crouches into the surfing position.

'Now you try. Pop.'

The English backpackers laugh and jump up at his command, making their own popping noises as they bounce upward. Joy is like a cat in her movements, graceful and natural as she springs into position. Matt feels like an oaf in comparison. He clambers to his feet each time, dragging his knee.

'Okay, let's hit the waves!' Dan announces, picking up his board and leading the pack into the water.

Laughing, hooting, swearing and panting, the group of learners swish around in the sea. Dan moves like a fish between them, darting and dodging stray boards, pushing some people into waves and shouting encouragement at others. The English girls are already standing up and riding waves to the beach. Every time they finish a wave they squeal with happiness and start guiding their boards back out for another ride.

Matt finds it difficult to negotiate his way through the breakers with such a big board to hold onto. He tries to steady it in the water and push it along in front of him. A waist-high wave slaps the board up, which hits him in the stomach and knocks the wind out of him. Crouching over in pain, Matt wades back to the shallows to gain his breath. As he walks, Joy zips past him on a wave.

'Woooooohooooo!' she shouts, waving at Matt as she glides past. She takes it all the way to the sand and steps off onto the beach like an expert.

'Matt! Did you see that? Did you see it? I was like Kelly Slater!' Joy exclaims, running up to him with her board in tow, splashing her happiness into the air.

Matt manages to smile at her enthusiasm before returning to his world of pain.

'That was amazing, Joy. Really cool.'

'I told you it would be fun. Are you okay?' Joy looks at him with concern.

'Yeah, I'm alright. I'm just going to take a rest for a minute. I'll watch.'

'Are you sure?'

'Really. Go and get another one, I'll watch,' he repeats.

'Yes! Alright, you'd better watch me.'

Joy looks like a little girl, elated at the discovery of a new toy. She sticks out her tongue and wades away, heading back out to the line-up. Matt imagines her clicking her heels with glee under the water every time she jumps over a wave. The sight makes him forget that he's not having any fun of his own. It is truly enough for him that she's living out a new experience.

After half an hour of steady circuits, the group start to grow tired. One by one they return to the beach and join Matt, sitting on their boards, exhausted. Joy is the last one to come in. She catches a long roller, riding it directly past Dan who is standing in waist-deep water. As she sails past, he reaches out and she gives him a high five. As Joy skips up the beach, it looks like her eyes are going to pop with pleasure.

'Did you see that one!' she yells, running up to Matt. 'That was the best one yet!'

'Ten out of ten,' Matt laughs. 'You're a natural.'

'She sure is!' Dan adds, as he joins the group. 'I think Joy caught more waves than anyone today!'

The backpackers give a hoot of agreement.

'Ha,' Matt smiles. 'She certainly caught more than me. I couldn't even manage to get out the back!'

'What?' Dan's face turns serious. 'You mean you didn't get to stand up on one?'

'Nah, but it's okay,' Matt waves it off, 'I just enjoyed seeing Joy have a good time.'

'I don't think so, mate,' Dan puts his hands on his hips. 'It says on my brochure that we'll have you standing up, or your money back.'

'No really, it's alright.' The thought of going back out into the ocean seems too draining for Matt.

'Nonsense,' Dan persists. 'What do you think, everyone? Are you happy to hang here while we get Matt a quick ride?'

'Yeah!' the group clap in answer.

'Come on, Matt,' Joy chimes in next to him. 'Give it a go. It's incredible.'

Matt doesn't like group pressure. He has never been able to resist it in the past.

'But I can't even get my board past the breakers,' Matt protests.

'Easy!' Dan fobs it off. 'I'll paddle the board out, you can swim beside me. Once we're in green water we can swap and I'll push you onto one.'

Dan picks up Matt's board and starts walking down to the water.

'Go on, Matt.' Joy gives him a friendly push. 'It's my turn to watch.'

Unable to resist, Matt plunges into the sea. Catching up to Dan, he wades in silence next to his coach, who manoeuvres the board effortlessly over the waves. Matt's heart drums like a quickening death march. Without the surfboard as a hindrance, Matt finds it simple to swim in the surf. It's not long before he's bobbing in the ocean next to Dan, who is sitting comfortably on the foam plank of a surfboard.

'You ready for this, mate?' he looks down at Matt with a relaxed smile. 'You jump on and I'll get you on a good one.'

Dan's confidence instils some much-needed assurance in Matt, who is now terrified by the prospect of trying to get to his feet in front of a small crowd.

Wobbling onto the board, Matt finally finds the sweet spot, lying in a prone position facing the beach. He looks over his shoulder at Dan expectantly.

'Alright, now we just sit and wait,' Dan instructs him, fastening the board's legrope around Matt's ankle. 'I can see a set coming. We'll go over the first wave and take the second one okay?'

Matt nods.

'As soon as you feel the tail of the board lifting up, I want you to push up with your arms and arch your back to steady yourself. Once the wave has you, jump to your feet.'

These basic instructions make it sound like surfing is the easiest thing ever.

'Okay here we go, mate. Here we go, get ready!'

Matt lays flat on the board gripping the rails hard and Dan swings him into position. The first wave of the set rises and falls gently underneath them. Matt watches as its back rears up before folding down in a plume of spray, crashing into the sand. The sound is more violent than Matt expected. No, this is a bad idea.

'Ready, set, here it comes. Start paddling!'

'Wait...' Matt says weakly.

Dan starts kicking behind Matt and they gather some momentum. The swell lifts the tail and Dan gives the board a shove.

'Paddle, paddle, paddle!'

The wave pitches up hard and Matt feels himself being propelled forward.

'Lean back!' he hears, above the hissing roar all around him.

Matt can't respond. Instead, he grips onto the board tighter, hugging it as the tail rises up. The nose of the board starts to dig into the base of the wave, sending jets of water into his eyes. As if in slow motion, Matt becomes weightless. Then, time catches up in a rushing whoosh and water explodes around him. Matt's feet kick up into the air and he tumbles like a scorpion over the front of his board. Crashing down beneath the surface his limbs are pulled in opposite directions by the washing machine around him. Matt opens his eyes, but everything is a blur of sand and water. His lungs start to cry out for oxygen. In the tumbling mess, Matt's feet somehow find the bottom. With a desperate lunge, he kicks off and propels himself upward. Breaking into the light, he sucks in air a fraction too early, sending watery foam shooting into his windpipe. Gasping and struggling with himself, Matt tries to get life into his body. He is kicking frantically to stay above the surface.

'Matt!' he hears Dan yell. 'It's okay, mate, just put your feet down and relax. Relax, you can stand up here.'

In confusion, Matt probes downward with his toes. He hits hard sand. Thank God. He draws in crisp, life-giving air. Dan is right next to him, with a staunch look on his face.

'Matt, you should have leaned back. That was a cracker of a wave. You'll get it on the next one, I promise.'

'Next one?' Matt lets out a wracking cough. 'I'm done.'

'Nah, you're alright.' Dan claps him on the back. 'Come on. Your lady's watching you. That was the worst possible wipeout you could have had today and look at you, you're fine. Just a little spin cycle.'

Dan's casual tone makes Matt think maybe he is overreacting. He looks up to the shore to see Joy standing and watching with the rest of the group. Maybe Dan is right; it was just a bit of a tumble. It was just water.

'Okay,' Matt gulps, swallowing his pride, 'just one more try.'

'Great!'

This time, Dan makes Matt paddle around a little bit out the back, just to get comfortable on the board. He instructs Matt to do laps, building up enough momentum to glide for a few seconds in the cobra position before lying down and paddling again. Gaining familiarity with the surfboard helps Matt calm down.

'Matt, you're going to get into this one yourself I reckon,' Dan encourages him. 'When I tell you to go, you face towards the shore and paddle with everything you have. Don't go until I say so, okay?'

Matt nods his determination. The last wipeout had invigorated him somehow, as if by surviving that, he could survive anything. He watches the horizon and waits for his chance. A few faint lines start to appear out the back.

'Is this the one?' Matt asks Dan, who looks out toward the set.

'This is the one alright. Are you ready? You're going to nail it.'

'I'm ready,' Matt says, stealing a quick glance at the beach to make sure Joy is watching.

'Here it comes, Matt. Wait. Wait. Now! Go! Paddle!'

Matt puts his head down, digging his arms into the sea. The craft gains speed and the same rising of the tail begins to lift his board. He scratches in hard, paddling to match the speed of the wave, soaring already. Bringing his hands up, he leans back and sets his sights on the shore. This is it.

As the wave peaks, Matt leaps to his feet. He wobbles, but the shooting speed of the board catches up with him and offers some stability as he streaks down the green face. Churning behind him, the wave lifts up and dumps, but Matt outpaces the white water. It surges to catch up and abruptly shunts the board forward again. The burst of speed causes Matt to lean too far forward and he loses balance. Before he falls off though, he gives a little salute to Joy who is jumping up and down on the beach. Matt is now a surfer.

The rest of the group cheers Matt as he drags his board up the sand. Dan is trailing just behind him, beaming at the success of his lesson.

'I told you it was awesome,' Joy says, as Matt approaches.

He can only smile his agreement. Lightning is tingling all through his body. His core is charged with achievement. If this is what he felt like just catching one small wave, what do those madmen feel like when they get a monster?

Matt hugs Joy tightly and lifts her a little bit off the ground.

'Thank you, Joy,' he whispers in her ear, hugging her again.

'Thank *you,*' she kisses him.

Even though there are clouds overhead, sunshine surrounds the pair as they bask in the triumph of the day.

Fifty Three

Joy's face is placid in the calm of sleep. Her long eyelashes curl upward toward her forehead, like a row of black vines searching for the light. As a result of the big outing yesterday, Joy had crashed in the afternoon. She fell asleep in the lounge room before Matt scooped her up and carried her to bed. Now at 9:00 a.m., Matt is beginning to think she might sleep forever. In her peaceful state, he admires her stunning features. They are a symmetry of perfection. There is a faint smile on her lips, like she knows something that Matt doesn't.

He thinks that if this were the picture of death, then he too would welcome eternal bliss. Wrapping his arm around her, Matt snuggles into Joy's body, absorbing the heat of her slumber.

Joy's room is spacious. Located at the tail end of the house, it faces north to capture all of the sun of the day. It doesn't matter what time it is, if the sun is above the horizon, its rays make it through this window that overlooks the backyard. Hanging above the bed is a large photo of a woman. At first, Matt had assumed it was Joy, but then noticed subtle differences. Without having to ask, he had concluded that it was Joy's mother, watching over her always.

Joy begins to stir, drawing Matt's attention back to his sleeping beauty. She still has her eyes closed, but her expression has turned to a frown.

'Are you awake?' he asks softly.

'No,' Joy answers grumpily, her eyes clamped shut. 'I'm still sleeping.'

'You stay sleeping,' Matt kisses her eyelids. 'I'll make us some breakfast. Are you hungry?'

'No,' she stuffs her head into her pillow. 'Sleeping people can't be hungry.'

'Okay, I'll make something anyway. You just stay here.'

Sliding out from under the covers, Matt slips a t-shirt over his head and pulls on some pants. Padding into the kitchen as quietly as possible, he fills the kettle and finds a pan in a cupboard near the fridge. Whistling softly to himself, he goes about preparing a modest breakfast. The aroma of coffee perks him up. Poached eggs bubble away in shallow water. Matt notices some mail on the bench addressed to Joy. He sees her last name is Hannigan. Matt shakes his head. He still has so much to learn about her. Fresh toast jumps out of the toaster with a clang. Pop! It reminds him of Dan the surf coach. After slicing some avocado, Matt arranges the meal onto a well-presented plate for Joy. He feels good about doing something special for her, even if it isn't a huge effort.

Still whistling, Matt carefully carries the laden tray into the bedroom, where Joy still has her head buried in the pillow.

'Room service. Did you ask for a handsome man with eggs?'

Rolling lazily onto her back, she opens her eyes and stretches her arms above her head with a yawn. Rubbing the sleep from her eyes, she starts to sit up, pulling the covers up to keep her warm.

'Wow,' she says, eying the food. 'Did I die in my sleep and go to Heaven? What did I do to deserve this?'

'Just being you,' smiles Matt, placing the tray down on the bedside table. 'Now, do you want salt or pepper?'

'No, thanks. Phew, I don't know if I can eat all of this, Matt. I don't have much of an appetite.'

'Just eat what you can,' he says casually, 'whatever you don't have, I'll finish. I'll be back in a second. I'll grab mine and we can eat here together.'

He returns to find that Joy has barely touched her food. Using the knife and fork she is cutting everything into tiny pieces and is spreading it out into sections. Matt sits down and watches her as he devours his own eggs in big gulps. In between mouthfuls he looks up at the photo above the bed.

'What was your mum's name?' Matt asks.

She turns to see the image, staring at it for a while. 'Lucinda.'

'Lucinda,' Matt repeats the name. 'It sounds beautiful.'

'She was in every way,' Joy says. Staring at her plate like it's Mount Everest, she chews another small mouthful of food, then takes a small sip of her coffee. She sighs.

'What's wrong?' Matt asks her. 'I'm sorry if asking about your mum makes you sad.'

'No, it's not that. I just haven't had any desire to eat lately. It's a proper effort to force things down.'

'But you have to eat,' he presses calmly. 'You're too skinny as it is.'

'I know, I know,' Joy nods, looking back down to the plate.

To appease Matt, Joy takes her fork and scoops a portion of food into her mouth. She chews and chews painstakingly, before taking a big swallow. After only a few seconds, Joy retches loudly, regurgitating the food all over the blankets in front of her. Egg yolk splatters the white linen.

'Oh shit. Shit,' Matt jumps to his feet, as Joy vomits again.

She struggles to move and the plate on her lap slides off the bed, clattering to the ground. Ignoring the plate, Matt rushes to Joy's side and starts patting her on the back,

'Shit, are you alright?'

Joy coughs a little, before waving Matt away.

'It's okay, I'm alright. It's just a little spew, that's all.'

Matt is shaking at the confronting display. *A little spew?* Everything had seemed so settled before she just brought it all up. Zero warning. It had just come up out of nowhere. He stands, not wanting to clean anything until he knows Joy is okay.

'Joy, are you sure you're alright? Do you feel sick?'

'No,' she shakes her head. 'This happens sometimes. It's nothing.'

'Nothing? Joy you just vomited. It can't be nothing!'

Joy casts the sheets aside and climbs out of bed, swaying on her feet. Matt jumps in to hold her up.

'It's fine, Matt,' she says weakly in his arms. 'I'll be fine. I just need some water.'

'Get back into bed and I'll bring you some. Just stay here.'

He forces Joy to sit back down. Gathering the dirty top blanket off the bed, Matt dumps it in the laundry on the way to the kitchen before hurrying back with a glass of water. Joy is sitting up, still a bit pale, but looking somewhat recovered. Taking the water from Matt, she takes a tiny sip and then leans back into her pillows. She stays there for a few moments before having another drink.

'Peter told us this would happen more and more, remember?' Joy says to Matt. 'You can't let it worry you.'

'How can I not?' answers Matt.

'It's nothing,' Joy repeats. 'The cancer puts a big strain on my lymph nodes. Sometimes they swell up and constrict my throat. It makes it hard to swallow solid food, that's all.'

Matt doesn't understand how she can take it with such grace.

'Isn't there anything we can do about it?' he pleads, feeling useless. 'Isn't there any kind of medication you can take for it?'

'I have those steroids. It doesn't treat anything though, they just keep me a bit stronger.'

'I think we should go in for a check-up,' Matt says.

'Nah,' Joy says, sitting up again. 'We should clean this up and then go and do something.'

Matt looks around at the floor. There is still egg and bread and avocado on the ground, splattered like a conceptual art piece through the carpet.

'I think maybe you should just rest for the day, Joy,' Matt says, concerned. 'Maybe we overdid it with the surfing. I'll clear this away. You sleep.'

'No way,' Joy says, swinging her legs over the side of the bed again. 'A little bit of vomit isn't going to stop me from living my life super-size style. Don't you have uni to go to today? We can do that.' she continues.

'I'm supposed to,' Matt gets on his knees and starts picking up the scattered remnants of breakfast. 'But I think we should just relax for the minute.'

'Let's go to uni,' she ignores him. 'I'll come with you. I'd love to see where you learn.'

'Joy, no. Come on. There's no way you're going anywhere. We can't keep pushing and pushing until you drop. Just stop and take a breath. Please.'

'No,' Joy says, crossing her arms over her chest. 'I'll help you wash this up and then we'll crash your lectures. They won't even notice I'm there.'

'They won't because we're not going.'

'Yes we are.' Joy stands up and walks to her wardrobe, flinging it open. 'So, what do students wear these days?'

Matt hangs his head down. He can't fight Joy while she pretends Death's impending hand doesn't already have its fingers on her shoulder. He may as well help her focus on what life is ahead.

Fifty Four

Dr Byron's voice echoes around the walls of the lecture theatre. Joy leans forward on her seat to capture every syllable being delivered. Rather than standing behind a lectern and microphone, the shorn-headed Byron stalks around the room. Her undulating tone keeps everyone captured on the subject matter. The lecture is supposed to be about Joseph Conrad's *Heart of Darkness,* but Byron talks about other works that it has influenced, like T.S. Eliot's poem *The Hollow Men* and Francis Ford Coppola's masterwork film *Apocalypse*

Now. The lecture ends not with a whimper, but with a bang when she plays a clip from *Apocalypse Now* set to Wagner's classical song *Ride of the Valkyries.* As the final shuddering explosions go off, helicopters bombing the fleeing Vietcong soldiers with incendiary napalm, Byron narrates the ending lines of the book: 'the horror, the horror'.

As her words die to a whisper, Byron promptly exits the theatre.

The entire audience sits stunned at what is better described as a performance than a lecture. Joy grips Matt's arm.

'I think I want to come to uni every day!'

Matt looks back at her, unable to speak for a few moments.

'It's not always like this,' he says, shaking his head in disbelief.

'It gets better?' she asks, wide-eyed.

'No. You should see my journalism lectures. They'd put you to sleep.'

Matt picks up his bag and shuffles out along the cramped row of seats. They follow the plodding lambs of young pupils into the brightness of the day, back to the reality of campus. People are walking around in all directions, like uncoordinated flocks of birds.

'So what are we doing now?' Joy asks Matt, as they make their way through the press of bodies.

'Well, we can probably go and get something to eat. My next tute isn't until two o'clock.'

'What? But there's so much to learn. Can't we just go to another lecture?'

'It doesn't work like that, Joy. The classes I'm enrolled in have a set schedule, you can't just turn up in any place at any time and hope people will be talking about something relevant.'

'What's relevance got to do with it?' Joy asks, halting their walk. 'What did you enrol in uni for?'

'To get a degree,' Matt answers, turning back to her impatiently.

'What about getting an education?' she counters, not budging as students walk around her in an endless mass.

'It's the same thing,' Matt huffs.

'No way. You want to get a piece of paper saying you passed something. You're looking at it all the wrong way. You should be here to learn.'

'I am!'

As Matt raises his voice, some of the passersby turn their heads at the outburst.

'Well let's go and learn,' Joy ignores the stares.

'Learn what?' Matt moves closer to her, trying to avoid a scene. 'I'm enrolled in an Arts degree. I can't go to the Law Faculty and drop in on a class about criminal legislation or something, it's not allowed.'

Joy smirks at Matt's comment, like what he's said is ridiculous.

'Matt, I'm not supposed to be here and no one has even looked at me sideways since we arrived. It seems like you can pretty much go wherever you want. It's not like we're stealing anything. The teachers are presenting anyway and there are spare seats in the room.'

'So?'

'So, I can get all the knowledge I want here for free. You're doing it all wrong. I don't even know why you're paying for this, or why you enrolled at all. You should be getting a guerrilla education. You should be taking advantage and just sliding in wherever you like.'

'A guerrilla education?' Matt asks puzzled. 'I think maybe you've lost it.'

'No. Don't you see?' Joy slaps Matt on the chest. 'You're not coming here to get a qualification. An Arts degree doesn't qualify you for anything anyway! You're coming here to be a writer. All the best writers know something about everything. You need to be going to every class you can, even if it's just for people watching.'

'But what would the point be?' Matt screws up his nose.

Joy throws her hands up in the air in exasperation, like she's speaking to a child.

'The point is that you *learn*. Who cares about passing tests, as long as you have the knowledge at the end, right? As long as you can figure out the necessary tools to become a writer, then you've achieved your goal.'

'I guess so,' Matt concedes reluctantly.

'I know so,' Joy smiles at her victory.

She looks around at the campus with a big grin on her face and makes a show of breathing air into her lungs.

'I wish I had been living like this all along,' Joy says excitedly, peering around at the people walking by. 'I wish I knew I was dying from a younger age. You need to realise it too, Matt. Start doing exactly what you want, because in the end, that's all you need to do.'

'I am doing what I want. Or at least I hope I am.'

Matt is confused at Joy's line of thought. He wonders if this falls under the category of 'mental abnormalities' that Peter was talking about. He shuffles closer to her, in case she's about to have another vomiting episode. She appears normal, if a little wound up.

'What if I said you could only do one thing before you die? What would it be?' Joy asks him.

'I want to write a book. I just don't know what to write about.'

'Then let's figure it out!' Joy yells, stamping her foot on the ground. 'We're not going to find out standing here like a couple of pork chops. Let's experience something different. Let's live!'

'What if I said you could only do one thing before *you* die, what would it be?' Matt says.

'Learn more!' she exclaims.

She grabs a passing student by the arm and stops him. The young Indian man looks completely taken aback by this wild woman with tiger's eyes.

'Excuse me,' she says, batting her eyes at him. 'What class are you heading to?'

'Ah, I'm on my way to a lecture on theoretical physics,' he stutters, looking at Joy like maybe he's supposed to know her.

'Theoretical physics, eh?' she says, looking impressed at the title. 'And what is the topic about specifically?'

'I think it's going to be about black holes,' he answers, looking from her to Matt, who is trying to pretend he's not part of the conversation.

'Perfect!' she exclaims, turning to Matt pointedly. 'We might learn about time travel. Let's go!'

Matt rolls his eyes and follows Joy, who is already trailing behind her new friend. If this is what she wants, then this is what she wants, but he has a nagging sensation that she's only doing and seeing the things that are right in front of her, rather than seeking out the deeper meaning for herself.

Fifty Five

Matt lies awake next to the slumbering Joy. He's been in the grips of insomnia all night. Staring in the dark with lifeless eyes, he thinks about the manic day they experienced at university. Joy had dragged Matt around campus, moving from lecture to lecture: ranging from education, science, law, marketing and even statistical mathematics. If they found the material boring, they would quietly exit out the back door. When it was engaging, Joy would raise her hand and ask some questions, even though it wasn't polite to do so in lectures.

In the end, Matt had missed his journalism tutorial. They were engrossed in a philosophy lecture about Aristotle and his theory that the best life is one lived in the virtuous pursuit of true knowledge. According to Aristotle, it was a person's goal to learn, since rationality is a unique characteristic known only to humans. Joy had interrupted, asking why thinking had to be the only thing unique to humans: why couldn't it be creating art? This had sparked a furious debate mid-lecture amongst the class. At the end of the session, the professor had thanked her for initiating the question. He said that learning was at its peak when in discussion, rather than in inert listening.

Everything is still. There is no noise outside. Not even a wisp of wind. Matt turns to look at the digital clock beside the bed: It's almost 4:00 a.m. Why hasn't he been able to sleep? He should be tired. Joy is certainly dead to the world. She's like an immovable log next to him. She was out like a light as soon as her head had hit the pillow. Matt tries to close his eyes, but they keep springing open. Out the window, a full moon hangs in the sky like a ripe, silver fruit. Its reflective light illuminates the night sky, without dimming the stars around it. Matt thinks that the moon would make a better person than the sun. It is less selfish. The sun has to be so bright that nothing else can even be seen in its direct presence. The moon, however, is happy to share the night with other smaller entities. It is a benevolent god.

Matt is restless while the world rests. Joy is completely inanimate. Her skin glows like the light of the moon: pale, yet radiant. Her body could be a statue it's so still.

Maybe she's a little too still.

Matt leans in close, trying to detect if he can hear her breathing. There is no sound. He puts his hand on her chest, to see if he can feel it rising. He can't perceive any movement. He waits. He's not sure if the heartbeat he can feel is hers, or his own thumping organ that is now throbbing in his ears. Matt becomes panic stricken.

Is she dead? She's not breathing. *But she's warm.*

'Joy,' Matt shakes her, 'Joy!'

A low moan escapes her mouth and she rolls over, away from Matt.

'What? I'm sleeping,' she mumbles.

Matt lies back down and pulls his hand away. He stares upward. Maybe he's going crazy. It's not like he's seeing things, but maybe it's worse that he's not seeing things that are actually there. Isn't that still some kind of delusion?

Matt tries to lie as still as possible, so Joy won't notice that he woke her. He hopes she'll think it was just a dream and drop away again. He forces his fingers to play dead. He makes his legs into tree trunks.

'What time is it?' Joy cuddles into him. 'Is it morning?'

'It's still dark,' he whispers. 'It's not even four o'clock.'

'It's the time for spirits,' Joy says drowsily. 'Why aren't you asleep?'

'I don't know.'

Joy props herself up on her elbow and looks down at Matt. She caresses his chest with her spare hand. Noticing the brightness of the moon outside, she stares at it for a while.

'Why don't we go outside and have a cup of tea?' she says, in a question that's not a question.

'Because it's bedtime.'

'Who says so?' she smiles, her eyes slowly losing their dreamlike character. 'Come on. We can have the world to ourselves for an hour. Just the two of us, alone in the suburbs. Let's do it.'

'But I'm tired,' Matt lies.

'No you're not. You woke me up. Come on. Let's go,' Joy throws back the blankets. 'Sometimes you need to step outside when you're not supposed to.'

Getting up, Joy retrieves a jumper from the floor and a pair of pants from her wardrobe. She slips her feet into a pair of ugg boots. Matt watches her, but doesn't move.

'I'll put the kettle on,' she says in a normal voice, like it's the middle of the day. 'I'll meet you out there. Bring the blanket with you.'

Staying in the cosiness of the bed for a bit longer, Matt looks out the window again. It seems illogical to be going outside for a drink at this time, but the idea does seem kind of thrilling in its own quirky way. He listens to the noise of the kettle boiling. In the quiet of the room, it sounds like rain floating down the hallway.

Matt drags the covers with him as he gets up, wrapping them about his body in a protective cloak. With bare feet, he walks into the lounge. Joy isn't there, but the front door is wide open. Poking his head outside, he sees that she has taken two chairs onto the nature strip and is sitting, waiting for him. She has her back to the house and a steaming drink is placed on the empty chair next to her, ready for Matt.

Still naked underneath, Matt pulls the doona tighter around him. Easing down next to Joy, he picks up his drink. A freezing draft of air wafts into his portable cave, but he locks the sheets around him again and the temperature of the tea in his hands helps dissipate the chill.

A thin layer of mist hangs above the road, which is devoid of any life. Frost twinkles under the streetlights on the manicured lawns in front of cookie-cutter houses. They squat like identical phantoms along the strip.

'It's like the Zombie Apocalypse has come through town and we're the only ones left,' Joy comments, slurping her tea.

Matt nods, assessing the scene.

'It *is* a bit like a horror movie, isn't it?'

'Horror?' Joy looks at Matt. 'It's beautiful. It's like this planet exists just for us. Imagine it. We'd be able to walk the streets naked and sing and dance and no one would stop us. Planet Joy.'

'Don't get any ideas,' Matt smiles at her.

They lapse back into silence. It occurs to Matt that a world without people might actually be a much better place. A world without people, except for him and Joy.

'What do you want most out of life?' Joy asks thoughtfully.

Matt looks down at the dwindling tea in his cup. He sets it down on the ground and shuffles his chair closer to Joy's, putting his blankets around her as well. Bringing his legs up, he puts them over hers.

'I don't really know,' he ponders. 'Maybe that's my problem.'

Matt kisses Joy subtly on the ear.

'What do you want?' he asks her.

She cradles her tea in her hands.

'I just want to be happy.'

It seems to be the only answer that could have come out of her lips. She leans in and rubs her nose onto Matt's.

'And what makes you happy?' Matt wonders after a while.

'I used to think having a purpose would do that,' she says, 'I used to want to change the world, just a tiny bit. I wanted to help people. That's why I became a teacher.'

'Has that changed?'

'Maybe. I'm not sure teaching people two plus two fundamentally changes kid's lives. Repeating facts from a book doesn't seem to alter their nature. I tried to instil in them a thirst for life, like my mum had for me, but I'll never really know if I ever got through. At the end of each year they drift off into the world and you don't really have any meaningful contact with them after that. Sure, you bump into them down the street. You can see how they live and fantasise that part of the good in their lives was because of you, but you never really know. You don't get to stop, sit them down and ask them what you meant to them.'

'That would be a little strange,' Matt says.

'It would be inappropriate at least,' Joy laughs.

'Well, you've made a difference to me,' Matt says. 'Maybe saved my life.'

Joy looks over at Matt, taking his hand.

'You don't have to comfort me, I'm content with what I've done. It's all I could have done.'

'I'm serious,' Matt squeezes her palm. 'I thought about killing myself before I met you, Joy. I even stood up on the lookout and looked down.'

'Oh, Matt,' Joy whispers. 'You didn't.'

'But you've pulled me out of that,' Matt says. 'That sadness might come back sometimes if you go, but instead of looking at blackness as the only way out, I can now look up. I can look forward. There's always something I won't have learned, or experienced and that's okay. But I'm going to try to do as much as I can. Life is about moments, like this,' Matt leans in and kisses Joy lightly on the lips. 'If you've taught me anything, you've taught me that.'

'I love you,' Joy whispers, nuzzling her face into Matt's neck.

'I love you too,' Matt whispers.

He wraps his arms tighter around the beautiful soul clinging onto him. He can feel the dampness of her tears running down his skin. In the distance, a rubbish truck rumbles and clangs into their planet. Matt looks up to see the sun is starting to impress its glow on the start of the day.

'Let's go to bed,' Matt says. 'I want you to myself just a little bit longer.'

Fifty Six

It's past noon before they wake again. Matt feels completely rested. He slept with a depth that can only be achieved by waking up and going back to sleep again. It's like his body has melted completely into the mattress and become a part of it.

Joy is still dozing. Her limbs are twitching in a dream. Matt finds it comical to watch her movements and hear the small whimpers that escape her lips. After one particularly intense shudder, she sparks awake and opens her eyes to see him watching her.

'Good afternoon,' he yawns. 'What do you want for dinner?'

Joy sits up quickly and looks outside.

'Oh no! Have we wasted the day? What time is it?'

'Relax, you needed the rest. It's almost two. I haven't been up yet either. It's too comfy in here.'

Matt leans in and pecks Joy on the cheek. She twists to face him, so their lips collide in a single breathtaking kiss, before pushing away again.

'We can still do something this afternoon if you like,' Matt offers. 'Skydiving, drag car racing, whatever you want.'

Joy slumps back onto the bed.

'I don't know if I'm up for action sports today,' she says, 'maybe we can do something a bit more romantic.'

'Oh really?' Matt muses, gently tracing his fingers over Joy's stomach, exploring tentatively under the waistband of her pyjama bottoms.

'Oi, I said no action sports!' Joy smacks his hand away. 'That's not what I had in mind. Romance first, reward later.'

Matt pouts out his bottom lip in mock sadness. He whines like a puppy dog, trying to look as forlorn as possible.

'That's a good boy,' Joy says sternly. 'You do what your master desires. Now, what can we do?'

'I don't know,' Matt gets up, snapping out of his act and stretching his arms in the air. 'Why don't we just keep it simple and go for a walk. We haven't been up to the cliff since our first date.'

Joy stares out the window thoughtfully. A smile plays on her lips.

'It seems like a long time ago, doesn't it? Remember that guy chasing us? He had no idea what was going on.'

'I was crapping myself,' Matt scoffs. 'I thought he wanted to beat us up for stealing his chips.'

'Beat you up maybe. I'm too pretty to get in a fight.'

'Really?'

Matt picks up a pillow and playfully hits Joy in the face with it.

'Hey!' Joy protests, grabbing the pillow and throwing it at him. 'I'm frail, you need to look after me.'

Matt drops his pillow to the floor with instant remorse.

'I'm so sorry,' he says.

'Just kidding,' Joy jumps up and swings her own pillow, connecting with Matt's stomach. He doubles over in surprise and Joy tackles him back onto the bed.

'Come on,' Joy says, straddling on top of him. 'Let's go for a walk then. No hot chips this time. You need to leave room for dessert.'

She runs her hands over her body, teasing him with her sexuality.

Matt pulls her down for another kiss. He's glad Joy is in a more subdued mood today.

The mid-afternoon light plays off the bark of the moonah trees around them. Last time they were here later in the day, so everything was more obscured. Now the sun still has a good few hours before it sinks into night, so the only shadows are the ones deep within the scrub. Matt spreads a rug out on the clearing, covering the patches of brown leaves and sticks, which have been blown down by the prevailing westerly. Clouds are scattered across the sky, as though they don't know how to find each other in the great blue expanse. The dark waters of the Southern Ocean are in the process of changing their mood to suit autumn. The colour has shifted from summer blue to a more dramatic green. Out to sea, the breeze has ruffled the surface to look like a massive school of fish is migrating east. In close, the surface is as smooth as an oil slick. Joy sits near the edge, looking down over the precipice at the kelp beds far below. They protrude like rubber strands of hair from the rubble of sandstone erosion.

'I really love our planet,' Joy says. 'It's a free place, full of wonderful things.'

'Is this Planet Joy or Planet Earth?' Matt smirks at her.

'Is there a difference?' she asks, walking back to him and sitting down on the rug. 'This life is what we make of it in our own minds at the end of the day.'

'I think that philosophy lecture might have gone to your brain,' Matt jokes.

'I hope so,' she lays on the ground next to him. 'Really though. That cloud up there,' Joy points up into the sky. 'What is it to me? It's certainly not a bunch of water particles bunched together into a useless shape. It's a wild horse, flying away from that gigantic dragon that's chasing it over here.'

Matt laughs as he follows Joy's line of sight. The cloud does indeed resemble what she describes.

'But with the wind, that horse will probably look like a cow soon,' Matt says. 'Everything changes with time.'

'That's my point,' Joy says, looking up to the sky. 'Everything changes with time, but we can still fix things in our minds and keep them that way forever. As long as we can remember, we can make our own world.'

'Like a photo?'

'Yeah kind of, but photos don't have a taste like memories. They lack dimension. In my mind, this Polaroid has a dragon in the air and a sweet man at my side. The air smells like wet trees and dirt, and the ground is hard on my back.'

'It sounds uncomfortable.'

'It is a little bit, but it's bearable. I don't want to change it to be soft in my memory, because then it wouldn't be real. I'd just be kidding myself. Do you know what I mean?'

'I think so,' Matt nods, sidling in right next to his love. 'Tell me one of these multidimensional memories of when you were a girl then. Were you always this much of a weirdo when you were young?'

Joy slaps Matt on the stomach playfully.

'Maybe,' Joy says, 'I remember going to an art gallery on an excursion for school once. The teacher told us that as long as we had our buddy with us we'd be safe. My buddy took it seriously. She held my hand all day. I dragged her around doing what I wanted to do. We were supposed to stay in the 'Angels of the Renaissance' exhibit, but there was a gothic hall about Hell that I wanted to see. I made her sneak out with me to see the skulls. My mum had only recently passed, so death held a special fascination for me. I remember being absorbed in this black and white etching of a skeleton holding a scythe in one hand and an hour glass in the other. The air smelled like old books. My buddy wanted to go, but I kept telling her we were fine as long as we held each other's hands. It calmed her down. We stood there for what felt like forever. I can still feel the warmth of her hand in mine, as I look at the picture in the book.'

Clasping Joy's hand, he notices that her skin feels cold. Matt wishes that he could transfer some of his time through his skin into hers. He wishes he could pass on days, hours and years until there is a balance that suits them exactly. They could live here in the clearing, until they grow old, looking up at the sky. When the moment came they would die in their sleep together, still holding each other's wrinkled hands.

Joy shifts her weight to lie directly on top of Matt. She brings her legs to rest over his and spreads her arms out so they join at the palms, like a big starfish. Lowering her head, she nestles it into the groove of Matt's neck and shoulder, so their ears are touching. The ocean beats rhythmically into the cliff.

Up above, the dragon is catching up to the horse. It won't be long until they dissolve into a brand-new creature.

Fifty Seven

Pasta bubbles on the stove. The aroma of garlic and onion mixes with the scent of the fresh tomato that Joy is chopping on the wooden board in front of her. Matt is sitting on a stool watching. He had wanted to cook, but Joy insisted that he'd done more than his share of caring this week. After a few days of steroids, Joy's appetite has improved and she's looking rosy in the light of the kitchen globes. A throat-warming glass of pinot noir sits in Matt's hand, as he salivates over the food.

'What about some cheese?' Matt asks. 'Do you want me to grate some cheese?'

'No!' Joy says firmly. 'Get away, you're annoying me. Go and put some music on and relax on the couch, or do some more study. It's my turn to do something for you.'

'But I haven't done anything really. I've just been here.'

'That's plenty. Now go!'

Bowing to her wish, Matt takes his glass of wine and wanders over to inspect Joy's record collection. They are all still in the original cardboard sleeves. The only complaint that Matt has about the collection is that there isn't anything past the 90s. It isn't a huge concern, since Matt's parent's love of The Beatles and The Rolling Stones had groomed his taste for more retro sounds. Matt slips a record out of the stack and looks at the cover. It's a Led Zeppelin album called *Houses of the Holy*. The cover art is a strange scene, showing a group of naked but androgynous children climbing a pyramid of oddly shaped stones, into an orange sky. Matt has never heard the album himself. Looking at the track listing, he thinks the *Rain Song* sounds like an interesting title. He takes the big black disc out of the jacket and places it onto the turntable. Soothing strums of electric guitar meet Matt's ears. It's not the hard rock 'n' roll he expected, but the swaying twang of the chords suits his mood. He lets the record run.

Fifty Seven

Taking a big sip of wine, Matt lies down on the couch and lets the music wash over him. The heady vocals of Robert Plant send Matt into a swoon. He thinks he might even fall asleep.

'Matt?' Joy's voice says, just over the top of the record.

'Mm Hmm?' he answers dreamily.

Music fills any answer that Joy might have given.

'Matt?' he hears Joy say again more insistently. 'I'm feeling a little...'

Before Matt can sit up, the crash of a breaking glass penetrates the soundscape of the room. Matt leaps to his feet, spilling red wine on the carpet.

'Joy?'

He can't see her. He turns his head frantically, looking to see if she's down the hallway.

'Joy, where are you?'

Matt steps out from behind the couch and spots her convulsing on the ground amid shattered glass.

'Joy!'

He runs to her side and crouches down. Her whole body quakes in spasms. White foam sputters violently out of her mouth. Instinctively, Matt puts one hand under the back of her head, to stop it from smacking hard into the tiles. He sweeps the glass away from her, so she doesn't cut herself. The shards slice his palm.

'Shit!'

Matt's mind is racing. What can he do? He clutches the back of her head with one hand and grips his shirt with the other, trying to avoid getting blood on the ground. Joy's convulsing starts to subside and then suddenly stops. Matt turns her on her side, wiping the foam from her mouth. He makes sure she hasn't swallowed her tongue. He feels her neck for a pulse. She's alive. She's breathing.

Standing up, Matt searches for a phone. He swears inside his head, over and over again. It doesn't help.

Seeing Joy's handset on the bench, Matt grabs it and dials 000. It feels like forever before someone picks up.

'Hello, emergency assistance. Do you need Police, Fire or Ambulance?'

'Ambulance,' Matt blurts, rushing back over to Joy.

'Ambulance. What's your emergency?'

Joy is starting to groan on the floor. Matt kneels down next to her.

'Joy? Are you okay? Can you hear me?' he says to her loudly.

'Sir, what's your emergency?' Matt hears in the phone.

'I need an ambulance. My girlfriend just had a fit. She has cancer. I think she might have hit her head.' He's on the verge of tears.

'Okay, sir, I need you to please calm down,' the woman says in a steady voice, which helps him gather his wits. 'What's your location?'

Matt gives the address, looking into Joy's face, hoping she'll stir again.

'And you say she may have a head injury?'

'I think so,' Matt says, looking down at the blood drips around her head. He doesn't know if they are his or hers.

'We'll send someone out right way. Just stay calm and make sure she is comfortable and doesn't move.'

Matt drops the phone as it cuts off. Joy groans again and moves her arms.

'Joy.'

'Dad?' she moans, trying to sit up. One of her pupils is fully dilated and the other is a pinprick of black inside a sea of green iris. She gives a lopsided smile. 'Daddy, you came to visit,' her words are slurred.

'Joy, it's me, Matt,' he holds his hand down gently on her shoulder, stopping her from moving. 'Stay there, Joy. You've had a fall. An ambulance is on the way.'

'What? No,' she tries to get up again, brushing Matt's hand away, but she's weak.

She looks confused, but she does as she's told. Her breathing slows to normal and her eyes come into focus. Looking up, it's like she's seeing him for the first time.

'Matt?' she says. 'Why am I on the floor?'

'You had some kind of fit. Are you feeling alright? Are you hurt?' he tries to keep his voice steady.

'My neck is killing me. I've got a bit of a headache, but it's not bad.'

'Please stay there. There's an ambulance coming.'

'No, I'm fine!' she says, real clarity coming into her voice.

'They said not to move. I'll get a pillow. Watch out for the glass.'

'What glass?' Joy starts to sit up and looks around her.

'Don't sit up,' Matt says crossly. 'A glass smashed.'

Spotting the blood on the floor, Joy gasps.

'I think it's mine,' Matt cuts in, before Joy can say anything. 'I sliced my palm.'

'Oh my god, are you okay?' Joy props her back up against the cupboard.

'Don't worry about me!' Matt snaps 'Lie down!'

Seeing his concern, Joy does as she's told. Matt gets up and takes a cushion from the couch and brings it back to Joy.

'Can you turn the pasta sauce off?' Joy says, 'I don't want to ruin it.'

Matt shakes his head and turns the burner off on the stove. He finds a tea towel and wraps it around his throbbing palm. The cut is deeper than he thought.

He doesn't say anything. He just wants the ambulance to arrive.

There is no wailing siren, but flashing lights through the front window alert Matt that the paramedics have found the house. He gets up and opens the door as a robust woman in uniform and a dark-haired man with a medium build walk quickly up the drive.

'She's in here,' says Matt in the way of introduction. 'I'm the one who called.'

'Is she conscious?' the woman asks curtly, following Matt inside.

'Yes. Actually, she won't shut up. She had a seizure. She has advanced cancer, so maybe that caused it somehow. I don't know.'

'I'm fine,' Joy calls from the ground. 'Really, you shouldn't have come out. I'm sorry.'

'We'll be the judge of that,' the woman breaks in impatiently.

The man, who has still yet to say anything, crouches down next to Joy and gently puts his gloved hands on either side of her head.

'How are you feeling?' he asks kindly, looking into each eye purposefully.

'I'm alright. A headache that's starting to get worse and my neck hurts. I don't think I've broken anything.'

'Whose blood is this?' the woman interrupts.

'It's mine,' Matt answers, holding up his hand with the now crimson tea towel wrapped around it.

'I think he's worse off than me,' Joy smiles from the floor.

'Okay, you don't seem to have any major injuries,' the man says in his soft voice to Joy, 'but considering your medical history, I think we'd best take you into hospital for some more tests. Just sit tight while Laura here goes and gets you a trolley. He looks up to his partner who nods and turns to leave.

'Now,' he continues, turning to Matt. 'Let's take a look at that hand.'

Beginning to unwrap his makeshift bandage, Matt lays his arm down on the counter. Some red plasma seeps out onto the bench top as he unclenches his palm. The flap of skin folds back to reveal white sinew. It doesn't upset Matt too see this. As least he knows what's wrong. He'd rather a visible enemy than one that attacks in the dark.

'You've done a good job,' the paramedic says, leaning over Matt's hand. 'Put some pressure back on it. We'll have to stitch that up.'

'Matt?' Joy says from down on the floor. The paramedic looks down to her casually.

'Matt, I think I'm going to have another one.'

Fifty Seven

The words have barely escaped Joy's lips when her body starts to shudder again. A choking wail fills the air.

'Laura!' the paramedic yells out the door. 'Laura, get back in here, now!'

Fifty Eight

Matt sits next to Joy's hospital bed, staring at his cut. Four stitches and some painkillers is an easy fix to patch up a slice of the skin. If only the same patch job could work for her. In the ambulance Joy experienced yet another seizure. Matt had been horrified, pressed in the small cabin of the van while her slender body thrashed in the padded trolley. There had been little warning this time. The paramedic woman was taken unawares and it had taken her a minute of scrambling before she pulled the situation under control. Matt felt completely impotent watching on, unable to do anything to help. The woman just told him to sit down and shut up, while Joy jolted and swayed with a foaming mouth, before slumping into lifelessness again. Her moan as she woke up sounded like she had died and come back to life. Matt cried silently as he watched her. He felt worthless. It was the longest drive of his life as they raced up the highway to the city hospital.

During the night, Joy had gone in for an emergency MRI scan. They had sedated her afterward with morphine. Matt filled out the appropriate medical forms with shaking hands while she slept. It was a small blessing that Joy had private health cover, so she had a room to herself. Matt was able to sleep on the floor next to her, waking up every hour as a nurse came in to check everything was okay.

Matt now waits for Dr Peter to come. Part of him is thankful that Joy hasn't woken up just yet. He's not sure he can stand being alone with her while there are so many questions unanswered. The other half of him hopes that she will actually wake up. He hasn't had enough time with her. It feels like there are still universes to discover by her side. Forever still wouldn't be long enough.

There is a soft knock at the door. Dr Peter's grim face comes into view and he walks in holding a folder.

He meets Matt's eye and inclines his head in a shallow nod. His black eyes have faded completely, but they're still etched with concern.

'Hi, Matt. How's she doing?'

'She's sleeping,' Matt answers flatly, standing up to greet the doctor. 'It was a rough night.'

'And how are you?' he asks, looking at Matt. 'How are you holding up?'

'I'm fine,' Matt replies automatically.

'You know it's okay to not be,' Peter says earnestly, patting Matt on the back. 'This isn't easy. If you need someone to talk to, just let me know. I'm here, or we have counselling staff that can help you through it. It's not only Joy who we need to look after.'

'So, what happened?' Matt changes the subject. He doesn't want to talk about himself. 'Why did she collapse like that?'

'Maybe you'd better sit back down,' Peter says, looking at his folder, rather than Matt. 'The news isn't good.'

Matt grasps backward and finds the chair with his hands, not wanting to take his eyes off Peter, who takes a seat on the foot of the bed, watching Joy sleep.

'Unfortunately, there's no easy way to break this to anyone, let alone a friend,' Peter sighs. 'The cancer has spread to Joy's brain. She has secondary tumours the size of oranges near her pituitary gland and in her left frontal lobe. That's what sparked the seizures. It's like trees falling on power lines. They cause a short circuit and send her body into shock. We've given her a good dose of anti-convulsants to stop the seizures. Otherwise, the more she has, the more they cause. It's called kindling.' He looks down at the paper in his hand, like it's helping him speak out loud. 'We think we have them under control but it's just a symptom of the bigger problem we are already aware of.'

The news is devastating to Matt. He had secretly hoped that Joy might recover miraculously and that they'd live together and get married. He knows they are foolish dreams, yet he still wants them to happen.

'But she seemed so healthy,' Matt whispers.

'Yes, but inside she's black,' Peter says. 'I'm sorry, but know it's only a matter of time until the rest of the body begins to shut down.'

'Is there anything we can do?' Matt asks, lifting his head to look at the doctor.

'I'm sorry,' he apologises again, shaking his head. 'She'll last maybe a week more. I want to say it'll be alright, but she won't be going home this time. She'll have to stay here. I've put her on some painkillers to help her rest. I wish I could do more.'

'You've done what you can,' Matt bows his head.

'I just wish it was enough,' Peter says softly. 'It's never enough.'

The two stand and watch over Joy, who sleeps on with translucent skin.

'Someone needs to call her dad,' Matt says, remembering her reaction after the first seizure. 'He needs to come and see her.'

'I've called,' Peter shakes his head. 'He won't pick up. I'm sorry, but I don't think he'll come to visit.'

'What?' Matt's anger leaps out of him. 'What kind of father is he? He can't just -'

'Oscar's been through a lot, Matt. His wife and now Joy. You can't blame him.'

'Like hell I can't,' Matt says, 'What's his address? I'll talk some sense into him.'

'You know I can't do that,' Peter says softly.

Joy stirs in her bed, making the two of them look up simultaneously. Her eyes crack open a little and she smacks her lips together.

'Water,' she says weakly.

Peter walks over to her side and picks up some water that is already sitting next to the table. He holds it to her lips, while she sips. The liquid seems to revive her and her eyes open completely. She sees Matt and manages a brief smile.

'Hi Joy,' Peter says down to her fondly. 'It's terrible to see you again.'

'It's terrible to see you too,' responds Joy half-heartedly. 'When can I go home?'

'This is your home now,' Peter says, looking back at the clipboard in his lap. 'I'm afraid I don't have the best results here.'

Silent tears slide down Joy's cheeks as he delivers the news. Matt moves to her side and she reaches out to touch his fingers with hers. It's unclear who's consoling whom.

Fifty Nine

M att walks down a narrow side street, with high timber fences on either side. The road is cobbled stone. It makes Matt feel like he's in some back alley of a medieval town. Overhead, flat grey clouds mute the sky in a doleful haze. Checking the numbers on each gate, he makes his way along the odd side. Matt hopes this is the right place. The last O. Hannigan he tried was a dead end.

Joy is at hospital, going in and out of more tests that she insists are a waste of time. They only confirm what everyone knows - time is a dwindling resource. The routine has given Matt a chance to head home and gather some fresh clothes for them, meaning he can set up camp in her room for the long haul. This extra detour is one Matt can't help but take. Despite Peter's insistence that him seeking out Oscar is inappropriate, Matt begs to differ. If this can draw even a lopsided smile out of Joy it will be worth it. Luckily the phone book was more forthcoming with address options than Peter.

Finding the house he's looking for, Matt presses the ringer on the gate. A metallic bell sounds inside the compound and after a short wait he hears some shuffling inside.

'Hello?' a male voice asks from behind the barrier.

'Mr Hannigan?'

'Yes?'

'I need to talk to you about your daughter, Joy,' Matt says, opting for the direct approach.

The only reply is silence, but Matt can see through the hand hole of the gate that the man is still standing there, listening. This must be him.

'Can you let me in?' Matt asks softly.

Again silence. Matt waits, looking through the gap to see the man hasn't moved an inch. A crisp wind blows down the alley, rustling some fallen leaves around Matt's feet.

'I just want five minutes,' Matt tries again. 'If you don't let me in, I'll be back here every day, knocking until my hands bleed. Please,' Matt adds. He doesn't want to appear rude.

A rattling behind the gate indicates the latch is being unlocked. The wood swings back to reveal a pale man dressed in a navy, woolen jumper. His black hair is peppered with flecks of grey all over, like whitecaps on a night-time sea. His shoulders are hunched, as though he's trying to be shorter than he really is.

'Oscar?' Matt asks, holding out his hand. 'I'm Matt.'

The man looks at Matt's hand for a while before he clasps it in a strong grip that takes Matt by surprise. His skin is warm like Joy's used to be. Oscar drops Matt's hand, avoiding eye contact as he steps back to let him in. He leads Matt through a small courtyard and into a rundown house. There are photos strewn all over the floor, falling out of old albums and ramshackle picture frames. Images of Joy as a girl look up at Matt. Pictures of her with her smiling mum, pictures of her as a blossoming teenager, pictures of her camping with her dad. Oscar sits down into a recliner chair and picks up a yellow envelope. It is branded Kodak on the outside and stuffed with memories within. Matt doesn't sit, he just watches as Oscar takes out the photos and starts flipping through them, a sad smile hanging on his face. He seems to find what he's looking for and leans back, turning the photo around so Matt can see.

'Her sixth birthday,' he says proudly.

On the image is Joy in a red party dress and paper crown, surrounded by other girls and boys all gathered trying to blow out some candles. The cake beneath looks like a swimming pool filled with green jelly. Chocolate biscuits make up the sides and there are little candy men and women floating in liquorice tyre tubes inside.

'Lucinda used to make one of those creations every year,' Oscar explains, pointing at the cake. 'She had this Women's Weekly Birthday Cake Book. She and Joy would look through it for hours, trying to figure out which one it would be each time.'

Oscar picks up another envelope and rifles through the contents. He holds up another photo, 'her eleventh birthday.' This time it's Joy giving two thumbs up, with a weak smile on her face. There are no other kids in the photo, just a deformed train cake that looks more like Matt's Holden, if it had a giant Mars-Bar chimney sticking out of the bonnet. 'I had to make that one,' Oscar says, putting the photo away.

Oscar looks around at all the images on the ground, seeing one in a frame. This one is of Oscar and Joy together. They both have Black Sabbath t-shirts on and are pulling twin 'horns up' signs with their hands. They look like they're out the front of a rock concert. 'She called me Ozzie for months after this one,' Oscar laughs. 'Did you know she used to play the guitar?'

Matt shakes his head.

'She was in a band. The Flaming Blimps. She stopped playing after the drummer broke her heart. Smashed up his kit with her Fender Telecaster, then set her amp on fire and threw it through his car windshield. Can you believe that?'

Matt nods. That sounds like it might be something Joy would do when upset.

'She didn't let many people into her heart after Lucinda left,' Oscar says. 'I'm afraid she got that from me. You must be a special man to have gotten past those defences.'

Oscar picks up yet another frame. This time it's of Joy dressed in a graduation gown holding a degree in her hand.

'You need to come and see her,' Matt says, finally getting up the courage to talk. 'She's not long for this world, Oscar. She wants to see you.'

Oscar shakes his head, still looking down. A teardrop splats onto the picture in his lap.

'I don't want to remember her like that,' Oscar says in a quaking voice. 'This is Joy here,' he caresses the image tenderly. 'Not some skeleton in a hospital bed.'

'She's not dead yet!' Matt snaps, his anger rising. 'You've still got some moments to live with her. Don't rob her of her dad's love, just because you're scared of saying goodbye.'

'What would you know?!' Oscar growls, looking up at Matt with pain in his eyes. 'I watched Lucinda waste away. Sat by her bed every day. Held her hand. Kissed her lips, even as they grew cold with death. Now when I close my eyes to think of her that's all I can remember. Nothing else. Just a sack of bones. No spirit left. I won't let it be the same for Joy. She deserves better.'

Oscar grips the photo in his hands so tightly Matt thinks it might shatter.

'You're right,' Matt says between gritted teeth. 'She does deserve better. I'm glad I didn't tell her I was coming today. I wouldn't want her last memory of her dad one where he willingly turns his back on her. Better she remembers you as a distant figure, huddled in the corner weeping for a past long gone. Better to see you as simply pathetic than as a coward too.'

Matt shakes with rage. He waits for a reply. Oscar stares down, as still as the photos around him. The hiss of his voice almost feels like it's coming from the walls. 'Get out of my house!'

'I will,' Matt says, making his way towards the door, not caring where he steps. 'I'll go back to the hospital to see Joy. Because every single memory I can get of her is precious. Even the ones that hurt like hell. I want to remember all of her, not just the pieces I like.'

He walks out, leaving the door and the gate open behind him. The cobbles of the street are hard under his feet, matching the feeling that's steeling his heart.

Sixty

M att creeps into Joy's room carrying a gym bag full of clothes. The sterile white walls drain any trace of character from the space. A vase of plastic flowers in the corner and a crucifix hanging above Joy's bed are the only hint of decoration. It's like a prison cell. Matt sets the bag down, opening a faux wood cupboard in the corner to see if he can put some things away.

'Oh hello, doctor,' Joy says from the bed, taking Matt by surprise. 'Have you come to take my temperature?'

She's even paler than usual, but seems in good spirits. The sight of her smiling face helps Matt wipe away the residue of the confrontation he'd just had with Oscar. He decides to focus on the beauty of now, rather than dwell on things he can't control.

'How are you feeling?' Matt asks, walking over to give her a kiss. Matt lets his lips linger for a second and Joy pokes her tongue in his mouth. He jumps back, laughing with the shock of it.

'Like I should be out practising my mad surf skills instead of surfing this sorry excuse for a bed,' she says. 'Can we go home yet?'

'Peter says no,' Matt shakes his head. 'But I brought some paintings and a few other things from your place, thinking we might be able to make this room a little homelier. They're in the car.'

'Don't you dare,' Joy says, giving Matt her best angry tiger glare.

'What?'

'Don't you try to dress this cube up as an adequate place to stay. We're heading back to the coast as soon as possible.'

'We'll see,' Matt says, trying to appease her. 'I'll talk with Peter again.'

'You tell him if he doesn't let me out, I'll break out,' she glares.

Sixty

'Do I need to go and buy some handcuffs?' Matt raises his eyebrow, trying to lighten the mood. 'I saw some pink fluffy ones in the sex shop on the third level.'

'If only this place was that liberal,' Joy huffs. 'It's all Jesus and salvation in between getting jabbed with needles. What else can we do?'

'We could probably hug and watch TV,' Matt offers, 'Or I could regale you with stories about embarrassing moments from my childhood?'

A beeping in his pocket interrupts the conversation. He takes his phone out of his pocket and looks at the screen.

'Who is it?' Joy asks.

'It's Z. She and Gerard are downstairs. They've offered to help me out with a few things. I'd better go down and see them.'

'Tell them to come up here,' Joy says. 'I want to meet them.'

'You sure?' Matt asks.

'I want to see the people who are giving you your first writing job. Make sure they're above board.'

Matt rolls his eyes at her tone, but texts G and Z to head up. It's not too long before Gerard tentatively knocks, poking his head in the door. Z saunters straight past him like she owns the place, coming up to the edge of the bed ignoring Matt.

'So, you're the other woman in his life,' Joy says, looking Z up and down.

'And you're the one he won't shut up about,' Z sniffs.

The pair stare at each other, neither of them looking away, as if whoever drops eye contact first will lose some sort of contest. It's Z who breaks first. She glances up at the crucifix on the wall. Stepping forward, she adjusts it so it's hanging upside-down.

'Let's see how long it takes them to notice that,' Z says.

'I like her,' Joy smiles at Matt.

Gerard steps forward, introducing himself. Joy holds out her hand to shake and he takes it in his hands, kissing the top and then cradling it between both of his palms.

'Nice to finally meet you,' G says, 'I wish it was under better circumstances, like maybe running away from a bogan whose fish n' chips we've just stolen.'

'He told you about that, did he?' Joy looks at Matt. 'Anything you guys can think of in here to have some similar fun, I'm all ears. I've been going stir crazy lying here and going in and out of MRI machines all day.'

'Maybe we could go and watch a surgery or something?' Z suggests, 'Like in one of those open theatres.'

'I don't think this is that kind of hospital,' Matt says, 'plus, Joy's been ordered to rest.'

'Right, rest,' Z says, her mind clearly ticking. 'I need to go to the rest room.'

She walks out into the hall without any further comment, leaving the other three staring at each other.

'Gerard?' Matt asks, before Joy can plant any ideas into his other friend's head. 'I wanted to ask you about how I can maybe defer uni for a little while, without losing Austudy.'

Gerard purses his lips, thinking while he continues to hold Joy's hand in both of his. 'I'm not sure if you can, at least not for any significant period of time. But if you give me your student number I'll ring the uni direct and see what kind of compassionate grounds you can get leeway on. We'll find some kind of loophole for you.'

'You're a champ, thanks' Matt says.

'We've booked in a client too,' Gerard adds, 'looks like you'll be writing some customer service scripts for an airline. Hello writing and travel all in one hit on your résumé.'

'Wow!' Matt says, 'well done mate, that's amazing.'

Z clatters back into the room and any discussion about the new client is instantly forgotten. She's pushing a wheelchair and is wearing a doctor's coat. With her lanky frame and thick-rimmed glasses she looks like a bona fide medical professional. Joy sits up in her bed, a big grin forming on her face.

'What on earth are you doing?' Matt asks in a harsh whisper, 'where did you get those?'

'Cool your man tits,' Z says, 'There was a staff break room up the hall that was very unprofessionally deserted.' She looks down at her jacket. 'One Dr Carey must have left her jacket in there for some reason and I was getting a bit cold in this air-conditioning, so I thought I'd borrow it.'

'Oh my god, that's Peter's jacket!' Joy claps her hand in soft applause. 'Where are we going?'

'Not too far,' Z says, 'next wing over. I want to show you something.'

'You can't, Z!' Matt protests.

'That's Dr Z to you, Pearce,' she says. 'This is my hospital and I'll go where I want.'

'You sound like a super villain,' Joy says, limping out of her bed to sit in the wheelchair. Gerard helps her settle in and puts a blanket over her lap.

The three of them move to head out of the room when Matt stops them.

'Wait,' he says, in a resigned voice.

They pause.

'Four of us can't go. It will look too strange. Gerard, can you stay here in case Peter comes back? I want to make sure beanpole here doesn't do anything stupid.'

Matt ignores Z's incredulous look. She pushes Joy out of the door and Matt pauses quickly to speak with Gerard.

'Text me if the doctor comes asking for Joy. Stall him and say we've just taken her to get some fresh air.'

Matt takes a piece of paper out of his pocket, handing it to Gerard. 'And here's that list of potential interviewees I was telling you about. I'll give you a call later, just in case we don't get a chance to chat about it when we get back.' Gerard nods, pocketing the paper. He takes a seat next to the empty bed.

Matt strides out the door, looking left and right, seeing the retreating form of Z pushing a wheelchair down the far length of the hallway. It takes him a few twists and turns to catch up, making his way from the oncology ward through a connecting walkover that arches right across the top of a busy city street. When he finally gets to them, they're strolling through the maternity ward. No one gives Z or Joy a sideways glance. The confidence Z is projecting, like she's knows exactly where she's headed, means she blends into the hospital pace without missing a beat. Matt pulls up next to them. He decides not to ask any questions, in case he blows their cover. He's simply along for the ride.

Z glances left and right as she walks, like she's making sure everything is in order. Matt suspects she's searching for something but doesn't know what. It becomes apparent when she picks up pace, making a bee line for a room with a long window. Inside are rows of cribs with new born babies in them. Z wheels Joy right up to the door, stopping to get the attention of the midwife on duty. A woman in her early 30s with a round face, kind eyes and plump breasts comes over.

'Yes doctor?' the midwife asks, approaching with a smile.

Z's eyes go down the name tag resting on top of the woman's ample bosom.

'Hi Joan,' she says with soft authority. 'I know this might be a little bit of a strange request, but I have a cancer patient here who's not going to be around for too long. It's one of her last wishes to hold a newborn baby. I was wondering if we could bend the rules and let her nurse an infant whose mum is getting some much-needed rest?'

'Oh, I'm not sure doctor,' her eyes flick back nervously to the mostly sleeping babies. One gives a light cry and grasps the air with tiny pink hands.

'Please, call me Karen,' Z says. 'I promise it will just be a few minutes. Joy here is more at risk of infection than the bubs, so we'll keep it quick.'

Joan's eyes go back to the babies one more time, before resting on Joy's face. Joy's eyes are only for the babies. Her mouth is hanging half open in wonder and her hand is unconsciously outstretched a touch toward the one who is crying in its crib. Seeing the reaction, the midwife's resolve breaks. She heads back to the baby and picks it up, cooing and shushing as she rocks it gently from side to side.

'This is Emily,' Joan says, to Joy. 'Have you ever held a baby before?'

Joy shakes her head. She tentatively holds out her arms, as Joan shows her how to support the infant's head and neck as she lays her down onto Joy's lap. Z pulls Matt back a few steps, out of the room, giving Joy some privacy as she starts whispering hello to the child, introducing herself. When little Emily wraps her hand around Joy's finger and starts sucking the tip. Joy lets out a small giggle, looking to Joan for support. The midwife moves to get a small bottle of milk, warming it up for a few seconds before bringing it back. Joy takes it and ever so softly lets the baby start to feed. She looks back at Matt and Z, mouthing a 'thank you' with glassy eyes.

'How did you know?' Matt asks, watching the pair, seeing a window into a future that might have been if things were different. Part of him wishes he could have a hold as well, but he knows he can't.

'Please,' Z says, 'even a middle-aged dyke like me feels her ovaries ache when there's a fresh one in the vicinity.

A young, vibrant girl like that - her body will be filling with so many endorphins right now she'll be walking on clouds for a week. Without the chafed nipples to boot.'

Matt's phone starts to buzz in his pocket. He looks at the screen and hits silent. Nothing needs to interrupt this moment right now. Not Peter. Not Gerard. Not cancer. Joy leans down and rubs her nose gently on the baby's forehead. She stares down into its half-closed eyes, taking in the miracle of a new life. Matt puts his arm around Z's shoulder, giving her a squeeze of thanks for adding an extra memory into his and Joy's bank of dreams.

'You know that midwife doesn't have any ring on her wedding finger,' Z whispers into Matt's ear. 'I wonder if she has a thing for tall, handsome doctors.'

Sixty One

Some days are okay. Others are not. This is the most basic way that Matt can articulate it in his head.

Joy's face is grey today. Her eyelids barely open and when they do, the usual zest behind her green orbs is dim. Every morning she asks if she can check out and go back to the coast. Every morning Matt speaks with Peter to see if they can somehow leave, but he politely refuses. He says it will be easier on everyone if she's here. Matt doesn't care about easy; he cares about Joy's happiness. Yesterday they had inserted a stent into Joy's oesophagus, opening it up so she can eat properly. Without real food, she's starting to waste away. The operation had gone well, but it had left her weak. While she was out, Matt took the time to work on the customer service script Z and G needed. Tapping his fingers relentlessly on the keys of his laptop helped keep his worry at bay. G had been able to arrange some special considerations at university as well, so he can hand in assignments late and not receive any penalties. He still has to do the reading.

Now, Joy rests quietly in her bed. Matt reads aloud to her. She finds it hard to talk on days like this and he finds it hard to sit in silence. He doesn't know if Joy is listening half the time, but occasionally she turns her head and nods at him. The communication is enough to keep him narrating. The heavy pages of Bram Stoker's *Dracula* sit in his hands, weaving a romantic gothic tale into the air as the afternoon wears on. Matt didn't know when he first started reading that it was a love story. He finds it oddly beautiful.

Finishing a chapter, Matt looks up from Transylvania to see if Joy is awake. She is staring at him with half-closed eyes.

'You're going to be an author one day,' she says faintly. 'Someone is going to read your words aloud to a loved one just like this.'

Matt lets the book drop onto his lap and closes the cover. He looks at her black hair, which has lost none of its lustre. Standing up, he walks over and leans in, kissing her on the forehead.

'I hope so,' he smiles. 'I just need to come up with a good story.' Straightening up, he puts *Dracula* down on the table next to his wallet and keys.

'Why don't you write a book about a girl named Joy, who lives forever?' she blinks up to him.

'Is she a vampire?' he smiles, thinking she's talking about what he has just been reading to her.

'No,' Joy shakes her head. 'She's not evil, she's good. She lives inside a book. As long as someone reads about her, they bring her back to life. When the pages are closed, she sleeps.'

Joy closes her eyes for a few breaths, before opening them again and continuing her sentence.

'She loves being immortal. She loves falling in love again and again with a gorgeous writer called Matt, who thinks he's not good enough to construct a novel, but is secretly amazing inside. She brings out the best in him.'

'It sounds like a good story,' says Matt, stroking her cheek gently with the back of his fingers. 'Does this Joy have green eyes? Is she pretty and different from everybody else and have small ears?'

Joy nods, animation coming into her features as Matt rubs her neck.

'But she has a disease that can't be cured,' Joy adds. 'Matt thinks it's a tragedy that she's going to die, but in the end, all he has to do is open the book he's written and she's there with him again, in his arms.'

Matt sits down on the bed and lets Joy wrap her hands around his. He tries with everything he has not to cry. He can't let her know he's breaking inside. He looks at the white walls, trying to compose himself.

'Promise me you'll write it,' Joy says. 'Promise me you'll put your soul into it.'

'I will,' he nods, turning his face back to hers, a lump rising painfully in his throat.

'Make sure you write it in the present tense,' she looks at him intently. 'I want to be active, not someone in the past. It needs to be Joy does this, not Joy did that. You can't write Joy said, Joy ran. It has to be Joy says, Joy smiles, Joy runs with the kite, Joy kisses Matt, Joy loves Matt, Matt promises Joy.'

'I promise,' Matt whispers, his exterior finally cracking. Salty tears drip down onto their entwined fingers. He squeezes her palm tightly and leans down to press his lips against hers.

A nurse clears her throat in the doorway. The lovers look up from their embrace, resenting the intrusion.

There is a moment where the woman looks like she's about to walk out. She glances to her left before clearing her throat again.

'I'm sorry Joy, but you have a visitor. He wanted me to check if it's alright to come and see you.'

'Who is it?' Matt asks, puzzled.

The nurse appears somewhat nervous as she looks at Joy.

'He says he's your father.'

Sixty Two

Matt almost jumps off the bed. He's not sure why he's so startled. Even though he'd begged Joy's father to come the previous week, he now doesn't know if it's a good or bad thing. He turns to his companion. She has sunken back down into the pillows and is looking at the nurse silently.

'Joy?' asks Matt.

'Of course,' she coughs. 'Tell him to come in.'

Matt drops back to her side, immediately in protective mode.

'Do you want me to go?' he asks, hoping she won't send him away.

'No,' Joy says firmly. 'I want you to meet each other.'

Matt stays silent, not wanting to go through the awkward explanation of how they'd met already. A noise at the door causes Matt to look up. Oscar is standing in the doorway holding a small bouquet of multi-coloured flowers in his hands. He cups them gently, as if they might fall apart if he doesn't nurture them. He's wearing the same navy jumper he had on last time Matt had seen him.

'Hello,' Oscar says, looking past Matt directly at Joy. 'I brought you some violas. They were always your mum's favourite.'

'I remember,' Joy nods. 'I always thought they looked like little speckled butterflies next to her bed. I love them.'

Oscar diverts his eyes back to the flowers and draws in their scent. He waits in that position, as if studying each petal for imperfections.

'Dad, this is Matt,' Joy breaks the tension. 'He's been looking after me. Matt, this is Dad.'

'Oscar,' her dad corrects.

Matt rises from the bed and faces up to Joy's father.

'It's nice to meet you, Oscar,' he says, shaking his hand in greeting.

Oscar gives a slight nod to Matt, indicating that he too would rather pretend that their first meeting never happened. He looks at Matt with his hard face and blue eyes, which bear the scars of eternal regret. Carefully, he passes the flowers into Matt's possession and grips his forearm firmly.

'It's nice to meet you, Matt,' he says. 'These are very delicate and precious. Can you take good care of them for me?'

Matt nods.

'Thank you,' he says.

Releasing his hold on the violas, Oscar looks back at Joy again. He pauses, leaving a space between them. He stares at her like she's a ghost.

'Do I get a kiss?' she asks him, smiling.

The words make his features soften.

'Of course, dear.'

He approaches the bed and eases down next to his daughter. Bending down, he kisses her on the cheek and again on the forehead. He looks at her face and then up to the crucifix on the wall. He reaches up and adjusts it, so it's hanging the right way around.

Matt waits quietly, holding the flowers that were entrusted into his care.

Oscar turns to look out the window. Outside, the afternoon is bowing to the evening as shades of amber fade on the horizon. Wispy clouds hold the last of the day's light. The three of them seem like strangers in a waiting room, with nothing in common. Matt is uncomfortable, but dares not move. He doesn't feel like he belongs in this scene.

'I'll say hello to mum for you,' Joy says to Oscar finally.

Without turning around, he nods slowly.

'I'll let her know you haven't forgotten about her,' she adds.

Joy's father looks back down to her. He kisses her on the head again, keeping his eyes on hers.

'I love you,' he says tenderly. 'I'm glad I got to see you again.'

'I'm sorry,' she replies in barely a whisper. Her cheeks are wet with tears that her father won't cry.

'It's not your fault,' he whispers back, giving her a long silent hug. Joy's hands clasp her dad's back, pulling him into the tight embrace.

'Can you sing me a lullaby?" Joy asks when she finally lets go.

Oscar stares at her for a while with a sad smile, before nodding. 'Your favourite?'

Joy nods and settles in. Matt takes it as his cue to leave. As he walks out the door, Matt hears Oscar start a slow version of *I Hope That I Don't Fall In Love With You* by Tom Waits.

Matt wanders the halls for hours cradling the violas in his hands. He peers into rooms from time to time, wondering about the stories behind the people lying in the beds. Is every one a tale of sadness and redemption and endurance of the human spirit? Matt decides that they are, and that love and strength are more common than most people realise.

When the clocks show that visiting hours are over for the day, Matt makes his way back to Joy's room. Oscar is still there, watching over his sleeping daughter. His eyes flick up briefly to Matt, before watching her again. He leans in and gives her a soft kiss on the cheek.

'Goodbye, for now,' he whispers in her ear before straightening up.

Oscar steps away from the bed, letting his fingers trail along the wall as he turns to leave. Walking past Matt, he pauses, looking down at his feet. Without raising his head, Oscar reaches out and pats Matt on the shoulder, clasping it for a few moments.

'Good luck,' he says, looking ahead to the corridor. He finally turns to meet Matt's eyes. 'And thank you.'

Matt doesn't watch Oscar depart, he simply inhales the scent of the flowers in his hands. Removing the fake bouquet from next to the bed, Matt puts the living ones in their vase and pours some water in to make sure they're nourished. He then picks up *Dracula*, sits down in his chair and reads aloud. Visiting hours don't matter. He'll stay here as long as Joy does. As he reads, Matt hopes that she can hear the words in her sleep, keeping the idea alive that there can be an afterlife, even if it takes strange forms.

Sixty Three

Midday sun streams into the hospital room. Joy lies silently in bed. She hasn't said a word all morning. All Matt can do is continue to read, even when he's sure Joy's mind is in another place altogether. Just having their bodies present in the same room is enough for now.

Matt's phone beeps on the table next to him. He picks it up, smiling at the message.

'Hey,' Matt says, 'Z and Gerard are here. You mind if they come up to say hi?'

'Huh?' Joy asks, letting her head turn to the side.

'Z and Gerard have just popped in to say g'day. Mind if they come up?'

'Oh, sure.' Joy says, sitting up a bit and propping her back against her pillow. 'I don't think I'm up for any tours around the hospital though. I'm so damn tired.'

'No worries,' Matt says, giving her a kiss on the lips.

'I'd say get a room you two,' Z says from the doorway, 'but you already have one. Maybe lock the door if you're gunna get busy.'

'Hi guys,' Joy says softly, managing half a smile.

Z and Gerard walk in together. Z has a DVD player under her arm and Gerard has a tangle of black cords in his hand. He puts them down on the foot of the bed, before giving Matt a clap on the back hello and kissing Joy on the forehead. Z doesn't offer any other greeting. She just drags a chair underneath where the TV is mounted on the wall and starts checking the back for connections.

'Pass me those white and yellow tipped audio cables,' she instructs Matt.

'What's all this then?' Joy says, perking up a little more at the action.

'Matt told us you like surprises,' Gerard says.

'Good surprises I do,' Joy replies, as her eyes watch Z hook up the DVD player to the TV.

'I hope it's a good one,' Gerard looks at Matt. 'My editing skills aren't great, but all those addresses you gave me were perfect.'

'What addresses?' Joy asks, her head turning from Gerard, to Matt and then Z.

'You'll see,' Matt says, 'it will be another mystery of the universe solved.'

'Once I get this shitbox of a TV to cooperate,' Z says, jiggling some cords in the back and clicking the remote. The screen flicks to an all blue screen. 'Boot up the player and put the disk in, G.'

Matt sits next to Joy on the bed, holding her hand. Gerard takes a disk out of his back pocket and goes to the DVD player, balancing it in his hands as he inserts the circle of plastic. When Z jumps off the chair, Gerard rests the player on it and stands next to the bed, waiting for the show.

'Can you see alright, Joy?' Gerard asks, making sure he's not in the way.

'Just hit play,' she says, 'the suspense is killing me.'

On cue, Z pushes a button on the remote and the screen flicks over to black. Gerard's face appears.

'Are you filming?' he asks.

'Can you see the bloody red light on the front of the camera, idiot?' Z's voice says off screen.

'Don't swear in front of the kids,' Gerard whispers sharply.

'I didn't fucking swear, I said bloody!'

There's a giggle in the background and the camera zooms out to see two young boys sitting on chairs. They look like they're about twelve or thirteen and are clearly twins.

'Oh my god, that's Robby and Danny,' Joy gasps breathlessly. 'How did you?'

Matt gives Joy's hand a squeeze and she falls silent.

'Sorry boys,' Gerard says, turning to the kids and moving to take a seat next to them. 'So, like I said, we're doing a little documentary on what Miss Hannigan taught her students, so she can know how much of a difference she made.'

Joy's head turns to Matt, her mouth wide open.

'Just watch,' Matt smiles, nodding toward the screen.

'You mean Joy, don't you?' one of the boys interrupts Gerard onscreen.

'Didn't you call her Miss Hannigan?' Gerard asks.

'Nah, she said that calling teachers mister, or sir, or missus was a social construct designed to maintain power relations in the classroom. She preferred Joy. It helped remind her she was learning along with us as well.'

'Right,' Gerard says, looking at the screen.

'I can't believe they remember that,' Joy whispers, almost to herself.

'She was the best teacher ever,' the other boy on screen adds.

'And what do you think was the most important thing she ever taught you?'

'Ummmmm,' the boy on the left thinks, his eyes looking up as he does.

'She taught me double double,' the one on the right says.

'Double double?' Gerard asks.

'Yeah, it's a trick to remember your four times table. You just double the number and double it again. I couldn't bloody get it before then, but Joy made it stick with that.'

'Don't swear!' his brother says.

'I didn't! I said bloody. The other man said that's not swearing,'

'She's a lady!' the other laughs.

'Really?' the boy looks above the camera.

'Sorry about Danny,' the boy on the right adds, 'he's a bit slow.'

'I am not!' Danny snaps.

'Double double,' his brother shakes his head. 'Surely you can come up with something better than that.'

'What's yours then, Robby?' Danny asks.

'She taught us to always be ourselves,' Robby smiles.

'Unless you're a dickhead,' Danny adds.

'Unless you're a dickhead,' Robby confirms, 'then you should pretend you're a gentleman.'

Joy mouths the last words along with the boy, like she remembers telling them exactly that. She shakes her head in disbelief. Before she can say anything, the boys continue on screen.

'You do act like a gentleman most of the time now,' Danny says to his brother.

'Thanks!' he beams.

'But I guess that means deep down you're really a dickhead.'

'Hey!' Robby says.

'Just kidding, mate.' Danny adds, winking at the screen. 'He's still too easy to bait, Joy. I promise I do go easy on him like you asked.'

'Is there anything else you want to say to Joy before we go?' Gerard asks the boys.

'Just that we'll never forget you,' Robby says looking directly at the screen.

'Yeah, we'll never forget you, Joy, you rock.' Danny adds, flipping his hands into a 'horns up' gesture.

His brother mirrors the gesture, then the screen cuts to a teenage girl, looking down into her lap. She's wearing tight black jeans and a black singlet top. It's almost like she could have taken the items directly out of Joy's wardrobe.

'I think maybe the most important thing,' the girl says, raising her head to look at the screen. 'Is that she said even in tough times there are still things to love about the world.'

'Oh, Jodie,' Joy whispers.

'That really meant a lot to me,' Jodie continues. 'Now whenever I'm down I start looking for a tiny bit of beauty around me. There's always something interesting to find, just like she said there was. It helps, you know?'

Gerard nods to himself, both on screen and standing by as he watches.

'And is there anything you want to say to her?' onscreen Gerard asks.

'Just thanks.'

'Just thanks?' Gerard prompts.

'Just thanks,' Jodie nods and smiles at the screen. 'She knows. We've been through a lot of the same stuff.'

'Her mum,' Joy starts to explain, but stops when yet another girl comes on the screen.

'Joyyyyyyyyyy, it's Marissa! Remember me?' the girl says at the screen. She has a curvy figure, seemingly on the far side of puberty even though she has youth in her eyes. Her confidence and energy oozes through the TV into the hospital room.

Joy's face lights up. She even straightens in her bed some more, gripping Matt's hand tightly.

'I miss you!' Marissa smiles, showing a row of braces as she beams. 'You taught me so many things! I don't even know where to start. So, before I go blabbing like I always do, I'll just say six. The first!' she holds up her finger. 'Love your body, because it's the only one you get! And what a body hey?!' she winks, plumping up her breasts at the camera. Next to her, Gerard averts his eyes. 'Number two through to six!' she adds, holding up her fingers in the peace sign, then counting with her fingers as she says the words in a short burst. 'Why. Are. We. Doing. This?!'

The screen cuts to small boy. Looking at the camera he says with a big grin: 'Why are we doing this?!'

Again, the screen cuts to another boy, then a girl, repeating the same phrase: 'why are we doing this?' Another five different kids appear in quick succession, their faces up close on the screen, each of them saying a single word: 'Why. Are. We. Doing. This?'

Joy lets out an involuntary laugh.

'It took me a whole day to get that cut right,' Gerard beams from beside the bed.

The screen returns to the curvy girl, Marissa, who is recovering from a fit of laughter. She wipes a happy tear from her eye.

'What does that mean?' Gerard prompts her as the interviewer.

'Well,' Marissa says, adjusting herself in her chair and staring down the barrel of the camera like she's a news presenter. 'Every time we had a lesson at school, didn't matter if it was maths, or P.E., or English or whatever, Joy would explain what we were going to learn and then ask the class why we were doing it. If we couldn't come up with a good answer together we wouldn't do it. She said that's how we should go through life. If we can't think of a really good reason why we're doing something, then just don't do it. Full stop. I live like that now, you have no idea how much time it's saved me and I'm only 14.'

'Sounds like good advice.' Gerard says.

'The best,' Marissa agrees. 'She changed my life. You changed my life, Joy!' she yells happily at the screen.

Another cut goes back to the small boy.

'Yup, changed my life. No doubt.' He says thoughtfully.

The screen goes dark and Z clicks the remote. Silence falls over the room and everyone turns their faces to Joy. She sits, tears streaming down her cheeks, shaking her head, struggling to talk.

'I can't. How did? Thank you. How?'

Matt rubs her back helping her settle down as she looks to Gerard and Z, then him.

'You said you wanted to know what you meant to them, remember?'

She nods.

'Well, I figured, why couldn't I just ask? I rang the education department and explained the situation. They gave me the name of the school you taught at for a few years in the city. I rang the school and asked the principal. She said to say hi, by the way, and that when you kick cancer's ass then please come back to the school.'

Joy laughs, a big smile settling on her face behind the sheen of tears.

'You,' she says at Matt. 'And you guys too,' she adds to the others. 'You guys are amazing.'

'Yeah, I know.' Z agrees, before Matt and Gerard can say anything. 'Now, you feeling up for another trip to maternity? I want to visit that nurse again.'

Sixty Four

Matt's eyes flutter awake. He must have fallen asleep reading. His back is stiff from spending the night slumped in the chair. Outside, hot air balloons drift along the dawn sky. He sits up quietly and stretches, watching them float like colourful giants on a dreamtime ocean.

The steady breathing in the room is a metronome of souls. Matt keeps time with Joy, just as he always does when they sleep together. It helps him feel closer to her, like they belong in the same body. He wonders how he'll find his own natural rhythm when she stops breathing. He can't remember it ever coming as easily as it does now.

'It would be a nice day to go to the beach,' Joy's sleepy voice nudges Matt out of contemplation.

He turns to look into her jade-coloured eyes. She seems well today. Joy smiles at him hopefully.

'It might be windy enough down there to fly kites,' she adds.

'I'll have a talk with Peter, maybe we can do a day trip,' Matt responds, knowing what the answer will be. He doesn't have the heart to say no directly. 'You need to have some breakfast first.'

Joy rolls onto her side and props herself up on her elbow. Her cheekbones are more prominent than ever because of her weight loss. She frowns at Matt.

'The food here is rubbish' she says.

'I know,' he sighs. 'Maybe it will be better today.'

'It's the same every day,' she whines. 'Breakfast will be overcooked eggs and bacon that's too stiff to swallow. You'd think that they'd give you something nutritious in a place of healing. God, even a freshly-squeezed juice would be nice.'

'Do you want me to go and get you one?' Matt seizes the opportunity to help. 'There's a place down the road. They do good coffee as well.'

'Do they have any blueberry muffins?' she asks eagerly. 'I might be able to stomach a muffin.'

'I'll check,' he says, jumping into action, happy that he can do something. 'Do you want me to tell the nurses to save your eggs for someone else?'

'Yes please. And tell Peter I'm looking strong today. Tell him I'm going to eat something and that I could probably go running.'

'I will,' Matt shakes his head at her persistence. 'I'll be back soon.'

He pauses at the desk on the way out, letting the duty nurse know that he's going to get Joy her breakfast today. She advises that Peter will be on his rounds in half an hour. Matt has plenty of time to order whatever he likes.

The outside air is a welcome freshness from the stale interior of the hospital. Matt realises it's been a few days since he's actually been out in the open. The thought makes him feel a pang of sympathy for Joy. The only breeze she gets to experience now is a seeping draft from a rarely opened window. It doesn't seem fair that she has to be removed from her connection with nature. Matt resolves to convince Peter to let him take her out to the park for an hour in a wheelchair today. Surely, he can't begrudge her that basic happiness.

The vibrations of the juicing machine rattle the crockery on the counter of the café. Matt sits down and sips his coffee slowly, as he watches the waiter push fresh apples and oranges into the mouth of the machine, grinding its precious liquid into a waiting milkshake cup. A glass display case houses a selection of fresh muffins, which Matt orders to take away. He feels useful again. These may be small wishes for Joy, but they are ones that can be fulfilled easily.

Armed with his special package, Matt starts humming a Jeff Buckley song as he walks back to the hospital. The high notes buzz in his ears and give extra sensation to the routine errand. In the elevator up to the room, he keeps humming, knowing the entire tune by heart.

As the lift doors open, Matt is almost knocked over by a bustling Peter.

'Matt!' he looks worried, searching inside the elevator. 'Where's Joy?'

'What?' Matt asks, not really registering the question. 'She's in her room. I just popped out to get her some-'

'She's not there.' Peter interrupts. 'I stopped in to say hello before I started for the morning and couldn't find her. She's not in the bathroom either.'

Matt pushes past Peter and rushes down the hallway, barely resisting the need to run. It can't be right. Bursting into the room, Matt can see immediately that it's empty. The ensuite door is wide open and it's dark inside. Matt flings open the door of the cupboard, where he had hung some clothes for Joy. Two empty coat hangers swing alone on the bar.

Peter appears at the door.

'Where is she?'

'I don't know! Maybe she's gone down to maternity.'

'Why would she go down there?' Peter asks.

Not wanting to explain, Matt does one last scan of the room before he heads to the other ward. The violas are in their vase against the wall, but his book is on the ground. He strides across to pick it up and looks down at the table. His keys are gone. Matt pauses. He runs to the window. The hot air balloons are still floating in the sky, but his Holden is no longer sitting in the parking lot.

'Peter,' Matt says, turning to the concerned doctor. 'I'm going to need to borrow your car.'

Sixty Five

Matt grips the steering wheel with anxiety as he drives down the highway. He doesn't know how much of a head start Joy might have, but he doesn't expect to catch up with her before he gets to the beach. The straight stretch of road leads the way down to the coast. Down to home.

Blueberry muffins sit on the passenger seat. The fresh juice awaits its rightful owner in the cup holder of the BMW.

Thoughts are scrambling through Matt's head. *How did she get out without being seen? Was she planning this all along? Is she fit enough to drive?* None of the answers really matter. All that matters is that she's safe. Matt starts to laugh despite himself. Trust Joy to pull this kind of stunt. It's like she's giving the world one final salute, reminding them that she's not gone yet. Matt is not angry. He just hopes she's where he thinks she is. He trusts his instincts.

The wheels of the BMW skid to a halt next to Matt's Holden, which is sitting in the gravel car park, leading to the cliff-top track. Calming his nerves, Matt gathers the juice and muffins in his hands and steps out into the salt air. She's here. Matt feels relief that his intuition was right.

The wind is light and onshore, carrying with it the cold ocean temperature. The chill brings a strange mood into Matt, like the breeze is infused with a sense of resignation. He walks down the familiar path to a break in the scrub beyond the waist-high wire fence. Twigs scratch his neck and back as he pushes through the eucalypt-scented bush. He threads the path to their special spot.

Joy is hanging her feet over the edge of the cliff, looking down at the rumbling sea. She has a little red and yellow kite sitting next to her, its plastic wrapping lying discarded in the middle of the clearing.

Sixty Five

Matt steps forward, letting his footfalls announce his arrival. Joy turns to look at her visitor. She lifts her chin in a welcoming gesture, like she was expecting him at any moment.

'I've got your breakfast,' he smiles weakly, holding it up for her to see.

'I'll have it in a minute,' she says, looking drained. 'Come and sit with me for a bit first.'

Matt puts the food down on the grass and warily approaches the cliff. Instead of sitting next to her, he nestles in behind Joy, straddling his legs either side of hers and pressing his chest into her back. He rests his head next to hers, so they share exactly the same view of the endless expanse in front of them. A small boat bobs out at sea alone. It lists up and down, its sail limp. Matt and Joy watch the tiny waves meander in their direction, coming toward land, always moving forward until they reach the rocks. They have travelled across oceans to reach this shoreline.

'You couldn't help yourself, could you?' Matt says softly, hugging his arms around her body.

'How could I miss this?' she smiles against him. 'You should never waste an opportunity to return to where you belong.'

Matt chuckles gently in unspoken agreement.

'And what about the kite?' he says, looking down at the nylon toy.

'I thought I'd grab one on the way through, just in case,' Joy strokes it fondly with her fingers. 'This one seemed prepared to fly.'

'Well, there's not much chance today,' answers Matt, looking at the plate-glass sea. 'Maybe if we wait long enough, the breeze will pick up.'

'It doesn't matter,' she leans back into his body, letting him support her weight. 'It was just a silly thought. I'm just happy to see all of this one last time.'

'I don't know,' Matt kisses her cheek. 'You seem to be doing a good job of sticking around.'

'I'm tired of holding on,' she says. 'I'm tired of waiting. I'm ready to find out what's on the other side.'

Matt wraps his fingers between Joy's and rests their interwoven hands on her lap.

'Well, you have to promise to get a message back to me if you find anything. You have to let me know you're okay,' Matt nestles his head affectionately next to hers.

'I will,' Joy whispers, turning to kiss him. 'I'll do my best.'

'You do that and I'll write your book,' Matt says to her tenderly. 'That way we'll be together always, in this world and the next.'

Sixty Five

They turn their attention to the ocean again. Matt can just make out the sailor on the boat, sitting back on the deck, propping a fishing rod between his legs. He doesn't seem to mind that he's out there all by himself. Matt's lips rest on the lobe of Joy's tiny ear. He tries to match his breathing with Joy's like he normally does, but hers is too slow. It's like she's holding her breath between inhales and exhales. Matt looks at her face to check she's okay. She smiles sleepily and wriggles closer back into him for support. The rolling sound of the breakers below drifts lazily on and on, lulling the two together into a contemplative silence. Matt closes his eyes and listens to the thrum of the sea, keeping as close to his love as he can. As Matt shifts his weight to become more comfortable, the wind picks up a little, causing him to raise his head. The wind grows stronger still, sending an upward gust glancing up the cliff-side. Next to them, Joy's little kite catches the breeze and shoots up into the air, spiralling unexpectedly outward, into the open air above them.

'Joy,' Matt hugs her tightly. 'Joy, look!'

But Joy isn't there to share it with Matt. She has already slipped off, over the edge of eternity.

Epilogue

Bill's garden is awash with colour. Bluebells, peonies and other spring blooms peek their faces out from lush green bushes. Matt walks toward the sight, towing a wheelie bag behind him. His backpack bounces with each step, clapping him across the shoulders as if urging him on. Bill kneels with his hands in the soil, planting seeds. He looks up at the noise of the wheels on the pavement. Seeing Matt, he stands up and dusts his palms on the back of his pants.

'Howdy stranger,' Bill says with a smile as Matt pulls up to the fence. 'You look like you're headed somewhere.'

Matt looks down at his bag. 'Yeah, going to Tassie to see the folks, before kicking on to Europe for a bit.'

'That sounds like an adventure,' Bill grins.

Matt smiles back, nodding.

'I wanted to say thanks,' Matt says after a spell. 'For the gardening advice and everything else.'

'Please,' Bill says, waving the thanks away. 'I think I enjoyed it more than you.'

'Maybe,' Matt laughs, thinking back to the lessons on making fertiliser from seaweed and using garlic spray to ward off snails.

'Do you want me to tend the patch while you're gone?' Bill asks earnestly.

'Nah,' Matt says, 'I reckon you've got your hands full keeping this lot sorted.' He indicates the massive garden around the elderly man.

'Nonsense,' Bill says, 'I love the view up there. It's a nice secret hideaway. Special.'

'You sure?' Matt asks.

'Moonbeams and autumn joy might be hardy plants, but they'll still need a little nurturing in that salt air.' Bill says, like the discussion is closed.

'I don't know when I'll be home,' Matt offers Bill a final chance to back out.

'Then I won't hold my breath on you helping me with the Valentine's rush come February,' he smiles.

'Thanks again, mate, really,' Matt reaches out to shake Bill's hand.

Bill swats Matt's outstretched palm away and pulls him in for a hug over the fence. He claps Matt on the backpack.

'I'll miss our chats,' Bill says, then stands back, still holding Matt's arm.

'Me too,' Matt nods, moving to walk away.

Bill continues to hold Matt's arm firmly.

'And Matt,' he says, 'remember, they'll always be in here.' He rests his hand on Matt's chest and puts his other hand over his own heart. 'And here.' Bill adds, picking a tiger lily that's close by and handing it to Matt.

Matt takes the flower, looking down at it, fighting back tears. He's shed his fair share in front of Bill, but he wants this goodbye to be a happy one. Rather than risking waterworks, he simply nods, pats the old man on the shoulder one last time and starts wheeling his bag toward the centre of town.

As he walks, Matt smells the tiger lily in his spare hand. The scent reminds him of Joy's funeral. It had been a small affair. Matt, Oscar, Peter and his wife had been there to witness Joy being laid to rest next to her mother. Gerard and Z had come along for support, as had Z's new girlfriend, the midwife Joan. They each had their own special memories of Joy to share at the wake, which consisted of fish n' chips and red wine down on the Ocean Heads' foreshore. Matt's favourite story had been Oscar's recount of Joy's first live performance with her band. A girl in the audience had requested 'something poppy'. Joy had responded with a fifteen-minute version of War Pigs by Black Sabbath, complete with power chords played using her middle finger directed at the girl. Matt had listened to the song for weeks after to cheer himself up, whenever the hole of Joy being gone got too much. He would mourn her for longer than he'd known her, but increasingly it was with a smile on his lips, rather than tears in his eyes.

Matt takes a seat at the airport shuttle stop out the front of the tourist bureau. He takes out his ticket to double confirm he has the date and time right. It's the twelfth time he's made the check today. On the bottom of the itinerary are words he has written: 'For 24/7 wingman support call or message using the following options.' The company had been so happy with the customer service scripts that he'd provided, they'd offered a bonus of an open round-the-world ticket and space in any of their on-flight magazines whenever he felt like contributing. He'd taken up the ticket at urging from Gerard, but turned down the offer of being published until he was more confident in his prose. He feels lucky the university had been so flexible when he'd dropped back to part-time, online study. Dr Byron had gladly helped arrange the shift, saying that the most valuable experience any writer could have, was actually experiencing the world. "Without that," she had said, "you have nothing but hollow words."

The sound of a car horn makes Matt look up. A black Mazda 6 pulls up to the curb and the electric window rolls down.

'Thought you'd sneak away without saying a proper goodbye, dickhead?' Z leans out the window, giving Matt a surly look.

'I figured you'd be busy up in the city working.'

'Nah, G banned me from coming to a meeting with a potential new client because I might give the wrong impression.'

'You did tell that app company last month that they were a bunch of whiney bitches that were still sucking at their mummies' tits.'

'They wanted online-only customer service without any option to even chat with a real person!'

'Righto,' Matt backs off, smiling at her reaction.

'You getting in, or what?'

Matt stands and puts his bags in the boot of Z's car, before walking around to the passenger side. He settles down in the leather seats and she peels a noisy U-turn, heading out of town. They drive past the supermarket, past the shops and the school and the skate park. They drive past the lookout over the bay. Matt says a silent goodbye to the Great Southern Ocean that stretches out beyond the cliff.

'How's the book going?' Z asks Matt as she drives.

'It's going. I've got a bunch of chapters down and things are starting to take shape. But I'm not in a hurry. I just want to get it right, you know?'

'Yup,' Z pulls an e-cigarette out of the centre console of the car. She takes a long draw, blowing the mist it creates out the window. Matt gives her a strange look as she puts it back down in the console.

'What?' Z asks, keeping one eye on the road. 'Joan says that if I don't quit smoking then she'll never forgive me for pretending to be a doctor when we first met.'

'She's a good influence on you,' Matt smiles.

'I know, it's horrible, isn't it?' Z says. 'But she's got a tongue like a wind turbine and a rack like an eighteen-year-old school girl.'

'Z!'

'What?' she asks, picking up the Vape stick and taking another drag.

'It's nice to know some people never change,' Matt says shaking his head, looking back at the road ahead.

'And it's nice to know some people do,' Z replies, patting Matt's knee as she speeds up to over a hundred.

When they hit the highway at the edge of town, the feeling in Matt's stomach is one of nervous excitement. His smile mirrors those in the cars on the other side of the road heading to the freedom of the coast, while he is heading into the freedom of the unknown. He is uncertain what tomorrow will bring and is scared that without a script he won't know what to do. But then, that is half the fun and all of the adventure.

If you enjoyed this book, please head to Amazon.com and write a review (or send a letter to the editor of your local newspaper about it).

You can also spread the word on social media by tagging in @tim_hawken on Twitter or Instagram.

Better yet, do something old fashioned and lend a friend this copy.

For more by the author of
IF KISSES CURED CANCER visit:

www.TIMHAWKEN.COM